Praise for *Victor McGlothin* and *His Novels*

McGlothin's rugged prose captures the sultry locale, and the suspenseful edge is a nice complement to the story's social conscience."

—*Publishers Weekly*

"Victor McGlothin has written an amazing story of spiritual and emotional redemption. DOWN ON MY KNEES is a welcome addition to Christian fiction."

—Victoria Christopher Murray
#1 Essence Bestselling author of *Grown Folks Business*

"McGlothin unravels at a relentless pace a sexy and twisted story of marital and spiritual unfaithfulness, culminating in a shocker of a conclusion. Eric Jerome Dickey, watch out."

—*Publishers Weekly* on Sinful Too

"I found myself lost in the story, living the moment with the characters and feeling their emotions. I recommend this book to those who love post-civil war era stories and romance."

—*APOO Bookclub*

"The last few chapters had me furiously turning pages to find out what happens."

—*Laura L. Hutchison, The Free Lance-Star*

"A talented storyteller with a knack for telling a convincing story, McGlothin manages to weave an entertaining story that may indeed ring true to many readers... What's a Woman to Do will introduce readers to yet another new and refreshing voice in the world of contemporary African-American fiction."

—*QBR* on What's a Woman to Do

"The twists and surprises are both plausible and unbelievable, the novel both engrossing and entertaining."

—*Booklist* on What's a Woman to Do

"4 Stars... Victor McGlothin has written a superb, true-to-life book. With a masterfully created plot, it explores the turbulent lives of three courageous women. This book offers a gripping, emotional glimpse into the dark world of the unknown."

—*Romantic Times BookClub* on What's a Woman to Do

"A fast-paced, soulful, dramatic story."

—*The Sunday Oklahoman* on What's a Woman to Do

"An absolute page-turner...intriguing and thought-provoking"

— Kimberla Lawson Roby,
New York Times Bestselling Author, on Autumn Leaves

"Credible, honest."

—*Kirkus Reviews* on Autumn Leaves

"The pacing of the story and the storyline itself ought to keep the reader interested until the last page is turned since there's plenty of drama and secrets to keep you wondering and guessing until the end. Victor McGlothin has told a story that is sure to satisfy fans of his first novel, AUTUMN LEAVES, as well as new readers."

—*Book-remarks.com on Autumn Leaves*

"McGlothin creates a sizzling slice of life in 1947. McGlothin weaves convincing historical elements into a fast-moving caper, and Baltimore Floyd is a delightful scoundrel."

—*Publishers Weekly on Ms. Etta's Fast House*

MY FATHER'S SON

Happy Birthday
" Latonya Ammons "
from your by *girl Dakota ~*
Victor McGlothin

Best wishes,

Well Done
B o o k s

My Father's Son

Printed in the United States of America.

ISBN: 978-0-9667243-4-9

Victor McGlothin www.VictorMcGlothin.com

First Edition: August 2020

Special Dedication

I am very grateful for the book clubs, friends, family and fans who have supported me throughout my twenty-two-year journey as an author. I could not imagine returning to where it all began without you. Therefore, I dedicate this dual novella to y'all. Yes y'all. Thanks for making my Texas-sized dreams come true.

Also By Victor McGlothin

MY FATHER'S SON

by
Victor McGlothin

PART I

"Yea, though I walk through the valley of the shadow of death…"

ONE

Hot Buttered Soul

S econds before Humphrey's Drugstore & Emporium closed, the front door opened slowly. As two elderly women argued over loose change, a young man entered with a mean scowl and swagger to spare. His tortoise-green full-length trench coat, with artificial fur trimming the collar, fanned the floor as he disappeared behind the back grocery aisle. Jon Holloway, the store clerk, stood unwittingly at ease with his tall frame leaning against the counter. He chuckled softly, observing the women debate whose turn it was to spring for a bag of pork skins and *RC Colas*. Eventually they came to terms, paid for the items then exited the store.

Jon returned his attention to a college textbook behind the front counter. Still unaware of the man lurking a few feet away, he hummed to himself while making notes in the margins. It had been a good day; one spent earning an honest wage, which was uncommon to too many young black men in the frigid winter of 1968. Times were hard on Negroes throughout the United States, Dallas held no exception. In the throes of Civil Rights demonstrations, civil disobedience and wide spread unrest, the country was at disastrous odds with itself. Maintaining employment was a legitimate strain for black men who had half a mind to bare it. Many didn't bother with the burden.

Jon, a twenty-one-year old honor student at City College, considered the weight of responsibility when his watch read ten o'clock. He yawned then sighed wearily with a crooked smile. *Quitting time*, he thought, then headed toward the front of the store to lock up. From the window, Jon glared at the bank of frozen snow that accumulated on the sidewalk.

When the rotary telephone rang, he hustled back to answer it. "Humphrey's Drugstore," he announced in a somewhat breathy tone.

"Hey Baby," the caller's voice replied. "I thought I'd dial up with three reasons to hurry on over to my place." The woman's voice resonated like a slow and mellow love song. After Jon's hectic class schedule and a long day of discontented customers, it was beautiful music to his ears.

"Yeah? Say you got three of 'em?" he asked, anxious to hear more.

"Uh-huh, though I ain't gonna need but one. That's the sweetest honey you ever put in your mouth," she answered seductively.

Imagining her tasty proposition, Jon moistened his lips with a measured stroke from his tongue. "You know I got a sweet tooth. Keep that honey warm and I'll be right there to lick the jar. Give me a minute to balance the cash drawer then I'll be right on over."

"Hurry up now. I just climbed out of the tub. Had to make sure everything was squeaky clean just in case my man gets any bright ideas from those French books he's had his nose buried in."

Jon's expression softened when he envisioned what awaiting him. "Is that so?"

"You can tell me what you think after you're good and satisfied."

Overwhelmed by the innuendo, Jon fumbled the telephone. "Gimme twenty minutes Starla. Don't get started without me baby."

With bated breath and a hopeful grin, Jon hung up the telephone. His excitement evaporated when a man's deep voice startled him from behind. "Open that cash draw' and hurry up," barked the man in the trench coat. Then, he belted back a long-measured swig from the bottle of bourbon he'd pulled from his coat pocket. The stranger wiped at the excess liquor resting between his upper lip and ratty mustache then he hollered further demands. "I said open up that damned register! Are you deaf?"

Frozen on the spot, Jon reasoned the robber was more likely to blast him if he made any sudden moves. While weighing options that just might keep him alive, Jon contemplated his fate. Figuring he'd better do as instructed or take a chance meeting the wrong end of a bad situation, the nervous store clerk pivoted timidly with both arms hoisted high in the air. His six-foot frame was as taut as a tightrope while addressing the would-be assailant through squinted regretful eyes.

The man in the tacky green coat glared at the good looking clerk's awkward expression as he insisted on Jon's cooperation for a third time. "Open that register dammit! I ain't got all night! Oh yeah, and I want these here prophylactics and some Juicy Fruit bubble gum. Hurry up man, you move slower than my momma and she old." After shouting orders, he peered through the drugstore's plate glass window. Jon peered at him peculiarly when the man's lips puckered perfectly. He blew a kiss at the young lady applying a fresh coat of lipstick in the rear view mirror of an old La Salle coupe. "Come on now. If you take too long, she's liable to change her mind, man." The insistent customer didn't have robbery in his heart at all. He'd intended on nabbing something worth a whole lot more to him than money, a shot at a young woman's sweet surrender.

Jon was still shaking behind the counter with his arms extended. The man stared at him oddly again then shrugged after taking another healthy nip from his liquor bottle. "And put yo' hands down, fool! You'd think somebody was tryin' to stick you up or something. Jon, why you acting like a stick is up yo' ass?"

"Haz'?" Jon answered, his voice trembling. "Torrance Hazlon from Ms. Whitherspoon's tenth grade home ed. class? Man, I thought you were robbing me. Had me damn near about to piss my pants too." Now Jon was angry with himself for having been so easily shaken. "How'd you get in here after I locked up?"

Torrance Hazlon was a petty thief, who fancied himself as a crafty burglar with exceptional talents at stealing a woman's virtues as well. "Don't pay that no never mind," he shouted, more agitated than before. "How I got in here ain't as important as what I'm tryin' to get into out there."

Jon nodded that he agreed completely. "I see your point. Here, just take the stuff and have a good time. It's all on me."

Hazlon flashed a wide-mouthed grin and then accepted Jon's gracious offer. He waved a half-empty bottle of bourbon towards the store clerk as a gesture of gratitude. Jon refused the liquor but did take a moment to spy the girl in the front seat of Hazlon's car. "Don't do nothing I wouldn't do Haz," he said, smiling back at an attractive girl who was making eyes at him.

"Hell man. I'ma do everythang she let me do and whatever else I can get away with. I done already sprung for burgers at Good Lucks. I gotta get at least six dollars and two bits worth of somethin' out the deal." Without giving it another thought, Torrance Hazlon unlocked the deadbolt then bounced out of the door with renewed hopes of finding out just how far six dollars and twenty-five cents would get him.

Tickled at the previous turn of events, Jon laughed to himself as he reconciled the cash register receipts. He continued laughing when the notion of getting cozy with the woman he loved was pulling at his zipper. Starla was the kind of woman who made a man feel like a king, whether he deserved it or not. That alone was worth the sacrifices Jon made to keep her happy and by his side.

Once closing down the store, he slipped a nylon skullcap over his head and buttoned his would-be robbers. Although, he had never given it much thought before, Hazlon's visit had him watching his back. Once convinced there was nothing to fear, Jon tossed the canvass book bag over his shoulder.

He started his eight block trek, ducking into a howling wind and crisp darkness. Jon enjoyed a casual stroll which allowed him to ease out of a long day but the cold air was thick and unrelenting. Soon enough, his casual strides became shorten and hurried. By the time he'd traveled two blocks, there was nothing on his mind but braving the elements and a warm place to lay his head.

At the corner of Peabody Street and Forth Avenue, a shiny new Cadillac idled at the curb. Three young men smoked reefer inside and passed around a fifth of whiskey while crooning to music from the local soul station. Suddenly, the driver's-side window lowered. Odell Owens, a criminally mischievous neighborhood thug summoned Jon from the front seat. His extremely close-to-the- bone Ivy League haircut was not in any way indicative of his social status. However, the gold cap over his front right tooth was.

Odell ran the tip of his thick tongue over the gold crown and smacked his lips. He winked his good eye then settled deeper into the front seat to further solidify how cool he felt behind the wheel. "Hey Joe College," he yelled in Jon's direction, "You looking mighty cold standing there with your bony knees knocking. Come on and get in before you freeze."

Jon had known Odell since they were kids. He also knew well enough to be suspicious of the expensive car, seeing as how Odell never had a job to speak of but always found a way to be in possession of the finer things life had to offer. Besides, there were already too many young black men jailed for being a little less than stupid.

"I don't think so Cat Daddy," Jon answered eventually, as he studied the expensive white walled tires. "I'm gonna have to pass. Something this fine has got to have major consequences tied to it and I ain't trying to deal with any of them. I avoid the kinds of things that get a black man tossed in the slammer."

"Come on Jon," Odell insisted. "This here is my old man's retirement wheels, thirty years at the milk company. Now get yo' scary ass in this pride ride before I change my mind."

The other men in the car laughed dismissively. Jon couldn't deny the fact that his feet had begun to stiffen. With mounting reservations, peer pressure trumped his half-hearted appeal to morality and common sense so he climbed into the back seat for a short jaunt through the neighborhood.

Trying hard not to enjoy the amenities, Jon sat pensively with a book bag perched on his lap like a worried virgin on her first date. Eventually, he allowed his eyes to wander throughout the lavish automobile. He couldn't resist the temptation to run his fingertips along the thick leather, feeling the thinly veiled shadow of well being drawing him in. In short order, he was joined by a false sense of comfort as the other passengers swayed to the Motown sounds blaring from the car stereo.

The party was in full swing when the Cadillac glided passed a police squad car hidden within the backdrop of a quiet residential street. Two white patrolmen on a routine donut break admired the sleek Caddy. They were satisfied with doing something close to nothing, until one of them got an eye full of four Negros partying riotously as the expensive automobile rolled past.

Jon was crooning backup vocals during the sing-a-long with the others when the rear view mirror warned that police followed closely behind them.

"Hot damn, it's the law!" Odell shouted. "Hold on y'all. I'll lose 'em." He spilled whiskey in his lap when maneuvering through traffic. Barreling toward the end of the block, Odell kept that sedan roaring one step ahead of the police car sirens and flashing lights.

After dodging oncoming cars on the wrong side of a one-way street, Odell slammed on the brakes then darted through a shopping center parking lot. The fuzz was in heavy pursuit when the Cadillac traveled too fast to make the next turn. It sideswiped a Buick LaSalle parked near the rib joint on the corner. Tires shrieked angrily into the thick night air as both cars wheeled onto Forest Avenue.

Two of the joyriders belted out driving instructions to Odell. Jon was quietly regretful. Suddenly, he was sure the car couldn't have been Odell's father because he'd gotten his chest blown open during a loaded dice game 13 years ago. But, none of that mattered now. Jon was riding in somebody's very expensive automobile with young men who had been drinking and toking marijuana; not to mention being chased by two white police officers through the same neighborhood he lived in. Jon quickly realized then he wasn't a chump for getting talked into hot-rodding in a stolen car. He was a damned fool.

Odell understood how running from white cops often resulted in brutal attack if captured. "I'll fix them pigs. I don't intend on having the man's boot on my neck again. I'm sure as hell ain't goin' back to jail for nobody," he declared hotly.

Odell slammed on the brakes again, causing the police cruiser to ram the back of the boosted car. The riveting jolt startled all the passengers inside the Cadillac except Jon. He hurried to collect the text books that spilled out of his bag during the collision while the others stared out of the rear window to see if the squad car continued to give chase. Luckily, it had stalled in the middle of the abandoned street. It's busted radiator spewed steam into the air. Odell and his crew cheered with raised fists when the black-and-white patrol car faded behind a thick white cloud.

"Stop the car Odell," Jon growled, after catching his breath. No one blinked until he said it again with more conviction. "Stop the damned car now! Let me out. I should've known you was up to something. Talking about this was your daddy's ride. Let me out of this backseat before those donut dippers call in the cavalry."

Odell smirked like a man contemplating the consequences if he chose not to comply then he tossed back a long gulp to empty the whiskey bottle. When push nearly came to shove, Odell pulled the car over. The back door flew open.

Sweat streamed down Jon's forehead as he climbed out onto the street. Before he could regain his bearings, the shiny and now battered Cadillac bolted down the street then hooked a left onto Oakland Ave.. Jon's chest heaved violently as he slipped in between houses and hopped over backyard fences. His book bag, slung over his shoulder, bounced up and down in his shadows.

He finally reached his front porch and hurriedly forced the key in the lock. In the time it took to blink, he was on the other side of that closed door and thankful to be alive. His beautiful wife Starla stood in the middle of the large living room wearing a strained expression and a long sheer black gown with a revealing slit riding up her right thigh.

Starla's flawless toffee colored skin often awarded her a second look, as did her long thick hair and shapely frame. She'd received more than her share of lustful leers although it was no fault of her own. Orphaned at the age of nine and more streetwise than she ever cared to admit, Starla was forced into womanhood before she was ready to deal with the lessons that accompanied that dubious honor.

While Jon gawked out of the window between creases in the drapes, Starla was troubled by his uneasiness. The strained countenance on his face hardened his handsome attributes. There were no signs of the subtle dimples and charming bright smile. The glow of his soft brown eyes was absent. Instead, there was panic and fear. Understandably concerned, Starla cleared her throat to get his attention. "And just what are you looking for, baby? Who's out there?" As she sauntered toward him, her arms fell down by her sides. "You alright?"

Jonathan drew back suddenly as if Starla had been pulled out of a hat. Then, he nodded with a vacant expression. Knowing that his evening walk home usually delivered him cold and tired, Starla prepared hot tea for his arrival like she had done each night the weather dipped down in single digits.

While they sat at the kitchen table searching for normalcy and sharing cups of hot spearmint tea, Jon shared details of the perilous car chase. "Whew, you should have seen Odell wheeling that beautiful Caddy down Forest Avenue like he was running from the devil. Those cops almost got us too," he added in retrospect. "Shoot, you should've heard Odell spouting off about that was his daddy's ride."

"Daddy?" Starla blurted out, when Jon tried to slide a weak lie past her. "Odell ain't got no daddy. Everybody knows that. I can't believe you went joyriding around in a car you knew was ripped off." Jon's eyes drifted away from her disapproving stare. "Jonathan Holloway, you know these white cops are killing Negro men for less than that." When he didn't attempt to argue, Starla shook her head to display her fervent disappointment. Several moments passed before she tossed a labored smile at him. "Well, if those policemen had caught up to y'all, the devil would have been the least of Odell's worries too. I know y'all go way back but you have a family now. Don't let a bona fide thug like him take that away from us."

After conceding how ridiculous his decision was, Jon swallowed the last drop of tea along with his humility then leaned across the table to steal a kiss. As soon as their lips met, a faint cough came from an upstairs bedroom. Starla pulled away. "Why don't you go up there and see about Jon-Jon and then you rush on back to see about me," she suggested seductively.

Her husband wasn't ready to give up on their brief interlude. "Come on now sweetheart, Jon-Jon's gonna get by all right until I get there. I just need a bit of honey to take the edge off my nerves. I'm still stirred up after the run-in with the law. How's about you giving me something for my rheumatism?" he joked softly.

Jon continued to woo Starla until shooed him away. "Uh-uh. The longer you take, the longer I've got to wait and you know I don't like waiting. Besides, your son needs you."

"I thought his momma needed me too."

"She does," Starla confirmed. "But that ain't how things is. I can't concentrate on pleasing you knowing our child needs attending to more than me. Bless his heart. Jon-Jon fell asleep calling your name."

As Jon marched up the wooden staircase, the aroma of lemon scented furniture polish smelled like a citrus bouquet. Having a woman who took pride in a clean home made him happy, everything else about her made him glad to be a man.

After reaching the upstairs landing, he quietly opened the door to his son's room. The small child rested soundly like a chocolate cherub beneath layers of homemade quilts. His forehead seemed a bit moist when Jon stroked it gently so he folded back the top cover. "Good night son. You'll be better soon. Daddy's gonna see to that." Jon stationed himself at the child's bedside until the fever broke. Hours later, a tired but relieved father went to see about collecting on those passion-filled promises made by his wife. Starla stood by her word, satisfying each and every one of them.

TWO

Early Sunday Morning

On Saturdays, family outings to the nearby park and trips to the zoo typically followed household chores but it the air was too brisk that day for a recuperating three-year-old. Instead, their male bonding session was limited to the family room which allowed Jon a chance to delve deeper into his textbooks with expectations holding down a coveted spot on the dean's list.

By mid-afternoon, Jon-Jon had fallen asleep. He was sprawled across his father's chest with an open American History book covering his child's back. That picturesque scene brought joy to Starla's eyes as it did each time it occurred. *Perfection*, Starla thought, *a strong Negro man spending quality time with his son, comforted by a volume of history and his hero.*

When she returned downstairs, Jon greeted her with a warm smile interrupted by a long yawn. She handed him a note from their neighbor Ms. Willa Mae Harris. The paper-sack-brown colored woman lived alone since her husband passed away early in their marriage. She'd never gotten over his untimely death from pneumonia. Since Ms. Harris often bought more meat than one woman could possibly eat from the neighborhood meat delivery wagon, she gladly offered half of it to the Holloways.

Jon wouldn't have felt comfortable accepting handouts but the gratuitous meat wasn't one at all. On South Blvd. neighbors lent a helping hand when they could. That's just the way it was. Every time Starla handed Jon a note from Ms. Harris asking if he minded repairing another broken items around her house, he'd smile then get to it.

Ten minutes after Jon read the note requesting neighborly assistance, he slipped into a pair of faded work coveralls and a painter's hat. Soon after, he was fiddling around in his green toolbox on Ms. Harris' front porch. She stepped out of her door onto the landing with a thick knitted afghan wrapped around her narrow shoulders. "Morning Jon," she said, briefly surveying the overcast blue-gray sky. "They say it just might warm up today but they haven't done such a good job at predicting lately."

Jon glanced up for a moment to see what he thought of the dense cloud cover then he went back to rounding up long nails. "No, they sure haven't, Ms. Willa Mae. That's the only job that still pays off even when you're wrong half the time."

Ms. Harris smiled then looked at Jon before she spoke what was heavy on her heart. "Listen to me Jon and I know you're going to get embarrassed but it needs to be said. Your momma would be so proud of the way you keep up that house and how you look out for a particular neighbor lady who doesn't have a man to help with the handiwork."

"You're welcome Ma'am," he answered humbly.

Jon's mother died of a heart attack when he was in high school. He'd worked hard to keep up the taxes and utilities on the house she'd left him. And although Jon had heard his neighbor's commendations for the umpteenth times, he was still uncomfortable when she mentioned that footnote.

Ms. Harris leaned against the doorframe then surveyed the sky again. "Just saying thanks is all."

After a stiff breeze persuaded her to scurry back inside, Jon sawed off two evenly measured wood blocks then he sanded them to a smooth finish. While admiring his craftsmanship, he noticed a long moving truck pulling against the curb a few houses down the block. The massive U-Haul idled in front of a large brick home on the other side of the street, which belonged to a Warner Price, a prominent Negro doctor. Not many of Jon's neighbors moved around much in those days. Upper class blacks typically stuck together, stayed around their own kind. Jon back ended his way into the cozy cradle for upper-middle-class blacks when the wealthy family his mother cleaned house for suddenly died in a plane crash.

The highly respected doctor, however, gained recognition from the Dallas medical establishment after committing twenty years of his life to his community. It was quite a blow to when he purchased a bigger home on the north side of town. Before long, there would be more moving trucks pulling up and subsequently carrying off the best and the brightest men and women who led the Negro community from within but Jon didn't grasp what the first U-Haul truck represented that Saturday afternoon. It would become evident that Negroes were as unprepared for the tribulations that desegregation brought on. Like the Babylonians of biblical times, it raped the communities of their most precious resources, the means by which to sustain itself.

Sunday morning crept in nice and easy. The sun tapped on Starla's shoulder. She looked over at her husband and son, both sound asleep. She sat up and swung one leg over the side of the bed; hoping the other would follow. After stumbling out of the restroom, she rubbed her eyes and slid into a fuzzy housecoat.

Five more minutes under those warm covers was tempting but duty summoned Starla and she was always proud to answer the call. Family meant everything to her, everything.

Minutes later, the sun's relentless gaze forced Jon to rise and meet the day. The welcoming aroma of grits, fried eggs, and bacon met him as he approached the kitchen. He scratched his head wearily then kissed his woman good morning. "Hey Starla. It smells so good but a breakfast like that is liable to thicken a man up in the middle. I'd have to trade you in for a large sized woman to mash up against."

"Watch your mouth Jonathan Holloway!" she spat jokingly. "You ain't trading me in for nobody. Don't matter what size the heifer is."

Suddenly, a collection of hard raps banged against the front door. Jon was puzzled why anyone would be stopping by before breakfast on a Sunday morning. He tucked Jon-Jon tucked under his arm when the knocks became more persistent. Jon cradled his son with one hand while opening the door with the other. The moment his eyes met theirs, he wished he'd have peeked first. Two white police officers stood on his porch with their guns drawn.

"You Jonathan Holloway?" shouted the cop nearest to the doorway.

Jon's eyes widened. Instinctively, he lowered Jon-Jon to the floor in the event of an altercation. Nervous as hell, Jon answered reluctantly. "Yeah, I'm him. I'm Jonathan Holloway." Then he pressed his lips together and swallowed hard.

The same cop who spoke earlier holstered his weapon while his partner pointed a pistol at Jon's head. Starla eased behind her man, wearing naked trepidations.

"What's going on?" she asked when the officer threw Jon against the door frame. "Hold on a minute. Don't you hurt him,"

Starla begged, when the pistol pointer cocked his weapon. "He didn't do nothing. Hey! Hey!"

"Starla get Jon-Jon!" Jon demanded. "He don't need to be seeing this." Jon raised both hands above his head in a slow methodical manner. "Ain't no need for that gun. I'll come peacefully." It was the second time in three days he found himself with his arms hoisted over his head but this time he had a legitimate reason, this threat of bodily harm was real.

Starla snatched her son off his feet in one swift motion then secured him in her arms. She stepped aside begrudgingly when the officers barged into her home. They tackled Jon immediately onto the hardwood floor even though he was not resisting. Starla's eyes grew wide when one of the officers punched her husband in the back of his head just for kicks.

"Ouch man," Jon howled. "What was that for? I'm not resisting you."

"Don't make this hard fella. We don't want anybody to get hurt," answered the more level-headed of the two. He snarled with a wicked grin then reached for Jon's hands. "Just shut up and come quiet now. You're going down for grand theft auto."

"Hey man hold on!" Jon wailed anxiously. "Grand theft what?" His eyes darted back and forth until it came to him. *That damned Odell*, he thought. "Okay, I'm coming. I said I was coming," he insisted. "No trouble. I'll come quietly. No trouble at all."

Filled with a silent scream, Starla's mouth fell open. She turned her son's head away when they handcuffed his father like a career felon. Once the officers clamped steel bracelets onto Jon's wrists, one of them jerked harshly on Jon's arms. He was determined to get rough. His predisposition for aggression was likely ignited when he saw a Negro family sitting down to a hot meal in a nice home while he patrolled the cold cement streets; or maybe it was simply business as usual. In either case, the cop angrily swatted Jon twice across the back with an his nightstick.

Jon grimaced in pain. "Hey man! I said I would go peaceful," he reaffirmed. With no regard to common decency, the officers paraded him down the long walkway in his favorite pajamas and run over house shoes.

"That's in case you go getting any ideas," the cop replied. He raised his stick again for another gratuitous strike at Jon but his partner stepped in and grabbed the baton. He noticed their early morning arrest had to drawn a crowd of onlookers.

"Not out here in the open!" he countered. "You wouldn't want to give these good people something to talk about in church this morning, would you? Cool off and get a move on."

Jon tried to get his head wrapped around the thought of being hauled away from his front door. From the backseat of the dirty squad car, he tried to explain how the stolen Cadillac had nothing to do with him. The older officer, who seemed to be in charge, bragged how they had Jon dead to right. His Political Science textbook was found underneath the seat of the abandoned car. A wealthy white man's expensive automobile was boosted and wrecked, that meant someone was going to pay. And by the looks of things, it was going to be Jon.

A ton of regret shadowed him all the way downtown, regret for making a bad decision and more of it for missing out on the chance to enjoy that fine breakfast Starla had prepared. He was rushed off to jail instead, in the back of yet another strange car, as other respectable Negroes peeled their eyes at him from passing automobiles.

Adding insult to injury, Jon landed behind bars with a bleak and uncertain future sneering at him I-told-you-so fashion. The Dallas

County jail was steeped with more than its share of young Negros. As Jon waited to be assigned a public defender to clean up the mess he'd stepped in, he begun to count all the men locked away in that hellish hole who looked like him. Those who walked like him, talked like him and had the same struggles in life to face that he did. Those, whose mothers and fathers worked themselves into early graves just as his had. Eventually, he gave up wondering why there was such a disparaging percentage of Negros restrained in cages.

A circular wall clock counted the moments since he'd been pinched for foolishness and nothing more. He was saddled with plenty of time to contemplate his terrible mistake and hopes of squaring it somehow on the back end. Since hope was free, Jon grabbed all that one man could hold.

After two long days spent on a metal bed, Tuesday rolled in right on schedule. Jon's court-appointed mouth-piece was white, like most of the legal assistance downtown. The lawyer made his first impression by showing up late for the hearing. He seemed quite fidgety for a grown man, especially for a white one who was on the right side of the law. The fact that he couldn't sit still for longer than one hot minute at a time wasn't the sole reason to cast doubts Jon's way before the arraignment. He also noticed the lawyer's business suit was nothing more than a vast collection of wrinkles. Actually the suit consisted of a snug pair of polyester slacks and an oddly fitting sports coat that weren't close to being the same color blue. To make matters worse, he didn't seem sympathetic in the least after hearing Jon's story. True enough, the overweight apple-headed attorney, who apparently suffered from a persistent case of active hemorrhoids, had heard countless stories like Jon's and from too many colored men claiming to be innocent. Wrong place, wrong time, and the wrong skin color typically demanded a two-to-ten year sentence in a state facility despite the charge.

Starla managed to share Jon's charges with Ms. Willa Mae before breaking down in a pool of tears. "And Ms. Willa Mae, I just don't know what to do. We don't have enough money to be paying no lawyer who probably won't care what happens to a colored man no how," she sobbed. "I'm just sick about the whole thing."

"Don't you worry your head none, Starla. I'll carry you downtown and see exactly what Jon's up against."

Once they arrived at the county courthouse, Starla remembered going there once before but it appeared gloomy and lifeless this time around. There were no well-wishers or smiling faces offering congratulatory salutations to a young married couple in love. Instead, an overwhelming presence of sadness and desperation aligned those hallowed corridors. Starla's mood worsened when she saw Jon bound in chains at the mercy of an old judge sharing a striking resemblance to Abraham Lincoln. Only thing was, that seasoned judge wasn't about to set any Negroes free.

The wrinkle-suited lawyer stood up then anxiously read Jon's plea for dismissal. "Judge, my client is a college senior with an A average. He's a homeowner and a married man with a small child. Your honor, he hasn't even had a parking ticket before." Good thing for Jon, his court appointed legal aid was a promising defense attorney who actually cared about his win-loss record.

"Well, your client should have considered all he stood to lose before stealing another man's property," the judge argued curtly. "No counselor. I think this qualifies as a bit more serious than a parking ticket." He glared at Jon as if the accused had just dropped his pants in open court. "Son, I've heard your explanation as to why you allowed yourself to become a party to this crime after the fact. And, you may not be the one who took the vehicle but someone did. And unless you are willing to name your co-conspirators and help the court bring them to justice, the heavy burden of guilt will fall squarely on you." After the judge shuffled some papers and scribbled a few private notes, he peered over his bifocals and down his nose at Jon like before. "Tell y'all what, I'm feeling pretty generous today. I'll leave it up to you, uh Mr. Holloway," he said, reading Jon's name from the arrest report. "I'll hand you the keys to your future." Jon held his breath while the judge continued his thought. "You can either go to trial and believe me you'll serve the maximum sentence for this crime or you can enlist in the Army, go to Vietnam, and serve four years of duty for your country."

A thick knot lodged itself in the back of Jon's throat as he looked over his left shoulder. He caught a troublesome glimpse of Starla holding their son. Both options seemed like life sentences. Jon's lawyer watched him mulling things over.

"Take the deal Jon," the wrinkle-suit whispered. "If you go to jail, you'll be a felon and lose valuable rights as an American citizen. You won't be allowed to vote and forget about getting a decent job after doing time. Think about it. Do you want that little boy of yours to go through life cheated because of what his father got caught up in? Of course you don't Jon. Take the deal."

Jon's lawyer began to sway uncomfortably from left to right. He was concerned that his client might fail to heed sound legal advice and his flaming hemorrhoids were nearly unbearable. While the attorney wavered and squirmed, Jon stood firmly like a mighty oak. He considered the arduous decision put before him, thinking if it were really up to him, he wouldn't have been shackled about the wrists and ankles like a slave on an auction block. Starla's sad eyes and his son's likelihood of a dim future poked at Jon like a sharp stick, prodding at him to take the deal strongly suggested by his legal representation. Regardless of the outcome, the one thing Jon was certain of, Wrinkle-suit's; inability to withstand more courtroom deliberation unless he received immediate treatment for his condition. A brief image of his lawyer squirming uncontrollably for a two-day trial ushered in a hurried conclusion.

"Tell the judge I'll go for it," Jon whispered. "Choice between hell or jail, I'll take my chances in hell."

"My client will plead guilty providing the plea not be entered into the record and your honor's kind offer is still on the table," the attorney spouted hurriedly. "We feel the army is a good alternative. Thank you sir."

Jon wasn't thankful for anything. Besides what was all that *we* stuff about. The evidence against Jon was circumstantial at best. The lawyer could have easily argued the textbook was on loan to a friend or stolen before the car had been taken but the judge had his mind made up within the first ten seconds of laying eyes on the defendant. When it was all just about said and done, the judge winked at the prosecuting attorney who hadn't said a word. "The chains were a nice touch, don't you think? They always do the trick," said the Abe look-a-like. "They tend to weigh a little heavier on the Negro boys. Takes them back to their roots, I suppose."

It was excruciating for Starla to watch Jon being handled like a hardened criminal. Watching the unnecessary spectacle became more impossible when her husband's heavy leg irons jerked impulsively between each of his short restricted steps. Starla turned away, shuddering at the reality of losing her first and only love.

She cried hysterically as they led him away. "Don't go Jon! Stop! He didn't do anything! Judge you got the wrong man!" The bailiffs were forced to restrain her after she attempted to fall into Jon's outstretched arms. The nightmare continued when the state corrections officers led him out the door and out of her life. In accordance to Jon's unconventional plea agreement, he was immediately remanded into custody until the military police transferred him to boot camp at Fort Hood, in Killeen Texas. Starla feared never seeing her husband again. Losing him to another woman would have been easier to stomach, at least then she liked her chances of winning him back.

THREE

If There's a Hell Below

When the military bus docked at the Army boot camp intake station, Jon stepped off it thinking of himself as an indentured servant rather than an honorable soldier, considering the terms of his enlistment. However, he was forced to adapt to his new surroundings or risk seeing old Abe again.

Jon had been a college track star before becoming a family man. When he learned that Starla was pregnant with Jon-Jon, he rescinded a full scholarship at Prairie View A&M in order to hustle a living and raise his son. He wasn't a stranger to hard work or to the discipline required for top physical conditioning. After completing his first four weeks of basic training, he'd shaved two seconds off the obstacle course record and was offered a spot on the Army track team after returning from Vietnam. Spending additional time in *The Man's* Army was out of the question. All Jon could think about was his family and getting back to normal life as quickly as possible. And, sometimes on a clear day, he could smell that last breakfast Starla cooked for him. He could all but taste that hot plate of grits, fried cheese eggs, sizzling bacon and hot buttered biscuits. It was the best breakfast he never got the chance to eat. Something about that just didn't seem fair.

Jon's platoon was called up shortly after the eight-week training period ended. Hundreds of young men lined up to board the largest aircraft carrier Jon had ever seen. The flight to Vietnam was long and arduous. For nineteen hours, murmuring cries were heard during incremental bouts of strained silence. None of the men knew what to expect when they arrived in *the jungle* but they all had one thing in common, knowledge that many of them would not be catching a return flight home when the fighting was done. Fear of the unknown shook even the bravest soldiers. Jon tried to pretend he wasn't disturbed by the somber anxiety which infiltrated the aircraft but that was impossible to pretend. The blatant terror he witnessed kept reminding him how millions of hijacked and displaced Africans had endured far more ghoulish apprehensions during tumultuous voyages across the deep waters where uncertainty and death awaited them too—on the seas of tears.

When the plane Jon hitched a ride on finally landed in Viet Nam, most of the troops had no idea why they were in the middle of a war zone or where it actually appeared on a map. For two years, Jon had witnessed the blatant brutality of war. Malaria, Swine Flu, and Typhoid Fever were the least of his concerns. Blood was spilled daily in the thick humid sticks of Southeast Asia. Close calls were even more common, not to mention ambushes which occurred frequently. Each time Jon encountered another still body lying in the midst of swampy mush, void of life and breath, he drifted a greater distance from reality. Detachment from the real world was the best way to deal with the horror of such an atrocity against humanity. With each sunset baring close resemblance to the next, Jon kept a daily journal in order to keep a good record of how many days had actually passed. He took notes on man's malicious fury and diabolical schemes. Some of his entries described murderous plots that were so despicable; he winced when reading them himself. Beheadings, executions, and live prisoners of war being used for target practice were common occurrences. Good men, decent men, became monsters. Likewise, many of those good and decent men experienced the same shameful deeds they'd dealt, from the business end of enemy rifles.

One morning, the sun came up just as it had the day before but something eerie was in the air. Jon awoke to the sound of his own voice screaming as everyone else rejoiced due to the first blissful day of Cease Fire. When Jon realized he was no longer asleep although he didn't hear mortars falling or search and rescue helicopters hunting for those wounded in combat, he assumed he'd died during the night. It was the sound of deadening calm that whipped Jon into an unnerving frenzy.

Without thinking, he leapt from his bunk to rummage through his gear for a weapon to fight off whatever demons that might have followed him into the afterlife. Suddenly, James Brown singing *Please, Please, Please*, caught Jon's attention. Cautiously, he peeked his head through the barracks entrance then lifted his hand to shield his eyes from the blinding mid-morning sunrays. The entire camp seemed locked in a foray of euphoria. Soldiers made most of the opportunity to lick their wounds and reflect on managing to stay alive and in one piece. Some of the enlisted men played softball and sand volleyball, reveling as if the war was over. Others sought the chance to busy themselves by exercising their chosen addictions to drugs or alcohol. Their world stopped and for a brief moment and everybody found something to celebrate, something to laugh about, and something to help them forget. During the thin slither of time, there were no worries, no woes, no tomorrows.

Jon spent the better part of the day, writing home and reminiscing over letters he'd received from Starla. Since Jon hadn't acquired a taste for alcohol or desires of drug induced hazes, perfumed letters supplied all the natural highs he needed. One of his early parcels home explained how he'd missed Starla's sweet kisses, hot teacakes right out of the oven and his son's carefree giggles.

In one letter he wrote:

Starla,

You and Jon-Jon are the only things that reinforce the reasons why men dare to dream in the first place. Sometimes, when I find myself thinking of giving up, I overcome my selfish thoughts then smile when I envision our son and dream of you. Y'all restore the hope that my circumstance took away, so I persist and endure in the meantime with the thought returning to what makes me whole. And, in the depths of the darkness or in a heated afternoon, I still think of getting things back to the way they were and coming home soon. Sweetheart, I remember when tomorrow was only a day away.

"P.S., I LOVE YOU..."

He ended each of the letters in the same manner, in the event that he didn't make it home himself. Jon wanted P.S. I LOVE YOU, to be his final words to Starla. Despite the dreadful deeds carried out on the battle field, Jon was still one man in love – holding onto threads of the good man he always wanted to be.

During the three years he'd been in Vietnam, Jon obtained a battlefield education in the mechanics of weaponry issued by the government. However, he didn't acquire the degree of heartlessness that was all too common when it came to committing senseless murders for the sport of it. One unnecessary death was one too many despite the constant mantra of kill or be killed. Coincidentally, careless doses of sympathy sent men home in body bags faster than carrying an empty gun, so Jon continued his proficiency at killing and staying alive. War was hell and whoever said it first must have experienced it personally. Just when Jon thought the twisted trail of death couldn't have gotten any worse, it did.

As the sun peaked over the horizon, Jon's Platoon sat by the roadside packing up to push back to base after having been out in the field for three straight days. Suddenly a small Vietnamese child, who couldn't have been more than four or five years old, entered camp with a stuffed animal tucked under his arm. Several American soldiers took notice of the tiny dark haired boy wearing pajamas and a runny nose. Others didn't give him or his childish toy a second look as they made preparations for a shift change. Every man in that company should have treated that child with prejudice and fear. If they had, the small toy animal which was stuffed with explosives wouldn't have killed seven weary Americans while wounding five more. An innocent child on a suicide mission was unthinkable before it happened. The boy's smiling face was erased by a thunderous unsuspected blast, which sent dozens of armed men scurrying for cover.

After Jon had gotten over the initial shock of unbelievable catastrophe, the image of a smiling child was overshadowed by visions of bloody human fragments sprawled along the roadside. When his company returned to base later that afternoon with the dead and wounded in tow, Jon learned that he had been assigned to gravedigger detail. It hadn't occurred to him before then to cry for families of the fallen soldiers but unstacking lifeless limbs and stumped torsos rocked him to his core. A disturbing cloud swelled inside him, a cloud of doubt that he'd return home in one piece.

Shortly after the graves were filled and covered, the barracks were quieter than usual because of what had been witnessed first-hand. A blonde headed soldier, who didn't appear old enough to shave, sobbed uncontrollably in his beer on the other side of the room. He called out to get Jon's attention.

"Holloway, can you believe what happened today, man? I was there and I still can't believe it."

Jon had spent several hours replaying the sequence of events in his head as well. The images of flying bodies coupled with the smell of dynamite and burning flesh was more than believable, it was as real as real could get. "Yeah. Yeah, I believe it all right," he responded eventually.

"Holloway, I sat along the road waiting for orders to move out. I smiled at that little boy when he passed by me to hand Captain Moss that goddamned stuffed rabbit. I sat there wishing that he'd given it to me. I thought it would make a great souvenir, you know." The soldier's head fell back softly against the thin bamboo lining of the barracks wall. "Then boom, Captain and that little boy were gone. They just disappeared in a cloud of fire and black smoke. And to think, not a minute before, I was sitting there smiling and wishing it was me!" The young soldier resumed his pitiful outpouring of emotion before popping the top of another warm can of beer to drown his sorrows. "I was wishing it was me, man," he reiterated between sobs. "I was wishing it was me."

Ironically, Jon also remembered his bright idea of getting his hands on a souvenir when the tiny assassin approached the camp. He was willing to throw in combat pay to outbid his Captain for the toy rabbit for Jon-Jon before it occurred to him that his son had seen a few birthdays since he'd been away and was more than likely beyond the stuffed animal stage. In fact, the photos Starla sent him displayed how much his son had actually matured. Growth, which Jon regretted not having made a worthy contribution.

One day seemed to dissolve into the next, mere carbon copies of the previous ones. People died, lives were adversely affected and right on schedule the sun followed restless nights. "Don't make friends and you won't miss 'em when they get their heads blown off," was the advice Jon received when he arrived. He'd taken that recommendation to heart until a mind-altering experience blew in along with a warm Vietnamese wind. The chopper that delivered shipments of body bags also brought a relatively peculiar parcel, with a peanut head to match his nutted complexion.

Marlin Murchison found himself behind the eight ball. A strange girl's dead body mysteriously appeared in his room at a St. Louis boarding house, where he rented a bed from time to time. Even though he'd never laid eyes on the girl before stumbling onto her naked corpse, gagged and strangled on the floor of his closet, that wouldn't have mattered to the local authorities. When it occurred to him that it was another ploy of the St. Louis Police Department to rid themselves of what they considered a trouble making protest organizer, Marlin enlisted in the army later that same day and hopped on the first thing smoking out of union station. He'd signed his induction papers as Marlin Blade, taking his street handle for a surname earned via his effectiveness with a knife. His contempt for the U.S. establishment was unrivaled but Vietnam was as far away as he could get with only two rusty nickels in his pocket.

Once he checked in with the commanding officer, Marlin Blade accepted his quarters and immediately begun sorting out various personal items on the bunk he'd been assigned next to Jon's. The bed had been recently vacated by one of the men killed in the explosion.

Jon was instantly drawn to Blade for two reasons: the things he said and the books he read. Early one Sunday morning while Blade thumbed through books written about Marcus Garvey and Malcolm X, he inhaled a whole pack of cigarettes. Blade chugged a six pack of red cream soda, puffed twenty cigs into a clouded chain of smoke, polished both pairs of his government issued boots then cleaned his pistol. As if on cue, the dinner bell sounded when Blade finished reading his second book of the day then began lacing up his boots. He'd missed two meals already. He wasn't going to pass on dinner.

Looking on eagerly, Jon smiled. "Man, I didn't think you'd ever get done reading. Those must be some heavy books?"

Blade peered up peculiarly as if he'd been alone the entire time. "Yeah, some real heavy consciousness about strong black leaders. Can you dig it?"

Jon, the reserved Texan, wasn't real acquainted with the latest slang that recently transplanted soldiers tossed around but he caught on fast enough. "Yeah, I think I can dig it?"

During the next several months, Jon and Blade became the best of friends, helping each other to pass time constructively. Jon tutored him on survival tactics and how to get the best shine out of a pair of muddy boots. Blade shared his collection of literature written by, for, and about Afro-Americans and the struggles they were enduring back home. Blade also informed Jon of the struggles he would be certain to encounter if and when he returned to the states.

Late one Thursday evening, Blade debated the plight of the Black man in America with a renowned troublemaker feared by most of the enlisted soldiers and for good reason. Brown Lee was a brutish thug from Nebraska. He was a solid mound of muscle with a shaved head that added to his intimidating personality.

The fact that he often displayed his strength by ripping off one-hundred consecutive pushups didn't go unnoticed when he took personal items from other soldiers without argument. They'd all decided individually that losing their possessions was better than losing teeth.

At times, Brown Lee singled out Jon who refused to scrap with any fellow grunts for any reason. He fought on the battlefield to stay alive and was compensated for it. There was no benefit in fighting with his countrymen. That night however, a near fatal incident was inevitable.

Blade was lying on his back. He nimbly turned the page on a novel which stood on his narrow chest while holding a lit match to the end of another Winston cigarette. Brown Lee snatched the book from his hands then begun to ruffle the pages. The oversized bully was hell bent on drawing blood merely for the sake of it.

"This shit ain't sayin' nothin'!" he scoffed, at the much smaller man.

Blade casually lowered his dark sunshades to peer over the top of them. "Brown Lee," said Blade, just loud enough to be heard, "it's no mystery to me why you don't understand the nuances detailed in that there book. It's kind of difficult to make out what's going on without any pictures. Now give it back before somebody gets their feelings hurt."

Brown Lee exhibited disdain with a tight lipped smirk. Blade raised his glasses with a pointed index finger and then demanded his book be handed over although it was obvious that the cocky tree stump was looking for a fight. All he needed was another body to accompany him in a dangerous tango of skill and strength. "Little nigga," Brown Lee hissed, through a large gapping grin, "you want this book back, you gotta ask me nice. Let me hear you say, may I please have my book back, Mr. Lee."

Blade sat up on his bunk, hunched his shoulders then opted for the path of least resistance. He stood up, bowed and shuffled dramatically like an imbecilic simpleton while using an exaggerated submissive but sarcastic tone. "Mr. Lee, may I please have my book back? Uhhh, Mr. Lee, suh?"

Several of the soldiers snickered when the intimidating dolt had been overwhelmingly outwitted. Brown Lee was embarrassed. His immediate snarl suggested that he was resolved to make Blade pay for his blatant defiance. He rather enjoyed further baiting the trap. "Yeah, that's real funny. This time, ask me from down on yo' knees. Chump!"

Jon had been watching the ill-matched chess game of intelligence and he knew that Brown Lee was about to make a decisive move. While Blade stood firm in the barbarian's shadow, not about to back down, Jon stepped in.

"Heyyy fella's, it's not that serious!" he offered cordially, in attempts at defusing the situation. "I have lots of books you can have Brown Lee, and shoot… some of 'em even got pictures. Let this thing go, right where it is, and you can have 'em all."

The humorous crack Jon hurled at the muscle bound menace brought unbridled laugher from the growing number of curious onlookers. Brown Lee was furious. The veins in his neck bulged when he averted his attention toward Jon. Blade was tough for his size, and skillful with the butterfly knife he kept hidden in his boot. Jon figured Brown Lee just might walk away from the disagreement if he stepped in.

In the time it took Jon to work it all out in his mind, Brown Lee had tossed the book across the room and started over toward him in a threatening huff. "Ooh, Holloway wants to take the midget's ass whoopin'. I'm tired of you anyway. Always bein' a do-gooder and printin' letters for these fools who can't write they own

name. Let me tell you what you can help me with." He snatched
a picture of Starla off Jon's makeshift headboard then proceeded
to antagonize him with it. "Yeah, you go on and write home to
tell yo' pretty lil' woman about this ass whoopin' you about to get
then she can start sendin' me some of her panties in a plastic bag
after the milk man gets 'em wet."

Without notice, Jon leapt to his feet from the writing desk.
Brown Lee grabbed him tightly by his shirt. Cheering erupted in
the barracks. Servicemen liked a good fight. In peace-time or war-
time, they liked a good fight. Blade pulled the dark sunshades
away from his thin face before climbing onto a folding chair.
He dove onto Brown Lee's back and held on for dear life. Before
the intimidating hulk could react, Blade had a chrome-plated
fishing knife pressed against his throat. Brown Lee's expression
warned that he intended on seeing this skirmish through to the
bitter end. Relentless, he carefully moved his hand upward to
separate the shiny steel from his neck. Jon was certain that one
or both of the men would be dead in moments if he didn't inter-
cede. In a swift maneuver, he spun from Brown Lee's grasp then
pulled a service revolver from the waist band of his fatigues. The
barrel of Jon's weapon was nestled firmly against Brown Lee's
right temple. If someone had to die, Jon figured Brown Lee to
be the odd man out.

Jon swallowed hard then proceeded to enlighten the man who
was about to get himself croaked. "Corn Fed, there's two things
saving your life right now. Love for my ignorant brothas and the
simple fact that God looks after children and fools. You ain't no
child but you're still covered. Now, don't you go and make me out
to be no liar 'bout God and have to kill you on the spot."

The room brewed with anxiety as emotions ran high. Brown
Lee held on to the fringes of contemplation and the thought of

fighting his way out of the no-win situation. Jon understood the difficulty in Brown Lee's dilemma so he made one last attempt at reconciling it before there was nothing left to say but the last rights over another man's dying corpse. "Now look, you said something about my wife that I didn't particularly care for and I'm gonna let you slide 'cause you don't know no better. But you'd want to ease up, go over there and sit yo' big country ass down before I change my stance on apologies."

After Jon cocked the hammer on his gun and prepared to pull the trigger, Brown Lee's eyes widened. He was caught somewhere between rage and redemption, both boiling inside his barreled chest. Sweat beaded up on the top of his shaved head while he measured his life expectancy. And just when the room begun to spin and didn't appear as if it was going to let anybody off until a body dropped, Brown Lee squeezed his eyelids shut. He grimaced furiously then slowly lowered both his hands. When he slinked out of the room in defeat, a chorus of cheers rang throughout the camp. The bully had been broken, once and for all.

A few days later, Brown Lee approached Jon with his tail still tucked between his legs. He readily admitted that his reading skills suffered miserably and that he was jealous of the assistance Jon had given to other men. He'd been too proud to ask the same help for himself. Jon and Blade both agreed to look past their disagreements. They set up daily tutoring sessions until Brown Lee read well enough to pass a high school equivalency exam although their toughest challenge was getting him to add, subtract, multiply and divide without taking his shoes off.

Over the next the six months, Jon indoctrinated himself with the strategies of black revolutionaries on the front lines for equality. As his social awareness grew exponentially, his view of the world became more grossly distorted, with each passing day. He developed a bond with the movement in Black America and ingratiated himself with literature written about the militant movement in full bloom back in the states. Jon had just completed a letter to Starla, explaining how he had evolved instead of wasting away like so many of the men he'd served with, when a first lieutenant stopped by with unexpected news. His tour of duty was shortened by 97 days due to the pressure put on President Richard Nixon to begin evacuating troops by the thousands.

Jon was going home. Even better, he was actually going home alive. Every soldier who fought in Viet Nam had hopes of returning home to their families after the fighting ended but few of them counted on it. Since it was a foregone conclusion that Jon's hopes hadn't betrayed him, he decided to pass on sharing the good news in his last letter to Starla. Jon imagined her surprise when he showed up at her door unannounced. He even managed a smile, as he dropped the letter into the outgoing bin as already written. It read quite differently than all the love filled pages he'd mailed home earlier.

Starla,

The nights seem to drag on forever and the days live twice as long as I remember them lasting at home. I'm considered an old man here. A few months shy of a four year hitch and I'm still alive, I mean. Funny huh? The fella's gage your life by how long you've retained it instead of how much of it you've used. Blade is still helping me to fully understand why things are happening in the States the way they are and maybe one day I'll be back to help straighten things out. Baby, I read everything I can get my hands on, articles on black Muslims, black panthers and everything else black. They're making serious efforts at changing the way black folk are being treated in America, while we're over here meddling in other folk's business and being pimped by The Man, in the process. I'm sorry Starla, I didn't set out to get so heavy but that's just how things have turned out.

Please make sure Jon-Jon gets his lesson 'cause we need to raise more Bobby Seals, Huey Newtons, Malcolms, and Martins for the next generation. The revolution is upon us and preparation for any battle starts in the mind. Solid..."

Jon concluded the letter with, *"Power to the People"* written in the post script where *"PS, I Love You,"* was once a heartfelt standard. He'd endured changes from half way around the world, having no idea that the little piece of heaven on earth he was once forced to leave behind had experienced a multitude of changes without him as well.

FOUR

Soulville

Sixteen days after Jon received the good news, he found himself stepping off a Greyhound Bus at the Dallas station. It was a hot Friday afternoon when he exited behind several small children being escorted by an elderly white lady dressed in clothes that reminded him of a travel brochure. She wore a quintessential multi-colored tropical print blouse with Bermuda walking shorts and a big wide brimmed straw hat. The bus driver asked if she were going to transfer buses in Dallas and catch the next leg to New Orleans. The woman turned and smiled cordially as she took her last step off. "Naw, I'm going to Monkeytown," she yelled, to be heard over the rumbling bus motor. "You know… Montgomery, Alabama."

When Jon heard the woman's total disregard for social etiquette, he wanted to retaliate against her foul reference to the southern town heavily populated with black people. Racial attitudes weren't above reproach, by any means, but naked racism was well on its way to becoming socially unacceptable and dangerous. Black folk were fighting back. Jon imagined the world evolving but reality crept in alongside the cool shadow that engulfed the bus terminal. It was as if the afternoon sun took its time to wink at the woman's rude comment so Jon did likewise. He nodded kindly to the driver, refusing to allow a thoughtless bigot to steal his joy of being home.

Since government issued clothing were all that he'd worn for the past four years, Jon felt comfortable marching up the busy avenue in his dressed uniform, starched like a crisp dollar bill. He slung his heavy duffel bag over his shoulder then started out toward the local bus line to get acquainted with the city routes. While he wandered through downtown, Jon was amazed that so many buildings had been erected. He also noticed that the air smelled differently than he remembered. Thousands of new automobiles contributed to the unfamiliar and unpleasant odor but Jon was still proud that his hometown had prospered in the years he was away. Viewing the city from his vantage point gave him the impression it had matured as well, offering loads of opportunity for a young and ambitious war veteran. No doubt about it, Dallas was sure to open its arms wide and welcome him home. Jon could hardly wait to get settled in, find the perfect job and reclaim the life he was meant to live. If only it were that simple.

Peering out of the window as the city bus wheeled up one busy street and down another, he marveled at clusters of prosperous looking folks with expensive suits and fine cars. It appeared that all was well until the bus rolled nearer to his old neighborhood on the south end. The fine cars suddenly became older, less impressive models. Countless tribes of pedestrians, black people mostly, trod along the sidewalks. *Where are all those brothers and sisters going*, he'd thought to himself, *and why weren't they taking the bus to get there?*

No one warned Jon of the staggering realization that more people were out of work and below the poverty level than when he left. The pedestrian tribes hoofed it because the recent bus fare hikes cut too deeply into their grocery budget. Putting food on the table was the overwhelming favorite versus over inflated fares and bumpy bus seats. Something that was an obvious contrast, were the buildings on his side of town, the ones without shiny finishing or cutting edge architecture. More than half of the buildings were vacant, indicating how badly the neighborhood was struggling.

As Jon journeyed even closer to home, he couldn't help but feel that someone or something had gang raped the entire area then ran through town bragging about it. Liquor stores operated next door to churches and directly across the street from elementary schools. Devastation took root when the city officials neglected to include the south side in their zoning regulations for every other section of town. The city leaders that be didn't think enough of it to adequately separate books and bible beaters from bottles of booze.

Prostitution sprang up like rotten weeds. Some of the working girls were little more than zombies hyped and haunting the breezeways of run over tenements, firing up, getting high and going down on the next trick. Renegade cops made out like bandits, shaking down resident heroin dealers. Disowned sons of prosperity ran the deadly mule train. "Gravity for sale," shouted those uunscrupulous hustlers, spreading that jive among the poison they peddled corner to corner.

Jon's gaze was drawn to the sprawling federally-funded residential projects aligning the enterprising avenue. The new fangled bells and whistles of a depressed economy was explained thoroughly after a young woman took a seat behind Jon. She quickly slipped off her size nine and-a-half narrow shoes from her aching size ten feet. She started sounding off to another passenger, with what she thought of the news station's biased coverage of the Black Panther's participation in the citywide taxi strike.

As the woman massaged the corns on her left foot, she took a run at summing up the status quo from where she sat, tired and dissatisfied. Her point of view varied greatly from the television news anchors, who often missed the mark where black people were concerned. "Girl, I just don't know sometimes," she rattled off, in a syncopated rhythm for emphasis sake. "That plastic looking white man staring back at me through the TV set keeps on telling me about what he calls the 'hopeless predicament' of the black race but I just don't get it. Sure it's been tough, ain't no denying that, but behind these walls of discrimination seeing is believing and love is what I see. How dare they tell us about us on the news at eight when nobody knows our struggles better than we do. Behind these walls, they say we're depressed, desperate and helpless but I'd be willing to lay a stiff bet that I have more true friends than they do... and what's more, my neighbor is still my neighbor. Fences don't separate us behind these walls where every woman is my sistah and each man, my brotha. Honey let me tell you, we have just what we need in this here 'hopeless predicament' we have each other and ain't nothing hopeless about that, chile."

While Jon listened in on the profound monolog, he fought the urge to turn around and salute the outspoken woman with feet much too big for her work shoes but he didn't. However, he did study her through the window after the bus had reached her stop and she'd slowly stepped off wearing house slippers, carrying her run-over hushpuppies in a thrift store handbag. Her white hospital uniform, powder blue and neatly starched, suggested that she probably didn't hold a position on the medical staff. Jon continued to observe her, carrying a shopping bag under each arm, until she made her way through the entrance gates of a low-rent apartment complex.

From that brief encounter, Jon understood how important it was to maintain prideful while scratching an honest living. That was his second lesson since hitting town and it stuck in head as the bus wheeled back into traffic and closer to his stop.

There was a blatant absence of the black dollars where remnants of desegregation stood in its place. "Baccus Cleaners is still alive and kicking," he said to himself. "I bet they're still charging too much but at least they're still here."

Amidst the doldrums of hard times, Jon found himself enjoying the latest fashions on parade. Freedom of expression was in full stride. Women's bodies hadn't changed but the way they showed them off vastly improved, and after being out of the country for years on end, Jon didn't mind it all at. As far as he could see, self-expression was a good thing. A mighty good thing.

A two-toned late model Ford station wagon passed as he marched up Forest Avenue. Several young girls hailed, "Welcome home soldier boy!" from opened windows. Those words went straight through him like a strong wind slapping at the frays of a weathered flag. He felt it but it couldn't pull him away from the mission he was dead set on bringing to fruition. All the new-fangled ghetto attractions offered an over abundance of stimuli to sift through, as he turned left onto South Blvd., but he managed an eager smile when his eyes landed on his home from the corner. The well-built two story wood frame house stood sturdy and firm. It needed paint and a good deal of patchwork but it was his and he couldn't wait to get inside and surprise Starla.

Suddenly, a brand new tomato-red four door Cadillac cruised by slowly then slammed to an abrupt stop before backing up toward him. If Jon never saw another Cadillac in his lifetime, that would have been all right with him. Initially, he assumed the driver must have mistaken him for someone else. Then a man about Jon's age, decorated in a hip mint green velveteen jump-suit with a thick goatee hopped out of the expensive car, leaving the driver's side door opened. Decked out in party clothes, in the middle of the afternoon no less, Jon also assumed the man had to have been involved in something illegal.

The sharp dresser begun to jive strut toward the curb. He had a grand afro and the nerve to put a matching wide brimmed hat on top of all that hair. "Holloway?" he reveled. "Damn nigga, you a sight for so' eyes. When'd you get home? Awe blood, you lookin' righteous in yo' uniform. Man, let's go have-a-drank."

Jon eyed the hustler suspiciously but couldn't place him. When it dawned on him who the clothe horse was, Jon dropped his duffel bag to the ground then reared back and cracked him on the jaw with a stiff right hand. Jon's stinging punch shook the man down to his patent leather platform shoes and knocked that ridiculous hat clean off his head. He was rattled when staggering to his feet. "Hold on now! Blood, hold on!" He picked up his wide brimmed lid then rubbed his jaw, cautious that the soldier might take another jab at him. "I guess I had that comin'. Why don't we put what's in the past behind us and let bygones be bygones, with you makin' it home and all."

Both men stared each other down until a suppressed smile pushed its way through Jon's lips. The awkward climate thawed when he laid a firm soul shake on his old acquaintance for old time sake. "All right then… Bygones," Jon agreed, as he turned to get another look at the man's fancy wheels. "So Odell, whose Caddy you driving this time? It's sho-nuff laid."

"Hell, it'd better be mine. I had all my girls workin' Christmas to Easter double time so's I could tool 'em around in a righteous sleigh. Seventeen-thousand and change, cash money. Which reminds me, I need to be mindin' my bid'ness and my hoes back on the stroll. They on a lunch break at the free clinic. Them check-ups be diggin' in a nigga's pocket. Man, the streets get lonely if my girls ain't there to keep 'em company. So, you coming or not?"

Jon passed on the offer to toss back a few drinks but promised to look up Odell once he got settled. He knew that pimps had the 411 on all kinds of money changing hands because of their affiliations. It was common knowledge that prostitutes were privy to hearing delicate criminal matters before all the pillow talking was done. It was no secret they told their wrangler everything worth sharing.

Odell strutted over toward his red Cadillac. Drawn in by the allure of another expensive show piece, Jon couldn't resist so he followed closely behind. As soon as he peeked into the car window to view a seventeen thousand dollar sleigh up close, he caught a poignant whiff of a fat marijuana joint burning in the ashtray. After he declined to sample Odell's reefer, Jon snickered at the brazen disregard to conceal a felonious act in progress then he took a long reminiscent gaze down the quiet residential street. Odell didn't have to guess what Jon speculated, and likely had on too many occasions to count.

"Starla's been a good girl while you was away. I know you'd been wonderin'. What man wouldn't, fine as she is? And yo' son looks just like you did when we was kids. Man it takes me back when I see lil' Jon-Jon walkin' on his way to somewhere. I offer to give him a ride now and then but he always say he ain't allowed to take nothin' off me. Guess Starla ain't ever forgave me for what I got you into." When Odell's eyes turned away shamefully, Jon noted a glimpse of genuine remorse before he continued. "Yeah man, Jon-Jon got that same skinny frame you had. Gon' have big feet too. He's yo' spittin' image all right. Well hey, I'm a split before my ladies thank I don't care and you know I can't have that." Odell mumbled something about his bitches having his money as he glided away from the curb.

Watching him drive away, Jon reflected on the yesterdays gone by and tried to feel good about it for once. There was no benefit in harboring hate for Odell over all that transpired since an ill-fated joy ride. Odell was just being true to his own nature and that was all he knew how to be. In the neighborhood, a well-connected pimp had juice. He was somewhat of a ghetto superstar. Against Jon's better judgment, he actually planned on looking up Odell later with intentions of getting a line on some honest money. Odell owed him at least that much. Jon planned on cashing in.

As the memory of that cold night when his life took a dangerous turn began to fade, two boys strolling down the sidewalk drew Jon's attention. He pondered for a moment then tried to dismiss it as a fleeting thought. After feeling compelled to study the two boys further, he was mesmerized by the taller boy's bowed legs and long gangly arms. The child's stature caused Jon to see inklings of himself in the seven-year-old boy a third his size.

Pride filled Jon's chest as they approached on the sidewalk. When they came within a few paces from where he stood, Jon called out anxiously, "Jon-Jon?" The boys stopped in their tracks, staring at him curiously as they squinted into the midday sun. The taller boy opened his schoolbook then carefully eased out a photograph of a soldier dressed in battle fatigues. Jon had sent it to Starla two years ago. The boy, who favored his father more than he did himself, studied the picture for a moment then peered up at him peculiarly. With his eyes fixed on a brilliant smile identical to his own, the child asked cautiously, "Are you my daddy?"

Jon's reassuring nod was subtle due to slight embarrassment caused by failing to be readily recognized by his only son. He was overjoyed nonetheless when Jon-Jon proceeded to introduce himself. "I'm Jonathan Holloway Jr. but you can call me Jon-Jon. This here is my best friend Reggie Brown," the boy announced with his hand extended. "Pleased to meet you, sir." The other child continued looking on with both hands shoved into his pockets, not at all sure what to make of the irregular midday meeting on the on sidewalk. Odell's summations proved correct. Jon-Jon was the spitting image of his father.

Jon saw himself in the child who stood before him, a carbon copy of the boy he used to be. As Jon squatted down, he firmly shook his son's hand all the while marveling at how much of a little gentleman Jon-Jon had become. "You really are something else," Jon gushed, eyeing him head to toe. "It's like looking twenty years of yesterdays in the face without blinking. No doubt about it, Starla's been raising you right." His eyes watered when he lifted him Jon-Jon from the gray fractured cement in one swooping motion to hold him in a crushing embrace.

Eventually, the other child's suspicions bubbled to the surface. "Jon-Jon, you sure you know this dude? The teacher says not to talk to no strangers."

"He ain't no stranger, Reggie. He's my old man home from the war." The proud father hoisted his duffel bag then walked into the hazy Texas horizon with his son held closely with his other arm. It was good to be home, so good to be home.

Upon reaching the cusp of the front porch, Jon motioned for the boy to step up and ring the bell. "Jon-Jon, is that you?" a woman's voice answered loudly, from inside the house. "I know you didn't lose your key again?"

As the front door swung open. Starla stood there, in tight blue jean hip-huggers and a snuggly fitted pink alter top. Her hair was pulled back into a thick ponytail. She was as lovely as ever and more of a woman than Jon remembered. Smiling longingly at the handsome soldier on her front porch who held her son in his arms like a large sack of groceries, Starla was caught up in the moment that she dreaded would never arrive. Although speechless, the things she couldn't say were evident in the tears streaming down her face. Thoughts of dragging Jon inside zigzagged through her head. Overwhelming elation held her at bay.

The soldier lowered his son onto the landing, preparing himself for the encounter he'd dreamed about since being dragged away. He reflected on all of the smooth lines he'd practiced if fortunate enough to be in Starla's presence again but the beautiful young bride he'd left behind had become a sensually fetching knockout. When the words he'd rehearsed faltered, he said the next thing that came to mind. "Woman, are you gonna come over here and kiss your husband or just stand over there looking like you want to?" It was difficult to discern whose case of the nerves trumped the other. Both of them had been reduced to memories and mere words on stationary, read repeatedly over nearly a four year span; which seemed like an eternity.

"Jon, I just can't believe you're home," she whispered, inching closer. "Thank you Lord for bringing him back to me in one piece." She kissed his full lips and angular face then pressed herself against his muscular chest. Warm tears flowed into the wells of her perfect smile. She squeezed him as tightly as she could, sighing as if the world had been made right with his return. Starla gripped Jon's shoulders firmly then melted like butter in his arms. "I'm sorry for acting like a silly schoolgirl but I can't help myself. Ohhh, you look so good baby. Welcome home Jon, back where you belong."

As the surprise of Jon's homecoming subsided, Starla's carnal interests began to swell. She felt perfectly justified while her mind wandered deep into the pools of desire, those she'd swam in alone while craving satisfaction. Starla chuckled softly then drew her face away from his chest.

Jon caught his breath as well. He didn't mind smeared makeup staining his dress uniform. There were no lingering intentions of wearing it again. Not ever.

After what seemed like hours of holding one another, Starla finally released her embrace to invite her man into his own house. "Come on in baby. Let me get you inside. Can I get you anything? You must be hungry. You need a drink to knock the dust off? Maybe some fried chicken and mashed potatoes. I just made some Kool-Aid. Remember how you love Kool-Aid? I'm sorry Jon. You're probably tired and need to rest. Can I run your bath?" Starla didn't know what to do first but she was certain of one thing, an overwhelming desire to please that man of hers. She had experienced more than her share of woes, being abandoned and making ends meet the best way she could. Jon sent every penny home, doing his best to take care of business from thousands of miles away. He promised to come back and made good on his word to pick up where they left off, loving one another unconditionally.

Jon-Jon sat at the kitchen table watching his parents getting reacquainted. Eventually, he became disinterested with the lewd glances thrown back and forth across the dinner table. He excused himself then climbed the stairs to his bedroom. Jon watched his ascent and thanked God for all his blessing, including Starla's maturity. He stared into her eyes then nodded his head approvingly. The adoring grin that anchored his face evolved into a sexual leer. He couldn't remember enjoying the way her breast pressed against her blouse, her hips tightly wrapped in faded denim, and her eyes piercing through him with uncertainty. His smiled shifted awkwardly when her expression displayed a tinge of uneasiness. It was easy to see that Jon was undressing her with his eyes. "I'm sorry Starla, do I frighten you?" he asked, not sure how he'd react if that was in fact the case.

"Yeah," she answered honestly. Her words were barely audible. "I am a little scared but I like it. It reminds me of the first time you looked at me and right away I knew you had to be mine."

"I remember. But you've changed," Jon replied. "You're so sophisticated now. I mean you really got it together. See you've taken good care of yourself too, put on a few pounds in all the right places."

Starla's big brown eyes sparkled as she took careful inventory of the welcomed stranger in her midst. She studied Jon like an abandoned lioness auditioning a potential mate then arose up from her chair to stalk her prey. Now stroking his back with her outstretched fingers, she squealed seductively then took a calculated step back. "Jon, would you please excuse me while I go and check on something? Please don't go nowhere. I won't be long. Just… please don't leave." She planted a soft smack on his lips then disappearing upstairs. Their brief bout of intimacy was hot and inviting, saying all the things that didn't require words.

Jon's nervous energy commingled with the excitement had him pacing the floor. After a few minutes passed, Starla reappeared. Jon-Jon traced her steps with a Fat Albert backpack harnessed behind him. He giggled while waving goodbye to his daddy before being rushed out of the house on an impromptu sleepover. Yearning for the passion-filled reunion she awaited, Starla wasn't in the mood to tolerate interruptions, limits or restraints. The time had come for catching up on grown folk's business, without any inhibitions getting in the way. She'd often fantasized of letting go, swinging from the bedposts and trying the sorts of bedroom tricks she'd read about in adult in *Reader's Digest*. Once they were alone, there'd be no holding back.

She tore at Jon's shirt, ripping buttons with her unrepentant lust. He lifted her by the waist. Starla locked her legs around him, shoving her moist tongue into his mouth. Jon climbed each step, slowly nibbling her ample breasts with sensual kisses. Tawdry kisses evolved into naughty nibbles.

"Come on baby," she cooed seductively. "I've waited a long time for reason to scream out loud."

"Yeah? I'm about to give you a whole bunch of 'em."

After reaching the bedroom entrance on the second floor, Starla climbed down off him momentarily. She hurried to the far side of the room to close the curtains then she began to unbuttoned her pants. Jon protested with a sexy growl.

"Uh-uh, let me. I've been waiting just as long to do that," he said softly.

Starla noticed the bulge in Jon's slacks growing bigger still. "Oh my goodness Jon. Let's get it on before I bust."

"You and me both," he sighed anxiously, before closing the bedroom door to mute the light inside. His penis throbbed while his hands eased Starla's jeans down past her hips. Her bikini panties, tie-died in a funky rainbow print excited Jon. "Oh yeah, I dig your style," he mouthed, while removing them. Jon began planting warm subtle kisses just above her naval then worked his way down.

Starla arched her back, spread her tender thighs then clutched at the bed sheets. "Damn it Jon, you got me trembling baby."

"Uh-huh," was his quiet reply. Jon slid one hand under her halter top and the other beneath the pillow used to raise her hips closer to his face.

"Oooh ooh. You didn't forget how I like it," said Starla, her clitoris aching with anticipation. Consumed with the wetness soaking her hairy vagina, Jon separated her labia with his firm tongue. He began licking honey from her sugar walls just the way enjoyed it most, slow and deliberate. "Ooh-wee," she gasped, with both hands guiding his head. Starla's hips grinded back and forth as her guttural groans deepened with each calculated stroke of his talented tongue. "Oohhh-weeee. Keep on doing it. You gonna make me pop. I can't hold it. I can't…, she panted ferociously. "You're taking me there baby!" she screamed, her fountain of love gyrating against Jon's welcoming mouth. "I'm going all the way!" During Starla's climax, Jon lapped up her juices like a man dying of thirst. Starla's back arched again when she heard his lips smacking noisily. It always did boost her orgasms, sending her to another stratosphere altogether. She was walking on sunshine with the deep seeded need to reciprocate.

Starla pulled Jon toward her on the bed. Her heart raced when she caught a glimpse of his long veiny shaft, hanging like a broken table leg. Jon chuckled as he wiped her wetness from his lips and studied the wanton look on her face. "You forgot what I took with me?"

She fondled him with an impish grin. "What you brought back is more than a notion," she answered sincerely, "a lot more." Starla told Jon to lie down, take a load off and that she'd handle things from there. He obliged -- hot, cocked, and ready. She whispered sweet nothings and naughty taunts in Jon's ear as she stroked his soul every inch and soothed his soul. "Did you miss what I'm about to do to you?" she asked, biting playfully on his muscular chest. "You used to enjoy the hell out of it."

"Hmm, that depends on what you're getting at." Starla began licking his penis from top to bottom. "Oh, you mean that right there? Damn girl, you don't know how much." He kept on enjoying it until Starla felt a twinge between her legs.

"Mind if we get back to that later? I need you to do something."

"Just name it."

"Don't move," Starla demanded. Jon agreed wholeheartedly when she eased herself on top of him, wiggling gently all the way down. "Don't move, not yet." She rocked his anchor back and forth at a leisure pace, taking time to enjoy what she'd missed just as much. With her knees locked, Starla worked up the tempo and then the courage to mash on the gas. She glided steadily for a moment before encouraging Jon to take all he wanted.

"You sure it's good and oiled?" he asked, with a strained tone.

"Right on baby, have at it."

Starla spent half the day and most of the night gasping, sputtering and screaming out loud. She was grateful to learn that her man had really grown, in several impressive ways. During unselfish bouts of getting reacquainted, they shared intimate thoughts and secret struggles that couldn't have been explained appropriately in the letters forwarded between them in the mail, some better received than others. Starla found herself intrigued by Jon's conscious transformation, his strategies for making a living, his strengths, hopes and dreams. During a multitude of cuddling, tickling and talking, Starla realized just how much she liked this new Jon.

"Baby, I don't even want to know where you learned that last thing you did to me but it was righteous." She didn't want to think about the time they'd spent apart or who he may have spent it with. None of that mattered now that he cradled her tightly, as if she were the last woman walking the planet. "I'm so glad you're back," she admitted solemnly. "I don't think I could have lived if you'd died over there. I mean, I tried so hard to hold onto what we had, praying that I didn't get one of those horrible yellow Notice of Death telegrams informing warning me to make arrangements for your body to be picked up at the airport. Uh-uh, I probably would've just shriveled up into a ball and wasted away." Although it was comforting to hear how Starla's love ran so deep, her heart felt testimony troubled Jon dearly.

"Starla, God knows I didn't want that for you. No woman should have to deal with that alone but I don't ever want to hear you say that again," he whispered back, staring into the darkness. "Don't ever think like that. I'm home now and that's all that matters. I'm home now." Jon's was point was well taken. He had been through hell and lived to tell about it. At last, all was restored in paradise. There would be no more watered down promises or black-eyed never minds refusing to be forgotten. Jon was home.

FIVE

Do Your Thing

The bright morning glow shined through the master bedroom. Jon's eyes fluttered, giving way to its menacing presence. He raised his head, unable to recognize his whereabouts. Hours of soul-stirring sex was intoxicating, it left him with the sweetest love hangover. The bizarre dizzying sensation subsided when it came to him where he was. He rolled over to kiss his angel good morning but Starla was already two steps ahead of him, downstairs and working on breakfast. Jon smiled again, thankful that some things never changed.

The smell of hot cheese grits, scrambled eggs and bacon rushed his nostrils, taking him back to another place in time, as fresh as it was then. That morning was the beginning of the rest of his life. There were no police officers at the door with arrest warrants, no deals to be made with a conniving judge and no one whisking him away to another corner of the world to fight for some God forsaken war. That morning, Jon enjoyed a breakfast fit for a king and prepared by his wife in his own house. It was great to be home.

After the breakfast dishes were washed and put away, Jon thanked his woman with kisses and playful affection. If Starla hadn't promised herself earlier to swing by the hair dresser, a couple of hours would have passed before Jon found himself heading down the block to the thank the neighbors for seeing after his son. Several four-door dedans and taxis parked against the curb, suggested the Brown's had a lot of visitors. *Must be popular folks*, he thought, while approaching his neighbor's door. Before Jon had the chance to knock, a barrel-chested man wearing a black beret, army fatigues and leather boots snatched the door opened. He stepped onto the porch with a tough scowl on his oversized mug, which reminded Jon of a bulldog that once chased him all the way home from the corner store.

The big man openly expressed his annoyance at Jon's untimely arrival. It was obvious that he had interrupted an important gathering. Each of the straight-faced brothers and sisters in the Brown's front room stopped whatever it was that they were meeting about when Jon peered passed the bulldog's thick head.

Jon spoke up quickly to diminish the likelihood of having a door slammed in his face. "I'm Jon Holloway from down the block. Didn't mean to bother y'alls meeting but my son stayed over here last night. I just came to carry him back home."

The barrel-chested bulldog didn't blink. Instead, he looked Jon over as if to size him up. The man's blank expression was meant to suggest that Jon wouldn't want to make the same mistake of interrupting them a second time. Then without any ado whatsoever, the bulldog with a body-builders physique motioned with his head that the boys were in the backyard. As the man stepped inside to close him out, Jon observed how the Brown's visitors jumped right back into their conversation as if his disruption was merely a sigh.

After asking around, Jon discovered that Reggie's father, Larry, owned and operated a small taxi company, which had issues with a rival white owned cab service. Larry Brown was warned to sell out his business holdings or expect retribution. A welder by trade, Larry put in over twenty years with a local construction firm until the white employees formed a union to improve their quality of life by demanding higher wages. Unfortunately, the black laborers weren't guaranteed the same pay increases, so Larry bought a half interest in a failing business. With sheer determination, he purchased the second-hand car company outright and began turning a profit within a few months. It wasn't a gold mine, by any means, but no white man's threats were going to shake him from it. The South Side Cab Co. was the legacy he wanted for his son Reggie. When it became apparent the threats Larry received were worthy of legitimate concern, he called on the local Black Panther chapter to strengthen his chances of holding onto his business. Two of his drivers were severely beaten when late night fares pretended to be drunk then lured the taxis into ambushes. The meeting at that Jon briefly interrupted was called to discuss what their mode of retaliation move would be.

Later on that day, Jon dug through boxes in his garage. While his son sat idly by, watching and waiting, Jon sorted out useless crap from valuable keepsakes. Difference between the two was based solely on Jon's perception. Digging through old memories and several layers of dust provided him the perfect foundation for getting to know his son. "So, Jon-Jon, what you been studying in school?" he asked, not knowing where to begin. He'd missed four birthday parties and the priceless moments which accompanied each one. Jon was determined to spend all of his spare time being what he didn't have, a good father.

"We study American history but momma don't like the book we use," the boy mumbled in a mellow tone. "She says that it only talks about famous white people and slaves so I don't bring it up

57

much. She'll only get mad all over again. But, I do like math. I'm the best in my class at adding and taking away. My teacher always tells me to help the other kids who don't do too good with numbers." Jon-Jon liked the way his answer made his daddy smile. He didn't know why but it felt like a tickle deep inside. "Yeah, I enjoy helping other kids the most."

"Son, that's great. We should all help one another get by. Lending a hand will make you a better man." He placed his strong hands on the boy's shoulders. "You know, you make your old man proud. As a matter of fact, I could use a hand right now. Reach over there and *hand* me another paint brush."

"Daddy," Jon-Jon sad, as a mature expression found its way on his son's face. "I'm real glad you're home. Momma's glad too. Yesterday, she was crying and laughing at the same time. It didn't make sense to me but I think she was mostly glad though. I heard her pray for you to never leave us again." Jon-Jon's eyes fell toward the ground. "You wouldn't do that, would you? I kinda like having a daddy all to myself instead of sharing my friend Reggie's with him."

Jon's eyes watered. His tough exterior softened at the sight of the man-child's solemn but hopeful face now peering up at him. "Nah, I promise that I won't be going any place that y'all can't come with me. We're a family again and there's nothing that could take me away from you and your momma. Nothing. I promise. You have my word on that." Jon watched his son walk away from their first man to man discussion, hell bent on keeping his word. While working out the details of fatherhood deferred, Jon also needed to restore more than just order in his son's life. The threat of abandonment still haunted Starla, her tearful prayers affirmed just how deeply rooted her fears were. Jon had something to prove, to his son, to his wife and to himself.

After he had made one last trip to the junk pile that mounted near the front of his house, several of the cars parked at the Brown's home begun to pull away one by one. Feelings of jubilation flowed through Jon's veins when carloads of militants rolled slowly by. Jon-Jon also looked on while listening to his father's summation of what he saw.

"Just look at them. Black leather jackets, shades glaring, and those afros-- as wild as their attitudes. Rolling down these rough streets four brothas deep, demanding respect where ever they go, huh, they're in the news more than the president. Untamed, street educated, unreal. Just look at them! Who would ever think you'd see Panthers in south Dallas." Jon had come to admire the somewhat confrontational organization and what they stood for. Political affiliations aside, he stood for finding a job.

Monday followed Sunday like it always had but this time Starla strolled through the shopping center arm in arm with Jon, enjoying one another's company like distant lovers on a holiday romp. It reminded Starla how inseparable they had been from the August evening they met until the morning he was carted off in hand cuffs. Conversely, their shopping expedition reminded Jon just how broke he was. After he'd purchased two new business suits, the search for job-hunting clothes was over, leaving a sizeable hole in their struggling bank account.

By Thursday, he managed to set up two job interviews after studying want ads in the classifieds section of the newspaper. Jon approached each opportunity with optimism and prayer. He was sharply dressed, poised, and prepared but it took each of the interviewers less than a total of eighteen minutes to discount him as a candidate for the positions he'd arrived on time to get. "What jobs have you held in this particular field?" they asked, well aware of his military background and war record. "Please explain any specific training you're had in the last two years." Nearly identical interviews disqualified Jon with thumb-on-the-scale requirements. Both questions shot him down before he could get started. Once the hiring managers laid eyes on him, they neglected to review the college credentials listing him as a senior honor student. Men with the power to bridge Jon's past and future saw what they wanted to see, a black man they couldn't use.

Bent but never broken, Jon strapped on his alternate suit then hit the pavement again. A downtown office tower lured him in as he read the numbers on the building twice, just to be certain. "Yeah, this is the right place. It sure looks like somebody's making money in here," he said, feeling better about his chances. When he caught an elevator going up, Jon was determined to put his other best foot forward. He'd heard a woman at the bus stop discussing that a particular company was in a rush to hire healthy young men for door-to-door sales positions. The woman even went so far as to show him their advertisement in the newspaper which sought to recruit salesmen with college backgrounds to market a new brand of shoes polish. With Jon's college credits and his familiarity regarding shoe treatment products in the military, he was more than qualified. It appeared he had stumbled onto the one thing he really needed, a can't miss opportunity.

When Jon entered the office suite, he approached a white lady covered in canary-yellow polyester. Seated up front at the reception desk, she glanced up from her crossword puzzle then greeted him eventually. "Yeah, what can I do for you?" she offered flatly. There was no mistaking the irritated tone. Those words weren't meant to be taken literally.

Jon overlooked the woman's lack of decorum. "Ma'am I understand this company is seeking enterprising young men with experience in the leather-goods treatment industry. Now, I don't mind working hard and I sure am healthy enough to walk miles a day to introduce potential consumers to your fabulous products."

She glanced at him peculiarly, replayed his eloquent pitch and then immediately informed him otherwise. "Sorry, you must have heard wrong. We're not hiring today."

Smiling cordially, through yet another rejection, Jon nodded his head in a slow deliberate manner. He'd heard her clear enough but he was not willing to be turned away that easily. "Uh-huh, I understand. I'll just come back tomorrow and apply then. What's a good time?"

"I'm sorry but *obviously* you don't understand. There is no need for you to come back tomorrow because we won't be hiring then neither."

It took a while to register but Jon eventually caught on that the receptionist was merely towing the company line, which would have come out differently had she said what she actually thought. *Sorry Black man, there must be some misunderstanding. Yes we are seeking enterprising young men 'though none of which, in any way, will resemble you.*

Jon pressed his lips together tightly then turned to walk away. As he pushed on the glass exit doors in the reception area, he overheard the same woman, who'd moments before told him they were not hiring. She cordially communicated to someone over the telephone that they were excepting all walk-in applications.

"Hey! I heard what you just said," Jon barked as he raced toward her desk, with the confidence of a prosecuting attorney who had just discovered the smoking gun. "You told someone on the phone y'all were accepting all walk-in applicants. Well, I'm an applicant and I sure as hell am walking."

"You-youuu must've misunderstood me," she argued none too convincingly, turning a bright shade of red. "And anyway, you shouldn't have been eavesdropping. Listening in on private conversations is a federal offense."

"You're kidding me right? *Wiretapping* is against the law. But, let me tell you what's offensive. You sit here in this nice air-conditioned office and decide who gets seen and who don't get seen. I'll bet my last nickel that you haven't ever, wait… scratch that, *ain't ever* seen the inside of a college lecture hall or studied all night long to disprove a mean old professor's assumptions that you couldn't past muster on his toughest calculus exam. And if you do have a high school diploma I would be extremely surprised. Now that's offensive!" Jon's jaws tightened. The entire situation headed toward a bitter end from the moment he entered the suite and it left a bad taste in his mouth.

The woman pounced from her desk. "I don't have to sit here and take your mouthing off. When I call the security guards on uppity Negroes like you, they'd just love tossing you out on your smart butt." She flopped back down in her chair, flustered and mumbling to herself in a low tone.

Jon stared the woman down. His stinging gaze measured contempt by the ton. Disgust was the order of the day and when he had too much of it, he picked up the clipboard holding the applications then flung it clear across the room. "Now, you can go run and tell that." Jon stormed toward the elevator with a little less resolve than when he arrived.

"Oomph, I would've graduated high school if I hadn't gotten married so young," was the woman's muted reply.

Two bus transfers later, Jon found himself staring out the window of yet another bus headed for the disenfranchisement zone. Corporate America had snubbed him again, this time using an uneducated woman to do their dirty work. After she had squashed his chances of getting ahead in the work force, Jon experienced another day of slammed doors and covert hell no's. And, every time that vision popped in his head, he got mad all over again. It wasn't fair to his family. Bills had to get paid. Legit hustle or otherwise, they had to get paid.

Jon didn't look forward to going straight home to his wife, who was undoubtedly anxious to hear how well he'd he made out. There wasn't anything to report, not worth hearing anyway. Jon counted on receiving the last of his combat pay, which would carry him another month if he budgeted right. After that, he'd be staring into the jaws of dismay, flat broke and busted.

Deciding to give himself the chance no one else would, Jon started a small shoe repair business out of their garage. It was enough work to keep him busy but failed to stack up well against his mounting debts. Starla, a seasoned veteran in the art of getting by, acquired part-time employment at the market. With an employee discount, her weekly paycheck covered the grocery bill, just the grocery bill. Jon dealt with the downturned economy as best he could while his self-esteem plummeted. Starla understood that a man's income and his success with putting food on the table was a measuring stick that most of them subscribed to. It challenged Jon's fortitude when he proved incapable of pulling together resources to sustain his household financially. There had to be something he could do to get his hands on some real money, without putting his freedom on the line.

SIX

For the Good Times

A ngelo's Market was a massive grocery store that catered to the needs of community. Outrageously high prices catered to Angelo's wallet. There were bins stacked with second tier produce and an assortment of dented canned vegetables greeting Jon as he entered the warehouse of necessary household items. He planned to pick up a few pounds of ground beef after the price had been substantially reduced. Grocers were notorious for lowering the cost of meats that neared the 'must sell by' date before spoiling. Jon searched the butcher's rack for packages that weren't too picked over. While picking over the questionable meats himself, he recognized Larry Brown debating whether or not to take his chances on a thick heap of questionable brisket. Larry was a stocky-built fair-skinned man in his early forties. His midsection was round but solid, as was the rest of him. His receding hairline made him appear to be a few years older than he actually was. Jon approached him with a raised brow and a suggestion to bless the brisket twice before sitting down to take his chances.

They chuckled like old friends, made small talk about their boys and complained about inflation. Eventually their discussion hinged on the difficulty Jon experienced finding work. Upon learning of Jon's unemployment, Larry took his thick fingers and rubbed the top of his head, where his hairline had retreated. "Young brotha, I know you're a good man and it's been a damned shame how they treat servicemen after y'all been doin' the politician's bidding. I'll tell you what... I just might be able to help you out. South Side Cab could use a good driver who knows his way around." He paused briefly to give Jon an appraising stare as if he were inspecting a suspect cut of romp roast. "You didn't come back from that war with no uh... problems did you?" There was legitimate cause for concern as many soldiers returned home with cocaine and heroin addictions.

"No, not me," Jon replied. "I don't even smoke."

"Just one thing though," Larry advised, "you gotta keep it under your hat about the position 'cause I've had to turn some other fellas down who asked before you. Meet me at the house about nine o'clock tonight, we'll get you started."

Their gentlemen's agreement sent Jon on his way feeling optimistic about securing gainful employment. He felt so good in fact that he made a visit to the butcher's counter, exchanging the aging ground chuck for two fresh chickens. A decent opportunity powered him like the engine of a runaway locomotive. Having empty pockets and opportunity was better than having pockets full of money and no inroads towards achievement.

Jon double-timed it all the way home with additional vigor in his step. He sauntered through his front door with a jive soul brother lean then swung the grocery sacks on the kitchen counter as if they were bags of previously buried treasure. Starla couldn't see what the bags contained but they had her man buzzing with excitement. Jon kissed her on the lips to stifle any impending questions then he broke into a spirited dance routine equipped with improvised 360 degrees spins. Jon-Jon took it all in, trying to figure out what the strange behavior meant. He was getting to know his father as a loving but serious man. This hyper dude with dynamite dance moves was a new twist. The young boy sat at the bottom of the staircase scratching his neck and wondering what could have made his father so happy.

Eventually, Jon unwrapped one of packages wrapped with white butcher paper. He held it near Starla's nose. The fresh chicken was presented like a trophy, with confident assuredness. Starla twisted her face and turned away. "Jon Holloway!" she shrieked, "if you don't get that dead bird's behind out of my face…" Reveling in Starla's embarrassment, he proceeded to chase her around the house, squawking and clucking like a crazed lunatic. Jon's animation pulled the boy from his perch. Jon-Jon joined in, imitating his daddy's antics until Jon pulled an about face. With the business end of the chicken pointed at his son, Jon closed in on him. Unbridled laughter filled their home again. At last, it began to feel like old times.

After the laughter subsided, Starla pondered a while as she put away the groceries. "Baby, are you sure we can afford this?" she asked. "I know you're working hard but things are still slow in your shop."

He nodded assuredly, staring down at his son who was now busy with homework at the kitchen table. "Sweetheart, I was saving this for an after dinner treat but I may as well tell you now because I know how you worry. Larry Brown had an opening for a driver. I know carting people around town isn't the kind of gig we counted on but it's a start and honest work. It'll be all right. I promise it will."

Starla's smile was tainted with a hint of apprehension. She'd heard some scuttle-butt about the trouble South Side Cab experienced with a rival taxi service. Being alarmed over gossipy street talk wouldn't put a single dime in her husband's pocket, Starla decided, so she let it go then prayed for the best.

Dinner was delicious as usual. The sautéed onions over baked chicken, mashed potatoes covered in white cream gravy, macaroni with three cheeses and emerald-green snow peas was delectable. As it grew closer to nine o'clock, Jon kissed Starla goodnight then made sure that Jon-Jon was tucked in his bed. Afterward, he strolled down the block with a carefree swagger, one that hadn't accompanied him since his ride in that police squad car some years ago. Under the clear sky he thought back on the many nights he laid awake in another man's country where the stars didn't seem to flicker nearly as brightly as they did in Texas.

At nine o'clock on the nose, Jon knocked at the Brown's front door. He wasn't fazed when the man with the bulldog's face appeared again. He stood in doorway wearing the same hard scowl as before. Jon didn't flinch or offer any explanation for his visit this time around. Larry stepped in when he sensed a testosterone explosion in the making. Good thing he did, for bulldog's sake. He wasn't man enough to deter Jon from starting his new job.

"He's cool Rock," Larry declared firmly. "This is the vet I was telling you about. He's the weapons expert, Jon Holloway. He made it back from the war a little bit ago and we could benefit from his training."

Jon didn't catch Larry's meaning. He was too busy keeping his eyes on the massive fellow blocking the door. Jon was also short on the facts concerning the death threats leveled at Larry and the intimidation tactics his company had recently been putting up with. Larry Brown was a business man, who also looked out for his own best interest when he hired Jon. If a battle was imminent, an army vet fresh from the jungles of Vietnam was worth his weight in gold. It was a savvy business decision to stack the deck with men who could handle themselves in the trenches when the time came to stand firm and fight.

Having been the first to arrive, Jon sized up all of the other men who reported for duty after him. It had become second nature from facing his own mortality day after day although he kept telling himself to relax. This was merely a job, not an adventure. He'd had enough of those for three lifetimes. Rock, the bulldog, slipped a black stocking cap over his head then rolled it up from the bottom until it fit snugly atop his thick skull.

When a loud knock at the backdoor drew everyone's attention, Larry nodded for Rock to check it out. Jon observed protocol for attending to the door each time another driver arrived. Rock didn't move unless Larry instructed him to do so. Jon understood their paramilitary chain of command. Rock was the sergeant at arms for their small group and more importantly its gatekeeper. He took his post seriously, like the enlisted men he'd fought with shoulder to shoulder for over three years. If looks could kill, Rock would have been facing life in prison for murder.

Jon kept an eye on Rock. He watched the brawny bodyguard make a subtle gesture to Larry, signaling that he wanted to be followed out of the room. Larry trailed closely behind him all the way to the backdoor, where four more men stood out on the rear porch waiting for the all clear sign to be let in. When Rock casually removed his cap, the new arrivals knew it was safe to enter and take their seats.

Rock resumed his role, studied Jon intently before discussing his concerns with the boss. "I ain't so sure about that Holloway cat. College boys don't have the nuts for what might be going down tonight."

"Other than you, he's the only man in this house who has killed somebody. Hell, he's killed plenty without a damned bit of thanks either. He needs us and we sure as hell need him."

Rock was forced to admit Larry's comments held substantial merit so he gave up on arguing about it. "You know I'm with you no matter what but I don't have to like it," he threw in, for the sake of getting the last word. "I guess we'll see soon enough if he can pull his own weight."

Larry sighed deeply. "Soon enough we'll find out more than we want to about all of us."

When Larry and his henchman fell back into the meeting room, the atmosphere had soured. Jon felt a host of nervous vibes. It reminded him of the missions that required locked and loaded weaponry. Intuition nagged at him. Something hot and heavy was in the mix and he'd found himself smack in the middle of it.

One of the four men, who previously waited out back, removed his dark shades and thin windbreaker. Some of the others in the room grimaced at the sight of his injuries when they caught a gander at swollen eye, the size of a golf ball, and rows of ace bandages bound around ribs. His hardened indigo face seemed to be pushing that bulging eyes away from his head. Julian Hampton came from the small town of Newberry, Louisiana. He'd been in Texas for a few months leading a nearly respectable life after fleeing capture from troopers in his home state. He had no intentions of spending his thirties on a prison farm after the stint he served years ago. Southern state penal farms took the most incorrigible black-hearted men and tamed them. Prison mules had it better than Louisiana state prisoners.

"Y'all know that ain't right!" one onlooker grunted, regarding Hampton's gruesome appearance.

Another frustrated taxi driver chimed in. "See, that's the kinda shit I'm talking about. They didn't have no business putting they hands on him. Damned crackers!"

Hampton was bushwhacked by white men associated with, Cane Cab, the rival company for strikebreaking. Two of Larry's drivers had also been beaten a few nights before but it hadn't been publicized. A third employee was laid up over in Parkland County, the hospital John F. Kennedy's body was rushed after being gunned down in Dallas. Larry anticipated a different outcome for his comatose employee, beaten within an inch of his life.

Hampton struggled to his feet from the end of the sofa. He held his ribs sorely due to a spike in pain then he peered around the room to look each man in the eye. "My brothas, y'all know me. Y'all know some of the things I'm capable of but ten against one just ain't right. We all know what happened to me and Jake and why Herman is in the hospital not knowing if he'll see tomorrow. We can't let it go down like that again. I'm sick and tired of playing the good nigga', behaving and keeping it cool. I don't look for trouble no more than the next man but those white boys started this and they done messed with the wrong brotha. They set me up and now they gots to pay!" Nearly everyone applauded his grievance until he raised his hand to stifle them. "Keep watch out there. I picked up this old white dude on Elm Street. He played drunk all the way over to Greenville Avenue on the north side. When I pulled over to drop the hunky off, he told me to pull around to the alley so's he could bust in on his old lady he said was cat'n around on him. Hell, after he stumbled out of the car, a gang of white boys surrounded the cab and pulled me out. They started kickin' and sluggin' away at me. They were sayin' how drivin' for Larry Brown was bad for my health." Hampton gasped deeply to catch his breath. "I wanna know what we gon' do to get even!"

Bolting from the room crossed Jon's mind more than once. He realized the level of commitment he'd have to pledge if he remained, fully aware that men's lives were at stake. Jon's army buddy, Marlin

Blade, made him promise that he would help brothers and sisters when he got the chance. Likewise, Jon assured him that he would be on the front lines when it did. All things considered, running out on the men who'd probably need him wasn't an option. He couldn't see turning his back. Not then, not ever.

After mapping out a strategy, it was agreed that four taxis would hit the streets that night. Each car transported two men strapped with revolvers. Other drivers waited on standby with walkie-talkies, prepared to be onboard for whatever transpired. Jon signed his name on the declaration binding the men together for a common cause, feeding their families. Come hell or high water, Jon was in the middle of it, all the way up to his neck.

SEVEN

Never Gonna Give You Up

Jon marched down the sidewalk with determined strides, feeling duty bound to do the right thing. When he opened his front door, Starla looked up from the daily newspaper. Her relaxed expression hit him like a haunting reflection in an old dusty mirror that he'd forgotten was there. Suddenly, he seemed lost in the contemplation of what exactly the right thing was.

"Jon, you forget something?" Starla asked. It was strange to see him wearing a somewhat perplexed expression.

"Yeah, yeah… but it's cool. I figured you'd be asleep. I didn't want to disturb you is all." His words softened when he changed the subject. "'Jon-Jon been stirring?"

"No, he's had a long day. All he wanted to know was what time your shift ended?"

Jon nearly showed his teeth at the thought of his son missing him. "I'll be back by the time he sees the sun. Expect me home by six or seven."

Starla approached her husband from the other side of the room. Her body was wrapped in a sky-blue satin nightgown that accepted the light from the outside street lamps and tossed it back happier than it was when making her acquaintance. The scarce illumination more than adequately accentuated her shapely silhouette, against the pale darkness. "I would love to… uh… send you off on your first night of work with a little somethin' special," Starla wooed seductively. "We can get started right here in the middle of this floor and see where it ends up."

Jon took notice, swallowed hard then quickly shook it off. "Come on now, I got to get back before Larry changes his mind. Anyways, what about Jon-Jon?"

"He's in dreamland. Why don't you send me there too? It won't take too long to get me going. I'm already hot and bothered."

"Dayyyum baby," Jon said regarding her offer. He kept cutting his eyes at the door then back at her. "Maybe just a little piece of…" he'd begun to say. Before he could get the last word out of his mouth, Starla pressed her soft body against his then guided her wet tongue comfortably into his mouth. She groaned sensually when her hands found the front of his work pants stretching against them.

Bam-bam-bam! Someone rapped on the door with three quick strikes. Starla stepped behind Jon as if the caller could see her sexy nightie through the curtains. One soft brush of the bay window drapes concluded that it was someone from the cab company.

"Starla, I'm sorry but I'm gonna have to catch that train of yours in the morning. That's one of the guys and you know I can't be late, being my first day and all."

"Go on then, but don't count on any raincheck 'cause it ain't even rainin'," she yelled playfully, as he opened the door to leave. "Don't work too hard baby. Save some for me," were the last words he heard her say before stepping out onto the porch.

Having no idea what fate laid in the balance, Jon ducked into the garage then rambled through his army duffel bag. He collected his service revolver and a long steal plated knife with a serrated edge. It was the same knife he'd taken off a Vietcong officer after ending the man's life in a hand-to-hand skirmish. Jon was glad now that he didn't accept the fifty dollars that Brown Lee offered him for it. Making a quick dash to the front of the house, Jon nodded assuredly at the cabbie who was sent to hurry him along.

After the job assignments were issued, Jon partnered up with Hampton. No one could have stopped him from getting a shot at revenge if the competition figured on trying their luck again. Preparing for the worst, they drove to an assigned post and as instructed checked in with Larry on the half hour. Their taxi fares were legit through a quarter of three a.m. As the hours rolled deeper into the night, the more it appeared they were in for a quiet ride throughout.

Jon thought it was a good time to break. He got clearance from Larry on the walkie-talkie then cruised by a local spot for sandwiches and sodas to go. Just as the food arrived, Hampton felt a knot swelling in his stomach. He told Jon that he needed to make a necessary pit stop to the men's room. The medication he took had irritated his stomach something awful. Hampton's pants were half way down before his skinny butt hit the slop jar stool.

While peeping at his watch and keeping look out for his partner, Jon headed back to the cab to check in for the three o'clock hour. He whistled a carefree tune as he cradled two smoked turkey sandwiches and twelve-ounce bottles of Big Red soda when climbing into the taxi parked curbside, next to the all-night diner.

As soon as Jon relaxed behind the wheel, someone sprang up in the back seat. A thin white man with a pickle-sized nose and child-sized teeth attempted to slip a piano wire over Jon's head. Years of combat training and Jon's sixth sense alerted him just in time that someone wearing high dollar cologne had climbed into the car with him.

The rear view mirror revealed the well dressed pickle-nosed attacker when he exposed himself by rising too high from his strike position. Jon managed to get his left hand underneath the wire, impeding the lasso from circling his neck. Two turkey sandwiches went flying inside the automobile as Jon wrestled feverishly. He pulled the man toward the front of the cab as far as he could. The assassin held on tightly with the resolve of a professional killer. Jon had been through a living hell battling the Vietnam army. He vowed not to let this man separate him from his soul. He gasped and grunted with the attacker doing likewise. Jon stretched out his right arm, frantically reaching for the glove box for the revolver hidden inside. He pulled forward quickly, anticipating his aggressor would be forced to move with him in order to maintain his tight grasp.

As expected, the executioner lunged forward with the notion of holding on. Jon rammed his head back sharply, smashing it against the bridge of the man's nose. The assassin grabbed his meaty beak with one hand when he heard the cartilage snap in half. He yelled out from the backseat while thick trails of blood spewed from his nostrils down past his narrow chin. His other hand casually released the piano wire altogether as he buckled onto the floorboard, anguishing in pain.

Jon gawked out of the cab's back window for Hampton, who was obviously still stranded on the toilette. His hands trembled when he realized they were covered with his own blood. The piano wire cut through his skin like a razor. He couldn't tell how badly they were injured but it didn't matter. Jon needed information. He needed it now.

As the bloody trespasser moaned loudly from sheer agony, an angry set of fast fist made their violent introduction. "Who are you working for?" Jon barked, with a vicious onslaught. Whack! "Who sent you?" Whack! Whack!

Jon demanded answers between each powerful blow to the man's face. Although bludgeoned, the attacker disregarded Jon's questioning. He was more distracted by the blood pouring from his head and his own timid voice pleading for the beating to stop. Jon continued looking for Hampton to return because he suspected that people who made their living in the killing fields didn't usually work alone.

Vigilantly, Jon reached for the glove box but his fingers ran across a full bottle of soda instead. He held it by the neck as he slammed it over the man's forehead. The assassin was useless if he refused to talk. Conversely, his whining, begging, and pleading was annoying as hell.

With a quick turn of the ignition key, Jon started the car engine then checked once more through the diner window for his estranged partner. He wondered if Hampton would ever reappear from the men's room before something happened that would send Larry to his doorstep with a boatload of apologies to Starla. Thoughts of leaving Hampton danced through Jon's troubled mind mixed with what to do with the lump stretched out and unconscious in the backseat. Larry and Rock would know the next course of action, so Jon decided he would deliver his hostage to the others for interrogation.

Before Jon had completed his thought, he felt a sharp punch land against the back of his head. The hard blow knocked him away from the driver's door. Jon's hunch was right. The assassin hadn't come alone. His partner was a much larger man by at least a hundred pounds. He was dark haired, with an olive complexion and dressed in an all black suit as if he were going to a funeral. If he was efficient at his business he would have been responsible for Jon's. This killer had more Italian features than the first, but it was unmistakable, the two were cut from the same cloth.

While Jon worked to regain his faculties, the meaty mauler slung open the car door then attempted to climb into the driver's seat. Jon tucked his knees then planted both feet in the middle of the man's abundant chest. That sent him straight to the pavement, rolling around on the street top. Jon slammed the door then fiddled anxiously with the ignition key.

The night had been calm as a lazy river but the wave of disturbance taking place in front of the diner roared louder than a hurricane. If Jon allowed the fat man to gain access to his car, he wouldn't live to see the sun rise or be there for his son as promised. That thought came to mind when the car stalled. Jon pumped the gas pedal profusely to get it started up again. "Come on! Come onnn!" he demanded, while continually patting his foot.

Bang!

Bang!

Two shots rang out, both hitting the driver's side door. The fat man reached inside of the car. He latched his thick and callused hand onto the steering wheel. Suddenly, the car started up. Jon threw the gear stick into drive and mashed the gas pedal against the floorboard. The car sputtered, rolling forward slowly. Jon fended off the black Italian suit through the car window while trying to pry the man's hand off the steering wheel. Pounding on the man's huge paw with his balled fists wasn't enough to force the killer to loosen his grip.

The taxi jerked, accelerating forward but the second attacker vehemently refused to let go. Jon was desperate. The broken blood-splattered soda bottle rattled beneath his feet. He franticly reached for it while dodging the hefty man's free hand. Eventually, Jon grabbed the jagged-edged bottle. He plunged it into the man's beefy chest and shoulder repeatedly until he relinquished his hold. Wounded and bloody, the second assassin still refused to give up.

He ran beside the moving car, sticking his other arm inside the car window for something to grab on to. When Jon pressed the accelerator again, the old taxi surged ahead. The mountain of beef panted desperately. Failing to keep pace, he began to stumble until he lost his footing. Jon made a hard right at the next corner. The man's stumpy legs dragged along the street like a heavy load of wet clothes. He tried to let go but his suit coat was caught in the door. Once the rambling taxi traveled a quarter mile in the business district, he was unconscious from being dragged on the hard concrete.

During his getaway, so many thoughts circled Jon's head. "Think ! Think! All right, all right. I gotta turn off the main road. If I get caught with two half dead white men in this car," he sighed nervously. No two ways about it, Jon had to dictate terms in order to survive the night. He pulled into a nearby alleyway. After hopping out, he paced nervously back and forth in the darkness. "Think soldier! This is war! Think!" he ranted.

"Holloway, this is home base!" Larry's voice shouted from the two-way radio. "Jon if you can, pick up. We got reports of shooting. Please respond!"

Jon didn't know how to respond, seeing as how he had unfinished business to deal with first. He noticed the first attacker moving about groggily in the back seat. Jon figured the situation called for survival tactics. Instinctively, he reverted back to the mindset he counted on in the jungles of Vietnam. He steered the old taxi off the well-lit street, detouring toward an undeveloped subdivision, cleared to make way for a new block of expensive homes.

The concrete disappeared beneath him. It was replaced by a dark narrowed one-lane dirt road where an interrogation would go undiscovered. He opened the car door on the driver's side then reached back to grab the .45 caliber pistol resting on the front seat. He tucked the gun in his waistband then dragged both battered men out into the open field before pushing them down on their knees. They should have been terrified of reprisal but neither of them appeared worried. Most Negro men in the South were more likely to run and hide rather than take a chance on killing a white man, let alone two of them. And that's what they counted on. What they failed to realize until it was too late was Jon's uncommon valor. He'd killed for a living too, once. Only it was the government who'd paid his fees and he was much more accomplished at it than either of those men would ever live to be.

After questioning the men with no relative success, both of them shared similar smirks that suggested they'd be going home afterwards. Unfortunately for them, Jon's reasoning wouldn't allow for their release. A prisoner who elected to withhold valuable information became a casualty of war. Uncooperative prisoners generally became dead. When a last futile attempt to obtain the names of their employer faltered, one of the men spit blood on Jon's shoes and the other laughed about it. As they cackled relentlessly, Jon pumped one large caliber slug into each of their heads at point blank range. Warm blood splattered against Jon's face although he hadn't noticed. Two dead bodies fell against the hard ground like heavy trashcans pushed over by starving dogs. Jon wasted no time before rummaging through their wallets. He found two out of state identifications which led him to conclude they were connected hit men, probably with mafia ties. Stunned by the new revelation, now he needed time.

Jon wandered over to the taxi and searched it, like he'd done to the wallets, until he found what he was looking for; the long steel plated knife hidden beneath the front seat. With the slow deliberate pace of a gravedigger, Jon headed toward the motionless corpses. He took a quick abbreviated breath, recognizing how quickly he'd come to hating those men. Not for the confusion and suffering their actions would surely introduce to his life but because of the senselessness that initiated them. The men were simply sent to snuff out his life, for profit. It was a simple case of murder for hire. Just as the U.S. troops were commissioned to kill over sees, it was business. No more, no less, just business.

Jon often wondered how the Vietnamese people felt when strange men from foreign places intruded on their villages and hunted them down like animals. He didn't have to wonder any longer. When that rage overcame him, he experienced with one hundred percent certainty, exactly how the villagers felt. Realization of the agonizing pain he'd caused those people was undeniable. He internalized that pain when he drew the long blade. With several swift chops, the dead men's heads rolled away from their bodies like ripe melons. Severing them, he figured, gave him the extra time he needed to sort things out.

He collected their wallets, jewelry, and other identifying articles from the decapitated bodies then placed the carcasses inside of the taxi. After circling the car, Jon ventured to the rear then nonchalantly opened the trunk. He shook his head slowly, warding off remorse and disbelief. The task at hand had to be carried out whether he wanted to or not. It was a necessary evil. He kept reminding himself of that when dousing the car in gasoline. He presumed correctly that it would take the local police longer to investigate the incident if they thought the victims were black. There'd be no rush for answers then, Jon reasoned further as he dropped a lit match on the trail of gas leading away from Larry's taxi.

Jon walked away from the burning car carrying a vinyl gym bag and the weight of what he had done to survive. It was nearly four a.m. when he scatted down back streets and off the beaten path. He'd run another four miles until reaching his own neighborhood.

His clothes were soaked with sweat, gasoline fumes and harmful evidence. Jon had grown numb, mentally and physically. He could have run all night if there was cause to. He felt no physical or emotional pain. The U.S. government created the less than human side of Jon when they dropped him into Asia's armpit. The real problem resided in their inability to de-program him once he'd returned home.

Having motored on autopilot since the killing begun, Jon instinctively turned up in Larry Brown's backyard with a blank stare and dirty grit masking his face. Rock thought he'd noticed movement through the back window. He used the flashlight to get a better look when easing out the door. By the time it closed, Jon appeared directly on the other side of it. His war torn appearance and lacerations were so disturbing that Rock's eyes reflected the fear he couldn't keep hidden deep within. Hampton exited through the back door as well, only to recoil when his eyes landed on his bloodstained partner. The sight of Jon was equally appalling to the other men who had been waiting there, with hopes his appearance. Jon didn't look human. And, after they learned what he'd been through, they wondered if he was.

"Man, what's happened to you?" Hampton asked hesitantly. "I heard the shots but by the time I could get my pants up, you and the taxi was gone."

Jon staggered into the kitchen. He plopped down at the breakfast table where he filled everyone in on the gory details. One driver vomited when Jon ripped the gym bag opened and two bloody heads bounced across the kitchen floor.

"Jon, you get hosed down out back," Larry directed, for all of their sakes. "Dispose of that damned evidence until we figure out what the hell we gonna do now."

They had expected trouble and waited for the fallout. What Jon delivered was a bomb wired to explode, again. As it turned out, the men he'd killed weren't the regular garden variety good ole boy racists. They were contract killers as Jon suspected, with established Mafia affiliations.

Within the hour, all the instructions Larry handed down had been carried out. "You're gonna have to lay low for a while soldier," Rock warned Jon, "at least 'til we can be sure your tracks are covered."

"You telling me I'm supposed to hide in my own neighborhood?" Jon protested. He didn't readily adjust to the thought of crawling in the shadows. "Two dead white boys might spook y'all but not me. I won't do it! I won't!" He didn't know how to be afraid, that common humanistic character trait had been drummed out of him.

Larry attempted to calm him down. "Just listen to me Jon. I know you don't like it but you gotta disappear for a few weeks. When the pigs find out those damned I-talians sent two pop you got smoked instead, it'll get real hot around here. Everybody's gonna be looking for a way to even the score but don't worry bro', they'll have to come through us first." Reluctantly, Jon agreed with keeping a low profile. He headed for home dressed in his neighbor's clothes.

Two hours later, Starla came down stairs to make breakfast with the thought of celebrating her husband's new job. She was pleasantly surprised when she saw him sitting with on the sofa with his back to her. Starla eagerly anticipated hearing all of the boring details of his first night on the job. As the clock hammered passed six a.m., she kissed Jon on top of his head then placed her arms around his neck. Jon inherently grabbed her arms tightly then spun on his hills to defend himself. Starla shrieked. She stared past the blade of her sharpest carving knife held closely to her throat.

When peering deeply into her loving husband's eyes, she didn't see in them anyone she recognized. Jon appeared possessed, callous and cold. Starla called his name tenderly. Non-responsive to her voice, Jon continued to aim the tip of the blade her way.

"Oh my dear God, you're hurt!" she whined. Her words were flanked by tears streaming down her wounded expression. "What happened tonight baby?"

Jon held his silence initially, gawking into his wife's eyes as if searching for something himself. Eventually, the hurt on Starla's face penetrated the hard defensive shell he'd manufactured to deal with an onset of horrific circumstances. "I'm sorry Starla Faye," he whispered in a strained, hushed tone, before removing the blade from her neck. "Sorry baby, sit down. I need to explain a few things." Jon shrugged as he paced in front of Starla. She held herself tightly, suppressing all of the emotion bottled in her chest. Jon stopped on a dime then kneeled at her feet. "You might not understand this but I need you to hear me out."

"What… what's got you torn up like this? Who beat on you?" she cried.

"I couldn't help getting involved. Two killers were sent for me. I had to defend myself." Before he said another word, Starla pulled his face against hers. She refused to listen although Jon made grave attempts at filling her in.

Starla continued pushing him away. The thought of his near death experience sent her reeling. She wanted to get away, pretend that his words were lies. Believing that her man was injured at the expense of two dead gangsters was horrifying. Starla couldn't stop herself from weeping loudly in long dry groans. She rocked back and forth with her knees pulled against her chest. "Why Jon, why?

You just got hommme. Please don't leave me again. I can't take it. Please don't leave meee agaaain."

"Shhhh-shhhh. It's gonna be alright," Jon swore compassionately. He stroked her hair while offering a calm assurance. "Shhh… sweetheart, it's gonna be alright. It'll all be just fine."

Jon had been half world away for nearly four years, and in one fail swoop Starla was in danger losing him again.

EIGHT

Going In Circles

J on kept his word. He hid out for nearly a week. He didn't leave his home to attend meeting when the Black Panthers gathered to discuss the cab company's next move. Policemen, detectives, and federal agents repeatedly dropped in on Larry Brown, all asking the same question. "Tell us how two dead white men ended up in one of your cabs, without their heads?" Mafia hit men or not, justified homicide or wrongful death; white men had been beheaded and tied to a small black outfit. High ranking law officials wanted to throw a blanket over it before the newspapers spun the story into a race riot certain to tear the city apart. Larry flipped the same answer each time a new cop darkened his door.

"I reported that car stolen weeks ago but the police don't come around here that often to protect and service us. Unless y'all come to kick in somebody's door and haul them off to Harmsway or to collect a shake down, then we can count on y'all for dinner. So tell me officers, should I set two more places at the table tonight?" Since Larry's affiliation with the Panthers wasn't public knowledge, the police were forced to back off until they had a solid lead.

A relentless Federal agent continued to visit Larry when most of the other entities moved on to other crimes they had a shot at solving without stepping on a suspect's civil right. Special Agent George Morrell was a twenty-eight year old, hot-tempered, dark headed, federally sponsored red neck. His swagger, personified by an irritating bravado, made him a dangerous man. He was resolved to become a constant irritation until blowing the lid off of the case. With the federal law on his side, he could push the envelope closer to the edge than any of his contemporaries. Morrell had only been in the Bureau a few years but he had lofty aspirations of moving up the ladder fast. A federal cop with soaring ambitions could become hazardous, to himself and to those who were foolish enough to get in his way. Morrell wanted to solve the 'taxi murders' case. More importantly, he had sights set on earning points with the national office and the local crime family by handing over all the parties responsible for the double homicide.

Late one evening, special agent Morrell, sat in the downtown Dallas office digging through a stack black and white photos resting on his desk. Carefully studying the mug shots of Afro-American men associated with South Side Cab and the Black Panther Party, Morrell sorted out pictures while taking the time to cast derogatory comments about each one. "Anthony Gagglio. Get a load of this guy, a spook with a guinea's name. Tell me Anthony, did you knock off two of your distant cousins? Huh? Nah, you look too stupid to crack that nut." He sorted through the stack methodically until he came across another picture which held his interested. "Let's see here, Varron Kelly. What wayward roads have you been down? Armed robbery suspect 1970 and two counts of burglary. No, you don't look tough enough to come out on the good end of a double homicide. Besides, you don't kill people. You might steal things from 'em but you don't kill 'em. Do you, Varron Kelly?"

After studying nearly thirty profiles, George Morrell realized that he spent more time than he planned on giving those dark faces had passed. The nearly empty office indicated just how late it was. Agent Morrell was frazzled but he continued his unorthodox photo analyses and barrage of rude remarks. "You won't do either, Herman Washington. They got to you first. At least the beaten you took improved your looks." Herman's photo was stamped with red oil-based ink, which read *Deceased* in bright blocked letters. Herman never found his way out of the coma after Cane Cab employees worked him over.

Morrell lit a cigarette, watched the flame burn down on the wood matchstick and then picked up the last photograph. It was a picture of Julian Hampton with a note attached regarding a bank robbery in Louisiana, in which he was a suspect wanted for questioning. The note was three years old and the trail had grown cold on the investigation. Something about the mug shot warranted a second look. Maybe he thought the suspect's head was too small or maybe his eyes were placed too closely together but Morrell continued leering at it. "Julian Hampton... yeah, you look like a natural born killer. If it weren't for your busted ribs, I'd run your skinny ass in tonight. I'm sure the great state of Louisiana would love to have you back in prison stripes." Morrell considered sending Hampton back simply to make his life miserable but there were bigger fish to fry.

A telephone anchored to the right corner of the agent's desk rang loudly. The surprised late night summons slapped him out of a brief daydream. The junior agent poised himself then answered the phone routinely as always, "Special Agent Morrell." When he realized who was on the other end, he sat up in his chair as if the caller could see him slouching. He peeped over his shoulder to see if anyone was in earshot of his conversation. There was only a hand full of agents on the floor keeping late hours but none of them close enough to listen in.

"Oh, Mr. Santone," Morrell responded excitedly, while trying keep his voice down. "Yes sir, I'm on it right now. Yes sir, yes sir. I promise you, I will personally take care of the matter to your satisfaction. It was unfortunate but I assure you that I can handle it. Yes, Mr. Santone. If you would just hold your boys off for a few days, I'll finish this. Just a few days… thank you. You won't regret it. Good night sir." Agent Morrell's lower back felt extremely stiff after all of the bowing and scraping he'd done to satisfy a very powerful man.

Sweat beaded on Morrell's forehead after he lowered the telephone receiver. Taking a call with a crime boss could have meant expulsion from the bureau and jail time for the rising star if his phone line had been tapped. Gus Santone was the Mafia godfather for the Dallas family and most of the larger Texas cities. A working relationship initiated by Morrell was nothing short of irreprehensible, as far as the FBI was concerned. A special agent on the payroll of an organized crime chieftain was inexcusable.

Mr. Santone demanded a swift resolution to the deaths of his contract killers. Emotions ran high on both sides of the tragedy. Rumors of warfare and race riots warranted several news crews from up north to cover the expected showdown, all of which were bad for business and for those who made their living in the streets. Coincidentally, Morrell made a couple of promises which could have easily resulted in his own demise if he over promised or under delivered.

After two hours of steady drinking in his car, Morrell found a perch outside of the busiest nightspot in the city frequented by black patrons. He continuously harassed people as they exited the blues joint, questioning them about the murders and what they'd heard about it. Each time he was met with uncooperative harsh stares and pockets full of "I don't know." Morrell felt the noose tighten around his neck when it seemed that digging up viable information was close to impossible. No one from the neighborhood was in a hurry to divulge anything to a government agent and burn one of their own.

Once Morrell had come to face to face with too many dead ends, he was prepared to call it a night until crossing paths with a dirty police detective who kept a pimp named Odell on a short leash. Tom McGruder was as underhanded as they came, making a fortune rousting dope pushers and other late night opportunists. McGruder suggested that Morrell pull on Odell's coat because his stable of working girls exceeded any other pimp in the area. The odds were favorable that he'd know more about the murders than most. McGruder's tip was the break Morrell had been waiting for.

After searching all the usual after hour haunts which catered to big spenders and thrill seekers, agent Morrell darkened the doorway of Rooster's Tavern on Metropolitan Avenue. Throughout the smoke filled room, red was the color of the day, every day. Chairs covered in red vinyl made for stylish commentary but the addition of red checkered table cloths with thick plush red shag carpet created an overdone crimson motif. Just about everything in the club was red and so was the owner. Rooster was an extremely broad man with light freckled skin and a thick reddish goatee. Although he had an easy way about him when his money was right, men often made the unconscious mistake of gawking too long at Rooster's hair. He'd served hard time for beating a man to death with his bare hands on account of making cracks about the worst head of naps that God had ever cursed a human with.

Bartending was just one of the hats Rooster wore during a busy Friday night. He didn't trust anyone with the cash drawer when drinks flowed endlessly. Likewise, there was no one better at busting up a fight over a woman with one too many boyfriends. While Rooster wiped down the bar with a damp rag, nearly hidden beneath his hands which were as big as baseball mitts, he kept an eye on the thin white man who tried to slink in unnoticed.

Since there were no other white faces in the jumping joint, within mere seconds everyone became aware of his presence. Even though desegregation had made itself at home on paper, the color barrier was still wide and deep on both sides of the great divide. If a white man had the stones to come down to Rooster's, he had to be crazy or carrying the kind of clout necessary to keep breathing. Rooster had seen this kind of white man before, the kind who was likely to double back with reinforcements if he got in over his head. This white man didn't know better or have enough sense to be afraid and it showed. He was the worst kind.

"Hey, let me have a Jack Black with coca-cola," Morrell ordered. It sounded more like a statement than a request. Rooster eased his hand off a loaded forty-five caliber revolver he kept behind the counter. Morrell grinned. He agreed with Rooster's decision. "You did the right thing, big fella. I'd hate to have to come back here with the health and fire departments. I'm sure they can find a couple of code violations if they really tried and I know for a fact that you're serving more people than this place is slated to hold."

The mammoth barkeep thought about putting his hand on the gun again then thought better of it. Instead, he tightened his jaws and poured Jack Daniels to the agent's specifications. After Rooster sat the drink on the bar top, he snarled his displeasure. "Anything else?"

"Yeah, you can point out someone for me. Tell me which of these fine upstanding gentlemen happens to be Odell Owens."

Rooster shook his head. "'Never heard the name. Think you got the wrong place. This ain't the information bureau."

Morrell flirted with his bourbon before pouring on a measure of soda to concoct his favorite elixir. "So you want to do this the hard way?" he huffed. "Either you can finger him for me or I'll have to call the cavalry down here to check everyone's identification and I know you're too good a business man to let all this fun and hard earned cash walk right out the door when we're finished."

Sensing the inevitable, Rooster felt compelled to give in. "The one on the end," Rooster told the man, sipping his liquor from the other side of his red marble topped bar. With that tidbit, Morrell chugged the drink fast then started off in the direction he was given. Several people watched his short jaunt to see who's night on the town was about to take a wrong turn.

One of Odell's working girls was parked on a barstool beside him. "Look honey, why don't find your pretty self another place to rest that money maker or yours," Morrell suggested. His gruffness left no question that he didn't expect an argument. "I've got some business with Odell here."

The prostitute was attractive and petite, with skin as dark as a long winter's night. Tula Lovejoy was the name she was using at the time. She had a slight frame to be in that line of business. The hardness in her face accentuated her good looks in a peculiar way. Her rough around the edges demeanor drew men like bees to honey. She was willing and able to dish out as much grinding as she took. Tula wore her melancholy expression like a former good girl whose dreams hadn't gone according to plan. At a hard twenty-five, she was woman enough to ride out her failures, one paying customer at a time.

Tula wasn't putting on a show when she went out her way to disregard Morrell and his demands. It was almost comical the way she took a healthy drag from her menthol cigarette then blew a stream of smoke in his face. Odell laughed riotously over his main girl's disrespect toward the pushy lawman. Morrell, feeling a bit put off, moved his dark jacket aside to expose the insurance tucked in his waist holster. His badge accompanied a shiny non-government issued handgun. The rules had just changed. Although Tula appeared more annoyed than threatened, she glanced over at her pimp and awaited instructions before moving an inch.

Odell reasoned that whatever the white cop wanted, he didn't have it to give so the conversation shouldn't take too long. "Baby-girl, why'ont you go on and powder your nose. This won't take but a tic."

After the well-trained prostitute stood up slowly, staring down the man who was too insistent for her taste, she strolled to the back end of the afterhours club. Morrell eased onto the stool she vacated. "Odell Owens, how's tricks?" Morrell quipped. Odell, outfitted in an orange two-piece polyester jump suit, ignored him. "See, I was just thinking," the agent continued, "how the stock exchange has been pretty weak lately but I'll bet you could care less about that, huh? Seeing as how your line of work is always steady despite all the ups and downs on Wall Street, I'd also bet the Dow Jones hasn't affected your earnings at all this quarter."

Odell fingered a highball glass a moment before finishing his drink. He attempted to get up from the bar without acknowledging the agent's questions. That was his first mistake. Morrell kicked the stool from underneath him. That sent that hip orange suit barreling to the floor with Odell in it. His tangerine colored platform shoes waved in the air as he flailed around from his back. Customers who hadn't decided to mind their own business continued with their awkward glances. Odell rose to his feet then dusted off his expensive threads. He wanted to kill Morrell on the spot for disrespecting him that way but white cops were above the law so he was forced to deal with it as best he could.

With clenched teeth, Odell peered straight ahead. He had been belittled on his own turf and couldn't do a thing about it. Not many officers of the law were willing to go that far out of their way to harass industrious businessmen in public. George Morrell was a strange animal. His mean streak had nothing to do with justice. He simply hadn't learned to accept no for an answer from black men and never planned on having to.

"Now why did you have to go and be all rude like that," Morrell asked. "It ain't good manners for you to just up and leave right in the middle of a conversation. Didn't your mammy teach you better?" That last comment was a message of how little respect Morrell had for Odell and everybody who looked like him.

Odell sucked his teeth then cut his eyes at the Morrell as he contemplated the precise words on which to make his stand. "Look, honky cop," he spat venomously, "I don't know no damned Dow Jones, Davie Jones or none of them white dudes. Matter of fact, I don't know nothin'. So get off my case, chump!"

Several people in the crowded club continued observing their interaction, anticipating a nasty show down. Morrell scratched casually at his at his five o'clock shadow with his the tips of fingers. He leaned in closely to Odell, who thought of a hundred better places he'd rather be right then although he refused to reveal that he was more scared than embarrassed. Odell reached his hand inside his pants pocket, came out with a thick roll of twenty-dollar bills then used them to fan his nose. "You smell something? I think I smell stank-ass swine. Next thang you know, I'll have pig shit on my shoes and that's a real muther' to scrape off."

Disgusted and tired of Odell's defiance, Morrell took the gloves off. He was capable of much more than barroom banter and willing to leave a trail of broken heads if he had to. "Well Odell, I guess we'll just have to take a little trip downtown for a while and I'll interrogate the hell out of you until you do know something."

The frustrated pimp returned the same degree of smugness, making a grave attempt at preserving his reputation. "I ain't no punk nor one of these street crawlers neither. I'm a rich nigga and threats don't move me. Take me to jail. They know me down there. Hell, I gotta damn good understanding with the county. Matter of fact, five will get you ten that I'll be out the ink dries. Shiiiiid, lemme get my hat." Odell chuckled to himself, feigning the confidence he lacked.

"You think I'm playing with you, huh?" Morrell scoffed. "'You think I've got time to hang around in the ghetto toying with you? To hell with this. I'm done." He slid his hand under the bar rail and rammed it between Odell's legs. Before Odell knew what hit him, his testicles were clutched in another man's fist. "Now that I've got your undivided attention, we need to come to an understanding and I mean right now." The excruciating pain running up Odell's groin rendered him speechless. "Odell," Morrell whispered, "I can arrange it so the local police find a dead body at your place by morning."

With no reason to doubt the agent's words, Odell believed him wholeheartedly. A trail of saliva dangled from his chin as he fought to bridle the yelp he'd held in. Odell nodded his agreement, unsure if Morrell was suggesting he'd be framed for murder or killed himself. Either way, he knew the man wanted something from him and wouldn't quit until he got what he'd come after. And whatever that something was, Morrell made it crystal clear that Odell would be responsible for providing it. Suddenly the agent released his tight grasp on Odell's jewels. The hustler choked back tears while catching his breath.

"Listen up, you nigga pimp! They say don't nothing go down on the south side without Odell hearing about it. So let's hear it. Lemme hear what you've been hearing."

Odell pleaded ignorance to what Morrell inferred. Despite the Black Panthers warning to keep a lid on the incident, every black man in south Dallas had heard about the headless bodies. And despite all the police attention, no one had given up a single lead to help the authorities break the case. Odell's attempt at playing dumb wasn't well received. A federal officer three sheets to the wind had his fill of being jerked around and that was more than enough to get a black man erased at the hands of a white cop, whether he was overly ambitious or not.

Severely agitated now, the agent drew his gun. He pointed the barrel at the willful sex trafficker. Odell slid off the barstool with both hands shielding his face defensively as Morrell dragged him out of the club by his wide collars. Murmurs grew loud when several men witnessed a total disregard for Odell's civil rights. Morrell drew closer to the door with a hand full of orange synthetic jumpsuit clenched in his knuckles when a slick dressed patron took the initiative to charge at the white man who'd gone too far. Morrell aimed the gun at the man's crotch, stalling his brief stint of bravery. "Sure you want to get involved in this?" Morrell challenged. After the man's eyes followed the tip of the gun barrel, his nerve abandoned him. That was Skeeter Tyler. He quickly remembered never liking Odell all that much anyway. Still, he was less than thrilled having to watch a brother from the neighborhood being handled like that, considering it could have easily been him at the business end of the agent's wrath. It was a noble gesture until Skeeter fully analyzed the situation. "I didn't think so," Morrell continued boldly. "You people can get back to minding your own business now. This is between me and my good pal, Odell."

When the two-some emerged from the darkened tavern, Morrell laid it on thick. "You still think I'm joking? Yeah you do. I can tell when somebody's laughing at me on the inside and I don't like it. Maybe I should beat what I want out of you and find a… hell, create a murder to saddle your ass with and still make it home before breakfast." The agent was serious and playing every move as if it was his last.

Odell enjoyed his ghetto-fabulous lifestyle, the money and frills commonly awarded to sharp dressed hustlers. He wanted the episode with Morrell to end as quickly as possible. He glanced left and right to see if anyone watched them before explaining the ramifications of helping the FBI. "Hey man, don't you get it? I ain't got no problem with you but I can't tell you nothin' either. If the brothas knew I talked, they'd come down on me hard!"

Morrell grabbed Odell's arm then proceeded to pull him toward the car. "You have the right to remain silent. If you accept that right to remain silent, you will remain silent permanently," the agent barked. He had too much riding on this case to accept Odell's reluctance. Bracing his platform shoes against the concrete, Odell wrestled with Morrell to hold his position near the curb. There was no guarantee he'd return from a dark ride in a bureau car.

"Hold on man! Hold on!" Odell hollered. He stared at the sidewalk as he weighed his options. "Okay. Okay. I'll tell you what I know but you didn't get this from me."

"I don't want to know what you know," Morrell interrupted, "I'm after what you've heard."

"The word is… those dead white boys tried to put my man Holloway in the ground. That's when thangs got too hot and I guess they lost their heads," he chuckled.

"Ha ha, that's funny. I get it. Things got hot… and lost their heads. That's brilliant. I'm trying to investigate a double murder that could flip this city on its ear and I got a second rate soul brotha making jokes. You *Afro-Americans* never cease to amaze me." Morrell pulled a small note pad from his inside coat pocket. "Holloway… Holloway. So, who were the other *brothas* involved?" he asked, using a watered down street vernacular.

Odell hunched his shoulders. "Hey man that's it. Jon was solo," he testified proudly. "Or at least that's what I *heard*. Sounds about right, two dead honkies at the hand of one pissed righteous dude. It usually takes more than three crackers to kill one nigga. Why is that, special agent Mo-rell?"

Without dignifying the last question with a plausible guess, Morrell wrote the name down then patted Odell softly on the back. "You did good. Real good. One thing though, if I find out you're jivin' me, this'll be the last lie you tell." The stern warning was followed by a promise of safe passage if the information panned out. "You hear what I'm saying? If you're straight with me, everything will work out fine." Although concerned about a civilian with the talent to stave off two professional hit men, the special agent smiled oddly while altering his disposition. "Lighten up Odell, nobody's gonna know where I got the information." Then as nonchalantly as you please, Morrell strolled to his car with both hands pushed into his suit pockets as if he'd just taken a casual walk in the park.

Odell was glad to retain his freedom from a man who appeared unrelenting. He'd recognized Morrell the very moment the agent entered the nightclub. A man in Odell's business had to keep his ear to the ground in the community. He also knew that a whole slew of people saw him dragged out of Rooster's with his tail between his legs. Showing up inside the bar again without as much as a scratch indicated either he'd convinced the tough white man of his ignorance or that he was quick to give up everything he knew. A barrage of foul sneers thrown at him after he ventured back inside, presented frightening cause for concern.

After Odell sufficiently drowned his guilt beneath several glasses of gin and tonic, Rooster cut him off. It was hard to watch Odell leaving the bar in a drunken stupor, declaring his innocents to anyone who listened. "That pig didn't get nothin' outta of me!" he sniveled. "Nothin', Jack! Nothhhin!" Odell sold his soul when he gave up another black man, a good black man. Knowing that Jon was hailed as a hero after what he endured in that taxi, selling him out was an unforgivable sin.

NINE

Jive Turkey

The next evening, Morrell returned Mr. Santone's phone call notifying him of the progress he'd made then he headed for the side of town where most of the trouble was bound to take place. Morrell planned on causing most of the trouble himself.

He stopped by Larry Brown's house again. This visit wasn't meant for gathering information. This time he presented Larry with a few recent discoveries and a handful of flippant remarks of his own.

Morrell stood on the Brown's broad front porch like he paid the mortgage. His conceited behavior was so bazaar that it dumbfounded the puzzled homeowner. "Hey Larry Brown from the south side of town. Tell me something, what's going down?" the bigoted agent joked. "I like it when I put a rhyme together like that. Did you notice how it had a nice ring to it, Larry Brown from the south side of town? Sounded pretty good to me. Think I could make any money doing that? Huh? You think there might be a demand for a rhymer somewhere? Naw, guess not. That would be ridiculous. Nobody would ever pay good money to stand around watching some guy saying rhymes but hey, it was just a thought."

Not at all amused, Larry was trying to figure out why the agent seemed to be so confident or was he simply on a fishing expedition hoping to get lucky and hook something for his troubles. During all the other visits, Morrell was anxious and uptight as if a time bomb was ticking inside his boxers but those previous signs of exasperation had moved on. Morrell continued when he saw Larry backing against the ropes. "Oh that's right. I've been coming around here all week but Mr. Brown ain't seen nothin' and don't know nothin'. Well let me tell you what I know. Your boy, Jon Holloway, is the spook we're looking for… for the double homicide that everybody's all hush-hush about." Larry started to open his mouth to refute the charge. Agent Morrell cut him off. "Ahh-ahhh don't lie. You were going to stand right here and lie to my face but I already know. See, my pal Odell… you know Odell the pimp? Yeah, he told me that you told him. And you know he's a very reliable source. When Odell rats someone out, I can always count on the charges to stick. His word is good as gold and it makes you appreciate it more when you own it." The agent enjoyed having the upper hand for a change but he went and got all beside himself and overplayed it.

When Larry displayed his annoyance by pressing his thick lips together, Morrell knew Odell's tip was solid as a rock. Holloway was the man to find although Larry denied knowing any pimps. Jon was the key to Morrell's case since it was rumored that he was solely responsible for the murders, although the agent still had difficulty believing a common taxi driver pulled it off alone.

"You wouldn't want to help me out by telling me where you've got him stashed would you?" Morrell. "And I know that you do because I've been asking around and nobody's seen him since the day before the incident occurred." Unyielding, Larry sustained his silence and defiant stare.

Morrell issued a firm warming. "This thing is going to blow up in all your faces if you don't give him up, Mr. Brown." With the dumbest move Morrell could have made, he stepped right up in Larry's face with a fierce challenge. "So you'd better get me Jon Holloway before I kick down every door on this side of the tracks to find him myself."

Larry's eyes narrowed due to Morrell's blatant disrespect. "If you're feeling that froggy, why'ont you jump?" Larry replied calmly.

Such a hostile act of solidarity hit Morrell like a right cross so he jabbed back. "I just might do that." He stuck his chest out like a prized cock at a county fair. "You think you're proving something Brown, huh? You're only proving how stupid you are. I'm going to get him anyway and then your little house of cards will come crashing down. And, when I do find him, I'll charge your black ass with accessory after the fact. You both can share a cell together, won't that be cozy."

Larry tilted his head back, somewhat stunned by the gall of the agent's continued disregard for his property. He casually moved in closer to his thin trespasser, who had been a nuisance since he'd arrived. Without notice, Larry grabbed Morrell by his red neck with both hands, hoisted his feet off the porch and squeezed. Larry was so angry, he shook with bitterness. Contempt formed in the corners of his mouth as the edges of Morrell's wing tip shoes desperately reached for the floor. "Now that I've got *your* attention, let me tell you something. We're tired of y'all kicking our doors down any time you run outta things to do. The next time you *think* about coming around here, you'd better call first to make sure I feel like takin' comp'ny." Larry grunted as he heaved the agent off his porch. The agent landed butt first on the dusty front lawn.

Coughing hysterically to catch his breath, Morrell climbed to his feet then swatted at his business suit to loosen the dirt. When he'd gathered himself, he reached under his coat for a revolver. The thought quickly faded as two of Larry's men appeared on the porch, brandishing double-barreled shotguns. Morrell was pissed off but he wasn't stupid. He cautiously withdrew his hand along with the bad idea altogether. After dusting himself off further, he backed away with both hands in plain view until he reached his car.

Larry's jaw line softened to rebut the agent's unwelcome visit. "Sorry but I don't feel like takin' comp'ny today."

"Don't get yourself confused into thinking this ends here!" Morrell shouted back, with his head poking out of the window. "You'll will give Holloway up, Larry Brown, you will. Trust me!" As the agent pulled away from the curb, he waved cordially to the three men, like an adventurous child leaving for summer camp. Larry knew that the man he'd just thrown off his property was a big problem. Special agent George Morrell beamed strangely at the men while muttering to himself. "What has this country come to? *Afro-American's* pulling guns on decent white folk." It seemed he rather enjoyed having been flung onto someone's lawn as he hummed a carefree melody between gulps from a pint of cheap bourbon. The bottle was half empty by the time he merged into traffic onto the interstate, seven blocks away.

Larry told Rock what happened then summed up what he thought of Morrell. "It's bad enough being a fool, that a man shouldn't have to go around trying to prove it. He's like a bothersome housefly, Rock, a housefly that's been trapped inside too long. But understand this, some flies don't have the sense to get away even if you leave the window opened. Sometimes, the only remedy is a quick death with a heavy swat." Drastic measures, Larry had decided, was the only remedy. A heavy swat.

By nightfall, Morrell discovered that Jon Holloway wasn't listed in the local police files. Since he took the deal for grand theft auto and served a suspended sentence, his case was dropped the moment Jon enlisted in the military. Therefore, no charges were found in the system. He hadn't been in the states long enough to receive any mail and the house was still listed in his mother's name. Searching for Jon wasn't so easy, finding him would be a terrible mistake.

When the special agent remembered how he'd forgotten to ask Odell where Jon lived, he figured the pimp's plush apartment was a good place to start making up for the oversight. The same tune blew from his lips as he trotted up two flights of stairs in an apartment building on Peabody Street. His carefree tone fell flat when he found Odell's door slightly ajar. Instinctively, Morrell drew his gun. He proceeded to nudge the door opened with his left forearm. "Odell," he sang softly, "you forgot to lock up. That could be dangerous… in this neighborhood… all kinds of people looking to do bad things." Morrell paused to take in the apartment's zodiac motif. Astrological black light paintings and animal print furniture dominated the small front room. "No wonder you left the door opened… probably wanted someone to come over and steal this butt-ugly couch." Morrell's game face returned when he found what he'd come for but it was too late to get anything out of Odell. Someone else had already stopped by for a chat.

Sprawled out on a black imitation leather recliner, was Odell's motionless body. His left foot had been hacked off and stuffed in his mouth. It was difficult to determine whether it was the beating he'd taken that killed him or the considerable blood loss that took him out. There was no mistaken the outcome, Odell was dead. Real dead. The lasting expression on his face was remorseful, like a repentant drunk who wanted to confess how he couldn't shake the nagging urge that made him what he was. A brand new color television hummed while flashing an off-air test pattern on the screen. The TV witnessed the mess that someone made of Odell's overly decorated apartment and now it watched Morrell step around in the leftovers.

Tracking through the pool of blood that Odell no longer needed, Morrell leaned over to read a note pinned to the dead man's silk night shirt. It read: "Good bye cruel world. Woe is me. I stuck my foot in my mouth again."

Woe is me, is right, Morrell thought, frowning unsympathetically. "Odell, look at yourself. How thoughtful of you to leave a suicide note," he mused. "It's a travesty but you got what you deserved. You shouldn't have told. Guess I'm not the only one who can't stand a snitch." Morrell continued agonizing over the crime scene and the trail to Jon Holloway that had suddenly grown cold.

Now the federal agent was antsy. He'd promised a notoriously vindictive mobster that he would resolve all issues relating to the murders. He also wanted to solve the case then present it to the heavyweights at the FBI regional headquarters. Morrell was being pulled from both sides. He was forced to hit the streets again, shaking up one prostitute after another along the busy boulevard. Morrell questioned each of them in the front seat of his car. He threatened to arrest the women until he was convinced they didn't know anything that could help him.

Midnight showed up just like Morrell expected and Mr. Santone had demanded good news by morning. Morrell was fit to be tied until he stumbled across the woman he recognized from Rooster's afterhours club. "Hey, get in," he offered kindly, after idling next to the street corner.

The dark-skinned streetwalker hopped in. She was glad to rest her heels. "Hi'ya baby, I'm Tula. Thanks for pulling over. I'm real lonely tonight. So you wannna date, handsome?" she propositioned, while adjusting her brazier straps at the shoulders. She hadn't looked at the driver's face once, before talking business.

"You don't remember me do you? I remember you though," Morrell told her, grinning arrogantly. "I could never forget the way you blew smoke in my face over at that ridiculous, everything red, late night spot."

Morrell had studied her from head to toe by the time she'd finally gotten around to taking a look at the man she'd planned to open her legs for. "Oh, you mean Rooster's. Can't say that I recall your face mister but if we can find a clean room, I'll do my best to duplicate whatever it was that's got you looking me over like that."

Obviously, Tula misread his questioning leer. Morrell was surprised at how differently she looked from the first time he saw her with Odell. The other night, she was full of confidence and carried herself as if she was accustomed to getting whatever she wanted by negotiating with her tools of the trade. This time around, she was a bundle of nerves and it was apparent by her puffy eyes that she'd been crying. An even closer look confirmed that years of rented time in rented rooms had shown through her thick coat of *Covergirl*. The agent's excitement waned when he became less thrilled about getting revenge. Since Tula wasn't in her top form, he decided to pass on his chance to even the score.

"Tula, was it? Nah, I'm not interested in a date," he answered finally.

The woman tossed Morrell a long gaze for the first time. "Awe man, hell. You that white dude who was rousting Odell. What... now you gone kill me too?" She winced after realizing that he may not have known about the murder and by admitting that she did, she'd just implicated herself. Morrell had already noticed drops of blood on Tula's high heels as soon as she climbed into his sedan.

Since she'd let those words slip from her mouth, she went on with her thought. "Well, go 'head. I'm too tired to run and too hurt to fight you."

"Hurt, what do you mean? You look fit as a horse. Well, in a good way," he added when she openly objected to the back handed compliment.

"My heart, Cop. Somebody done killed my man and it broke my heart. He was good to me and now I ain't got no place to go but down. Figured it might've been you who done it. I saw how you treated him that night."

"I'm sure it wasn't you who did it but you'd better change your shoes before somebody else gets other ideas about you offing your pimp... uh your man? Looks like you'll be needing another one but that's not my concern. I'm in need of something else. You help me, maybe I'll help you and we both come out on top." Since Tula hadn't chased any of Morrell's pitches, he lobbed one right over home plate. "Jon Holloway, you know him?"

Tula seemed confused by the question. "Yeah, I know him. We went to high school together," she admitted. "What business you got with him?"

"Believe me, you don't want to know. It's official."

"O-ficial. Honey please, my time is too valuable to be sittin' in here with you playin' cops and hoes. Anyway, you must be talkin' about another Jon Holloway 'cause the one I know ain't the type to have no o-ficial business with the feds. He still owns a house on South Boulevard and pays his taxes like y'all do but I ain't got nothin' to tell you that's gonna do wrong by him. Even heard he's some kind of war hero."

Tula's answer helped explain to Morrell why Jon's name was the only one associated with the murders. He was skilled in the art of hand-to-hand combat. Morrell begun to sense that it was all coming together. Out of the blue, he pulled a gun from his shoulder holster then used it to raise the front of Tula's dress. He shoved it between her legs but the hooker didn't blink. Not once. Tula pushed the gun away then casually pulled her dress back down like she'd done too many times to remember. "That won't get you nothin' from me. It'll take a bigger pistol than that to get me going."

"Dammit. I'll pay you for your time but I don't understand this," Morrell said, shaking his head. "Why is everyone working so hard to protect this man? What's with this stupid code of silence?"

"Jon Holloway. You never met him, huh?" Tula asked tenderly. Her eyes glazed over as she thought back on much simpler times. "Jon is special, always was. He's a college boy, like you but a real goody two-shoes and shit." For the first time, a smile creased her lips.

"So that allows him some kinda special privileges?"

Tula stared past the agent's windshield then directly into his eyes. "Let me ask you something Cop. You ever try to pull up a shrub by its roots?"

Morrell's perplexed expression verified that he didn't comprehend the question. "What's that, a ghetto riddle? No, no I've never tried to pull up a shrub by its roots. So what?"

"Guess you haven't. But if you did, you'd know that even the smallest tree with shallow roots can wear down two or three of the strongest men. Sometimes they figure it's smarter to quit tryin' and give up because the earth ain't ready to let go of that little tree. Jon Holloway is a big tree and his roots run deep. He's always been special like that. Maybe you ought to quit tryin'."

Morrell thought to himself for a moment, *just wait until I catch up with him. Then, he'll be a dead tree and his roots won't matter.* When he stopped the car to let her out at the next corner, she stood on the curb insisting on the money he'd promised for her time. "Hey, that'll be ten dollars and an extra five for the rough stuff you pulled. All of you federal dudes are freaks." Tula stood there with her hand out. The agent winked at her, then sped away. "Hey you weirdo!" she screamed after him. "My money!"

"Whudda you know, a philosophical whore," Morrell snickered. "What's wrong with these people?"

Once Morrell learned where Jon lived, he was livid. He'd been driving circles around the man's house, simultaneously jumping through hoops to find him. During that time, he'd been lied to, choked, body slammed and threatened. Most of all, he was exasperated with Larry for concealing the fact that Jon lived on the same street, only a few houses down from him.

TEN

Never Can Say Goodbye

"Precautions have to be taken," Larry rationalized, when Jon refused to stay hidden for another minute. "Jon, we can't just have you walking around like nothing's happened. Your name has been linked to two murders, two dead white men. If the Dallas Police didn't have so many idiots running the force, they'd have brought you in by now. The smartest thing you've done is kept a low profile."

"Larry, my whole life and my family's lives are on hold and for what?" Jon argued. "I'm running out of excuses to tell my son why he can't go out to play, not even around the house. Man, I haven't been sent to prison yet and dammit I'm tired of acting like I have."

"Things will die down soon Jon, just hold on. Besides, there's this other thing. There's this white boy that's been...." Larry nearly choked on what he was about to say.

"What about some white boy?" Jon pressed. His concern mirrored Larry's. "Is there something you've been keeping from me while I've been locked away and climbing the walls?"

Purposely avoiding eye contact, Larry allowed his troubled gaze to drift up to meet Jon's. "He's a federal agent, a real bad shit heel too."

"So, we expected the FBI to sniff around for a while. If that's the least of my worries then I'm getting my ass some sleep then tomorrow I'm going out to find me another job." Jon stood from his kitchen table and extended his hand. "I am thankful for what your people have tried to do though. Much obliged to you."

Larry accepted the firm handshake then offered one last proposition. "Okay, okay... You're right. It's time to make something happen instead of waiting on it to happen to us. I'll send for a man I know, from Houston. He fixes stuff and he's done this kind of thing before."

Extremely interested now, Jon wanted to hear more. "A fixer, huh? Just what kind of thing are you talking about?"

"The kind of thing that makes a problem disappear," he answered solemnly, "without a trace."

"Sounds good but how long would it take to make this... problem go away? I'm already getting jumpy and Starla's losing her grip. You know how women worry."

"Yeah I know alright, can't catch a break from mine either. But, what I need from you is to sit tight one more day. My man from out of town is as fast as he is good. Hell, I can't turn a corner without seeing that fed on my heels. Tell you what... let me set up a guard around the house until I can neutralize things. Give us two days at the most then you can do whatever makes you feel real."

"Cool," Jon sighed. "I can dig it."

"Solid."

Although they had reached an agreement, Larry's left with a headache the size of Texas. He couldn't get past the thought of ridding himself of the pesky problem, who he felt wielded too much power for one man.

For the first time in a week, Jon begun to feel better about his situation again until he closed the door and found Starla standing on the staircase with tears streaming down her face. He knew right away that she'd listened in on the entire conversation. Since he didn't have the words to eradicate the fears that mounted inside her, Jon wasn't foolish enough to try. Instead, he eased toward Starla. Her arms were folded tightly across her chest. With a fair amount of gentle coaxing, they fell by her side then eventually found their way around Jon's neck.

"I'd rather be locked up in this house with you forever," she whispered, "than spend another day without you. That wouldn't be freedom, that's not life worth living. You're here now and that's all I've ever wanted. Please don't let them take that away from me."

Jon pulled her hands close to his face without taking his eyes off hers. He planted the softest kiss imaginable on her wedding band. She vowed to remember that kiss for the rest of her life, and all it stood for. She also had to believe everything would be all right or lose her mind in the process of worrying about it.

Three days had passed since Jon had eaten a thing and two days since he'd managed to sleep a wink. During the week before, his biggest concern was figuring out how he was going to keep the lights on and now this. When a man has worries beyond his control, sleep never comes easy. Much like the time he spent in Vietnam, sleep only came when he needed it, when he could no longer sustain consciousness. Sure, he wanted to tell Starla that everything would be over soon but he didn't believe it himself. He'd learned by watching countless numbers of young soldiers torn head from limb to think that tomorrow was promised to anybody. His wife hadn't come to know life as he had, taking one day at a time while being very uncertain about anything in it.

Guards were posted outside Jon's house around the clock. Wise to expect retribution, Larry positioned two men out front to patrol continuously from the sidewalk to the front door. Two additional guards occupied the backyard, keeping a watchful eye on the sides of the house as well. A lazy crescent moon hid behind a thick herd of cumulous clouds that night. By morning, a certain fixer was due to report in from Houston and get down to business by eliminating the arrogant agent by noon. Larry Brown had made all the right moves. However, a rogue federal agent had a few tricks up his sleeve as well.

Special Agent George Morrell parked his tan sedan one block behind Jon's house. He had until morning to make something happen or take a leave of absents before Mr. Santone's personal hit team steamed rolled over him. With the address of Jon's home in his pocket, he surveilled the area. Morrell expected a patrol to keep closely by. After watching the comings and goings at the Brown residence, he followed all the activity surrounding 2053 South Boulevard. When he sneaked beside the neighboring house, the agent saw two armed guards dressed in Para-military fatigues and black leather jackets. Morrell wanted to get a closer look but didn't dare risk getting caught and subsequently tortured or worse. He needed a diversion, something to steer the guards' attention away from their posts.

Morrell returned to his car, thinking how much of a nuisance this case had become. He'd made promises, to unforgiving people, that he would handle things. If there was a chance to make good on them, he had to take it regardless of the outcome. There would be no acceptable words to explain to Mr. Santone that he couldn't get near the man he wanted dead after giving his word. Suddenly it came to him that he had to kill Jon Holloway or be willing to die trying.

Mumbling to himself quietly, the agent took a half full pint of bourbon from his glove box and turned it up until it was nearly empty. Then, he reached inside his coat pocket and came out with a white handkerchief before stepping out of his car.

The sky was a peculiar pitch of indigo. The only light cast upon the neighborhood emanated from the dim lamps along the street. Morrell tilted his head back and rolled it counter clockwise while stretching his shoulders like prizefighters to do work out the kinks once they've climbed into the ring. After glaring down at his brand new wingtip shoes, he walked to the rear of his car cussing all the way wishing that he'd remembered to bring an older pair. Still cussing up a storm, he ran a rubber hose into the gas tank and the other into the liquor bottle. When he wrapped his lips around the hose, he wished for a better way to siphon out the gas but there wasn't one. He inhaled on the hose. Gasoline came rushing out of it. He spat on the ground then shoved the hose inside of the bourbon bottle. Morrell started cussing all over again as it filled faster than he anticipated, spilling onto his clothes. Foul words poured from his mouth as he stuffed the handkerchief down into the full pint bottle with a few inches of cloth hanging out.

Once more, Morrell skillfully sneaked beside the house directly across from Larry Brown's. From his vantage point, it was easily to spy on the men down the sidewalk guarding Jon's family. Morrell kissed the bottle before striking a match. He held hold it to the tip of the handkerchief. As the cloth caught fire, he uttered smugly, "Cocktails anyone," before throwing the flaming bottle. It soared high in the air from one side on South Boulevard to the other. Initially, it appeared to be headed for the roof of Larry's home but it started to descend. Smash, went the bottle against a bright orange colored South Side cab parked along the street. The firebomb found its mark. Flames covered it. "Outstanding! Now it's time for some fireworks," Morrell cheered triumphantly, before disappearing into the darkness.

Larry bolted through his front door with a rifle. "Water, water!" he shouted. "Help, it's a fire!"

When the guards stationed in front of Jon's house saw the commotion down the street, they abandoned their posts to attack the blaze. One of the men posted in the backyard took it upon himself to watch the front, vacated by the other two. Confusion created the window of opportunity Morrell needed to get close to his target. When he tipped behind the house, the remaining guard patrolling the parameter heard him step on a dry twig. Cautiously, he headed toward Morrell's general direction. Unable to determine exactly where he'd heard the noise, he ventured deeper in to the yard to investigate. The last thing he remembered was excruciating pain racing through his cracked skull before fading to black.

The agent used a milk crate from Jon's garage to reach the kitchen window. He placed his hands on the glass to peek in. Darkness filled the house. Morrell felt time racing against him. It seemed like the perfect place to slither in and take a look around so he carved a circle in the windowpane nearest to the lock with a small glasscutter. After unlocking the window, he raised it quietly then crawled inside.

Jon stirred when he thought he heard a noise downstairs. Morrell hid on the other side of an antique grandfather's clock when the bedroom door opened on the second floor. Jon eased down the stairs, looking for any signs of trouble. He became increasingly more relaxed when it appeared that all was well. When he pulled the drapes aside to check for sentries posted out front, he didn't see any of the guards armed with a semi-automatic machine guns or anything else for that matter.

After pacing toward the kitchen to check the rear post, Jon approached the back window to peer out back. Sharp pain jutted throughout his right foot. He'd stepped on fragments of glass left behind by the intruder's entrance. "What in the hell?" he clamored, hopping over to the light switch on one foot. His contorted expression transformed into a disturbed frown as the illuminated room revealed the window had been broken from the outside. He inhaled through clenched teeth while picking two sharp pieces of broken glass from the sole of his foot. Realizing that the rear guards were nowhere to be seen, concern for his family outweighed droplets of blood splatter on the linoleum floor. It was clear that someone had breached the security and infiltrated his home.

Jon's heart pounded as he raced up the wooden staircase fearing an assassin laying harm to his wife and child. He reached the top of the stairs, looked in his son's room and didn't find Jon-Jon asleep in his bed. Jon tracked blood as he crept down the hallway to locate the boy, scared that someone had abducted him. With looming trepidations, he peeked in the master bedroom. Breathing a short sigh of relief, he found Jon-Jon nestled beside Starla in bed. Both of them were sound asleep. Jon assumed his son had climbed into his parent's bed after hearing noises coming from downstairs too.

Still speculative about the broken glass, he took a key from the dresser box. He used it to lock the bedroom from the outside before sliding the key underneath the door so that it could have only been opened from the inside.

Without a weapon in hand, Jon headed back down stairs to confront whoever was stupid enough to threaten his family. He searched out of the front window again, hoping he wouldn't have to take on two attackers like he did before. The yard was still desolate but the poignant smell of gasoline and cheap liquor alarmed him. Jon panicked as he tracked back through the house toward the kitchen to get his hands on a knife. As he crouched past the grandfather's clock, Morrell swung the baseball bat he used on the guard. A powerful blow struck against Jon's chest, knocking him to the hardwood floor.

Gasping for air, Jon was hurt. Although taken by surprised, his outrage wouldn't allow him to waiver. He looked up at the man standing over him, taunting with his son's baseball bat. Morrell sneered and scoffed. "You sure I've got the right house? You're not so tough, not tough at all." Then the intruder kicked Jon in the side when he seemed to be catching his breath.

Jon fell over, holding his ribs. As he struggled to his knees, the agent circled behind him and wrapped his right arm around Jon's neck. Morrell wrestled feverishly to maintain his chokehold. While Jon attempted to free himself, Morrell pressed a thick white cloth over his nose and mouth. He grabbed at the intruder's wristwatch, using his own weight to judo flip the agent over his shoulder. Morrell's body slammed against the floor. His pistol fell out of its holster and scooted across the room.

Starla heard a loud thud downstairs. When she couldn't locate Jon in the bedroom, she jumped out of bed to look for him. Reaching the locked door, she pressed her ear against it. It was clear that someone was rumbling on the first floor. Starla pounded on the door. "No!" she screamed. "Oh God, help us!"

Staggering toward the white man, who wreaked gasoline, Jon threw both hands around his neck and squeezed with everything he had left. Morrell twisted and gasped. He was turning a peculiar shade of reddish-blue but wouldn't give up. He dug his fingers into Jon's face. In turn, Jon cracked him on the jaw with his fist. Another jab landed against Morrell's nose but he continued to scuffle.

Jon held him down. "Who sent you?" Whack! "I said, who sent you?" he demanded, between powerful blows to the bewildered agent's face. "Oh yeah, you're gonna tell me if I have to beat it out of you." Whack! Whack!

When Morrell began to gag on the blood flowing from his mouth, he reached for the other gun he kept in an ankle holster.

He couldn't get to it. The beating Jon handed the agent was taking a weighty toll on both men. As a wave of nausea coupled with dizziness eventually swept through Jon like the raging fire, he knew then the cloth Morrell had placed over his nose had been soaked in something debilitating, maybe even poisonous. Jon begun to grow weary. His head spun woozily. Jon, weakened by a heavy dose of chloroform, fell onto his knees.

With muted slurs, Jon swung erratically. "Get... out of my house! You hear me? Get out!" The chloroform's foggy haze forced Jon's respiratory system to seize. Starla continued pounding and screaming as her husband's unresponsive frame collapsed on the floor, answering the drug's haunting call.

The agent's chest heaved violently. He'd inadvertently applied the white cloth against his own bloody lips to stop the bleeding then immediately removed it when he realized what he'd done. Moments later, Morrell propped Jon's limp body against the sofa then took out a small brown leather case. The agent worked fast to secure a thin rubber tube around Jon's forearm. Agent Morrell wiped sweat from his eyes with the cuff of his sleeve. He panted irritably while injecting Jon's arm with a hypodermic needle filled to heroine. There was enough smack to stop a horse.

"See you later, Sambo," Morrell spat, wiping at his eyes again. "You're going to the big plantation in the sky."

Jon scarcely heard Starla's voice calling his name before his body began to writhe as if it were strapped into an electric chair. Once the assassin's poison ravaged his veins, it cooked his body from the inside. Jon's life was over.

Morrell heard Starla's cries growing louder. He scurried to the kitchen window, leaving the house in the same manner he'd entered it then he disappeared silently into the darkness.

After the commotion ended, Jon-Jon discovered the key underneath the door. He handed it to his mother. Starla struggled to unlock the large oak door. Void of apprehension, she stumbled downstairs shouting her husband's name. When she reached the bottom, the sight of Jon's lifeless body hit her like a brick wall. The worst fate imaginable had overcome the only man she ever loved.

Starla sank to the floor shaking her head in disbelief. "God no!" she cried, beating his chest with her balled fists. "Damn you, Jon!" The faraway look in his eyes caused Starla to reflect of all he had seen and experienced without her and what he had to endure by himself now.

After the blaze that consumed the taxi was extinguished, Larry fell into deep deliberation over who might have started it and why. While fuming over the smoldering vehicle, he noticed the guards, who were supposed to be watching Jon's family, milling around the torched automobile. Through the smoldering ashes, he could see the Holloway home in the distance. It already seemed different somehow, less than what it used to be. Larry stared up toward the sky, littered with clouds. He feared the worst and for good reason. "Dammit!" he shouted, in disgust. "Y'all get on back to Jon's place. Make sure he's alright." The words were meant to disperse the troops but they were as empty as the burned out car in front of him.

Shock met the men straight on when they crashed through the front door. One of them ran toward the kitchen and out the back door to see if anyone were still on the premises. Another one tried to revive Jon in the living room but Starla resisted. She wouldn't allow anyone to touch his body. Within minutes, the others arrived with Larry. He was too distraught himself to console the young widow holding the remains of her slain husband. Larry was reminded that Jon's determination to put food on the table and help a neighbor hold onto his business had cost him his life. The heavy burden of guilt prohibited Larry from saying anything to Starla directly. The deep chasm eating at him from the inside gnawed at the pit of his stomach. From that day on, he was merely half the man he used to be.

Before the police and medical emergency vehicles made it to the scene, Rock removed the needle from Jon's right arm. The ambulance driver spotted the puncture mark. He knew a drug overdose when he saw one as Jon's body laid there, still and traumatized. He wore death like a poor man's borrowed suit, it wasn't a decent fit at all. Jon-Jon sat at the bottom of the staircase the entire time, with his knees tucked against his chest. He was a seven year-old child but possessed the maturity to understand there was something wrong about the way his father died, something tragically wrong. He watched black men fussed over his daddy's body until some white ones came and carried it away.

The funeral was attended by a few close friends from the neighborhood. Black Panthers brandishing rifles and white reporters vied to get photos of Jon's home going printed on the front page. Starla was sedated in order to deal with her grief stricken emotions although there was no such prescription to suppress her tears; which flowed throughout the service. Jon-Jon watched mostly, and wondered why all those people came to see his daddy get lowered into the ground. At age seven, he attended his first burial. The suffering and heartache he witnessed that day made it his last.

Weeks later, news of Jon's death traveled to his former troop in Vietnam. The men he'd counted on in the grittiest war of our time assembled in a broad circle, symbolizing a continual and unbroken chain of brotherhood. Marlin Blade blessed the assembly with profound sentiment. "Brothas, soldiers, men. Our fallen comrade, Corporal Jonathan Holloway Sr. is no longer with us.

He passed on to a much better place than any of us are likely to see. Let's remember his bravery and the compassion for his fellow man. For, no truer friend was even known. You will be missed… Jon." A single tear made its way down Blade's flat cheek. Brown Lee, who once threatened to kill Jon in Viet Nam, wept openly like a newborn baby. The solemn bond they'd forged had not been forgotten.

ELEVEN

A Slow Burn

The next twelve weeks were filled with accusations and uncertainty. The local Black Panther chapter blamed a rival taxi company for Jon's murder although Cane Cab vehemently denied it. Larry Brown didn't want to believe agent George Morrell had anything to do with it but he felt down to his toes that the self-serving agent was somehow involved. Unfortunately, Larry didn't have one shred of evidence to prove it. Local newspapers featured a myriad of stories from differing points of view, none of which reflected the truth. Most of the articles seemed to have been written for the sole purpose of discrediting Jon Holloway's name.

FBI Special Agent George Morrell was quoted, "Even though (Jon) Holloway returned from Vietnam a decorated soldier, his long time addiction to heroin and continual run ins with local law enforcement agencies may have aided in his outright beheading of the two men he killed in cold blood. All they wanted was a cab ride across town. It's so sad how drugs ruin everything it touches. If Holloway had only admitted his problems with heroin, maybe none of this would've happened. On the other hand, the way he ended his own life saved tax payers from shouldering the cost of

prosecuting him." A major outcry ensued behind those unsub-
stantiated words. The community was up in arms demanding the
Dallas Times Herald, the leading newspaper which ran the quotes,
print a retraction regarding Morrell's statement. Neither the out-
cries nor demands of the people were ever addressed. To most
of the community, Jon was a martyr. To those who didn't know
him, reading slanted bi-lines in the daily paper made it believable.
There was no way to stop the lies, to stop the pain.

Starla was beside herself. Her world had dissolved into a fraction
of what she'd hoped for after Jon's return. The bottle she climbed in
to drown her sorrows summarily eroded what was left. At times she
found it impossible to face Jon-Jon because he so closely resembled
his father. Mental decay worked itself from the inside out coupled
with sleepless nights on end transformed the beautiful woman Starla
was into a mere shell of her former self. Her internal fire burned
low, leaving behind a cold impenetrable heart.

During the bouts of sobriety, when Starla was sober enough
to remember that she still had a shot at being an outstanding
mother, the thought of living a shatter life without her soul mate
dismantled it. Plagued with the stinging pain of loneliness, Starla
was finally confronted with the reality that Jon was gone and subsequently so was money needed to purchase groceries.

Starla awoke to a dusty bedroom reeking of liquor. She cried
when it occurred that her home was filthy and so were the clothes
she'd worn for days. Miserably hung over, Starla stumbled into the
restroom. She rushed toward the toilet then held her head over
the rim. Foul vomit spewed from her mouth. Groaning sorely, she
held onto the toilet bowl. As she purged into the bowl again, she
noticed her son standing in the bathroom doorway.

"Momma, you forgot to get me up for school again," the
third grader said, careful not to speak to loud. He'd seen Starla in

this shape before, in fact too many times to count. Jon-Jon was dressed in denim jeans which were worn through at the knees and a faded wrinkled shirt. "I'm running late so I'd better get going," he added sadly.

"Wait a minute baby," she uttered, wiping at her mouth with the back of her hand. "Let me put you some food on for breakfast."

"That's okay momma. They got free breakfast at the school for kids like me."

"What you mean, like you?" she grunted.

"Boys and girls with nothing at home to eat," he answered honestly. "Got go now. I hope you feel better momma."

Jon-Jon was out the front door by the time Starla managed to climb to her feet. She leaned against the sink, splashing water on her face. Afterwards, she leered at herself in the bathroom mirror. Too grimy to see things clearly, she scrubbed at the glass with a damp towel. When her startling appearance shown through the smug she'd washed away, Starla's mouth fell opened. Pulling at her wild hair, matted and grubby, she felt ashamed that her child had seen her that way. Within the hour she found another bottle of liquor and cried herself to sleep on the bathroom floor.

Late that afternoon, Starla picked herself up, showered then threw on some clean clothes. She remembered her son commenting about free breakfast for kids *like him*, making him a candidate for free lunches. "I'm so sorry Jon," Starla whimpered. "You haven't been gone a year and I been messing up already. I never meant to have our son begging for meals. I'll do better. I'll fix it," she chuckled oddly, with a bottle of brandy held to her lips. "I'll show 'em I can feed my own child."

Starla strolled down the aisles of Angelo's market carefully keeping watch as she tucked a box of noodles and pork shops under an oversized sweater. When Cookie Mitchell, an old childhood girlfriend, spotted her shoplifting packaged meat she made her way toward Starla. A surprise tap on the arm nearly caused Starla to jump out of her skin. She's assumed the store manager had witnessed her best attempt at obtaining a five-finger discount.

"Starla, I thought that was you." Cookie looked her classmate over thoroughly. Her accusatory eyes said what she didn't have to.

"Damn girl, you scared the hell outta me!" Starla shrieked. "I thought for sure I was busted for lifting dinner." The wrapped package of chops poked out beneath Starla's thick clothing. "Ooh, this is getting cold."

Starla exhibited zero remorse for ripping off groceries. Her long time acquaintance was stricken with enough shame for the both of them. "I know you didn't just pull a stack of pork chops out of your underwear. Honey you have too much class to be boosting anything from this store. If you need some real bread, I can turn you on to a few bucks today then we can discuss how you can bake your own." Cookie reached in her leather handbag then handed Starla a twenty dollar bills. "You know where to find me."

While removing all the stolen items from her undergarments, Starla watched as the attractive woman with a high yellow complexion, wrapped in a tight blue silk ensemble strutted off toward the exit. Cookie moved with the grace of a runway model, rocking four-inch platform heels and a perfectly shaped afro wig.

Luckily for Starla, Cookie had heard about her situation. In fact, everyone had. It was no secret that her husband was gone and her money was tight. Fortunately, the house had been paid off years before she'd moved in although the methodical manner in which she'd once kept the large home spotless was no longer the case. The house, as was Starla, had begun to waste away.

Before her old friend exited the store parking lot behind the wheel of a new Ford Cobra sports car, Starla was out of breath and pounding on the car window. "Heyyy! Hey Cookie! Stop!" As soon as Cookie through the gear shift into Park to stop the car, Starla jumped in the passenger seat hoping to engage in the kind of deep conversation she would later be sorry for. "So tell me, how I can get my hands on some sharp threads like yours and have some left over to pay my bills at the same time?"

"Use that money I gave you for starters," Cookie suggested eagerly. "Buy yourself some decent food and get yourself into dating shape. It's a lot of money to be made for keeping the right kind of company."

Starla knew what that insinuated. "Oh, I'd better give you back this then. I'm not so desperate that I have to throw my legs opened to make grocery money," Starla responded quietly, handing the twenty dollar bill across the console. Her voice elicited more pride than she actually had left.

"Oh you don't? But you're desperate enough to steal meat though? Girl, don't be no fool. Keep that money. You'd do the same for me." Cookie tossed the money in her passenger's lap. "Wouldn't ya?"

"Shoot, you know I would." Starla's eyes drifted downward then back up at Cookie's. "It's just that so many things have changed since…. Hell girl, how am I gonna pay you back?"

"Don't worry, we'll work something out," was Cookie's sly reply. "Yeah, you'll do just fine."

Their lengthy conversation hinged on providing adult entertainment at exclusive parties, hustling after hour clubs to pick up drunken high rollers, who had a lot of extra spending cash and didn't mind spreading some of it around. Despite her reservations, Starla was persuaded to meet some of Cookie's friends over at Rooster's Tavern. Conflicted with uneasy feelings, Starla declined initially. Her friend persisted by reminding Starla of late bills and disconnection notices arriving at the house daily; not to mention a son she couldn't feed.

It wasn't long before Starla was introduced to a number of legit businessmen who liked to get a little wild on the south side. Cookie was a top-notch hustler and didn't mind alternative life styles in order to make a living. Everyone liked the new girl she introduced into the *circle of friends,* as she called them. Their appreciation came in the form of gratuitous finder's fees. Each time they greased her palms, she split it right down the middle then worked the room for additional money to keep all to herself. For Cookie, getting her kicks and paying bills went hand and hand.

Within a few weeks, Starla found herself enjoying the circle of friends and all the trappings that went along with being associated with the fast crowd. Fancy new clothes and a spoon up her nose both suited her better than an empty cupboard. A newly acquired wardrobe and her renewed star-like appearance awarded her a befitting street name. Every night was the same. Men waited in line to get a private taste from the newest toast of the town, the Boulevard Star. Although she was humiliated by her new career, Starla was more afraid of being alone with her thoughts. And, more afraid that she might have rolled over in bed and expect to find her husband, whom she loved more than life itself, only to be reminded that her love of a lifetime had withered away. Knowing that no other man could adequately replace Jon, Starla tried to find solace at the bottom of the deepest bottles she could get her hands wrapped around. Cocaine provided a pick me up she'd convinced herself was necessary. What began as a prop had transgressed into a crutch, seemingly overnight.

Soon enough, Starla found it difficult to roll out of bed without a hit. The void in her heart became evident on her face. The bright smile Jon loved so much was a distant memory as were the

circle of friends who once welcomed her association. It was a pitiful spiral downward. A lower class of men took up the slack after
her "A" list refused to continue sponsoring her expensive drug
habit. There were always men, bottom feeders who loved the Boulevard Star; regardless of how dimly she shined.

Ms. Harris, the caring neighbor, was appalled when she
noticed how Starla thoughtlessly consumed herself with making
money and getting high above keeping an eye on her son. The
older mentor grew weary of pulling Starla out of parked cars in
front of the house and Jon-Jon learned to despise men who summoned his mother out front for a quick hand job or something
a bit more sinful. With a toot of their car horns or a toot of their
blow, Starla provided curbside satisfaction without hesitation.

On a rare occasion, Starla pulled herself together long enough
to prepare a hearty meal amidst a filthy cluttered kitchen. While
stumbling through an existence that could hardly be considered
functional, she inadvertently sat three places at the dinner table.
When it became unnervingly clear what she'd done, reality hit her
like a bone chilling wind. She wrapped both hands around herself, plopped down in a chair then wept uncontrollably. Jon wasn't
joining them for dinner, not then not ever. Starla's life was rapidly
diminishing without him, just as she prophesized it would.

Hiding behind closed doors with strange men and getting
high had all but scraped away the dignity Starla held sacred during Jon's tour in Viet Nam. Sharing her waking hours with drugs,
alcohol, and nameless faces provided welcomed alternatives to the
visions haunting her dreams. She considered it the lesser of two
evils until one fatal night, when a wild orgy flooded with narcotic
party favors sent her on a bad trip she didn't come back from.
Her life, filled with love and happiness inspired by hope of better
days, ended as a shadowy Jane Doe dead on arrival at the county

morgue. Despite efforts to separate Jon from her memory, Starla failed miserably. Her spirit died with his. Ms. Harris claimed her remains then ensured Starla was put to rest with the proper and descent send off befitting a loving wife and mother. A year after she'd given up, almost to the day, she was buried too.

Orphaned and nowhere to turn, Jon-Jon's life had changed so much that he didn't recognize it. Nights spent tossing and turning in foster home beds swiftly evolved into years of difficult adjustments. Making the best of bad situation, Larry Brown took in Jon-Jon for a short time until his taxi business toppled. Expenses required to clothe and feed two growing boys became too much of a financial strain. As much as he wanted to do right by Jon and raise his child, a sluggish economy wouldn't allow it. Ms. Harris worked tirelessly to give Jon-Jon what she thought a young man needed, visiting on weekends and providing a constant reminder of the best Starla had to give. Despite all of her good deeds, Jon-Jon struggled with separation anxiety and a refusal to forgive both parents for abandoning him. Problems with authority figures and bouts of criminal mischief chartered a path of destruction. The path was steady and sure, as was his inevitable collision course with tragedy.

Two weeks after Jon-Jon's twelfth birthday, the angels above must have held a prayer meeting on his behalf. Shuffled from house to house during the past five years, he learned to use his hands rather than words to express his anger. Just when it appeared only a matter of time before Jon-Jon ran up against the wrong somebody with a meaner streak than his, something amazing happened.

Moments after beating the snot out of a kid his age, who unwisely called his father a dope head, Jon-Jon's attention landed on a much older boy's ridicule from the far end of a recreational game room.

"What you laughing at punk?" Jon-Jon snarled.

"That snot hanging out of his nose is a trip but that's not the funny part. He should have called your momma a hoe too. Now that would've been funn…"

Before the older kid popped off, Jon-Jon crack him twice across the face. Fortunately for both boys, he was caught in the act. Officer Rideau, a white Dallas Police officer intervened as the older boy begged forgiveness and pleaded for the relentless thrashing to stop.

Reggie Brown, Larry's son, had a ringside seat for the violent incident. He shook his head the way he always did when someone brought out the worst in his best friend. "I told that fool not to run his mouth about Jon-Jon's folks. That boy loved his people. Better hope he don't lose that tooth hanging out his mouth."

The cop ended the brawl although Jon-Jon's tantrum didn't subside until officer Rideau slammed him against a row of lockers. "Son, what's gotten into you? We don't allow fighting down here at the community center. You could have hurt these fella's pretty bad."

"First off, I ain't your son and second, if y'all don't allow no fightin' down here then y'all shouldn't allow people to say things that might get their ass whooped."

Officer Rideau forced himself to contain the smile pushing through his thin lips. "What did they say to make you want to stomp them like that?"

Jon-Jon pointed to his first victim, still grimacing on the floor. "Him, I only socked once. He said something that wasn't true about my daddy. My daddy was a war a hero." Then he pointed at the older boy clutching at his swollen face. "Now him, I stomped. Shouldn't have called my momma a hoe."

Rideau scratched his head, understanding how the twelve-year old was provoked to rage. "Well, if what they said isn't the truth then you're just gonna have to look past the lies. The truth can never hurt you." After contemplating the officer's advice, Jon-Jon wiped away tears that escaped his almond shaped eyes.

"Well, it was the truth about my momma but that didn't give him the right to say it to my face. I ought to stomp his rusty butt again!"

Jon-Jon received a three week ban from the community center but much like a small animal, he returned in search of the cop who'd set him straight concerning the use of violence to make his point. One kind lecture moved Jon-Jon in a manner he hadn't imagined possible; it caused him to consider options when things went awry.

Days later, the officer persuaded Jon-Jon to join the Police Athletic League's summer boxing program. Having seen too many young boys with lethal degrees of hostility, Rideau redirected Jon-Jon toward constructive avenues which built character instead of those further preparing them for prison. That was the summer of change, change that created incentives that fulfilled Jon-Jon's need to feel like he belonged. More importantly, the coping skills he learned added years to his life. Just when it seemed highly improbable, Jon-Jon found peace after the storm.

PART II

"Vengeance is mine…"

TWELVE

High Finance and Hood Fantasy

Twenty years had come and gone. The *Power to the People* generation was replaced by *Generation X'ers* boasting mantras of *I* and *Me* instead of *We*. Two decades later, the masses insisted on counter-productive self-serving agendas, inflated egos and even bigger cars to accommodate them. The revolution was summarily boiled down to better jobs for women and minorities and equal rights for gays under the law. America underwent drastic growing pains in order to move the entire country forward rather than securing wealth for the privileged few like is had in the past. Things changed more than some readily admitted while other argued it still had a long way to grow.

"The weather man says it's going to be hot and he hadn't lied all month," the radio personality announced. "The breeze index is a negative ten and it's a sticky-icky seventy-nine degrees at eight thirty-five in the a.m. That's right, get your weave tight. You don't want to be caught outside without a retouch. Now, more R&B hits to get you there on time if you're not already late. Thanks for listening to your home team on K104 Radio."

As the announcer cut to a commercial, a handsome ebony-skinned man killed the engine in a shiny luxury car. He checked his hair and teeth in the rear view mirror, cracked the window in his cobalt-gray Lexus 400 then stepped out onto the pavement of the bank parking lot. Standing over six feet at two hundred and twenty pounds, the distinguished gentleman amounted to a nice, tight package. His neatly trimmed haircut fit him almost as well as the tailored banker-blue suit which hung elegantly on his sculptured body. In a word, the man was *together*. He exuded strength without the pretense of arrogance, the epitome of black and beautiful.

A collection of customers grumbled as the branch manager of American South Financial Bank made his way through the gathering to reach the front door. The day was Monday the 3rd, Social Security disbursement day. And, those who had worked enough years or suffered from various health conditions prohibiting their employment awaited the bank opening at nine o'clock sharp.

"When y'all gonna open up?" shouted an elderly woman, who'd decided to rest her tired behind on the broad hood of somebody else's 1978 hand-me-down Impala.

"How is everyone this morning?" was the manager's charming reply. He greeted the early risers with a doting smile before acknowledging the woman's question. "The bank opens at nine o'clock. That's twenty minutes from now." Subsequently, he checked his watch to be certain. "What brings y'all to the bank so early anyway?" he said, as if he didn't know. Every third of every month was the same. An eager pack of account holders nestled close to the entrance like anxious race horses awaiting the starting gate. It was the same month after month, year in and year out. Nothing would ever change about that.

A short round woman wearing thick pink foam hair rollers and a tight outfit which could have easily been mistaken for pajamas, snapped back. "What's got *you* so late this mornin'? You must have got dressed in the dark 'cause you got on black shoes with a brown belt. I know yo' daddy taught you better 'cause I knew him. Humph, now he was a man with class." The entire ensemble of customers erupted with unbridled laughter, like a classroom filled with high school freshmen responding to a wise-crack about somebody's mother. After the banker acknowledged his accessory mishap, he realized that he was no match for the quick witted fashion detective. He humbly conceded defeat with a noble head nod while strolling inside the bank. He flashed a smile of surrender before relocking the door behind him.

Each of the early risers had one thing in common; direct deposit accounts through the Social Security Administration Office across the street. Having access to their monthly source of income a.s.a.p. also cut out the middleman, the postman.

The manager entered the spacious lobby. Immediately, he began to straighten various account brochures, withdrawal and deposit slips at the freestanding check isle. Since the local branch was barely three years old, attractive mauve colored furniture complemented the architectural design of the building. Other than the two-inch thick bullet resistant window separating the tellers from their customers, the American South Financial Bank (ASFB) on M.L.K. Jr. Blvd. was an appreciated getaway, as well as a coveted neighborhood meeting place.

As the manger made his way to his conservatively decorated office, he noted that his banking staff was poised and prepared to endure a long business day. The 3rd of the month always was the most demanding, no matter which day of the week it happened to fall on.

Deidra Williams, the new accounts supervisor, welcomed the manager near the customer sign-in kiosk. She gave his expensive suit a slight once over before handing him the previous week's financial reports and forecasts for the next sales period. "Good morning Mr. Holloway, glad you could join us," she mocked, using the manager's sarcastic remark reserved for staff members when they arrived late for work. "Ha-ha, I just love it when you're late. It reminds me that you're human... *just like the rest of us*," Deidra added, accompanied by a sly wink.

Mr. Holloway responded casually, neglecting to raise his eyes from the reports. "I have been late two times in three years," he contended. "However... you, Ms. Williams, are late on a weekly basis." They exchanged abbreviated glances that quickly dissolved into good-natured grins.

"Oh, by the way Jonathan, what's up the black shoes-brown belt combo? You get dressed in the dark or what?" she joked.

Once again, he'd been reprimanded for his lack of detail. This time around, Jonathan felt it necessary to strike back. "Nice observation, I'll give you that. And I would be a bit embarrassed had I gotten dressed in the dark, alone." Jonathan flashed a winning smile as Deidra turned red.

"Uh-uh, too much information," she replied, as if she didn't care in the least. "I'm not trying to hear about the little hoochie fest you probably got going on over at your player palace. But if you did let some cross-eyed chick put that outfit together for you, get an upgrade."

"First of all, men don't wear outfits," Jonathan answered matter-of-factly, "and second, it ain't your business."

A senior teller watched the entire interaction between Jonathan and Deidra from her window. "They need to go ahead and knock boots and get it over with. All this cat and mouse stuff adds unnecessary stimuli to a simple situation," she said, before returning to the horoscope section of the daily newspaper.

Sitting in the next station, a junior associate added her unsolicited two cents. "Tell me about it. A child could see that she's in love with him like she's in love breathing. It's kinda too bad that she works here though. Mr. Holloway would never mix it up with an employee. God is my witness I've thrown it at him enough to know. Hell, if I even thought I had a shot at a fine ass brotha like that, I'd quit today then work him like a full-time job. Amen chile!"

"Speak on it, sistah," was the older woman's spirited reply. "You're preaching to the choir."

One of Deidra's fantasies was in fact a romantic affair with her boss but she knew better than anyone it would never happen. Their relationship was forged with respect and tempered with mutual admiration. Besides, she owed Jonathan far too much to put his career on the line for an inter-office fling.

Although Deidra lacked a formal education, her intelligence and natural propensity for solving other people's problems served her well in south Dallas's biggest bank. The petite, rich southern-brown twenty-four year old account manager loved her job almost as much as she loved to shop. Relationships had often been associated with heartache in her past but a new outfit always left Deidra feeling fabulous. She was adamant about looking the part of a consummate professional. That refreshing quality aided her in appearing more seasoned for her position than she actually was.

When Jonathan returned to Dallas, from his Houston assignment a little more than four years before, a street-wise female hustler was discovered outside the bank. Complaints from neighbors of a frail crack addicted prostitute caused quite a stir and police involvement. That was Deidra then. Jonathan happened to be surveying the construction of a new banking center when he was forced to settle a dispute between Fruit Of Islam and Dallas' finest. The police officers who arrived on the scene were not about to let a group of well-dressed Muslims rescue a wayward prostitute trespassing on private property. Deidra had been arrested twice on solicitation charges but the Muslims were determined to save her from another stint in jail. Within moments, a bad situation teetered on disaster. What seemed like a small army of black men donned in pressed suits and bow ties converged from every direction. Police officers on the scene intensified matters by summoning for emergency backup.

Jonathan realized someone needed to intervene before a typical summer afternoon reached a boiling point. Shouting, finger pointing and threats ensued. Jonathan stepped in, introduced himself as a bank official then immediately began reasoning with the police. He pretended to employ the hooker with an admitted drug addiction, who was on the bank's property with his consent. Furthermore, he added she was there to meet him for an appointment with a substance rehabilitation facility. The police didn't buy his explanation. However, they could appreciate Jonathan's underlying agenda, preventing a front-page public relations nightmare. Somewhat reluctant, the frustrated officers released Deidra with the stern warning. There would be no room for discussion if she was ever caught propositioning men in that neighborhood again.

The blistering hot August afternoon presented a challenge as well as a new beginning for Deidra, who had no idea how she'd fallen so far or how fast. Subjecting herself to Jonathan's guardianship was facing a difficult dilemma but she agreed that undergoing rehab was a far better outcome than county lockup.

After completing the drug program, she was the first employee hired for Jonathan's staff. Clean and sober for over three years, Deidra was one of the lucky few. She broke her painful addiction to crack and turned her life around. Within a year, she'd become one of the branch's most valuable assets. For Jonathan, it was an easy decision. He recognized the despair in Deidra's eyes, the hope she'd lost somewhere along the way. It was the audacity of hope that saved him as a child, hope that betrayed his mother but never abandoned him.

THIRTEEN

Not My Type of Hype

The vast teller cage was anchored at the far end of the building between the ATM deposit room and employee break area. The manager's office, positioned near the front door, was enclosed by two large glass-framed walls which facilitated an open door environment for both employees and customers alike. Jonathan loved his personal space, despite its fishbowl appearance. On the southern-most wall of his office, was a book shelf aligned with banking literature, policies and procedure manuals, and a litany of autographed novels signed by his favorite contemporary authors.

African artwork adorned the adjoining wall. Each piece was an original, completed by students from the Lincoln High School Art Club. ASFB commissioned the paintings, donating ten thousand dollars to the school's scholarship fund at Jonathan's behest. On the credenza directly behind his desk were numerous awards. Some of which were acquired via an affiliation with the 100 Black Men of America Mentorship Program. Numerous honors celebrated his participation and leadership in the city's anti-drug crusade. His most endeared gift of appreciation was the Illiteracy Extinction Tribute for a campaign he pioneered. When his efforts were publicly acknowledged by the Governor and captured by a barrage of cameramen, Jonathan felt as though he'd finally done something his father would have been proud of. Helping the community that gave him a second chance was icing on the cake.

Jonathan nearly knocked over a large plant arrangement placed on his desk. Oddly, no name appeared on the card. Instead, the word, *Congratulations*, was hand written in block lettering. Jonathan shrugged his broad shoulders assuming the sender would eventually contact him to see if it had arrived. *Congratulations for what*, he wondered.

As soon as the thought left him, Jonathan was back to work. He reviewed emails from the corporate downtown office, prioritized his morning then began to bang out a business letter with personal implications. The correspondence was addressed to Walter Delaney, Dallas Regional Manager of ASF Bank regarding budget allocation to the South Side YMCA Building Improvement Fund. Distracted by the chatter of brooding customers entering the bank, Jonathan peered up from the computer monitor.

Theodore Manus promptly barged into the manager's office without having been invited. Tee-Man was one of Jonathan's childhood acquaintances, who had grown up in a nearby run down tenement building. Even though he was Jonathan's age, his frame hadn't managed to produce a single muscle since the tenth grade. His sagging blue jeans and "Rehab is for Quitters" t-shirt were properly exhibited his youthful personality.

Although rudely interrupted, Jonathan couldn't resist the wide grin spreading across his lips. "Tee... Man, where've you been? Looks like you've been working out," Jonathan lied. "The sistahs better watch out. A hard body and a winning smile can get a man in a whole lot of trouble." The irony in Jonathan's compliments had the customer showing all twenty-one of his remaining silver-capped teeth. Jonathan had the knack of finding diamonds in the dirt.

"I'm just trying to be like you," Tee-Man joked, returning some of the man-banter tossed at him. "You know you my super hero, Super-Negro."

Jonathan stifled his laughter with a concerned smile. He found himself searching Tee's face for tale-tale signs of his on-again off-again drug use tailspin. The abrupt change in Jonathan's demeanor disturbed the man sitting across his desk. "What's up Jon-Jon? Oh, you're trying to see if I'm high. After all I been through, you think I'd get twisted up in that sin again? Thanks for your vote of confidence."

"Are you trying to play me *Theodore*?" Jonathan said, not sure whether to believe his instincts.

"Man, I'm all played out. I thought you knew."

Tee-Man appeared to have steered away of the haze that almost took him under. When his words matched the hurtful look on his face, Jonathan inhaled a sincere dose of remorse.

"I'm sorry Tee-Man, just checking," Jonathan apologized.

"Now that we got that outta the way, let's get down to bidness. I need you to do me a solid." He purposely lowered his eyes then conjured up a pitiful expression. "I need you to initial my payroll check this ONE LAST TIME." Tee-Man persisted with full knowledge of Jonathan's distaste for irresponsibility on any level. "I still haven't got my new I.D. yet... but I called the city and they swear it's in the mail." He jutted out his chin then held up his left hand over his heart. "They swear! I swear they swear! And, I'm kinda in a hurry so could you please...?" Still swearing, Tee-Man nudged the wrinkled paycheck closer to the bank manger with his long thin antennae-like fingers. "Ms. Williams been giving me hell, with her cute self. She say she won't let the tellers cash it unless you hook me up. Come on now, you know I'm good for it," he added optimistically. Jonathan wrote his initials on the left top corner, stood up then circled to the other side of the desk.

"Trade Mark Foods is one of our biggest customers. *They're* good for it," Jonathan argued, then extended a strong handshake followed by a brief soulful embrace.

"Thank you Jon-Jon. Gotta-go-bye." Tee-Man snatched the check from his hand then darted toward the teller cage as if on roller skates.

Jonathan grinned, just like he did each time their ritual played out the same way. He didn't know who got the better part of their short visit. Some of his customers provided constant reminders of where he came from and why he would not trade his job for the world. "You're very welcome, Theodore," he said, moments later.

"I need to talk to yo' boss then!" shouted a mountainous black man, as he pounded his fleshy fists against the thick teller glass partition. He was at least six-five and tilted the scales at three hundred and fifty pounds. Green jogging pants drooped off his behind and his 'I'm too sexy' tank top was at least two sizes too small. "This is some bullshit! If I was at a white bank on the north side I wouldn't be getting hassled this way. Where's your boss? I ain't going for this!"

When Jonathan heard the man's thunderous outburst, he sprang from his desk before Deidra had the opportunity to ring him Code One. Jonathan made a beeline through the busy lobby to address the loud mouth, who turned toward the long procession of customers waiting to transact business. "Just because this is a black neighborhood don't mean y'all can treat us like niggas," he spat, even louder than before. Pacing angrily back and forth, with both flabby arms raised, it was obvious he'd hoped to build an allegiance. The other customers sneered directly in his face then either gawked irritably or turned away. All of them were burdened with enough of their own issues to be concerned with his.

"Hi'ya doing Sir? I'm Jonathan Holloway," the manager said cordially, amidst the giant's shadow. His extended hand was not met with a welcomed response. Instead, the overbearing pain in the butt spent a few moments sizing up Jonathan from head to toe.

Suddenly he became more exasperated than before. "I said, I want to see the boss!" he hollered, directed at the junior teller on the safe side of the thick glass. "I want to see the man who runs this place. Not some assistant flunky." That insult was hurled at Jonathan.

Management Protocol 101: Keep in mind that many customers and valued employees are observing the situation and won't soon forget how angry outbursts are handled.

Having been a well-schooled student of protocol, Jonathan flashed an amiable smile then exhaled slowly to compose himself before agreeing to give his guest what he'd requested. "Well then, by all means. Let me direct you to the manager's office. I'm sure he'll be more than gracious to visit with you."

As the men headed to the other side of the spacious building, resembling an animal trainer walking a dinosaur, the junior teller exhaled her disgust. "Too bad this bullet proof glass ain't funky breath proof. His raggedy mouth is so stank." She held her nose while spraying a half can of air freshener throughout her immediate area.

Tee-Man presented his check under the small opening in the glass. "I'd have beat him down!" he ranted, playfully. "Better be glad Mr. Holloway's a peaceful man. Me, I'd have beat him down."

Management Protocol 102: Isolate the problem.

"Please have a seat sir," Jonathan offered kindly, behind closed doors. The windbag took a seat, grinning like a Cheshire cat, thinking now he'd get to see the head cluck who ran the coop. He made an unsuccessful attempt at crossing his meaty legs while Jonathan slid into his suit coat from the other side of the desk. The man stared at Jonathan peculiarly with wide-eyed curiosity then noted the angular granite name plate sitting on the desk. JONATHAN HOLLOWAY- MGR. Before he could voice the humiliation strewn across his pie shaped face, Jonathan flashed a close cousin to the cheesy smile, the visitor manufactured when calling the manager a flunky. After Jonathan had successfully made his point, he clasped his hands together on the desk.

"Look sir, I asked you to come in here so we could talk as men, without everyone listening in. You got to know, I can't have you going off, loud-talking my staff and bringing drama up in my place of business. This community needs this bank. This bank wants this community to grow."

The angry man rolled his eyes toward the ceiling. Jonathan continued despite the obvious protest. "There are a lot of people in this city hoping this bank fails so they can say I told you so and shut this place down but that's not going to happen. It won't happen because brothas like me have something to prove. The money down here is just as green." Jonathan had no idea how menacing he looked, his face flush with righteous indignation.

"Yeah, whatever," the big man mumbled. "My money is green too and I can't believe y'all trying to keep me from it." When it appeared he was getting worked up all over again. Jonathan held up his index finger to stifle him.

While peering down at the man's seven-hundred, twelve dollar and seventeen cent payroll check, Jonathan came across the reason why his teller wouldn't cash it. "Mr. Taylor, I didn't mean to cut you off but I need to show you something. You don't have an account with us. And, we don't have a business relationship with your employer."

"So?"

"So, there's no recourse if the funds are not available and this check bounces."

"And?"

"And, that's like you owing me money but telling me to get it from some dude who owes you," Jonathan explained further. He expected some form of repentance after delivering his patented dissertation. Instead, he found a cold pair of eyes staring back at him.

"So that's it Mr. Manager? You ain't gonna cash my check, even though this here is a bank? Thanks for nothin'... brotha." After the lecture, the mountain grumbled. He climbed from the chair, slammed the check into his pocket then stormed away with long contemptuous strides. He exited the office defeated but he wasn't quite ready to let it go. "I don't know why y'alls standing in line. The manager ain't nobody but an Uncle Tom. You put a nigga behind a desk and alls you got is another spook by the door."

Jonathan watched from his office doorway with his arms folded until the man left. It required a certain degree of intellect and patience to deal with people who felt unfairly disenfranchised, especially when their lack of banking industry knowledge rivaled their lack of opportunity make bank. Jonathan was accustomed to dealing with customers experiencing enormous shortages of both money and opportunity. He fully understood that money and opportunity won't stand for being separated.

Jonathan spent fifteen minutes reading over the weekly reports before it occurred that he'd been studying the same column of numbers. He couldn't get pass the angry man incident but knew why so many black people were angry; especially black men. At the outset of building this country, economic structures weren't designed with them in mind. Slaves didn't figure in nor did the idea of their descendant being free, educated, and ambitious. Jonathan couldn't help wondering if the angry giant was mad because he was black or just a black man who was mad about everything in general. Either way he was a lot of both, mad and black.

"Brian, come on in. It's open," said Jonathan, surprised at the rare visit from a white colleague. Brian Tillman, a commercial lending officer from the downtown branch stepped in the office on cue. He was a rising star in the company, prided himself on having the best of everything, and he didn't mind taking questionable measures to maintain it. The impressive Rolex he flashed every chance he got, was boosted from a jewelry store in the wholesale district. His extensive wardrobe of Armani suits, all black market acquisitions. Although his stature left much to be desired, he more than made up for it with an oversized ego. At five-foot seven, Brian Tillman proved undoubtedly that he was the perfect height for center stage.

Jonathan saluted his latest visitor with a crooked smile when he saw a fake one beaming back at him. Tillman respected Jonathan's abilities as a banker but he made his position known on several occasions that he didn't particularly look forward to traveling to the 'hood or transacting business deals there.

Jonathan was well acquainted with the golden boy type, the right Ivy League education and all the hype that it presented. He also knew than men who worshipped the all mighty dollar above all else couldn't be trusted. Greedy, paled in comparison to characterizing Tillman's love of money.

Tillman took the seat he was offered then wasted little time before inquiring about the disturbance that previously occurred in the lobby. "What was all that about, Holloway? That *homeboy* sure was pissed off but I guess that comes with the territory, huh?" He gave less than a damn about the territory but couldn't pass up on an opportunity to remind Jonathan that he was glad to far removed from the common man in his posh high-rise office.

"Yes, he was… pissed off. And yes it does come with the territory," Jonathan answered, as he peered out of his large window toward the parking lot. "Brian, I don't see your Benz outside. Did you catch the bus?" Of course he meant it sarcastically. A man like Tillman would rather walk than be subjected to taking Dallas Area Rapid Transit.

"I don't do buses," Tillman smugly replied. "I'm in that Rover 9000 parked next to your Lexus." He swayed back in the chair as if to admire a large chunk of the world that belonged to him.

Business must be good, Jonathan thought. That SUV was priced at over seventy thousand. He was impressed but refused to give Tillman the satisfaction of asking how he could afford such an expensive vehicle. He also noticed his visitor's sparkling new timepiece, solid gold cuff links, and the snazzy three button designer suit tracing his tanned body. Jonathan had no idea what was going on behind Tillman's veneered teeth but he was beginning to feel the itch. The same itch Jonathan experienced as a troubled youth which usually resulted in name calling, fists flying, and bodies falling.

"To what do I owe this distinguished visit?" Jonathan asked, with that itch still in the back of his mind.

Brian Tillman leaned in with his pricey grin that was inherently different from his flawed personality. "I just came down to see the only man who gives the brass in this company a bigger hard on than I do," he answered. "My sources tell me that you're the first from ASFB to get nominated for the Dallas Man of the Year Award. That's a great honor. Hell, I'm impressed and that ain't easy to do."

Suddenly, Jonathan became even more annoyed. The conceited little jerk was deliberately baiting him with privileged information concerning his career. Jonathan unclenched his teeth to calm himself. "Are you going somewhere with this or do you plan to sit there until your car gets jacked?" Locals at the bus stop began to gather around Tillman's new utility vehicle to get an innocent closer look. The new car owner rushed over to the office window.

"I got this covered," Tillman responded smartly. He slid his right hand into his pocket, pulled out his car keys then pressed a red button on the car alarm remote. Headlights flashed, the car horn blared and the alarm chirped. When it appeared the show was over, a loud automated voice sounded off. "Please step away from the car! You are too close to the car! Please step away from the car!"

Tillman reclaimed his seat then sank deeply into his comfort zone as the onlookers stepped back, marveling at the alarm system. His lack of insensitivity registered like a slap in the face. "I didn't know I'd have to arm the damned thing here at the bank."

"That comes with the territory too," Jonathan enlightened him. "But they don't want your car."

Tillman glanced toward the window again. "How do you know that? Look at how they're gawking at it."

Jonathan was so tired of the white privilege that had them thinking every black person wanted to steal their belongings when the truth was black people like shiny objects as much as the man who considered it his prized possession. "You really want to know how I know. Because it's still out there... Brian. If they wanted it, your new whip and that ridiculous alarm would already be gone. Just the same as if some white car thief wanted it badly enough, they wouldn't think twice about taking it from you."

Sensing the conversation had taken an ugly turn for the worst and wasn't likely to be restored, the downtown banker stood up and straightened his silk necktie. "Holloway, I didn't mean to upset you or insult your peeps," he explained, in a self-righteous tone. "But I've worked hard to get what I have and I plan on keeping it. I'm sure you feel the same as I do. Whether you'll admit it or not, you're more like me than them. You're young, educated, a star on the fast track, and you love it... just like me."

While peering into Tillman's eyes, Jonathan recognized that he was in the company of a stranger. His mouth became uncomfortably dry as he rose from the desk. There was that itch again, working on his nerves. "Brian, I'm nothing like you. I don't think like you. I don't feel the way you do," Jonathan replied, while shaking his head slowly. "My daddy didn't get me this job. And as an educated black man, I'm often feared more than I'm revered by white ones like you, those who are so damn afraid that if I do get the chance to make a big splash, I will. And, that scares the hell out of them. No, Tillman," Jonathan reiterated, while losing all familiarity, "I'm not like you and you sure as hell are nothing like me."

They stood mere inches from one another, both determined to hold their ground, as well as their points of view. Each of them felt the tension swimming inside of Jonathan's fishbowl. Dissension between them had thickened, neither willing to blink first. Both men were oblivious to everything outside of their sparring of words. Deidra wasn't the only person in the lobby interested in the peculiar standoff during business hours. A number of customers questioned the tiff with curious eyes.

When Jonathan's cell phone hummed, he hesitated then unclipped it from his belt to take a peek. Slowly, his eyes drifted away from Tillman's strained expression. After he looked at the screen, he wrinkled his brow. Mr. Holloway, this is a reminder to attend the regional community development meeting at one o'clock. The Maple Place location. Conference room number two. Jonathan jotted the information on a note pad then silenced his phone.

Subsequently Tillman's phone chimed as well. He held it in his hand, read the message then nodded arrogantly toward the exit like a gun slinger who knew better than to turn his back on a formidable foe. "I guess I'll see you at one o'clock."

Jonathan nodded assuredly. "Yeah, at one."

Moments after Tillman left the manager's office, Deidra came in and closed the door behind her. She scrambled to the nearest chair then plopped down. Jonathan was uncharacteristically quiet and wearing pent up hostility like a bad cologne. Deidra looked him over curiously then cleared her throat. "Uh-hmm. Sorry if I'm bothering you Jonathan but just the tellers wanted to thank you for standing up to that crazy man earlier this morning. I couldn't believe him banging on that glass like some kind of fool. Get me yo' boss! Get me yo' boss!" she mocked. "I can't stand idiot niggas!"

That last comment brought Jonathan back from his subdued daydream. "Don't say that," he mouthed just above a whisper.

Deidra stretched her neck to hear his reply. "What?"

"Don't say that. Don't use that word. It's poison." It took longer than it should have for him to regain his bearings because the trip he took was an arduous one. It started centuries before Rosa Parks refused to yield her bus seat to a white man.

"I know how you feel about that N-word. I'm just upset." Deidra was actually upset by the persistent thought of questioning Jonathan about Tillman's brief stop over until her curiosity overwhelmed her better judgment. "Uh, and I'm not trying to get in your business or nothing but I noticed that it got kinda heated up in here, between you and that fake white boy."

Finally, Jonathan's eyes found hers. "Deidra, I could have sworn you just said something about not getting into mine. Besides, I need to grab a quick bite if I'm going to make it to a one o'clock at Maple Place." With a lot on his mind, Jonathan methodically picked up his keys and his sunshades. "Text me if you need me. I'll be at corporate."

Deidra was well aware of Jonathan's struggles and the typical issues that most black men endured as they assimilated up the ranks of corporate America. She'd also learned from watching Jonathan, how distant he became when feeling pressed by forces beyond his control. Recognizing it was one thing but watching him go through it hurt Deidra as if his struggles were her own.

FOURTEEN

Get It Together

Brian Tillman hovered just inside the luxurious executive boardroom on the eighty-second floor while making small talk with the regional manager, Walter Delaney, a dumpy built fair skinned middle-aged ball of goo. He was also one of few black men, who had ascended high up the ladder by refusing to make strides at helping other qualified blacks get ahead as well. During his twenty plus years with the bank, he didn't make a single ripple. Although despised by most of the African-American employees in his region, he felt justified in doing nothing to bring about a change in the company's hiring practices, affirmative action, or in helping other cultures gain access to the brass ring held so tightly in his grasp.

Delaney and Tillman were the first to arrive at the one o'clock meeting. They discussed the direction in which the bank was headed since insurance company lobbyists challenged the legislature to place a ban on the sale of cigarettes at college campuses. Although the largest majority of the bank's holding were tied up in tobacco, employees were permitted to discuss how the bank made its real money, at least not in public. The rapid increase of generation X'ers incurring health problems related to smoking proposed a governmental stoppage of tobacco production until an in-depth Nicotine addiction study had been completed.

Delaney theorized what A.S.F.B. would be forced to do if the governmental sanction passed. "The bank is certainly going to have to divest into other industries. This work stoppage in our cigarette manufacturing plants could create a storm that'll shake up Wall Street but the big boys in Carolina had to have seen this coming. My bet is they're already working on something to recoup potential lost revenue. Losses could rise to forty million a month."

While Tillman salivated over Delaney's assumptions, eleven members of the bank's Community Development Committee began to fill the boardroom. When Jonathan entered everyone stood to applaud his arrival. The ovations echoed off the walls. Jonathan was at a lost. Panning the member's faces failed to offer clues as to the reason behind all the hoopla. When he took his seat, the others continued clapping around the magnificent cherry wood conference table.

Mr. Delaney welcomed the committee before announcing that Jonathan Holloway was the first nominee from ASFB for the coveted Man of the Year honors awarded to the most deserving male Dallasite who exemplified community service. Jonathan cut his eyes to inspect Tillman's expression but the snazzy-dressed yuppie refused to reciprocate eye contact. The nomination seemed to fall in his lap although he'd learned early in life that nothing worth having came easily or without expectations.

When Delaney left his chair at the end of the table to praise and honor his top producing manager, they all begun to cheer again. Jonathan acknowledged them with a quaint head nod, still unsure what to expect next. "We are all aware of what Jonathan Holloway has done for the south Dallas community, helping to establish ASFB in that sector, and becoming an intricate part of our Minority Business Development focus. His nomination and representation of the bank is an honor and we'll be pulling for him at the Chamber of Commerce banquet on Saturday night. Jonathan we're proud of you. Now let's get on to other business."

Wondering what all this meant, Jonathan prepared his mouth for a second glass of water from the crystal pitcher resting on the boardroom table. The meeting resumed but Jonathan's mind was miles away. He couldn't recall another black nominee, ever. Actually, the award had been jokingly referred to as the, 'Good ole boy of the year," *reward*.

Eventually, the meeting ended without any ground-breaking resolutions, but a series of promising suggestions were discussed then tabled to be voted on in the next session. As the group dispersed, Jonathan received further congratulations. Tillman gave him a stiff atta' boy pat on the back before scurrying out with the others.

"Jonathan, how have you been?" asked George Morrell, the chief security officer for ASFB and the same man who'd murdered his father over twenty years ago. He had gained a few pounds and the specks of gray in his thinning hairline suited his pale skin tone. "I just wanted to convey a special thanks from the security department for the work you do down there in south Dallas. M.L.K. is the only community branch that hasn't experienced a robbery during the rash of hold-ups. Good job son."

"We try," Jonathan answered aloofly. He hated it when older white men called him son, feeling it was one short step away from being called boy or worse. "*It probably has a lot to do with that two-inch-thick bullet proof glass you had inserted, which is an insult to my customers and the community in general,*" he wanted to add but thought better of it.

Jonathan didn't have the slightest notion that the man standing two feet away from him was the cause of his father's untimely demise and the subsequent ruin of his family. However, George Morrell was well aware of Jonathan's lineage and how killing his father boosted his FBI career into overdrive. Since the day he reviewed Jonathan's application for employment several years ago, Morrell kept a watchful eye on the young banker while gloating secretly each time their paths crossed. In due time, the gloating would end abruptly, once and for all.

Later that same day, Jonathan gathered a set of workout clothes, grabbed his gym bag and headed out the door of his modest rented townhouse. While maneuvering through the afternoon rush hour traffic, his conversation with Brian Tillman replayed in his head. "You're just like me. I'm nothing like you. You don't even know me. You'll never know me."

In the underground parking garage, Jonathan revved up the volume on his car stereo to get his mind wrapped around something positive. He roared from the garage toward his weekday getaway, Health Fitness Headquarters on Abrams road. After signing in, he stretched near an available treadmill to get the blood flowing before venturing into the pump room. "Marcus!" he yelled, spotting his workout partner entering the gym.

Marcus Gamble's complexion bordered the color of fresh pecans. Built like a truck and having recently turned thirty-two, he took a job with the Dallas Police in the Sub Force Unit, a special department that patrolled streets below the downtown district. Marcus settled for a law enforcement career once he finally realized professional football was not in the cards.

"Glad you got a hall pass Marcus. I thought your girl said you couldn't go nowhere but to work and church since some random female starting playing hang up on your phone," Jonathan amused.

Marcus smiled devilishly. "Nah, I handled that."

"What you do, have the calls traced?"

"I made it clear that if the hang ups didn't stop, I'd be forced to demote the chick who was doing it to my Monday evening slot. I think it was Tonja. She thought long and hard about all the time it took her to work her way up to Thursday's. Since then, everything's been biscuits and gravy." Marcus cut a wide-eye leer in Jonathan's direction. "You know I gots to keep my women separated. Give me some dap on that, playa'!"

Jonathan reflected on what his friend had just alluded to as two stationary bikes became available. "Yeah, you're laughing now. A week ago you were scared to go home."

"Hey, I'm Mrs. Gamble's baby boy. An honorable man... sort of. You know I like a variety and it pays to keep it complicated. Once a lady gets things figured out, I bounce then trade her in for two new ones."

"That's part of the reason there are too many fine single sistahs today, too many brothas working overtime to keep it complicated. Okay, take out the black gay men, the bi-curious, the down low, and the locked down."

Marcus shrugged his broad shoulders. "Yeah and that means more play for me," he chuckled.

"No, that means there's only you," Jonathan answered. "Well, black men like you and me actually. Running females and keeping it complicated, that ain't right man. It ain't right."

"Know what else ain't right? You acting like you don't have twice as many complicated relationships as I do. Your long ass sneak-sheet is damned near legendary."

Jonathan winced jokingly. "Why you gotta put this back on me? I'm not the one afraid to have a lady over while hoping the phone won't ring off the hook."

"Only because you turn the ringer off," Marcus suggested.

"That might may be true. I'm not saying it is," Jonathan countered, and not to convincingly. "Any way, how what you do is trifling."

"Negro please," Marcus snorted riotously. "And what do you call all that hopping and flip flopping you got going on?"

"That's auditioning." Jonathan considered his numerous on-again off-again romances, many of which matriculated simultaneously, before offering a response. Unfortunately it didn't change his answer in the least. There was no use in lying to himself when the truth was so glaringly obvious although he still felt it necessary to justify his sometimes shady relationship practices. "I, unlike you, am looking for someone to build something with, like my folks had. That's what I need. I'm tired of ego-tripping but don't know why I can't get enough."

"Cause you can't eat just one," Marcus howled. "How many times I gotta tell you that?"

"Man, that's just nasty. You're old enough to know that you can eat every sistah's cooking." Jonathan twisted his lips as if he'd just smelled something rank. "I'm starting to worry about you. You probably need some shots… and some extra-super-strength Listerine."

"Be careful Jonathan."

"Of what?"

"I'm just sitting here trying to figure out why you care about how brothas are getting over and who's getting the worst end of the deal. Sounds like hating to me. A little bit like hating."

With his hands up defensively, Jonathan stopped peddling. "Look, I don't even know why I brought it up. Just sometimes I think about my parent's. They loved each other as if nothing else mattered, my moms especially. A woman just wants a man she can be proud of and grow old with. That's all I'm saying. Don't be surprised if more black women start sneaking over to the other side to get that prescription filled."

"What? And sleep with the enemy? Nah, no way," Marcus vehemently objected. "Don't even play like that. I left New York because sistahs up there started bugging. It got so bad they didn't even want black coffee."

"What if there was a shortage of the high caliber females, are you telling me you wouldn't cross the line and get with a blonde haired, blue eyed, pink toe who was throwing hella vibes at you?"

Marcus pondered deeply for a moment. He considered his response before defusing the explosive hypothetical situation. "Yeah, I guess I see what you mean. You just mention three things on my Christmas list."

"Now you're really tripping."

"Maybe. However, I don't discriminate either. Booty-ful is booty-ful, in any color."

"True that. Likewise, I'd rather see a black woman happy with Country Club Chuck or Malibu Ken, than to see her heart-broken and alone because it stayed complicated too long with one of us."

"Dude, that was almost gay," Marcus chided. "You need to get whatever this Dr. Phil thing you're going through checked out." He climbed off the stationary cycle then hung a towel around over his shoulder. "Seriously though, see a doctor… or talk to a barber about it before you get your player card revoked."

Marcus spotted an old acquaintance, who at one time was a Wednesday evening regular in his weekly rotation. She was shout-ing distance in the busy health club so that's what he did. "Hey Moni! Monique, with yo' fine self." He wasn't opposed to a short conversation but hoped she wouldn't come over and stifle his chances to pick up something new for himself.

An attractive woman dressed in a black spandex whipped her ponytail angrily then scanned the gym to see who was shouting her name like a Country Bama calling the hogs. When she realized who it was, she stared through Marcus then continued on with the conversation she had going with another guy. It appeared she was into picking up a little something new for herself as well.

"You must be slipping Marcus," Jonathan teased. "Don't look now but Mrs. Gamble's baby boy just got benched."

"Monique, it's me. Marcus!" he yelled, louder than before. "Shit. Never mind Jonathan, let's go. She probably don't recognize me *with my clothes on.*"

Marcus followed Jonathan to the pump room to get into their heavy strengthening workout. "By the way, I called you at the bank today," the over-sexed cop remembered, "and some Deidra somebody took the message. She sounded fine too. Hook a brotha up."

"Man please, Deidra's a good girl. I wouldn't do that to her, if I didn't like her. Besides, today was not a good day."

As Jonathan shared the angry customer incident and the verbal altercation with Brian Tillman, Marcus wiped the sweat away from his brow. "Now don't go getting all upset when I say what I got to say. I know how sensitive you are about your old neighborhood but I always wanted to know something. You got open prostitution going on outside your branch on the 1st and 15th, gangs are killing each other over crumbs and can't none 'em read. Hell, they ought to be fighting over books, pencils and pens instead of some damned colors. Welfare has been an accepted way of making a living for too many families down there and half the kid's don't even know who their daddy is. I bet Father's Day in confusing as hell. It's a shame how all those people ended up there anyway. Look, you have a Master's degree and you don't have to put up with all that nonsense, Jonathan. You could have any ASFB branch in the city you want."

"So, was there a question for me in all that?"

"Yeah. Why are you still in the ghetto?" Marcus asked definitively.

Although Jonathan was somewhat disappointed in Marcus' ramblings, he was hardly surprised. It wasn't the first time someone suggested he take another position within the company, one with better scenery. He'd often asked himself that same question, especially after the day he had but something kept pulling him back, something a lot stronger than raw ambition.

"First of all, let me set the record straight and educate you on some things so you'll no longer use ignorance to fuel your foolishness. Secondly, nobody ends up in south Dallas, they begin there. Some of them just don't make it out and others would rather live in the same home their grandparents were born in than any other place on earth. The community is poor, true, but the ghetto as you put it is a state of mind not a physical address. I grew up in the 'hood and I still feel comfortable there, more comfortable than I would around a lot of people who don't look anything like us."

"Not me," Marcus objected, shaking his head.

"Not you. What' you mean, not you? Yeah, sometimes it seems hopeless but if I don't stay and try to iron some of it out, who will? I don't even know why I fool with your incorrigible ass."

There was a brief moment of silence and reflection until Marcus unfolded his arms along with his logic. "I'm not sure what incorrigible means but that sounds like a lot of work. What if I rush home and bake some freedom cookies or organize a boycott or something then can I get a hug?" Marcus wore a broad grin as he approached Jonathan with his arms opened wide.

"Man, you'd better gone with that before somebody's gets the wrong idea about us. And don't try to get back on my good side. You hurt me feeling," he jested. "Move now, I'm mad at you."

Later that evening, Jonathan returned home. After searching for his television remote, he sat down on his oversized hunter green leather sofa to catch up on the national news. An attractive brunette anchorwoman studied the teleprompter, with a backdrop of the U.S. capitol building prominently positioned behind her. "In this evening's national news, a special House sub-committee's in-depth investigation of the leading cigarette company's under reported utilization of Nicotine. For many years, tobacco holding companies have denied allegations that the drug is addictive but the latest studies show that many, who are hooked on cocaine and heroin, have experienced better success rates of kicking their habits than long time cigarette smokers."

Jonathan was amazed at how the story shaped up. He continued to listen on intently, well aware that ASFB had substantial billions of dollars tied up in tobacco. "Many illegal substance abusers have commented that rehab was a walk in the park compared to giving up smoking," the anchorwoman reported further. "After months of media debate and nationwide protest from the group calling itself *A Smoke Free You and Me*, government officials appear likely to buckle under the negative publicity. North Carolina Democratic Governor, Mitch Thornson, stated in an interview this morning: 'We just want to assure each American a chance at a drug free society. If our findings prove beyond a shadow of a doubt that cigarettes are as addictive as other debilitating controlled substance, it would be a great start at achieving our goal.'"

"A Carolina Governor selling out his own state, that's political suicide," Jonathan thought aloud. He couldn't believe his ears. The governor's stance was sure to make waves all the way up the White House. Since his state had always heavily considered tobacco crops as a staple income, he was literally biting the hand that fed him. The governor's photo faded from the screen before the female journalist rolled to the next story.

"In other news, the number of prisons under construction is down this quarter despite a rising murder rate among hardened..."

After he'd had enough disparaging news for one day, Jonathan staggered into the bedroom to shed the sweaty workout gear. He peeled off his clothes while listening to messages left on his home phone. He made mental notes of important calls he'd misses, saved some and deleted others. The last message cut off prematurely because it required someone to accept a collect call on his end. Jonathan couldn't come up with anyone who'd call him long distance, nonetheless collect.

FIFTEEN

Comphy and Natural Causes

B y the amount of sunlight piercing through the creases in the Venetian blinds, Jonathan realized immediately that it was much later than seven o'clock, his usual time to rise and shine. When he reached for a ringing telephone, it dawned on his that he'd fallen asleep the evening before without setting his alarm clock. With the wrong end of the telephone against his ear, he managed a garbled salutation. "Hello. Wait hold on. Yeah. This is Jonathan."

A woman's voice responded in a subtle voice. "Mr. Holloway, this is Deidra. It's nine o'clock and we're about to open. Should uh... we be expecting you today?" She was quite amused that Mr. Perfect was running late for the second consecutive morning. "Or will I need handle things for you? You know I will." Deidra's voice elevated an octave with the enthusiasm of a sixteen-year-old, wanting a shot at driving her older brother's sports car. In the back of her mind, she was really hoping for a shot at riding in his sleigh bed.

"No! I mean, no that won't be necessary Dee," he grumbled. "Nine o'clock? I'm sorry. I'll be there within the hour. Bye." Jonathan wasn't fully awake but he wasn't out of his mind either. His assistant did an adequate job in her assigned role but she was not ready to take on the responsibilities associated with running a banking center from top to bottom.

Jonathan felt disoriented. He had to pull himself out of bed. As he rubbed his eyes, he surveyed the room to gain a better awareness of his surroundings. The bed was calling him back, beckoning for extensive cuddling. The morning was already two hours ahead of him and moving fast. Eventually, he pulled himself together with a commitment to make up the stagger. Blowing off lunch came to mind but the thought passed quickly due to his standing 1st and 3rd Tuesday appointment at the Daniel "Chappie" James Learning Center. He volunteered for their reading laboratory and wouldn't skip think of disappointing the students and faculty.

"In the car. Down the street. On my way. Gotta get there. Come on… Move it people!"

When he finally approached the intersection at Malcolm X Blvd. and Grand Ave., the sight of flashing ambulance lights in the bank parking lot startled him. The sensational tingle began in his toes then moved up rapidly through his chest and then to the back of his neck.

"God, no," he mouthed quietly.

In his haste to reach the scene, he left his car parked in the street. "What's wrong? What happened?" he asked a bystander near the bank entrance.

The young man shrugged his shoulders then suggested the worst. "Man, I think somebody got shot or somethin'. Somebody's always gettin' shot up around here."

Jonathan surveyed the parking lot again. There wasn't a single squad car. Police always responded to shootings with a fleet of cruisers. His pulse returned to normal but perspiration had already begun to mount. A single stream ran down his face as he made his way inside the building.

"You got here just in time. Ms. Willa Mae Harris fell out," Deidra informed him. Paramedics were rolling the elderly woman out while securing her to the gurney with nylon belts. Her tired eyes found Jonathan's worried expression.

"I tried waiting for you this morning but this old body can't hold up like it used to Jon-Jon," she explained, hosting a troubled look that resembled her favorite banker's. "I'm so sorry for making a mess of everything." Jonathan had grown closer to the older woman, who'd taught his mother how to be more of a lady than her own mother had. She still owned the house adjacent to the one his parents owned in his youth.

Jonathan offered kind, reassuring words to his life-long friend. "It's going to be all right Ms. Harris. These men will make sure you get what you need at the hospital. I'll be right there to check on you." While he worked at clearing his head, concern for the woman's health resisted being put aside. Ms. Harris lived alone despite Jonathan's constant encouragement to obtain in-house care. She was a heavy woman in her golden years, seventy plus in age with high blood pressure and chronic arthritis. Like his father before him, Jonathan spent some of his free time fixing things around the woman's house that needed it or pruning the flower garden in her backyard. Sharing time with her always took him back to his childhood, before all hell broke loose in his personal life. Ms. Harris had a perfect recollection of the events that made that news over the past fifty years but she and Jonathan never discussed the disasters that changed his life.

"You okay?" Deidra asked Jonathan, as she watched Ms. Harris being wheeled away. "Everything is cool inside. She was just standing in the teller line too long is all. You know how these old people insist on handling their own transactions. She came in wearing this wide brimmed sun hat and I didn't recognize her or I would have helped her out like I usually do."

"I know Deidra, I know," Jonathan replied, wrapping his arm around her shoulder, letting her know she wasn't to blame. "Go on and keep the business flowing, I'll be with you in a minute." Jonathan left her side to approach a paramedic making notes on a legal sized triplicate form attached to a clear fiberglass clipboard. "Uh, excuse me. What hospital are you taking her to?"

"Parkland," the man answered sharply. He neglected to look up from his paperwork. Parkland Hospital was a county medical facility, a good one but known to have been vastly understaffed and overcrowded.

Jonathan noted the man's rudeness but let it pass. "No. You'll take her to Tri-City. She would like to be close to her home." Tri-City was only three minutes away and privately funded.

"And who are you?" asked the rude paramedic's partner. His tone was snottier than the first.

"I'm Jonathan Holloway, the manager here and if I tell you to take her to the moon, you'd better strap her on a rocket on that gurney. Just send me the bill and it'll be taken care of." The white men eyed one another with *whut-ever* written all over their faces until Jonathan read them clearly. "Fellas, today is not the day you want to try me on this one. Don't or you'll wish you hadn't." They stared at Jonathan as if sizing up his threats. When he didn't blink, they got the message. "Did you write *that* down?" Jonathan asked, returning the same whut-ever smirk they'd tossed his way.

Within minutes, business in the banking center returned to normal. Deidra filled Jonathan in on several reports from the previous afternoon then retreated to her desk. Jonathan opened the window blinds to invite more sunlight. He was greeted by an unkempt man dressed in old soiled clothing was urinating on the shrubs directly on the other side of the large glass window. "Hey!" Jonathan yelled, slapping against the glass to shoo him a way. "Get away from this building before I call the law! Heyyy! Awe, come on man," he complained.

The Urinator glanced up briefly, like a deer in the forest hearing a far off sound, before ignoring the manager's persistent pleas. After leaving the bushes dripping wet, he casually dragged a snaggle-toothed hair pick through his thick ratty mane while using the window's reflection as a mirror. Jonathan recognized when his efforts were futile so he closed the blinds with one hard jerk. The question Marcus asked about why he continued working in the hood flashed in his mind but only for a split second because the answer chased it away. "These are my people. Good, bad, or straight up trifling. These are my people," he heard himself say.

Moments later, a staggering slightly built homeless man loitered at the door way to Jonathan's office. Draped in recycled clothes two sized to big, he waited to be addressed like a small child, who'd learned his lesson about entering a room with grown-ups without having been invited in. He hung his head in a lowly position insinuating he'd been stripped of everything essential to be considered a man.

"Hi Comphy. How've you been?" Jonathan said eventually. "I haven't seen you around lately. Ahh, I bet I know. Some lucky lady has been keeping you busy?"

Comphy was a regular bank customer. His mental challenges were well documented after receiving a severe beating from over-zealous Dallas police officers during a desegregation protest in the late 1960's. He had been a brilliant Mathematician before the incident occurred. Since then, he resorted to roaming up and down M.L.K. Jr. Blvd., refusing to live indoors. When Comphy wasn't storming the sidewalk, he spent time reading everything he got his hands on including, discarded newspapers, magazines, and whatever he found lying on the streets. But he was often detached from reality, the same reality that mostly everyone else was hiding from.

"Which question do you want me to answer first?" Comphy asked with a sly grin, still avoiding eye contact.

"You joking with me Comphy?" Jonathan appreciated his visitor's quick wit. "You think you're slick don't you?"

"Slick? Naw, I use to be. A long time ago maybe but not now."

Jonathan knew right off that Comphy was having a good day as opposed to a bad one which occurred when he neglected to take his medication or had overindulged with wine between doses. The homeless man continued, "I've been good. Yeah, more good than bad. Yeah-boy, more good than bad as a matter of fact." Comphy smiled when he assessed how he'd been making out.

Jonathan spotted a fresh gash above Comphy's left eye. "Hey. Who've you been scrapping with?"

"I can't never remember. But I didn't win though," he mumbled, before lowering his eyes again, ashamed for doing something he knew better not to do. "Hey Mr. Jonathan, I need some money. 'Bout twenty dollars. That ought a hold me, uh-huh. Get me some lunch."

Narrowing his eyes slightly, Jonathan smelled something askew. "Your disability check came in yesterday. You know how to go up to the teller window and make a withdrawal."

Deidra learned through trial and error that Comphy couldn't handle more than twenty-dollars a day unless he desperately needed shoes or medication. The neighborhood pushers and pullers weaseled just about every dime out of him when he had his hands on any more than that. Impulsive and kindhearted to a fault, Comphy would find a way to blow his monthly allowance, all of his five hundred and seventy-two dollar monthly allotment.

"Ms. Deidra won't let me have none," Comphy admitted. "She don't like me much. But I like her. She cool with me. Uh-huh, she cool people."

After scouting the lobby for Deidra, Jonathan picked up the phone. "Let me see what's going on." He rang Deidra's desk for answers. She informed him that Comphy had come in the day before and emphatically demanded the total sum of his check. Since he was an adult account holder, she was forced to comply.

"Comphy, Deidra told me you came in yesterday and withdrew all of your money. "What happened to it?"

He raised his head peculiarly. "Oh I did? That was yesterday, huh? Well I need some more. You can loan me it 'til next month. I'm good for it."

"Not until you tell me what happened to the money you took out yesterday," Jonathan demanded.

The homeless man searched his wandering mind for a decent response then offered his best shot, the truth. "I misappropriated my funds."

Befuddlement zipped through Jonathan after Comphy explained his distress. "You did what Comphy?"

The maladjusted customer sat up in the chair and straightened out his clothing as if on a job interviewing. "I misappropriated my funds. I didn't use the money for what I was supposed to. You a college boy, you should know what that mean. Or was you joking with me? Now who's being slick?" He winked at the bank manager after making his point.

Jonathan was so amused by the interaction and exchange of wit, he chose to overdraw Comphy's account without penalty. "Here, show this to Deidra and she'll take care of it." He handed a withdrawal slip with J.H. initialed on it. Comphy hopped up like a toddler with a new lollipop. No more worries, no more cares.

Deidra rang the manager's office in a huff. "Are you serious Jonathan? I spent all morning running his silly tail out of here and you do this to me. Ooh, he gets on my last good nerve! I don't see how or why you put up with his mess." She slammed the telephone receiver down without allowing Jonathan to get a word in edgewise.

At the end of the business day, Jonathan visited the hospital. He ordered three large get-well-soon bouquets to be delivered from the hospital flower shop then he strolled off the elevator with one he'd picked up himself.

"Nice flowers," a middle-aged nurse commented, ogling the arrangement from her side of the registration desk. "Are they for me?"

Jonathan smiled cordially. "Actually, I'm looking for Ms. Willa Mae Harris in room three-eleven."

"Take this hall to the end and make a right. It will be on your left hand side," she answered in a faux disappointed tone.

Jonathan followed the directions which led him down a long quiet corridor, walled in soft yellows and pastel greens. He tapped lightly on the closed door with the name W. Harris placed above the number.

"Come on in, it's not locked," Ms. Harris bellowed.

Jonathan entered cautiously, hoping to avoid an awkward half-dressed older woman moment. "There she is," he cooed, after seeing her resting comfortably in bed.

"Unfortunately, here I am," she said, in the same warm tone.

Jonathan observed the bouquets delivered earlier as he approached her raised bed. He hid the flowers he personally delivered behind his back. "Would you look at that? If I'd known you were already stocked in the flower department, I could have spent my last dollar on something for me."

"What do you have behind your back there, Jonathan? I hope it's some fried chicken, biscuits, and gravy 'cause this hospital food is terrible. They need to let Ms. Harris in their kitchen and all these sick people would be going home today," she said in a huff. Jonathan's lips parted to reveal all of his teeth. "What's so funny? You know I'm right. Ms. Harris sure can tear it up in the kitchen," the woman said, referring to herself in third person. That way, self-gratification didn't sound so much like bragging.

With a subtle head nod, Jonathan offered his affirmation. "Yes ma'am. Ms. Harris can throw down in the kitchen, which is one of the reasons you ended up here. You just can't keep cooking with all that salt and grease and trying to keep that big house up all by yourself."

"You listen to me. I've been cooking that way every since my mother taught me how," she snapped back. "All these years later, I'm still here?"

He nodded again. "Yes ma'am, you are *right here*." Jonathan smugly referred to the hospital as being the here in question. "Oh, these are for you." He extended his arm, presenting the flowers like an academy award.

"You are so sweet. You were always a sweet one, even when you were a little boy. Remember, you would bring me flowers back then too." Realizing she had gotten too close to talking about the past, she abruptly changed the subject. "You shouldn't worry so much about an old lady like me. There are too many other things you should be focusing your attention on, like finding a wife," she suggested. "It's not in a man's nature to be alone. You've had enough time to…"

"Hey, how did we start talking about me?" Jonathan interrupted, shifting the conversation away from his personal life. "I came to see how *you* were getting along."

"Uhhh-huh..." I saw that move coming a mile away but I'll let him think you're getting away with something for the time being. I'll be just fine as soon as I can get out of here. My house is getting dirtier by the minute. I just know it."

"You'll be going home soon enough but first things first. Not until your tests come back from the lab."

"Tests, I'm not worried about any old tests," she quipped. "I'll pass them all. I always did well in school. Besides, my great niece is coming to visit me all the way from Oakland. That's in California, you know."

Jonathan wanted to meet this visiting niece as soon as she arrived. Ms. Harris's had several secret hiding places for harmful spices in that enormous house of hers. "It's a good thing she's coming to help out. Family's important in times like these."

"It's for her sake really. She needs to get away for a while. Got a few things of her own to work out."

After an hour passed, a doctor came by to make rounds. "Ms. Harris, how's my favorite new patient this evening?" asked the pretty black female doctor. She read over the chart then made a few notes.

"Can I go home now, Doctor?" Ms. Harris questioned eagerly.

"Well, not today. Maybe tomorrow. I haven't gotten a real chance to get to know you yet." The doctor glanced up from the paper work, toward the optimistic older woman, long enough to share an illuminating smile. "But things appear to be on the right track."

"Speaking of the right track, have you met my beautiful lady doctor, Jonathan?" Ms. Harris knew perfectly well he hadn't. "Jonathan Holloway, this is Dr. Tyler Quinn, just like the *Medicine Woman* television show. Isn't she pretty? Built up real cute, too."

Jonathan couldn't shield his embarrassment. He felt like a teenager being set up on a date by his grandmother. "Please excuse her, doctor. Maybe the fall she took rattled something in her head." He pinched Ms. Harris on her arm as payback for the overboard introduction.

"Ouch! Why'd you pinch me?" she yelp, rubbing her arm and frowning at him. "You just don't know a good thing or a real opportunity when you see one."

The doctor was also uncomfortable but she recovered well. "Thank you Ms. Harris. I believe I'm a good thing and I hope my husband thinks so too." When she extended her left hand, it displayed a brilliant princess cut three-carat diamond, surrounded by two marvelously crafted baguettes. Jonathan had no doubts that her husband knew a good thing when he snagged one.

Dr. Quinn collected her instruments then prepared to exit. "I'll check on you tonight. If you need anything, just buzz for the nurse and she'll be happy to get it for you." She returned the chart back into a manila folder then closed it. "Mr. Holloway, it was nice to meet you. Y'all have a nice evening."

Jonathan shook his head disapprovingly at the conniving patient. "You should be ashamed of yourself but I'll bet you're not."

"Jon-Jon, I love you like you were my own. There's no shame in that. And, if you really love Ms. Harris too, you would convince that pretty lady doctor to let me go home tonight."

Jonathan caught himself slipping. Ms. Harris's plea for sympathy was over the top. "That's twice today you've called me Jon-Jon so I'm watching my back. And yes, I do love you very much. Too much, to help you get out of here before the doctor thinks you're ready." He opened a thin metal case then slid out a business card. "I'll write my cellular phone and pager numbers on the back, you already know how to reach me at home. Call me if you need anything." Jonathan saluted her with a warm kiss on the cheek then prayed silently that her fall was not caused by a serious matter. Ms. Harris was his last remaining piece of family history and wasn't nearly ready to let her go.

The doctor who was treating Ms. Harris sat behind the nurse's station adjacent to the elevator. Jonathan walked towards her with his concerns in tow. "Excuse me, Dr. Quinn."

When she saw Jonathan approaching, she strained to keep from laughing in his face. "Yes, Mr. Holloway?" she offered, with a slight giggle. "You must be related to Ms. Harris because only family can throw shame to the wind in the name of match making like that."

Jonathan couldn't help but laugh himself. "No, not actually, but she is the closest thing to family I do have. I manage the ASFB branch on M.L.K. and we go way back. You could say that she's my favorite customer. When she fell in the bank lobby today, I almost lost it. Willa Mae Harris is very special to me," he added. "How is she, really?"

The doctor flipped through pages of a chart lying on the desk before she answered him. "Your favorite customer will be fine if she follows my strict guidelines that include lowering her salt intake, eliminating fried foods and adding more raw vegetables to her diet. Much is the same for a lot of my patients. Too many of our people don't eat to live. Instead, we live to eat. But, as long as she changes her eating habits, she should be around for a long time."

Jonathan thanked the physician for calming his worries then he caught the next elevator going down.

SIXTEEN

Muslims on MLK Blvd.

By the end of the week, Ms. Willa Mae Harris had been released from the hospital. Jonathan promised to stop in and check on her after work on Friday. In the meanwhile, he had become consumed with handling his own business, the mission of finding a date for the Dallas Chamber of Commerce banquet. He hadn't given it much thought until he received an email from the host committee requesting the name of his date. Jonathan panicked. Having been nominated for Man of the Year, it wouldn't have been fitting to show up without a princess on his arm. He considered calling Anastasia, who was always a cinch when he needed a last minute stand-in but then he remembered how she loved hearing her own voice. He couldn't envision subjecting others dinner guests to an evening dedicated to talking endlessly about nothing.

Sheila was next on the list but she refused to go along for the ride once Jonathan rejected a counter offer to rendezvous for an entire weekend. Sheila wasn't into one-nighters of any kind, if she could help it. "A brotha has to give up some real time if he wants some of mine," she meowed, before hanging up the phone in Jonathan's face. The last time he treated Sheila to a candle lit dinner, it required more than three hours and four policemen to convince her to leave his townhouse. She even began to forward her phone calls to his house and then brought along two Titanic-sized luggage, along with a bad case of separation anxiety.

Cheryl was absolutely livid when she heard Jonathan's voice over the phone. Because he hadn't called her for months after a sushi restaurant fiasco, she went off. "How dare you have the aww-dacity to think you can just pop up into my life any time you get good and ready. I'm too damned classy to go for this last minute bullshit!"

Three strikes later, Jonathan was out at the plate and right back where he started, on his own. Later that afternoon, he felt his chest tightening. He'd called Marcus, who insisted he had the perfect date in mind, a sexy playmate he couldn't get rid of. Jonathan laughed, considered how much trouble she must have caused Marcus if he was so ready to pass her on to him, then he rejected that idea altogether.

Jonathan was back in his romance rolodex again, dreading more of the same until he caught a glimpse of the Muslim Mobile. The spotless black Suburban with chromed wheels and tinted windows pulled in front of the bank. Style was not spared on the local Fruit of Islam member's mode of transportation. Brother Captain Darius X, the security officer for the Dallas Mosque, was the first to step out. He was a thick warrior-size man, not more than thirty years old. The serious scowl that always accompanied him resembled that of a much older man who had seen more than his share of regrets.

Minister Lawrence Muhammad slowly emerged from the passenger side of the newly waxed vehicle with two other men, each of them dressed in dark business suits and sunshades. Their daring apparel adequately complimented their deliberately staunch attitudes. The Minister was buttered biscuit brown, more yellow than anything else and his long gait and straight-backed stroll was all business. He could have passed for a male fashion model despite a checkered past including a stint in prison. He knew the evil streets better than any clothing designer knew his runway.

Jonathan offered first-class service and considered it a privilege when they chose to bank with him, despite other managers bidding for their business which guaranteed hundreds of home and automobile loans from loyal mosque members. It was an amicable business arrangement.

As the team of men approached Jonathan's office he noticed how they never appeared pressed or bothered. They were just plain serious.

"As-salaam Alaikum," the Minister hailed.

"Y-Alaikum Salaam," Jonathan replied, in a natural hi'ya been manner.

Minister Muhammad's diction was as eloquent as his disposition. Everything about him was impressive. Even his sun-toned complexion was unblemished. He'd been handpicked by the Chicago headquarters to head the local post. "Greetings, brotha Jonathan. Greetings." The leader grasped Jonathan's hand with vigor. The firm shake was reciprocated with a short military style embrace. The Minister exalted his banker and good friend. "Black man," he saluted, with an awarding winning smile.

"I am," Jonathan responded swiftly. "Minister Muhammad, you look well. Please have a seat."

The religious man was true to form as usual, always business first. "Brotha Daniel, would you be so kind to assure the amount on the deposit slip is correct and obtain a receipt? Thank you." He handed a black leather briefcase to one of the men nearest to him then took the seat across the desk from Jonathan. A forth dark-suited man accompanied the briefcase to the teller window while the security officer, Darius X, stood guard just outside the office.

"Minister, how's the building annex drive coming? By the increase in your deposits, I'm guessing your membership is bursting at the seams."

"Things are going as well as planned, although there are hurdles every now and then. We must anticipate peaks as well as valleys, of course."

Jonathan felt comfortable calling the younger man minister although he wasn't a member of The Nation' himself. It was a title, and an honor. The charismatic leader deserved a certain level of respect for the sacrifices he made to his flock. A young man with a master's degree could have earned a much larger salary than he was paid doing a servant's work. The Nation' offered what a lot of denominational churches in the community didn't, training for young boys beneficial to their manhood as well as to mankind. More importantly, Islamic principles demanded respect for one's self, respect for the black woman, and high regard for both.

After several minutes of casual banter between the two men, Jonathan nodded his head when a welcomed thought came to him. "It's always good to speak with you, Minister. You know, it helps to remind me why I'm here."

"What you do here is very necessary. I'm appreciative of that, however, your services and your blessings would be enhanced if you ran a financial institution for your own people." Jonathan flashed him the *not again with the African American Savings and Loan* smirk. "You know that we can do it and you are also well aware that we need it. We've taken the liberty to set up a board, comprised of good and successful brothas from the area. And we have contacted many Muslim athletes, whom have agreed to invest a portion of their earnings with us, once it's up and running of course. With your influence, leadership, and technical acumen, it would be correct and in check." After the sales pitch, he read Jonathan's face like a seasoned poker player, awaiting signs of allegiance.

Although quite interested, Jonathan was determined to conceal it. Such an undertaking would have required an uncertain degree of commitment and on someone else's terms, regardless of the presidential title on the table. "Well, it would take some lengthy deliberation," Jonathan told him, under no uncertain terms.

"You have the right of first refusal, remember that," the Muslim conceded. "Also keep in mind brother Jonathan, your consultation will be requested whether you join in this cause or pass on it."

"Consider it remembered."

Minister Muslim stood from his chair. "Well, I know you'll contact us soon, either way. I'm counting on that. Peace be unto you."

"Thanks, I could use some of that right now."

They shook hands with a fastened grip. The other men who waited outside the manager's office spoke in passing then exited in perfect step. The same sensation that sparked Jonathan's father each time he came in contact with Black Panthers years ago engulfed him as well. He remembered it vividly as he stood by his father's side, watching militants roll through the neighborhood like ghetto superstars. He always cherished those memories and the new hero's who helped keep them fresh.

Leaning against the window, Jonathan viewed the sun as it faded from bright amber to hazy orange. Forced once again to thumb threw a group of business cards that rested on the far corner of his credenza, he reminisced over all the eligible professional women he'd met since having moved back to Dallas from Houston. Unfortunately, he hadn't allowed himself to proceed any farther than the just-friends strata with any of them. There were the occasional overnight dates and too many meaningless nights on the town to remember, but his difficult divorce was hard to shake. The toxic relationship he endured for far too long left an indelible mark. The painful thought of it often reminded him to duck and pull away when casual romances produced too much heat. Getting burned twice did not appeal to him in the least.

As the evening began to slip away, Jonathan decided to take his mind off of his current dilemma. "Deidra, I'm going across the street for a trim." Jonathan's eyes closed for a moment, tired and dry, as he rubbed his flat palm over the top of his short tapered hairstyle. "Mind the store for me and try not to give the bank away."

Deidra frowned in his direction. "Ain't nobody gonna... All right, I'll handle things. Bring me back an orange soda."

"Anything else? A fish basket, rib plate?" he asked, halfheartedly. "Can I wash your car?"

"Nope, just an orange soda. You can run along now, I'm busy." Deidra cut her eyes at Jonathan then smiled playfully. "Well, I am busy."

"And you're pushing it."

"So," she whispered flippantly.

"I heard that!"

Deidra blushed as Jonathan exited the bank, heading directly across the street. Just because she couldn't have him in her bed didn't mean she'd have to stop thinking about it. He was her friend, which was enticing in itself. Five days a week, Deidra spent hours enjoying his company, sharing laughs and replaying the thought of loving him if things were different. Feelings Jonathan sheltered deep in his heart for Deidra were purely innocent. She was fully aware that he cared for her like a dear friend, and most times that was more than enough.

"Oooh girl! Here he comes. Come on to Momma. Come on over to my place," Sharisa panted seductively, as Jonathan crossed to her side of the street. She rubbed her thick thighs together behind the large tinted plate glass window of the Most Vicious Cuts unisex styling emporium. As he drew nearer, Sharisa started up again. "Y'all, he's coming. Just look at him!" She inhaled slowly through her mouth, making a slurping sound with her wet tongue. "I've been dreaming about you, with your fine self. Mmm-mmm-mmm! You want some come get some."

Charley, a male hairdresser abandoned the customer in his chair when he heard Sharisa's ravenous rants. "Ooh-where? Lemme see."

"China come here, hurr'up. Move Charley!" Sharisa yelled, when the male stylist darted in front of her.

"Excuse you, that's Charle'," he corrected her.

"Nnnn-eee-way, you need to go back there and see about your customer before you torch her scalp."

"Don't you worry about my business, I got this." Charley did an about face then sashayed toward the rear of the shop to resume work on his client's coif.

"Chiiiina! Come quick," Sharisa beckoned again.

China was blessed with a tight twenty-one-year-old's figure but also an adolescent's mentality to match, even though she was well into her thirties. Her sprayed-on hoochie-momma denim shorts exposed both butt cheeks when she bent over to get an eye full of what had her co-worker all worked up. See locked in on Jonathan's poised masculine strides. "Brotha-man is fine. All that and a Cadillac. He's got it goin' on like lotto. Ch-ching. Ch-ching!"

Sharisa pulled her gaze from Jonathan just long enough to voice her annoyance. "You can't even appreciate a man like that. Just listen to yourself. He got money! He got money! With your trifling ass." Sharisa was utterly dismayed by China's gold digging assertions. "Girl, if you'd put your purse down long enough, you just might notice his kinda package ain't for just paying the rent. Gear like that is made for plumbing too and he looks like a pipe laying man if there ever was one, I swear before Gawd."

"Oh, now some serious pipe-laying, I can get down for that," China quipped sensually.

Both women scurried away from the tinted window when Jonathan made his way toward the entrance. "Hellos ladies. Hey Charley. How's everybody?" he announced, as he strolled inside on the salon side of the dual all-in-one head shop. His salutation was returned with warm hellos and eager pleasantries. Sharisa was uncharacteristically speechless, staring at him with a stunned expression. Jonathan noticed her unavoidable leer. "Hi, it's Charlisa right?" Although he'd failed at getting her name correct she confirmed it nonetheless.

"Yeah… Charlisa."

"Good to see you're still on that training program. You look great," Jonathan complimented when nothing else seemed appropriate. "Don't overdo it now and disappear on us."

She attempted to wrestle with the lycra skirt riding several inches up her full hips. "I won't and thank you mister-uh…" She was so flustered by the compliment that she'd forgotten the man's name.

"Just call me Jonathan. Y'all be good," he said in a engaging manner.

Jonathan exited the room through and adjoining door which lead to the barbershop. Subsequently, an attractive woman with an aerobic instructor's curves raised her head from a rinsing bowl to get a substantial at Jonathan while everyone in the room, including Charley, watched his graceful departure.

"So that's Jonathan Holloway," she said, under her breath. "Mmm, now I understand what all the fuss is about."

"Yeah *Charlisa*, you look marvelous," China cackled. "That man is so fine, he made you forget his name."

"And hers too," Charley heckled. "He knows she ain't seen no parts of no diet. He was just being nice."

"He can call me whatever he wants," Sharisa admitted, with her stunned expression intact. "And he can call me however he wants. Bet he can make a sistah speak in tongues too." Sharisa tried to steal another glance through the partition. "Oomph… makes me want to holler."

Jonathan said hello to the barbers then waved hello to several customers seated along the opposite wall. "What's up fellas? Everything all right this evening?"

"Business is always good in the hood. You know that Mr. Holloway," answered Josh, the assistant manager occupying the second chair.

Two framed portraits of Martin and Malcolm were anchored above the barber's workstations. Full mirrors aligned the wall just beneath them. Between the portraits hung a black poster board which read: *In God we trust. Everybody else gotta pay cash.* The barbershop was a non-credit establishment.

The first chair belonged to the shop manager, St. Augustine Jones. He was an older man whose previous careers ran the gamut from professional gambler to an assortment of other questionable ways of paying the rent. He'd given up that lifestyle years ago when the illegal betting joint he managed over experienced a brutal robbery by dope fiends with sawed-off shot guns. Everybody in the place was forced to strip down to nothing then give up everything. Within a week, each of the gunmen were found tortured to death. After scarcely winning an acquittal behind the triple murders, Augustine turned his back on the gaming industry and took the barber trade. He was a high school friend of Jon's and served as Jonathan's personal barber since her could remember.

The distinguished older man emerged from the manager's office. His neatly trimmed salt-and-pepper goatee was manicured perfectly, as were his finger nails. "Jon-Jon," he shouted with paternal pride when he laid eyes on the son of a dear friend. "Boy, you is the spitting image of your father, rest his soul. Looking more like him every day." Jonathan heard the brimming comparison many times before but that didn't stop the barber from hitting him with it at least one a month.

"Good to see you, Mr. Augustine. Can I get a trim?"

"Yeah, you next," Augustine replied, before sneering at the row of patrons who were waiting ahead of Jonathan.

"Thanks but I'm not in a hurry," Jonathan relented. "I can wait." Actually, he enjoyed spending time in the barber shop. It offered him a chance to connect, to share in the lives of various people who still lived in the hood.

"What y'all arguing about now?" the shopkeeper asked, when the barber occupying the third chair disagreed on a hot topic with his headstrong customers.

"If that was my woman, I would've done the same damned thang. What she did was out of line y'all. If she wanted a maintenance man to tighten it up every now and then that's on her but you don't let no nother man lay his head where your husband catches his zees. That's just plain disrespectful. I mean, I can't see no nother man wearing my house shoes and scratching his nuts in my favorite recliner," the barber joked. "If you ask me, they both got what they deserved… that foul female and her dumbass side dude. At least, that's the way I see it." If someone's business was worth telling, it was often discussed in full detail at the barbershop.

After airing his disgruntled opinion, the man standing behind the third chair hesitated then cleared his throat. "Too bad Tank had to get caught up in it though. Any man stupid enough to sleep with somebody else's wife in her husband's bed needs to have his head broke on general principle alone. Hell, everybody's gotta respect the game. There's rules for a reason."

Somewhat intrigued, Jonathan wanted to inquire about the incident. It didn't take long to learn more about Tank, a former shop employee, and his grave misfortune.

"I heard when the cops showed up, Tank was covered in blood, butt-naked and balled up in the corner shivering like it was four below zero. I think he shot 'em first then beat the hell out of 'em until his arms got too tired to swing that bed post."

Augustine appeared unaffected. He continued to edge his customer's tight fade. "I told the boy to leave that crackhead alone. You can't turn a whore into a housewife. Many men have tried and failed. I warned Tank, warned him," Augustine recalled. "That girl was bad news from the jump. But see, sometimes you got to let a young brotha fall on his behind before he'll believe it hurts." He didn't bother to look up while throwing in his two cents. Not once. His electronic clipper kept right on popping.

Disturbed by the gory details, Jonathan felt a sharp pain in the pit of his stomach. The combination of women and drugs shook him each time he caught wind of a tragic story involving both. The outcome seldom varied.

"All my babies look like me!" shouted another customer, who sat a few chairs over. "I know they mine! They mommas know they mine! And the county damn sure know they mine. I'm reminded of that every time I get half a paycheck."

Jonathan was oblivious to the conversations that ensued. He had already begun to envision the haunting episode involving Tank, the barber whose name, photograph and barber's license still hung on the wall behind chair number four. Jonathan shook his head at the thought of how easily the fate could have found him in an affair gone sideways.

"Come on Jonathan, you're up," Augustine announced, after brushing away the trimmings from his previous paying customer. He and Jonathan traded stories about the good old days and the fact that not many of them were all that good. It often felt like stepping back into another era when they cruised over the same ancient tales, shared laughs and traded lies like old friends.

When the last story spun to a conclusion, Jonathan climbed out from the chair, said his good-byes then headed back across the boulevard. Deidra met him before he got past the entrance door. "Seem like every time you leave, something crazy happens," she said. "These gang-bangers chased this little boy into the bank." She whispered additional specifics while keeping an eye on the frightened child. "Who knows, maybe he wore the wrong color on the wrong block or mixed up stripes with plaids. Either way, the police won't even come to see about him so I called his mother. She's on her way. I had to choke it out of him but he says his name's Tariq."

Jonathan looked the juvenile over. His complexion was dark and even. Blue jeans hung off the thin boy's skinny behind. Jonathan checked the youth for signs of injury and trauma.

"You okay, son?"

The boy was obviously shaken but worked hard at not appearing so. "Yeah, I'm cooler than a fan but I ain't yo' son and you sure in hell ain't my daddy."

Deidra recoiled with a wide-eyed expression, not expecting the off-colored reply from an eleven year-old, twelve at the most. Jonathan recognized the same anger on the boy's small face he used to wear daily as a troubled youth.

"Well, we won't go getting into that but you'd better be nice to the pretty lady because she's meaner than those boys who chased you in here, bet on that."

"Yeah, that's right!" Deidra agreed. "So, sit your narrow tail down and behave before I have to get on that behind myself." Suddenly, the skinny kid stared up at Deidra. Tariq's bad-boy attitude softened after her words struck a chord although he was still play-acting tougher than he looked.

Jonathan excused himself to tackle some issues more prominent than the boy's problems at the moment, a few of his own. He read several messages stacked in his incoming mail tray. Ms. Harris had called for the fifth time by 4:20 a.m.. When Jonathan reached for the telephone receiver, he discovered traces of cosmetics on it. It was a sure sign that Deidra had struck again.

"Deidra! Stop using my phone!" he yelled, in the direction of the empty lobby. After wiping off makeup, he dialed Ms. Harris's line. Her telephone number had been the same for over forty years and she always answered by the third ring if she planned on answering at all. "Hello, Ms. Harris, that you? This is Jonathan. I'm good... good. I had a feeling that hospital couldn't hold you. Do you need anything? Uh-huh, large eggs, a pound of ground beef, six large red delicious apples, and shredded wheat breakfast cereal. Sure, it's not a bother at all. I'll pick up the groceries and bring 'em right over. See you in a few. Alright, then. Bye."

Jonathan rreentered the lobby. He couldn't readily locate the boy so he assumed the kid's mother had arrived and taken him home, until hearing Deidra's cheer. "You did it! I knew you were smarter than you act," she chided. Tutoring Tariq through a complex algebra problem was easy. Teaching him to stand up for himself in the face of adversity, was far above her pay grade,

Jonathan had mixed feelings about making another run at the boy but thought better of it to leave well enough alone. Just then, a willowy thin woman stood on the other side of the exit doors. Her worried expression sharply displayed a level of concern that only a mother's could.

"Come on in, ma'am. You must be Tariq's sister," Jonathan said, complimenting her youthful appearance. "I thought they said his mother was coming."

"How nice of you but I am Tariq's momma… Melissa Wrightsil. Is he still in one piece?" she asked with baited breath, while examining him for bumps and bruises. "I hope he didn't give y'all no trouble? I've told him a million times to watch his Bees and Cees around those bangers but he's hardheaded. Maybe now he'll listen."

Deidra grinned assuredly at the boy, who was pleading with apologetic eyes for a reprieve from his momma's wrath. "No, he's been a real treat. Those gang members were serious about catching up to him though. You might want to keep him in the house for a couple of days until they forget about whatever it was that had Tariq running in the first place," she advised.

Without warning, Ms. Wrightsil reached back and slapped Tariq upside the head after he rolled his eyes at the thought of staying in house for safe keeping. "Don't mind him. I'll straighten this out when I get to the house. And, I want y'all to know how thankful I am for what you did. Most people would have turned him away. I work for the city and they give us a hard time for leaving work. Tariq could be lying up dead somewhere and I'd still be catching hell from my supervisor about taking personal time."

Jonathan surveyed the area in front of the bank then escorted Ms. Wrightsil and her repentant son to the bus stop. Shortly after the city bus whisked them away Jonathan was in route to the market on Ms. Harris's behalf. Friday had nearly come and almost gone, and he was no closer to finding a date for the upcoming Chamber event than when it began. With a bleak outlook, he was dead set on finding a suitable candidate, even if it meant spinning the romance rolodex one more time.

SEVENTEEN

Man of Her Dreams

During Jonathan's brief excursion through the grocery store, he whizzed up and down the aisles collecting items Ms. Harris requested, paid with exact change then made a fast exit. He'd mapped out the evening in his mind. First, drop off the groceries and spend forty-five minutes making sure his old friend was getting well then get back to his townhouse to resume the dialing diva derby to secure a date. One, two, three—as simple as that.

Standing on Ms. Harris' porch, Jonathan couldn't have been more certain of his plan to duck in and dash out of her six-bedroom home. All the houses on South Blvd. were huge four to eight bedroom residences, which had once belonged to some of the city's wealthiest Jewish socialites before abandoned the block during desegregation. Now the small subdivision sat on prime real estate and greedy land developers wanted it back.

Jonathan wrapped on the door. Knock, knock, knock, "Ms. Harris, it's me. Jonathan." He tried to peek through the bay window but thick crème colored drapes only allowed mere glimpses of someone moving inside the house.

"Just one minute," an unfamiliar woman replied. "Who's there?"

"It's Jonathan Holloway. Ms. Harris is expecting me."

"Hold on, let me check." The woman on the other side of the door closed her eyes then smiled all the way down to her toes. Facing Ms. Harris lounged comfortably in her recliner. She watched her house guest muffle her nervousness.

"Well, let the man in before my groceries spoil, chile," said the older woman. Her halting command was followed by a warm prideful grin. The women had previously discussed Jonathan stopping by. Now it was show time.

Suddenly, the door swung opened, taking Jonathan by surprise. Drawn in by the woman's smooth mocha complexion, it took him a lot longer than it should have to make an initial assessment. Cold black, bone straight shoulder-length-hair framed her oval-shaped face. Full red lips and a narrow cleft in her chin anchored it perfectly. Jonathan couldn't deny that her snug faded jeans and teal sweater vest deserved a thorough once over. When he glanced at her statuesque build and regal shoulders. He assumed the woman cultivated her body through countless hours in the gym. *Nobody is born that fine,* he thought to himself. *What her parents didn't give her, this sistah came by later on her own.*

The woman blushed at Jonathan's flattering leer. "Um, come on in Mr. Holloway," she said, regaining her composure. "I'm Denise." Although she'd seen him hours earlier at the salon, this interaction provided a far more comfortable atmosphere. When Denise stepped aside to let Jonathan pass, her subtle citrus fragrance brushed against him like a housecat making an acquaintance.

"Jonathan?" Ms. Harris said, to summon him. "Come in and see about me and stop acting like you've never seen a pretty girl before?" Jonathan had no idea the niece would be so stunning. Despite the absence of her prescription bifocals, it was still very plain to see that Jonathan was attracted to Denise. "I want to formally introduce you two," Ms. Harris proclaimed, while having her fun with them. "Y'all are just like family anyway," she added, although it wasn't what either of them wanted to hear.

"Jonathan Holloway, meet my Denise Harris-Matthews. She's my brother's baby girl. I call her Niecey despite her thinking she's too grown for that now but I'm too far along in my years to stop, so she'll just have to put up with me for the next two weeks while she's staying here."

"Oh, two weeks?" he asked, feigning disinterest. "Denise, your aunt mentioned you'd be coming to visit and help her around the house. Thank you for stepping up. That's very nice of you." He felt utterly adolescent after having been quite taken with a woman he'd just met. And despite his curiosity, Jonathan understood that Harris-Matthews was a title. *Mrs. Denise Harris-Matthews, Married Lady.*

Suddenly his mind drifted back to sacks of groceries still weighing in his arms. He quickly reminded himself his plan to duck in and dash. *One, two, three and I'm out,* he thought. *Stay focused.* Jonathan sneaked another glance at his watch then disappeared into the kitchen. He was very familiar with the house and where the groceries belonged. After putting the items away, Jonathan began his regular routine check of mouse traps beside the ancient Frigidaire. It was the same ritual since he was a kid. Despite never having found a single mouse, it was expected of him so he kept up the routine.

As Jonathan rearranged can goods in the pantry to make room for the groceries he bought, he discovered a porcelain container labeled *Sugar.* The small bowl was pushed behind other cooking essentials on the middle shelf. It seemed to be an unusual storage place for spices so he wondered if Ms. Harris was up to her old tricks. Jonathan removed the lid from the container then collected a pinch of the white substance between his forefinger and thumb. Just as he suspected, it was salt. Ms. Harris had put one over on Denise, who was obviously overmatched in her aunt's *guest where I hid it the salt* game. Jonathan figured he would teach his old friend a lesson and have a good time laughing while he was at it.

He located a gallon size glass pitcher underneath the counter. He filled it with water then added Lipton powdered tea, two scoops of sugar and sliced lemon wedges. He collected three drinking glasses from the cupboard, then poured sweetened tea into two of them. In the third glass, he mixed in a small amount of instant tea then added water with two healthy spoonfuls of salt from the porcelain container Ms. Harris had disguised.

Being quite the southern gentleman, Jonathan returned to the living room with unsolicited refreshments. "I thought maybe you ladies would like ice tea." He lowered the serving tray to distribute drinks onto the coffee table, where Ms. Harris watched Denise set up the *Scrabble* board.

"Thank you handsome. You're so sweet to Ms. Harris," the lady of the house teased. "I can't remember the last time I had a nice glass of tea."

"Thanks, that was very thoughtful of you," Denise said politely, as she accepted the cool beverage.

Jonathan raised his glass and toasted to good health. The women did likewise and begun to drink. As soon as Ms. Harris gulped down a mouthful of bitter tea. She gagged and coughed. "Jon-Jon! You trying to kill me?" she complained, behind a pitifully sour expression. Her face was drawn up like a prune. "This is awful!"

"How is that?" Jonathan responded calmly, then took a congratulatory sip from his glass. "Ms. Harris, I used some of that special sugar for yours."

"What special sugar are you talking about?" Ms. Harris whined.

"You know, the special-sugar you keep tucked waaay back in the pantry, far behind all the can goods."

Ms. Harris grew more irritated by the second. "Jon-Jon, that's not sugar. That's where I hid the salt!" When she realized what she'd copped to, she grimaced but it was too late to recant her confession.

"I thought Dr. Quinn gave you strict instructions regarding salt," he reprimanded, like an over bearing nursemaid. "I care about you too much to lose you over some nonsense."

Denise watched the interchange between them. She was impressed with Jonathan's adoration for her aunt among other things. Eventually, Ms. Harris found the humor in the prank. Denise was delighted by his decision to stick around for a while longer.

When the game began, Jonathan's utter lack of *Scrabble* skills were exposed. He hadn't never played the game before. Denise, on the other hand was exceptionally good although Ms. Harris out-scored them both while he worked a crossword puzzle on the side. Quickly bored with word game neophytes, the neighborhood matriarch began to nod off.

"I reckon it's too late for an old lady to be hanging around with young folks so I'll turn in and leave y'all to practice," she added with a cunning smirk.

"Good night, Ms. Harris," said Jonathan. As soon as she headed towards the staircase, his awkward feelings about alone with Denise returned.

"Night, auntie Willa Mae," said Denise, with her eyes locked on Jonathan's.

He wasn't the type to overstay his welcome but regretted having to leave. "It's getting late and I've been here longer than I anticipated. It was nice meeting you, Denise. I really had a great time." In the eleventh hour, his dating expedition was well behind schedule. His *one, two, three duck in and dash plans* had experienced serious neglect although there were no visible signs of remorse.

"I thoroughly enjoyed meeting you too, Mr. Holloway," Denise replied, just this side of seductive.

"You've got to start calling me Jonathan."

"I think I can do that," she agreed.

Caught in between his desire to prolong the evening and respecting Denise's marital status, Jonathan took the high road. Unbeknownst to him, there was a detour ahead. "Listen Denise, I know you're a married woman and I don't feel comfortable saying this but I can't seem to get out of my own way. It might come across as too forward or presumptuous… but I was wondering if you would like to have coffee with me."

Denise found herself at a crossroad, contemplating just how cozy she was willing to get. "Jonathan… I don't think your friendly invitation is either forward nor presumptuous at all but is getting kind of late," she offered non too convincingly. "Let me get my purse."

During their leisurely drive, Jonathan's Lexus glided along the Dallas highways. Denise enjoyed the famous skyline featuring contemporary architecture as he pointed out the famed Reunion Tower, West End Market Place, and the Reunion Arena. Oddly enough, the last thing Denise needed to hear about was another basketball stadium. As far as she was concerned, hoop stars weren't worth a discussion in the least.

Eventually, Jonathan steered his car off the freeway onto a quiet street. They arrived at an out of the way coffee shop. Java Brew, was small and relatively empty, just as Jonathan hoped. A gray-haired waitress took their orders then excused herself. While the couple continued exchanging pleasant but somewhat nervous glances.

"So Mrs. Matthews, how do you like Dallas so far?" Jonathan was battling the idea of tipping around with a married woman, no matter how good it made him feel. "I'm sure it's much different from life in the Bay area."

"First things first," she objected. "Please don't call me by my husband's name. Denise will do just fine. Besides, I like the way it rolls off your tongue." There was a hint of innocents buried in her words. She knew exactly what she was doing. "As for Dallas, I really haven't had the chance to leave the neighborhood until now so thanks for showing me around. It's nice to get out."

After Jonathan stole a quick look at her impressive wedding ring, he wanted to convince himself that he wasn't interest in her. He wanted to believe that his short tour around town was nothing more than southern hospitality, trivial at best. However, nothing about Denise was inconsequential, not the way she pledged her undivided attention and laughed at his corny jokes, recited her favorite lines from Spike Lee movies or appeared utterly content with sharing his space. During the evening, it became evident how much they had in common. Too much in fact to let it all end with a few cups of Brazilian blend.

Amid the jokes and giggles, it was killing Jonathan to know why she wore her wedding ring on her right hand. He was reluctant to bring up Denise's husband again but the curiosity was annoying him like a pebble in his shoe. "It's kind of you to take care of Ms. Harris but I know your man must be sick that you're away," he said finally.

Denise knew where Jonathan was headed. She cut right to the chase. "Look, if you wanted to know my current status, you could have come right out and asked me. We're both adults."

"You're right," he answered softly, nodding his head back and forth. "That was lame but I didn't want to be misunderstood or worse, appear desperate. It's just that I'm more curious than I care to admit." When he realized how forward his comment sounded, even to him, he started to back pedal. "That didn't come out right either. Let me try it again. Everybody's got a story Denise and if you don't mind, I'd like to hear yours."

"Hmmm... my story? Okay, I'll bite. First of all, I'm from Atlanta but I haven't been back there since Christmas before last. Oakland has been my home for the past four years. Before that, was D.C., and before that..." She stopped when Jonathan's deflated expression suggested he wasn't concerned about where she collected her mail. "Okay, so I was stalling with that play by play but this isn't easy for me considering we only met a few hours ago."

"I don't mean to press. I'm just wondering if you're a bad girl on the run from her past."

"Oh, so you like bad girls?"

"No. I'm allergic," Jonathan replied, with a slight chuckle.

"That's great to hear because I'm a good girl, who enjoys a good time. I like to feed my mind as much as possible. I usually get lost in a few novels a month. I also love to sweat so I bought my own fitness franchise last year. And, as for *my man* as you put it, there isn't a Mr. Matthews any longer."

Yes! Jonathan thought.

"He was irresponsible with something I cherished greatly. I grew tired of that and tired of him."

Denise hadn't planned on divulging that much of her personal life, at least not that soon, but it didn't stop her. "He is a good guy," she continued, on her estranged husband's behalf. "I thought enough of him to become his wife so I won't dog him for being less than what I needed. Problem was, his love knew no limits. No boundaries. He had an unapologetic fondness for other women, his career, and partying hard with his teammates. It started out as recreational, the drugs I mean. An NBA wives tale, that's my story." Denise crossed her arms as she marched on. "It's funny how we used to be so in love back in college. Two days after we were married, he got drafted in the first round. The fame, fortune, and foolishness got the best of him. I was left with the rest of him. Our life together took seven years to build and one MVP season to destroy." Her eyes began to well up. Instinctively, Jonathan wiped away her tears with his handkerchief, in slow careful strokes. Denise exhaled deeply followed by a nervous laugh. "Bet you didn't know that I was a big baby?"

"It's all my fault. I should have let it go. It wasn't any of my business."

Denise found herself strangely endeared to a man she knew very little about. "Jonathan, it's alright. I didn't mean to hit you with all my baggage at once. It's hard to talk about things that matter without someone judging the mistakes I've made. Anyways, a girl has to be careful who she tells her business to. Never know when it might end up on the front page of some gossip rag these days. You probably wouldn't understand though."

"Love and bad choices seem to go together like coffee and cream. Most men get it right only once in a lifetime, if they're lucky. Me, I'm a firm believer that overcoming bad choices builds character. Everybody's got skeletons." His family chest was loaded with past indiscretions; most of which belonged to him.

"You got skeletons? No way. Not Jonathan Holloway. Word on the street, you're up for sainthood in this community."

Jonathan shrugged, looked away for a moment, before allowing his eyes to meet hers again. There, he found the warmest pair he'd ever seen. Still reserved, he wasn't sure if being candid about his own failed marriage was the safest avenue to travel down despite Denise having only minutes before laid all her cards out on the table. "You look like a woman I can trust," he said calmly. "Can you? Be trusted?"

"I don't know. Depends on what it is that I'm trusted with." She winked across the table at him.

"Trusted with my true confessions, I guess." He sipped from his coffee cup then grinned slightly. "I... uh, I've never told anyone this, not even your aunt, so it might sound a bit harsher than it should."

"Listen man, just because I took the lid off my Pandora's box doesn't mean you're obligated to."

"No, It's cool. My therapist, yeah some black folk do see therapists, my therapist suggested I talk about one of my bad choices in particular so I fired him before I the occasion to do what he prescribed."

"Wow, at least you didn't think you were too perfect to seek professional help. I had to come half way across America to meet a black man honest enough to admit he's not perfect."

"Did I say that?" he chuckled. "And all this time I planned on fronting that I was. Are you sure you want to hear this?"

"Oh yeah, I'm all yours. I mean, all ears."

EIGHTEEN

You Got Me Tripping

Jonathan fought off a stymied grin. He took a trip back down memory lane that seemed to be inundated with haunted houses on both sides. "I was married too, for about three years. Got married right out of college and made the NFL. Sound familiar? I played two seasons until I fractured my collarbone. That was enough for me. Those brothas hit a lot harder than they did in college. I managed to put away a little money then decided I was better suited for graduate school than the gridiron. When I went back to school, my accelerated course load required more time than I'd anticipated so getting released from the team was fine with me. NFL means Not For Long, right? My ex-wife didn't deal with it too well. She still wanted to hang out and hang on to the fast lane while I studied for the next year and a half. We grew apart, as they say. She lost her way and," he stopped to collect his thoughts and stave off the ill will which stood in his way, "those so-called friends she couldn't shake loose, partied until the money was gone. Being addicted to drugs that you can no long afford is the worst kind of reality. By the time I-do became I-wish I hadn't, we were like roommates anyway. I tried to help her kick but she wasn't having it. When I couldn't face her reality any longer, I bought a one-way ticket then put her on a plane to Baltimore thinking that maybe her parents could straighten her out." Jonathan leaned his head back and sighed heavily. It was still so unbelievable that all of the love in the world couldn't compete with cocaine. "By the time I returned home from class that evening, that woman had sold her first-class ticket. Yeah, she was chilling on the couch, getting high, and kicking it with the dope man. I was more hurt than anything else and wanting it to end so I shoved my 44-pistol in her dealer's face then invited him to take a ride with me. As soon as I jumped on the downtown expressway, I pulled over onto the shoulder then cordially threw his ass out. Funny how shoving a canon in a man's face forces him to reflect on who's worth doing business with." Jonathan laughed when he realized how dangerous it was tangling with a known pusher. "Crazy times call for crazy measures. I can still see him jogging down the freeway, wearing all that bling and thumbing a ride." Denise was tempted to laugh along with Jonathan but something told her the worst part of his story was yet to come. "Well, I made a beeline to the house, gathered my ex-wife's things and convinced her to get in the car with me. I must have been doing eighty all the way back to the airport. I actually watched her get on that plane then I called her folks so they would be there to pick her up when the plane landed. There was some sort of mix-up at the airport on the other end. They Cynthia two days later. She was killed in a crack house raid." Jonathan was still choked up about the weird way it happened five years later.

"Awe, that's terrible," Denise said softly. "I'm sorry Jonathan"

It was apparent that his pain was anchored deep inside him. Closure was still very far away. "It was rough. When I think about the last time I saw her, all the pleading and screaming, it's hard to forgive myself. Maybe I gave up on her too soon, probably what we had together too." Denise watched Jonathan fight through the harsh details of a love gone wrong as time and silence stood quietly between them. "Whew. I think I owe my therapist an apology."

"Yes, you do," Denise quickly replied, with sorrowful eyes. "There was a time I had my psychologist on speed dial."

Jonathan flashed a sincere smile across the table, thanking his new acquaintance for the much needed therapeutic conversation. Denise sensed that he wasn't the kind of man who readily revealed his troubles to a nearly perfect stranger but that's why it was allowed to happen. "Hey You," he said, eventually. "I'm glad we met."

"Me too, *Jon-Jon*."

His face lit up when she called him that. It reminded him of the way his mother Starla emphasized it when she was particularly proud of something he'd done as a child. "Jon-Jon?" he repeated. "So, you think you got it like that? A man pours his heart out and you run with it. You know that name is reserved for people who've known me for a long time. They know all the things I've done in my younger days but still love me anyway. I think I'll make an exception in your case 'cause you' so fine."

"'Cause I'm so fine?" Denise repeated, blushing at him.

Jonathan locked his eyes on hers. "Well that, and because I'm seriously feeling you right now."

The fifteen-minute ride to Ms. Harris's was a quiet one. Jonathan and Denise kept on feeling one another all the way back as his car stereo serenaded them with a mellow lover's tune performed by Duke Ellington and John Coltrane, eliciting a *sentimental mood* appropriate for the occasion. Jonathan looked over at Denise intermittently as his date nodded off, nestled in the front seat of his car. For that one moment in time, it was as if she belonged to him. For that one moment in time, she was his.

When the car pulled into the driveway at one-thirty a.m., Denise's eyes fluttered before she gathered her things to leave him. "I really want to thank you again for being the perfect host and the perfect gentlemen, Jonathan. It seems that everything I've heard about you is true. You are one of a kind. I hope your woman will forgive you for spending the night with a married woman."

Jonathan wondered when she'd get around to asking if there was anyone in his life who was significant enough to mention. He was delighted when she finally did. "I'm between women at the moment," he replied humbly. "Have been for a while now but I get out a little here and there. There's no one to check in with though. You thinking of applying for the position?"

"Hmmm," she sighed, "that sounds interesting but I don't think I qualify, not at the moment anyway."

"Then I'll just say good night. For now."

"Not yet."

As Jonathan headed for the front porch steps, Denise grabbed him by the hand. "Is there something else?" he asked, hoping there was. Before another moment slipped by, Denise leaned in closer to the man who made her feel as ease in her own situation. She planted a faint kiss on his lips then slowly pulled away. It seemed as natural as sharing the same air, space and time. "I guess I'll have to send in my membership dues?"

"Dues?"

"Jonathan Holloway fan club," she replied. "I want in even though I'm sure you have more than your share of admirers."

"How's honorary president sound?"

Denise was ready to be sworn in on the spot. Unsure if the timing was appropriate, she wanted to choose her words before going even farther than her common sense was willing to let her. "President? That's tempting. In the meanwhile, when should this candidate expect to see you again? Or is that too *forward* and *presumptuous?*"

Suddenly, he was reminded that he was still one woman shy of having a date for the Man of the Year banquette. "I'm booked solid for the next two weeks if I have anything to say about it. Actually, there's an office function I have to attend tomorrow night and somehow neglected to make arrangements for a dinner companion."

Jonathan's helpless expression drew Denise in like a moth to a flame, hopelessly attracted by the fire. "No date? Whuuuut? I don't know if it's a good idea to be seen in public with a man who couldn't muster one single, willing and able, female for dinner." She giggled at his expense. "Fine, I guess I could help you out this one time. I'm feeling rather charitable this morning."

"I'm not too proud to accept charity and I ain't too proud to beg if needs be. The event starts at eight. I could swing by and pick you up about seven-thirty unless we need to head out earlier to pick up something new. It's formal. My treat, of course."

Denise lowered her head bashfully, impressed at Jonathan's thoughtfulness. "No, I can cover that. Thanks for the offer though. When man starts buying a woman gifts and trinkets, he might think she owes him something in return. I wouldn't want to put that kinda strain on you, seeing as how the cost might be considerable." She looked him over, with half a mind to slip another kiss on his lips.

Out of nowhere, Ms. Harris stepped out onto the porch. She had been listening the entire time. "Y'all going to be out here all night? Niecey will be ready at seven," she said sternly. "Now get off my porch Jonathan Holloway before the neighbors think you've been here all-night catting around with me and I don't need that kind of scandal behind my name. I ain't too respectable for that kinda gossip but I am too old to deal with it." She pulled Denise inside to get the scoop on what took them all night to say.

Utterly infatuated, Jonathan doubted he would ever allow another woman inside his complicated world but it felt right. Some men never learned how to love, others chose not to. Jonathan had simply forgotten that an option existed for him. When he returned to his car, he turned the stereo off. Jonathan didn't want anything to disturb his thoughts of Denise, including the way she laughed, the things she shared or the way she was.

Still somewhat dazed, Denise shed her clothes and crawled into bed. She couldn't resist calling her closest friend Angie, in Oakland, as the sun peaked over the skyline. The excitement of this unusual man who seemed to stroll into her life like a hero from an old black and white movie refused to be contained.

Angie awakened with a bad attitude to the ringing telephone on her nightstand. "It's four o'clock in the morning!" she screamed. "If this ain't Denzel, somebody sure in the hell owes me a happy ending 'cause I was dreaming about getting me some."

"Sorry Angie, it's Dee girl. I'm sorry to be calling you this early but I can't get to sleep."

After a long wide-mouth yawn, Angie glared at the alarm clock again. "I was sleeping good and Denzel was just about to stroke my ego exactly the way I like but it can wait," Angie joked. "I thought you were supposed to be in Texas. Is your auntie alright?"

"She's doing great, funny as ever but that's not why I called. I have to tell somebody before I explode."

"Well... I'm up now," Angie said, in mid stretch.

"Girl, I met the most incredible man tonight, you should see him. He's the kinda fine that you see on another woman arm and wonder how long he's been putting a smile on that sistah's face. I'm talking a tall, dark, handsome, well-mannered, six-foot-two-inch chocolatey prince of a man. And you know what we say." The two women recited in unison, "The blacker the berry the sweeter the juice. The darker the skin, *the longer the root!*" They both burst out laughing.

Denise continued to rave on about the man who she was already thinking of as hers. "This man is something else. When he speaks, I find myself hanging on to every word and..."

"Oooh!" Angie interrupted, as she sat up in bed. "Wait a minute Dee. I recognize that tone in your voice. You gave him some, didn't you?"

Denise cooed like a schoolgirl with her first crush on a boy. "Uh-uhh, don't be ridiculous. He did make love to my mind though... and it left me wounded."

Angie's mouth fell opened. "Was it good? I hope it was 'cause I'm over here getting all worked up."

"Yes," Denise answered, reflecting on the time she'd spent with Jonathan. "Felt it down to my toes."

"Ooh-wee chile. Now, I want some." Angie responded sensually, imagining what that must have been like. "Why can't I meet some romantic man to stir up my juices like that? Shoot, Dee. You should've gave him some of that west coast booty. I probably would've been throwing it at the poor man," she confessed. "Lawd knows it's been too long since I've been blessed. Nowadays, brothas fall asleep before my hands are even tied up good."

Denise howled over Angie's scandalous testimonial. "Girl, you're gonna make me wake my auntie. I keep telling you there's nothing sexy about rope burns."

"That's why I got me a velvet rope," Angie replied bluntly.

"Uh-huh, you and Janet Jackson."

"A girl's gotta get her kicks. In the meantime, I'll be here alone with my undying devotion to Denzel. Yeah, my dreams are real as hell."

"Then I'll let you and Denzel get back to whatever it was you two were about to get into, with your nasty self. Sorry for waking you Angie but I just had to tell you about him."

"Oh, that's okay by me. Now Denzel can just get started all over again, from the beginning. Let me know if I can help. Living vicariously through you might be fun for a change but you know I'm your girl and I love you like a play-cousin so you promise me you'll be careful. Remember, you do have some unfinished business waiting on you here."

"You've got a point. I promise to watch my step. I'll keep you posted. Tell Denzel I said hello."

Denise chuckled over her friend's obsession with the famous movie star as she hung up the phone. However, her dream named Jonathan was real and off to a good start.

While lying in bed with the upstairs window opened, Denise considered Angie's advice. An innocent grin grew into a naughty grin as her newly devised plans made its way to her lips. "I might have unfinished business to deal with when I get home but I'm here now, and I like this opportunity a whole lot better." She reached for the lamp and bid goodnight to what little there was left of it.

On the following morning, all Jonathan could think of was Denise. The idea of getting to know her better fit him like a tailored suit. When Marcus Gamble met him at the YMCA where many Dallas police officers spent their Saturdays playing pickup hoops, he was still smiling.

"Gamble!" Jonathan shouted. The off-duty cop milled in slowly through the gymnasium doors wearing baggie blue sweats with a white towel draped over his head. "That you under towel? Late as usual."

Marcus pulled the shroud off his head slowly like it hurt. "Yeah, it's me. But please use your inside voice. I took a bus full of eight-year olds to the zoo yesterday then I tried to shake the memory of those screaming little monkeys with a bottle of Jim Bean. I don't know which did the most damage."

"By the looks of it, the bottle gets my vote." Jonathan was all teeth, despite his friend's dilapidated state.

"At least somebody's in a good mood this morning. What's the haps?"

"A certain fee-male," Jonathan hummed.

After rubbing his tired eyes, Marcus looked at Jonathan peculiarly. "Somebody I know?"

"Shiiid, I hope not," Jonathan argued. "Or I'll have to get some shot."

"Now that's cold. I had to go to the clinic one time and you won't let me live it down. But don't trip. I met some fine honeys down there."

Jonathan threw his hands up. "Hey man... that's too much information. Forget all the Band-Aid booties you keep running behind, let me tell you about something spectacular." He described Denise's physical beauty first, which was par for the course, considering men are visual creatures by design. And after Jonathan's eyes traveled to faraway place when he spoke of Denise's sense of humor and pleasant demeanor, Marcus agreed she sounded like a winner until Jonathan revealed one tiny glitch in the program. "Yeah, she's something special but there's just one... small... problem. Her husband."

Marcus tossed the towel aside and jumped to his feet. "Her husband! Have you lost your natural born mind? You're slapping skins with somebody's wife? Awe. Hell. Nah. This ain't good. Ain't good at all. This, this is trouble. And that means she's trouble." Marcus looked to his left, to his right, and then behind him in an erratic manner as if an angry spouse might have been waiting in the wings. "Dude, you have any idea how many brothas get killed each year by *her husband*?"

"Don't get bent out of shape," Jonathan insisted, trying to get Marcus to lower his voice by whispering. "Shhh! She's separated."

"Let me tell you how many playas get killed by her husband, almost as many that are murdered by *she's separated*!" Marcus answered, much louder than Jonathan cared for. Then, he polled fellow officers, who were warming up at the free throw line. "Kevin… Dre'… my man here is caught up over some sistah he just met. And get this, she's separated."

The taller of the two officers dribbled the basketball a few times before offering a eulogy. "Dead man walkin' here! Dead man walkin'!"

"That's what I'm saying," Marcus asserted. "Make sure your life insurance is paid up homeboy. It'd be a shame to leave your friends and family with the burden of burying your dumb ass."

Jonathan couldn't ignore Marcus's *I-told-you-so* stare. It cut him like a razor. However, Jonathan wasn't willing to throw the babe out with the bathwater so he was forced to face his dilemma head on and ride it out.

NINETEEN

New Jack Hustle

Saturday evening rolled around without a hitch. George Morrell and Brian Tillman faced the wall mirror in the large men's room of the Anatole Hotel, patting one another on the back before returning to the ASFB table in the main ballroom. "Mr. Morrell, I can't believe the time has finally come. You actually pulled it off just as you said you would. You're the Man!" Tillman cheered.

"All in a day's work young man, all in a day's work. And, after tonight, Jonathan Holloway will belong to me from his attitude to his ankles." The former federal agent made his proclamation with the confidence of a wealthy slave owner. "I've done it all before. You should have seen my operation in South Central Los Angeles. After five years of planning, the execution was brilliant if I do say so myself. I set up the whole operation from the outside in. The Columbians and Peruvians got more than they deserved when the homeboys learned how to rock up cocaine. As a result, I made millions by brokering the deals from my downtown office, just like I'm going to do here. Being a consultant to the LAPD had its advantages. When that imbecilic Mayor Tolbert wanted to double the police force to staff up for the war on drugs, I convinced him how insidious that was. Do the city a favor and double non-law enforcement jobs for the white instead by building twice as many jails I told the black and browns, and that joke of a civil leader has been a hero every since. He didn't even bother to thank me but the money I made won't ever compare to what we'll gross in Big D when our designer drugs hit the streets. The homeboys in Dallas won't be able to give crack away." Morrell noted the amazement on Tillman's face. "The way I figure it, we'll sample it on the streets to create a demand in the hood then ration the supply for a while. Just like Nike did with Michael Jordan basketball shoe, we'll start out by driving the price way up and make it hard as hell to get. That guarantees a large market share and maximize profits. Blacks always want that they can't have. Go ask Nike. You'll be a rich man Brian and I'll be on my way to the White House after a couple of years as the national drug czar. I'm just building a better mouse trap, no need to re-invent the wheel." Tillman checked his reflection, straightened his necktie then dreamed of all the millions coming his way. Moments later, both men congratulated themselves before exiting.

At the end of a long row of stalls aligning the other side of the men's room, the last door opened slowly. Walter Delaney, Jonathan's gutless boss emerged. He was frightened over what he'd overheard. Lasting effects of the startling conversation loomed on his face, reeking of contempt and control, which had been the demon and dragon that tormented his career during his twenty-one-year tenure with the bank. Delaney was provided yet another opportunity to do the right thing by one of his associates. Making the wrong decision would be his last.

The elaborately decorated ballroom was adorned with balloon monuments and glitzy ice sculptures. Each of the fifty dinner tables was decked out in yellow and coral colored tablecloths in an attractive overlapping design. Vivid flower arrangements made for stunning center pieces. Small candles placed over diamond shaped mirrors accented the setting's ostentatious appeal.

As the banquet attendants made their way inside while sipping complimentary cocktails, flickering lights reflected brightly off the shiny glass beneath them. Glimmering flames danced off the bright eyes of excited couples seated among tables sponsored by corporations which paid handsomely to be represented at the most prestigious function of the year.

Denise was awestruck when Jonathan escorted her into this grand affair. She'd attended her share of exclusive dinner parties but she couldn't hide the fact that it far exceeded her expectations. Now she was more than flattered to accompany Jonathan, whether she happened to be there by default or not.

"Jonathan, this is very nice. Y'all Texans sure know how to throw and wang-dang of a bar-b-q," she jested, with her best attempt of replicating his southern drawl.

"Ha-ha, I wish. No matter how good it looks, you can bet they've created another exotic way to dress up rubber chicken. It'll be rack-o-chicken, chicken a' la range, or baby back chicken ribs." He nudged Denise to step aside as he pulled her chair away from the table.

"Jonathan," Morrell saluted, as he stood to greet them. "Who's this lovely lady?"

Denise was wrapped in a gracefully painted on teal and black strapless evening gown that drew attention to her sculptured shoulders. Jonathan introduced her, somewhat reluctantly. "George Morrell, Denise Matthews." He'd often held reservations about the man who shook hands with his beautiful date, although he never fully understood why. Something about Morrell just didn't sit right with him. Intuition kept warning him to watch his back the same way it had whenever Brian Tillman was in the room.

Morrell simultaneously endorsed his younger colleague's taste in women while insulting Denise, all in the same breath. "I hope I'm not out of line but you are the prettiest thing I've ever seen on Jonathan's arm." Oddly enough, he meant it as a compliment.

"No, of course not. That was very flattering," Denise answered, dripping sarcasm. *Jerk!* "You're too kind."

Denise was funning beneath a three thousand dollar Vera Wang gown while warring against the urge to reveal her darker side. Unaware of the status Morrell held in the company or his affiliation with Jonathan, she decided to take the high road and play it safe. Besides, Denise had no plans of ever seeing George Morrell again, if she could help it. He left a bad taste in her mouth that contaminated her perception of the entire table.

"Good job sweetheart," Jonathan whispered in her ear. "Denise gets a gold star for diplomacy. Apparently, you've done this before."

"I've had more run-ins with the kind of white men whose leer says everything they wouldn't dare in front of their wives. They see brown skin and want to get invited in. I can handle myself with clowns like him."

While noticing twosomes around the table, Denise asked Jonathan why Morrell and Tillman were the only men without dates. "Probably because there isn't anyone on the planet better suited for each other," Jonathan joked. "My second guess would be Morrell's wife couldn't stand up long enough to get dressed. Uh-huh, too deep in the bag. At the last corporate function she got wasted, fell off her chair and then literally showed her behind after her mini-dress flew up."

Denise sneered, *that's-what-you-get* style, in Morrell's direction. "I just met him and already I can't stand him. Can't say that I blame his woman for trying to cope the best way she could."

The Master of Ceremony approached the podium to welcome those in attendance then commenced with a lame five-minute standup routine riddled with corny quips and recycled anecdotes. He was a talented TV talking head with impeccable blonde hair and a perfect tan, although his song and dance was laced with all the amenities of a grand introduction guaranteed to bore. "This year's list of nominees for the coveted award is perhaps the most diverse group of men ever selected by the Dallas Chamber. I wish that each of them could represent the city as well as they have in their respective fields of business and communities but the committee could choose only one. This year's recipient is a Dallas native, who has epitomized what this great city is all about. He has helped to implement the Illiteracy Extinction Program in association with the Mentor's Association of Texas. He has also established safety districts throughout the southern sector to institute drug free school zones."

As the News anchorman read a distinguished list of accomplishments, heads began to turn. People peered around the room for who the announcer was speaking so highly of. Dinner guests at the ASFB table traded whispers among themselves as anticipation swelled. Denise had no idea what was happening. Jonathan was too astonished to acknowledge the list of accomplishments belonging to him. The blank expression he wore was befitting a man caught with his pants down in a ballroom filled with onlookers.

The presenter caressed the award as he announced the winner. "And perhaps the most impressive of his achievements is the part he played in negotiations between the General Motors and The Car Builders Association to appropriate a 240,000 square foot automotive plant in South Dallas, creating over four thousand jobs in a community where such a great association will do wonders for that economy. If you don't know by now who he is, it is my pleasure to introduce you to Dallas' Man of The Year, Jonathan Holloway."

The ballroom erupted with applause. The ASFB table ignited in a standing ovation which quickly spread throughout the entire room. Denise was blushing amidst the hundreds of smiling faces and clapping hands, all praising Jonathan's efforts. After he received several 'atta boys', from his immediate congratulators, he leisurely strolled past a series of smiling faces on his jaunt to the elevated stage. The Emcee shook his hand vigorously then handed over an eleven-inch glass sculpture of a businessman leaning against a replica of the Reunion Tower landmark. The base of the award read: *Thanks to men like you, dreams do come true. Dallas' Man of the Year- Jonathan Holloway.*

Jonathan accepted the award with humility while letting it all sink in. He flashed a bright smile that illuminated his dark contoured face and allowed his charm to permeate the crowded room. He sighed deeply before expressing a few humble words of gratitude. "I would first like to know who I make the check payable to for receiving this city's esteemed honor." His joke produced a brief moment of levity as he pondered who was behind his name appearing on the award. "Seriously, I need to convey my thanks to you for thinking enough of me to acknowledge my work. Thanks to American South Financial Bank for their relentless support and to those of you who believe in me and what I stand for. Now, I must challenge all of you to get on the bandwagon and pledge assistance to the various communities you hold dear. There is still much work to be done." He paused to get another look at the award. "I had better sit down now before this begins to sound like a speech. Thank you." As Jonathan concluded, he hoisted the beveled glass high above his head to another wave of applause.

When he reached the ASFB table, Denise met him with a warm embrace. Some of the others stood, engaged in further congratulations and stepped in closer for first hand looks at the award.

"You deserve it Jonathan," yelled Tillman from across the table. As soon as Jonathan's back was turned, the devious conspirator raised a glass of champagne to George Morrell and winked. The diabolical plan they cooked up was one step closer to fruition now that Jonathan's prize had been delivered. Walter Delaney looked on, remembering what he'd heard in the men's room. The whole sordid scene caused a haunting vibe to creep up his spine although he made no attempt to warn his valued associate that he was being set up for serious corruption.

After the celebration waned, Jonathan enjoyed the moment, as he and Denise lingered near the valet stand for the car to be returned. "You ought to be shame of yo' self, *Mr. Man of the Year*," she scolded jokingly. "How're you gonna bring me out here to this thing all ignorant like that?" Denise pinched his side as she mocked his subtle invitation. "*Oh, I have to go to this company thing*. Why didn't you tell me you were up for such a prestigious award?"

"I'm sorry sweetheart but I didn't think I had a snowball's chance in hell of winning this thing," he apologized earnestly. "They don't usually invite us to these high fullutin parties so I figured my nomination was a simple plan to quiet the black newspapers that always rag on events like this."

Still harboring a faux pouting expression, Denise leaned in closer to Jonathan for a kiss. "That's the second time you've called me sweetheart. Keep on and I'll start to think you're up to something that might lead to trouble," she suggested.

Jonathan gleamed from the unexpected turn of events before his elation sputtered. "Alright then, I'll check myself. Guess I'm more like my old man than I thought. He used to call my mother that. Yeah, it lit her fire too."

When it didn't seem right to allow the evening end so soon, Jonathan convinced his out of town guest to extend it. Within minutes, they arrived at Dakota's, a quiet underground restaurant downtown. Denise ordered a bottle of champagne to commemorate the special occasion.

With raised glasses, he toasted to a promising friendship and taking more necessary steps to bring about positive change in the black community.

"Jonathan, I bet your family is so proud of your hard work. My aunt sure is. I can't wait to share the good news." Denise noticed his demeanor shift when she mentioned his family. "What is it? Did I say something wrong?"

"No, it's nothing really. During all the pomp and circumstance tonight, it hadn't occurred to me how my parents would be gushing right now if they were alive." Jonathan paused as his eyes drifted away from hers. "Actually, I assumed that Ms. Harris told you about my... family."

There were some things he wanted her to know in the event she altered her semi-detached marital status. Jonathan thought about sharing too much information too soon then he gave in to the tiny bubbles poured from the champagne bottle. "Obviously, there are some things you don't know about me and my past. I'm a complicated man with more baggage than most so you might want to run now while you still have the chance. Who knows, it might change the way you think of me." His eyes were inviting. Not in a romantic way but more in the manner of a train wreck that's difficult to turn away from.

"Jonathan, I know we just met but I want to know everything about you, everything that matters." Denise reached across the small café table to place her hand on his. "Our friendship means a lot to me and if there's something bothering you, I want you feel comfortable sharing it."

"More true confessions, huh? My mother would have loved you to pieces. Starla Faye was a lot like you, kind and beautiful. She uh… waited four years for my father to come back home from Vietnam. He was a lucky one to make it home alive and they looked forward to picking up where they left off before he was inducted into the army. As soon as he got settled, he became involved with an outfit involved with the Black Panthers. You know, down with the struggle and all that. It was all good for a couple of weeks until one night I woke up when I heard my father fighting violently with someone in our house. Later that night, we found him dead in the living room. Heroin overdose, all the newspapers said, but he wasn't a user. The Black Panthers blamed it on a cross town feud and some Italian mobster types but my old man was an ordinary working stiff. He didn't have any business with the Mafia."

Listening intently, Denise was caught between stopping him and allowing him to continue down a road of obvious sorrow. "Jonathan, forgive me. I didn't know."

"It's cool, I'm a big boy now. I guess it's old news anyway. The saddest part of it is, my mother died a year later of a broken heart. She was only twenty-five." He collected himself, staring at the golden bubbles in the champagne glass as he fingered it intimately. "But, I still have Ms. Harris. She's the only one who really knows what happened back then. She loved her some Starla Faye. You know, she taught my mother how to sew and made sure that we were in church every Sunday. Sometimes I think Ms. Willa Mae misses her as much as I do."

Instinctively, Denise gently squeezed Jonathan's hand. She had become irresistibly drawn in after hearing his story and begun to fall in love with his suffering. While she peered into his sullen eyes, she had a window view into his soul. Never before had she wanted to belong to a man as much as she did at that moment. "It must have been so hard losing both your parents, relatively at the same time. I'm sure it must have taken years to get over, if you ever could. You're really something," she whispered softly.

"I'm just my father's son. It's funny but after all these years I can still hear his voice ringing in my head. Son, this world is a bitter place sometimes and it treats black folks like we're cursed. Don't let other people's hatred stop you from being what you are meant to be, a great man. Look out for brothas and sistahs he preached. Help out those who need help from time to time. In spite of all the things this world might throw at you, do your part and serve your purpose." A reminiscent grin appeared where a weary frown had been for the past few minutes. "So, when times get a little bumpy, I remember that I'm expected to rise above it because my father said I didn't have a choice. That's my cross to bear. I can't seem to leave well enough along."

"Thank God for that."

Denise realized how the time had flown by and everyone under the Harris roof was required to be in attendance with the saints on Sunday morning. They finished the chilled bottle of Moet then enjoyed the walk back to Jonathan car parked on the quiet street above. With her head on his shoulder, Denise vowed not to think too much about the long goodbye, which was inevitable when time came for her to return home to Oakland. There was no way of getting around it. She was still some other man's woman.

On the west side of town, Morrell and Tillman entered an old building near the Trinity River landfill. The Dixie Dove Paint

Co. had been the area's most successful business for the past forty years. It was owned and operated by Shannon O'Brian, who suddenly forced his company into bankruptcy after losing a discrimination lawsuit. Unfortunately, the owner thought it more fitting to go out of business than to employ African Americans. Eventually, the building was purchased by a private investor then immediately gutted and refurbished to facilitate an even more lucrative enterprise.

From the outside, the monument of buff-colored brick and mortar appeared deserted but the lobby floor housed the White Sands furniture and upholstery service. The private investor was George Morrell. Fine furniture was shipped from all over the world to be refinished by White Sands. Craftsmen, who mostly consisted of ex-cons, worked diligently to recover extravagant sofas and chairs for extremely wealthy customers. Most of the pieces sent in for repair were returned to the client with special packages sewn into the cushions. It was just a little something extra for choosing White Sands. Morrell had been busy over the previous three years to fund his political aspiration. He managed the furniture business on the side while simultaneously maintaining an executive security position at the bank, one that allowed him special clearances and access to proprietary information at the airport. He knew in advance when random police sweeps were scheduled and which shipments would be spot-checked by drug sniffing dogs.

Watching closely, Tillman looked on as two men in dirty overalls stuff a large shrink-wrapped bag beneath a seat cover then reattach it to the antique mahogany chair had fallen off a moving van idling at the back of the makeshift warehouse. All of the furniture on the van was headed for Red Bird airfield, which was better suited for handling the smaller shipments of delicate items than the international airport.

"You guys do excellent work," Tillman complimented. "How much would a chair like that go for on the streets, I mean after you've *repaired* it?" He was getting some shady ideas of his own, a dangerous thing to do in Morrell's back yard.

"For the chair, a few hundred. For a White Sands cushion," one of the men began to answer until his voice fell silent when Morrell appeared.

"If you have to ask, you can't afford it," Morrell chimed in abruptly, for Tillman's sake. "Joey, don't waste time yapping. I have a schedule to keep. Clean it up and get it back on the truck. There's a very important soiree in Hollywood tonight and that chair will be the hit of the party. It must arrive in good condition and on time."

"Yes sir Mr. Morrell," the worker replied, hurrying to do as he was told.

The company thrived on offering excellent customer service and discreet payment arrangements for services rendered, all in monetary transactions via the secure ASFB computer network, monitored by none other than George Morrell. He had a pretty sweet set up with no one to scrutinize his actions. There were no paper trails, no bank audits, and no company records to be reviewed on the backend. As soon as large cash deposits hit a wire transfer, he'd move the money electronically to an off shore account in the Grand Caymans then erase any traces of the transaction. His operation was smooth, easy and extremely lucrative.

In the past three years, Morrell spent time formulating a way to become a major drug player without getting noticed by heavy hitters who might want to rid themselves of the competition. He knew that the illegal drug trade was the county's biggest industry. He wanted to become the undisputed king, without others feeling threatened by his success, until it was too late to do anything about it.

"Come on Brian, I've got something to show you," Morrell ordered. "It's about time you saw my brainchild at work."

On the way down a metal staircase, leading to the basement of the enormous building, Morrell voiced some concerns. "We've talked about this before and I won't say it again. I bought you in to secure a niche in the market and endorse my product. If I even begin to think you've started your bad habits again, you're finished." Tillman had a history of drug abuse but Morrell pulled a few strings at the state level to hedge his bets. He called in an old favor to have Tillman's arrest records deleted, for intent to distribute, from the Texas judicial computer system. Then the former FBI agent set Tillman up with a cushy high-paying job at the bank a week later. It was a well-conceived plan from the very outset.

"You don't have to worry about that Mr. Morrell, I'm clean now. Clean and sober. Word of honor." Brian Tillman had no honor but Morrell factored in the ex-con's loyalty, since he had paid for it. Morrell didn't think his ambitious associate was stupid enough to get greedy. It wasn't long before he'd be wrong on both accounts.

The basement floor was a vast contradiction to the upper level. This floor was slick spotless concrete. Specialized computation equipment and bio-rhythmic chemical mixing devices were mounted on stainless steel tables. Experiments were conducted in glass tubes as chemists draped in white lab coats concocted solutions which yielded illegal mind-altering money makers. Morrell surveyed their work in progress. "Webley, how's my star chemist this evening? Has the product reached perfection yet?"

Webley was a recent refugee from Huntsville State Prison. He looked more like an insurance salesman than he did a brilliant chemist. Morrell rescued him from a second strike which carried a twenty-year sentence for drug trafficking. Morrell had friends in low places, with the clout to make hard jail time disappear for the right price. The right price along with help from the Texas Department of Corrections staffed his underworld enterprise. Each of them was handpicked from a group of felons who didn't sell out their accomplices when the deck was stacked against them. Webley was no exception. By age twenty-three, he was touted as an award-winning honor student before walking away from a high brow graduate program Southern Methodist University. "Yesterday we just about had it," he replied, beaming with eagerness. "I almost pissed my pants. Here, look at this print out. You'll see the chronological dispensation I've been running over the past two days is narrowing down the precise equation to a level of potency we can control and re-create at will, without compromising the desired effects." He invited them over to another table where white lab mice were stored in glass cages. "Here's something else you'll want to see. Watch what happens when an ordinary mouse gets a taste of this solution."

They watched the mouse approach the water feeder. It sniffed the spout to detect poisonous elements. Webley squeezed the rubber end of an eyedropper. One droplet of a light blue tinted chemical mixture diluted into a container of normal drinking water. The mouse drank from the contaminated sample then casually moved away from the feeder. Suddenly, it scurried toward the remote corner of the glass cage and collapsed.

Looking on intensely, Tillman seemed fascinated by the testing procedure. "Hey-hey. You killed it," he whined.

"Where'd you get this moron?" Webley asked Morrell. "This is a bit more involved than playing baby banker. Just keep your eyes on him for a second. He'll come around."

Immediately, the mouse sprang up from its crouched position. It ran laps around the inner walls of the cage in an erratic manner. After it continued for a few seconds, the mouse hunched over in the same remote corner as before, simulating a mating act by itself. As the men observed closely, the mouse's heart rate continued to climb until it ultimately failed. When the mouse fell over dead on its back, Webley turned his eyes toward Tillman. "Now, I've killed it," he said, with a sheepish leer. "We're close though. Very close."

Morrell was not amused. Instead, he became more insistent. "I'm not paying you a million dollars to be very close. You're supposed to be the best but my patience is wearing thin." Morrell stormed off, leaving the chemist feeling substantially inefficient.

Tillman disassociated himself quickly then backed away. "That little experiment of yours didn't work and now you've killed a defenseless mouse. You're not a chemist. You're a mad scientist. You probably get off on it too. You should be locked in a cage instead of these mice."

The result of the experiment was the most favorable outcome yet. The solution was still too strong to be tested on humans although other outlaw pharmaceutical companies had already begun testing theirs on unsuspecting prisoners. Deaths were inevitable although occurring at a slower rate than any of the previous mixtures. In the science world, that was progress.

TWENTY

Strung Out Over You

During the next two weeks, Jonathan fulfilled Man of The Year obligations by taking luncheons at country clubs where black members were scarce. He was offered one token welcome package after the next. Congratulatory emails and telegrams from senior level executives in the ASFB Corporation poured into his office by the basket loads. Jonathan's private time was handled differently altogether. He spent his evenings sharing candlelit dinners and long walks with Denise. With each passing day, it grew harder to deny himself the pleasure of sharing his bed. Jonathan also wrestled with the temptation of discussing a potential future together and her immediately plans specifically. There was always the constant dread of her departure date approaching as the hours effortlessly dissolve into minutes. Denise and Jonathan had become very close in such a short time, falling too fast to put on the breaks. Even if they wanted, it was impossible to put aside their feelings. What started as a friendly coffee house sit-and-sip swept them up into something undeniable.

Sleeping alone didn't come easy. Jonathan was torn between giving Denise what they both wanted, bouts of window-rattling sex and reserving the passion until she was legally free to do as they pleased. Denise longed for Jonathan's constitution to weaken. She often hoped for a lusty proposition to throw caution to the wind and get what she craved every time he said her name. Each time he held her, she was reminded of how a woman in love was supposed to feel. Each time, another man's woman was dangerously close to getting what she needed, the way she hadn't received it before.

After cooler heads prevailed, Denise's fantasies manifested themselves while she slept. Her late night dreamscapes were exceedingly vivid. She felt Jonathan in her presence as she sat in her dimly lit bathroom soaking in a bubble-filled oasis. Denise watched the wind from an opened window slow dance with the iridescent flames of scented candles surrounding her. Jonathan kneeled beside the antique claw-foot bathtub. He held a basket of rose petals and scented oils. Asking how he appeared wasn't important. She simply knew he belonged.

While washing her hair, he gently massaged her neck and shoulders then whispered her name until she begun to drift deeper into a romantic trance. As Denise stepped out of the bathtub, Jonathan greeted her with an oversized shroud to wipe away warm droplets from her soft skin. He wrapped her tightly, raised her from the floor then cradled her with his strong capable arms. Intensity escalated when he marched toward the bedroom. Heat rising from her pores, Denise was spellbound as Jonathan lowered her limp frame onto the bed.

He applied oils to every inch of her body until it glistened in the light tossed from the candle's flames. Starting with her toes, methodically caressing each one, he worked his way up her thighs and stroked her from top to bottom. Denise gazed deeply into his dark brown eyes. She sighed deeply when feeling his warm breath on her neck. Her chest heaved to sustain consciousness as her pulse raced along with each accelerated heart beat. When her eyes begged for him to give an ample measure of what she desired most, he climbed between her eager thighs, now over wrought with anticipation.

Denise ran her outstretched fingers against his muscular chest, groaning as she looked past his chocolate rippling abs standing guard over the treasure below. She couldn't refuse him. The sight of his abundant manliness, coupled with the sordid inclinations of enjoying every inch of it intensified the yearning between her thighs. As Jonathan roamed her shapely terrain with his moistened tongue, Denise swayed innately with each additional stroke. She was overwhelmed by a deluge of passionate writhing when Jonathan maneuvered his fingers into her soaked vagina. She quivered and moaned until exploding into the palm of his hands.

Denise was awakened by her own passionate screams. When her eyes opened excitedly, her body was drenched in sweat and her long fingers dripping wet from self-induced satisfaction.

The mere thought of locking legs with Jonathan sent chills down Denise's spine. Until the other chapter of her life was finished, she'd have to rely on his frequent trespasses into her dreams. Sometimes the trip back to reality took longer than the joy of experiencing it. Two weeks came and went much too quick to catch her breath. She was a woman falling hopelessly in love with a man so different from her husband. Denise wanted to experience more time with Jonathan. She couldn't get enough.

After an eight o'clock meeting with Walter Delaney, Jonathan requested a personal day off before he and Denise were forced to say their goodbyes. "So, tell mamma how your meeting went this morning?" she flirted, after biting into a spoon of vanilla bean flavored ice cream.

"It was a good one. The fortune cookie I had last night called it." His Chinese dinner leftovers from the night before yielded a note. *Old troubles will bring new rewards.* Jonathan recapped the changes in his life since Denise had sauntered into it. "It's still hard to believe because I've requested a meeting to negotiate my pay increase for months, then this morning old man Delaney springs this impressive compensation package on me that almost doubles my current salary. He said other banks were sure to throw some lucrative offers my way so ASFB wanted to demonstrate their loyalty as soon as possible. They also offered an unprecedented four-year contract if I signed a non-compete clause, barring me from joining any other financial institutions."

"That's not so unbelievable. You're an exceptional manager with the refined interpersonal skills that other companies would kill for. It's just that they've finally recognized your talents and couldn't think of letting you get away. I'm proud of you Jonathan and it couldn't happen to a more deserving brotha."

Jonathan slipped his hand inside his pocket and pulled out a solid gold chain with two keys dangling from it. "That's not all. These are keys to the big time. This one goes to the executive washroom and this long one opens the door to a split-level downtown corporate apartment, which also came with a complimentary four-year lease. A brotha could get used to living free." He was lured into an executive lifestyle he didn't ask for and into a world he knew nothing about. Jonathan agreed to ascend to a place where rules changed continually, without notice or regard to anyone but the rule makers. Morrell convinced the other senior executives that Jonathan would soon require impressive incentives to stay aboard the ASFB train once aware of his new celebrity status. Morrell committed himself to clearing the path for Jonathan's ascension and better opportunities, all of which accompanied a heavy price.

Denise brushed her hand against Jonathan's. "You're my hero. Just thought you should know that."

"Yeah? Hero?"

"Uhhh-huh?"

"Does that mean I gotta run around in pantyhose, rescuing people from burning buildings and stuff like that?"

Denise laughed. "No, that sounds more like a gay fireman."

"Yeah, I guess it does. So what are my duties as a hero, seeing as how this is my first crack at it?"

"Hmmm... don't fool yourself. You've probably been one to a lot of people and just didn't know it. But your duties as *my* hero are as follows. Just continue being yourself and maybe I'll put in for a secret decoder ring for you. What do you think about a sexy Batman utility belt with gadgets and whatnot?"

"Okay, that's different. I can get into it."

"You could walk around butt-naked as often as you want, wearing nothing but that belt," Denise added, with sly giggle.

Jonathan leaned back in his chair to get a good look at this lady who seemed to say and do all the right things. "On the real tip, I would like to take you to see my hideaway though. I'll wear anything you want me to, as long as you take it off me."

"Well-well, lemme see... check out your new crib where I know I'll get into trouble. Or, be a good girl and try to preserve what we've worked so hard to maintain." She ran her tongue around her lips seductively. "I think I'll choose door number two this time." Her scandalous expression dissolved as she qualified her answer. "I'd like for you to hold door number one open for me until I'm can walk through it, for keeps." Denise was surprised at how serious her response sounded after it left her lips. When the awkwardness set in, she attempted to recover with humor. "Can you dig it, big daddy?"

He nodded assuredly with a delightful grin. "Sho'nuff, foxy mamma. I can dig it." He knew exactly what she was asking for, the same issues he wanted to discuss but couldn't bring himself to broach. Without having to massage the topic, Jonathan recognized he and Denise were on the same page. The page that began with careless whispers and led to exclusivity for keeps.

When time had arrived for Denise to leave, Jonathan loaded his car with her travel bags. They pulled away from Ms. Harris's home singing along with the Classic R&B station to avoid the bittersweet sentiment that accompanied saying goodbye.

"Make my funk the P' Funk. I wants to get funked up," Jonathan sang loudly and off key. "Make my funk the P' Funk. I wants my fun uncut."

"You are so crazy. If your boss knew this side of you, he would be too through," said Denise between hearty laughs.

"That's why he ain't gon' know," Jonathan replied loosely.

Denise stopped laughing abruptly when checking her bags curbside. The dreaded time had come. She asked that Jonathan pass on seeing her to the terminal as intended. After sharing his disappointment, he uultimately agreed that it might be somewhat easier if he didn't accompany her inside. Denise wanted to get through it as quickly and painlessly as possible. Both of them were uncomfortable when appropriate parting words came hard to muster. Jonathan was already in too deep and Denise was married to someone else. There were no appropriate words to reconcile that. Their long bout of silence was interrupted when an airport security guard leaned on his horn for Jonathan to move along.

"I'll miss you," she whispered, fighting back her tears. She promised to call him every day until she could get back to Dallas. After the security officer realized his presence was not going to ruin their special moment, he moved ahead. Jonathan nodded 'thank you' to the officer as he rolled passed their difficult departure.

Jonathan's words didn't come easy so he pulled Denise close to share how he felt without trying perfectly express it. "Remember when we talked about chance and how a man gets lucky only once in his life where true love is involved?"

The rain began to sprinkle them, she answered before losing the nerve. "Yes, I remember. And, that goes the same for a woman."

Another security car pulled next to Jonathan's Lexus. This officer wasn't as sympathetic to the lovers grasping at a fleeting moment. He leaned on his horn with an attitude. Denise collected her carryon bag and walked away. She tried desperately to resist the impulse to turn around but the desire to get one lasting glance overcame her. A single tear streamed down her cheek then disappeared in the corner of her weary smile. She marched toward the concourse wiping her face.

Jonathan considered running after her but knew that would have only complicated matters. He understood how things had to be. Unfortunately that didn't stop him from wishing it weren't so. As Jonathan maneuvered his car into traffic, accepting the idea of being alone again stuck in mind like a riddle he couldn't solve. Having no control over Demise's affairs in Oakland, he could only hope he'd have answers in due time. Until something definitive happened between them, Jonathan had to hold firmly onto the memories. Although two incredible weeks was hardly a lifetime, he couldn't wait to hold her close again. As suddenly as Denise appeared in his life, she was gone. Somehow it didn't seem fair.

TWENTY-ONE

Out of the Loop

J onathan arrived at the bank on Monday morning. Several construction workers carried supplies in and out of an opening in the wall where the conference office used to be. Massive equipment trucks were parked next to the gaping hole. Uniformed lackeys and dressed down high ranking officials from the bank's security team made their presence felt by surveying the progress.

Jonathan was taken by surprise at the vast production, apparently hours underway by the looks of things. He considered it odd that no one bothered to notify him of the work detail or how extensive it was going to be. He had previously asked for safe deposit boxes to be installed more than a year ago but he had been told several times that the budget wouldn't allow it. Perhaps his newly acquired notoriety had already begun to pay dividends.

Feeling better about the obstructive and unsightly work required in order to get what he had petitioned for, Jonathan entered the bank with a sense of calmness. As he sat his leather briefcase behind his desk, Deidra met him with the previous week's production reports just as she had for the past two years, but this Monday was different. After Jonathan received a neatly bound stack of reports, his assistant handed him a hot cup of coffee. He accepted it, looked at it peculiarly then rested the cup on the far corner of his desk, as if he were more interested in something else. "Thanks Deidra," he mumbled, looking past her. "You think it takes that many men to install safe deposit boxes?"

Deidra didn't have the slightest about any boxes but could tell that trouble was going to result from the workers tramping dirt through her lobby. The whole thing had a funny smell to it. When Deidra made her way into the office earlier that morning, she asked a man who appeared to be in charge what all the bulldozing was about. Much to Deidra's dismay, her demand for answers was quickly dismissed. She was rudely informed that the construction crew had their orders and that's all she needed to know. "I couldn't get anything out of them so I figured you must have known," she told him, with regrets. "The opening tellers said construction was going on when they got here at seven o'clock. Jonathan, there must be some protocol to inform you about things like this."

The idea that he'd been left out in the cold weighed heavily on him, too much in fact to let it slide. "Well, somebody had better come up with some answers."

Jonathan was hell bent on getting to the bottom of what purpose the commotion served and who'd authorized it as he stormed toward an unsuspecting construction worker. "Excuse me, who's in charge here? Who's the supervisor?"

An overweight white man in his fifties was reading a blueprint at a wooden makeshift desk reading a blueprint. "I'm the foreman," he answered. "You must be Mr. Holloway. I'm Buddy Eaton. You can call me Buddy." *Mr. Holloway*, that was very impressive, either that or extremely patronizing. The foreman had Jonathan by at least twenty years. Jonathan couldn't decide if Buddy was using *Mr.* to pull his chain or to get him to drop his guard.

In either case, he was not in the mood to exchange pleasantries until he'd gotten what he came for and felt comfortable with the outcome. "Yeah, nice to meetcha," Jonathan said, straight faced and serious. "What's going on here?"

"We were given work orders on Friday afternoon to come out here and…"

"I can answer that," Morrell interjected, as he ducked through the hole in Jonathan's building. He dusted himself off and removed his dark sunshades. "Jonathan, let's step into your office so I can fill you in on a few things."

Jonathan escorted the chief security officer into his domain, took a seat then peered over his desk waiting to be *filled in*. Morrell wasted no time getting to the point. "Jonathan, we've decided to make some changes and add a security vault with personal deposit boxes."

"Good, I asked for boxes a while back. It's about time."

"I've been aware of your request but these boxes are not allocated for regular customers. They've been requisitioned for some of the bank's special customers. Those who need to keep large amounts of cash available for emergencies or temporarily need to store delicate items from time to time. You know, for safe keeping." Safe keeping? That was a poor attempt at humoring up the situation.

Jonathan didn't catch on initially but he became agitated when Morrell's meaning smacked him upside his head. "Oh, I see. By special customers you mean wealthy white men hiding money from the IRS along with their girlfriend's jewelry. Yeah, I get the picture but I don't like what I see," he argued. "And, I won't be a part of it. Find some other front man to help your customers steal from the government or run around on their wives."

Morrell looked away briefly, disgusted at Jonathan's direct opposition to take one for the team. The security officer's grimace should have rattled Jonathan but it didn't. "Well if you didn't like that news flash, you'll probably take issue with this other thing too," Morrell added.

"What other thing?" Jonathan's posture shifted further when he tried to imagine just how pissed off he would be after hearing what that other thing was.

"I hate to be the bearer of bad news but the boys in Carolina have also decided to restrict final lending authority to commercial bankers exclusively. Someone else will be approving loans to these professional and executive customers who'll have access to the safe deposit boxes we're installing today. Sorry but it takes you out of the loop."

Jonathan was infuriated. His jaws clenched tightly. ASFB had stripped him of his decision-making authority and executed in such an underhanded manner to boot. He figured it must have been time come to start paying for that Man of the Year award as the construction workers hammered away at his business and his pride. "George, are you telling me that I've been busted down to babysitting? And to top that off you're going to, let me make sure I've got this straight, bring in another brotha to originate sizable loans in my bank." He sprang to his feet when his blood reached its boiling point.

"Please calm down, Jonathan. Don't blow this out of proportion. It's not a big deal. We've made sure your new incentive contract adds another fifty thousand to your salary so you wouldn't have to concern yourself with loan production. Your bonuses are guaranteed. Look at it this way, we need you as an ambassador to all of our customers, not just those who happen to live in south Dallas."

"Oh yeah, it's all so clear to me now. The fifty grand wasn't only meant to rid me of any production concerns. It was a payoff so I wouldn't be concerned about other things that might start to go on here." Jonathan's head throbbed. In his wildest imagination, he couldn't have seen this atrocity coming. As it panned out, Jonathan was worth more to ASFB with his hands tied behind his back, and turning a blind eye to suspicious transactions promised to the bank's *special customers*. It was a compromising predicament that had him at odds with his morals.

Morrell had the presence of mind to let Jonathan vent before planning his final piece to an intricate puzzle. "Look, we've done right by you and now it's your chance to," Morrell said, before pausing, "…show a little gratitude here."

Jonathan's head shook slowly. He was still trying to make sense of it all before he said what Morrell had danced around since the conversation began. "Show gratitude *and look the other way*?"

"Hell yes, some gratitude!" Morrell yelled, tossing those words back at him. His piercing dark eyes glinted with resentment. "Don't screw with me on this. Believe me, you don't want a pissin' contest. Listen Holloway, this is the way the game is played. This is how it's done. Always has been, always will be."

When Morrell resorted to calling him by his last name, it dawned on Jonathan that this wasn't about the bank's commitment to him, and his years of stellar service or friendship for that matter. Jonathan learned two valuable lessons that day. One, no amount of loyalty assured him that his pants wouldn't be down around his ankles if it benefited ASFB. Two, not everybody who yanked on his zipper was doing him a favor.

Despite on-lookers getting an eye full as the two of them went at it, Morrell became more insistent at overcoming Jonathan's defiance. "Watch yourself," he threatened. "Headquarters wants to provide this service for selected customers and this is the closest branch to downtown but far enough away to provide the discretion they expect. It's already been discussed and it's a done deal. We're not asking you to like it but it is going to happen and we want you to continue managing this office. You've built this branch and made it a huge success. You belong here."

"Oomph. I belong here? Is that the best you can do? Why'ont you tell me the real reason you don't run out and get a flunky to do your bidding here for half the price you're paying me? Man, you must think I'm some new kind of fool. Truth is, y'all know if I suddenly take up with another financial institution, there would be a real problem in the hood. The brothas and sistahs wouldn't go for that at all. Then the media would come around sniffing and interviewing decent black folk to find out what the shakeup was all about. Y'all know as well as I do that no other person could come here and unlock these doors without my endorsement. Folk around here ain't that trustin' of outsiders knowing how many pennies they keep stashed away in their checking accounts."

Morrell's silence confirmed there was legitimacy in Jonathan's objections. He was coming to grips with what they were asking their handpicked award recipient to do, and it wouldn't be as easy as he thought. In the past two weeks, Jonathan had been honored by the city then undressed and exploited like a carnival sideshow.

Jonathan continued to process the overwhelming news while holding firmly to his dignity. "Who is he?" he asked finally. "The new lending officer."

Not having the fortitude to look Jonathan eye to eye, Morrell stared down at his manicured nails instead. "Brian Tillman," he answered, in a much softer voice than he'd used earlier. "He starts next week."

"Tillman!" Jonathan shouted. "That asshole? He doesn't know a damned thing about what this community needs and besides that, he's white. White! These customers will eat him alive, especially when they learn that he thinks they're all low-bread car thieves." Jonathan wanted to aim his heated frustration at Brian Tillman who but he wasn't responsible for the turmoil. Tillman didn't have the clout to engineer something that diabolical. No, this huge undertaking was someone else's brainchild. Someone higher up the chain had his fingerprints all over this one. Tillman was only the residue, a pawn. Jonathan was sure of that. "Tillman of all people. Boy, y'all sure know how to pick 'em. Maybe, I ought to pack my bags and get as far away from this bullshit as I can. I should leave you and Delaney to explain it to the media after my customers picket your looney stash box idea and run you out of town."

Morrell didn't flinch. He was unscathed in a relentless pursuit of having his way. "You know as well as I do that's nonsense. This community needs this bank and your people need you. You wouldn't abandon them and we both know it." As he contemplated the bank manager's stubborn nature and deep resolve, Morrell recognized for the first time how much Jonathan resembled his father.

Suddenly, Morrell rose from his chair and drew closer to his prey like a Roman gladiator relishing another conquest then casually loosened his necktie. "Outstanding," he exclaimed, when sensing victory. "I knew we'd come to understand each other. This is a win for the team, Jonathan." He left the office to discussed matters with Buddy before stepping through the same hole he'd entered.

The end of their conversation had been overshadowed by the ranting of a scantily-clad woman dressed from the working girl's department of Whores R Us. She refused to take Deidra's advice suggesting it was probably not a good business decision accepting personal checks for time she'd spent on her back.

"Whutcha mean this check ain't no good!" the hooker screamed. "This lawyer dude pays me with checks all the time. He got lots of money."

"I'm sorry ma'am but there has been a stop placed on this check. Maybe you should call him up and see what the problem is." Deidra had to hold breath to keep from laughing at the woman. Obviously, the lawyer dude didn't feel the services she'd performed was worth the fifty-dollar check he'd written for them.

The woman huffed angrily then held the personal check up to the light. "That's all right. I'll fix his ass. This check has his home phone number on it. I'll just act like I'ma tell his wifey what he really likes in the sack. That ought to be worth at least a hundred, easy." She folded the check then slid it inside of her bra. "Thanks sistah. I'll handle this one myself." The prostitute smiled like everything was going to be all right. She sidestepped Deidra to deliver a dish best served cold, revenge.

As soon as the woman strutted out of the bank, the Muslim crew strolled in like always, serious. Their charismatic leader, Minister Muhammad, lead the assortment of well-dressed missionaries toward Jonathan's office.

"Black Man," the minister announced from the doorway.

"I am," Jonathan answered somberly. The pleasure that typically presented itself when his most conscious customers came calling, was absent from his voice.

"Brotha Jonathan, I sense that all is not well in paradise. But, I have a distinct feeling that I have a surefire remedy to correct that."

Jonathan looked toward the ceiling as if to suggest the impossibility of the Minister's comment. "Are you a betting man, Minister? Because I'd pay to see it."

"Well, I've given up on worldly vices or else I'd have you open your billfold because it's going to be worth every penny." The certainty with which he spoke caused Jonathan's brow to rise. "If I were to mention Reginald Brown, would that do the trick?"

Jonathan's face saddened when he heard the name. "Reggie Brown? Yes, brotha Minister, I knew him well but he's been locked up almost nine years now." He failed to see the rationale behind Minister Muhammad's questioning until a muscular, well-groomed man entered his office on cue then corrected him of the exact time period he'd been put away.

"You're close, brotha Jonathan," proclaimed the man whose face was very familiar. "But it's been more like ten years, six months, two days, eleven hours, fifteen minutes and some seconds that I can never get back," the man said assuredly.

Still dealing with the familiarity of his visitor's face, clean-shaven and smooth complexion, Jonathan studied it with reservations until the man's distinguishable smile displayed a gold cap over his right front tooth bearing a star in it. Suddenly, Jonathan chuckled. The capped tooth, he'd recognized, having been personally responsible for the chipped tooth underneath that shoddy dental work. It happened over twenty years ago when he fought with a sixth grader over a five cent returnable bottle they both happened to stumble upon at the same time. The familiar face and capped tooth both belonged to his closest childhood friend, Reggie Brown.

Jonathan sprang up from his chair with the renewed exuberance of a greedy plaintiff running to a lawyer's office after having had hot coffee spilled in his lap at a McDonald's drive-thru. "Reggie, is that you?" Jonathan could barely identify his long lost friend in the man standing before him. "Come over here and let me hug your neck. Man, you look great. I hate to say it but jail seems to have agreed with you. You've never looked better. And get a load of all that beef. What you been doing all that time? Never mind that!" Jonathan caught himself yelling over the worker's noise. "Let's move this welcome home party some place a bit more quiet. Let me take y'all to lunch so we can really catch up."

"When you're incarcerated," Reggie responded modestly, "time stands still. But I'm sure you can bring me up to date on what's been going on with you, other than you being a big time banker now and winning Man of the Year and all. Yeah, I read it in the papers before I was released. Man, your daddy would've been so proud of you... my old man too." Reggie's eyes drifted off Jonathan's, descending toward the floor. "He always said you had a little something extra that Allah held back from most of us. He sure was right about that."

"Yeah, well, you might have second thoughts once you hear what's going on now. But we'll get to all that. It's just so good to see you again, brotha."

The two of them followed the entourage' to the shiny black Suburban then climbed in. One block over, they arrived at the South Dallas Café on Grand Ave., a neighborhood landmark. They shared stories about their youth over coffee and tea. Jonathan was starving but the black Muslims limited themselves to only one meal a day and that was commonly reserved until after four o'clock, so he sacrificed his hunger for their tradition.

The Café's upper room was a clandestine meeting place for those in the community who needed a secure venue to discuss strategies and other matters requiring utmost privacy. The large room was once used by President Bill Clinton, when he visited with Dallas's black leaders during his first term in office.

"Damn, look at you Reggie," Jonathan reiterated. "I remember this scrawny, hard-headed scrub who said he couldn't make enough paper or have enough honeys if he had a hundred years to stack up both." As Jonathan continued to reminisce about the ex-con's checkered past, Reggie cut him off. "You were all about honey and money..."

"That was then. And believe me this is now. I almost died in lock down. Harmsway Correctional is for the criminally buster, disgusted, and definitely can't be trusted. I had to start hittin' the weights day one. Either get strong or learn how to braid hair. And you know I ain't one for havin' no grown man sittin' between my legs for no reason." All the men sitting around the oval shaped meeting table frowned at the thought of any black man maneuvering his fingers through another man's scalp.

Reggie described the infamous Harmsway he'd come to experience firsthand. "That place wasn't no joke. It's hell on earth if you ask me. Being told when to shower, shave and empty your bowels was bad enough to question your manhood but the sexual violence got so bad that inmates started killing each other and takin' themselves out when the ban on cigarettes hit a few months ago. I didn't think I was gonna make it out alive. The first month was like Armageddon. Tobacco became more valuable than life. If a man with a carton of smokes pointed his finger, somebody died that day. Jonathan, you haven't seen fiendin' until you've seen two thousand smoke-free murders, molesters, and thieves tryin' to kick nicotine cold turkey. They ran out of body bags and had to call in the National Guard but y'all didn't hear nothing about it 'cause the Governor didn't allow no news crews to cover the riots." The men listened intently to every word, shaking their head collectively.

Minister Muhammad, having experienced the inside of a state prison himself, was amazed. "How'd they stop the madness?"

"With drugs," answered Reggie. "They started giving away some experimental sex drugs that was s'posed to satisfy the urge but it didn't. Yeah, they used prisoners as guinea pigs and the drugs didn't even work. It made convicts hallucinate about getting buck wild then they got strung out on it. When the warden found out how powerful that stuff was, he cut off gen-pop without notice. Overnight, men started rapping each other and maturbatin' five and six times a day. Some of them developed nerve damage and sores on their privates that won't heal. At times, I wouldn't leave my own cell. They were forced to raise the ban on cigarettes to ease the strain but it was too late. The saddest part of it is, some of those maniacs are hittin' the streets now, worse than when they went in. Burglars, purse-snatchers and hot check writers... all potential sex offenders now. The cops on the outside ain't ready for what's about to go down. No way they could be."

"Like we need more problems," Jonathan muttered. He was blown away, along with the others.

"Enough of that. I've been free for two days but I couldn't catch you at home," Reggie explained. "I made a collect call to notify you that my parole was granted and I got my papers. Collect calls are the only kind you can make from the joint. The good Minister was gracious enough to receive me at the release station and assist me in getting re-established in the Free World. The Muslim's beliefs and the teachings of the Honorable Louis Farrakhan have developed and strengthened my mind while I worked on reconstructing my body. Now, I'm willing and able to contribute to society and help our brothas and sistahs like a real black man should." Reggie spoke with the pride and dedication of an African King. Jonathan was filled with admiration. His beaming smile adequately displayed it.

"Well then. All praises be to Allah, God and Minister Muhammad that you came home, whole," Jonathan concluded. "Black Man."

Reggie sharply responded, "That, I am." The other brothers looked on, nodding their heads in agreement. "It's just a shame that I had to spend my twenties getting to this point but I made it nonetheless."

Too many young black men spent their twenties behind bars instead of behind books. Reggie was just another sad statistical variable in the tragic paradigm of black men's epic struggles and likewise the black women's troublesome woes as a result. Jonathan was confident that Reggie had changed for the better and for good, unlike so many who used prison gates like revolving doors.

"Man of the Year," Minister Muhammad said, out of nowhere. "That's what I want to hear more about. That's the kind of positive fuel that'll inspire our people."

"Life's been good to me. God's been good to me. However, he must have blinked this morning." Jonathan explained the latest development concerning his position and the bank's idea of taking one for the team. "I do need to figure out a way to stop them from giving my lending authority to someone else. I haven't gotten all the details yet but this commercial lender named Brian Tillman will be running the show and I'm supposed to front for him. 'Be the good nigga by the do'." Although Jonathan didn't approve of anyone using that highly volatile word, it best described what ASFB thought of him.

The Minister had heard the name Jonathan mentioned before. "Tillman…? Tillman!" He's the one who turned us down for the building loan before we knew you had the power to make it happen, brotha Jonathan."

That added coal to the fire already mounting inside him. "And to think, they just gave me fifty grand and a luxury rent-free apartment in Uptown." Now Jonathan was embarrassed that he had so naively accepted the incentive package. The deal had a duck's bill and webbed feet but clucked the entire time. And since ducks didn't cluck, it had to be a lie masquerading as the truth.

Amidst the groans of discontentment which rang through-out the room, the situation became painfully obvious to Minister Muhammad, who voiced his disgust. "Fifty gees, huh? Isn't that something? That's *nigga be quiet and nigga behave* money. At least they didn't try to nickel and dime you. You said an expensive apartment downtown too? Awe brotha, they have you living in the Mastuh's house. Brotha Jonathan, we can't allow this." The manner in which the minister explained it, the situation was even worse than Jonathan initially thought. "Now, I know this is your thing but you think about how you want to handle it and we'll have your back, just as you've always had ours. One thing though, scrutinize who you trust and what you say over the phone at work. As a matter of fact, we'll be more than happy to stop by this evening when the bank closes to run a security check for wire taps, if you'd like."

After Jonathan had gotten over the astonishment that the men had access to such capabilities, it occurred to him that he'd underestimated his adversaries as well. "I wouldn't have believed they'd do something like that to me but after today, I guess I shouldn't expect any less of them."

TWENTY-TWO

Something Ain't Right

Jonathan returned to the bank after the impromptu meeting at the café. He located Deidra, pulled her inside the employee-only door then down a long corridor near a pair of private restrooms. He used his keys to open the furthest door. Wrestling with Deidra's objections was more difficult than Jonathan anticipated. "Hey, what the hell Jonathan! I ain't in to this," she complained. "I'm a lady. If you wanted a hem me up in your little hideaway to sneak and freak, you could have at least asked me to dinner first."

Jonathan flashed a 'get real' smirk before explaining what had transpired and what he planned to do about it. "So keep an eye on Brian Tillman when he starts working here and maybe we'll find out what's really going on, then we can come up with a strategy that'll straighten it out. Jewels, money, high rollers… I'm starting to hear clucking again."

Deidra didn't understand the clucking remark but she was on board with whatever Jonathan needed her to do. "Yeah, I'm with you all the way."

"I also need you to watch your step because this could get dangerous. So don't do anything you'll be sorry for. I wouldn't want anything to happen to you."

Deidra wanted to let his last comment slide but couldn't. "You've got your nerve. It's because of you I have a life. I'll ride or die for you Jonathan. Just say the word. I'll be the judge of what I let happen to me." She was actually willing to put her life on the line if it came to that. That was one more thing Jonathan had to concern himself with, Deidra's safety.

When he opened the door to exit the men's room, he felt her pulling him back by his belt loops. "Deidra, what is it?"

She glared at him disapprovingly. "How' you gonna straighten out anything and don't even check to see if anybody's coming before you and your Operations Manager get busted exiting the same restroom together. That's how rumors get started. You got to look around, look around." She peeked her head out then looked from side to side while adjusting her clothes before someone stumbled on them in a compromising position difficult to explain.

"I sure did pick the right woman for this job," Jonathan assured himself, leaving the tiny room shortly after Deidra's inconspicuous departure.

No sooner than Jonathan returned to his desk, a call came through from Lauren Stanton, a long time associate he'd known since their nine-month stint in the manager's training program. Lauren was an attractive petite blond with looks that caused most men to glance her way longer than deemed respectable. She was a cracker jack banker and as tough as nails. When she was only a child, she nursed her father back from a stroke when hard living on a strict diet of Red Hots candy and cheap beer took a toll on him.

"Hey Jonathan, its Lauren. Glad to finally catch you. I've got to talk to you about something that can't wait. Can you talk?"

She happened to be the managing assistant for his boss, Walter Delaney, which meant she was next in line for his regional position, but she held a stronger affinity for Jonathan than the man signing her checks. Remembering the advice of Minister Muhammad, Jonathan hesitated before answering. Lauren shared many personal experiences with him in the past. She was on the short list of people he trusted. "Yeah, but it might be better if I called you right back on a secure line. You got your cell? Good, take a coffee break and call me from the parking garage."

Minutes later, Jonathan hopped in his car with his flipphone in hand. His heart began to race a beat faster when the phone rang. "Lauren? Good, I'm sorry but I have to let you in on some things too. This way is a lot safer. What's going on with you?"

"There is some funny business going on around here at headquarters. All of a sudden, everything is so hush-hush and I've never seen so many documents being shredded in my life. Today, I overheard Delaney and that security guy, Morrell, arguing over something about your branch and it had to be heavy because Delaney stuck his head out of his office after they finished, then told me to hold all his calls. And get this, Delaney was as white as a ghost and scared as hell."

That information concerned Jonathan. Delaney was scared of Morrell. Now, it was clear that back room politics was pressing everyone involved, including his boss. "Thanks Lauren. That's good looking out. I owe you. Keep your eyes opened for me."

"Sure thing. By the way, that award they presented to you, I saw a carbon copy of a cashier's check, made payable to Ron Greer, the Dallas Chamber president. Sorry to be the one to tell you this but your Man of the Year honor was bought and paid for by ASFB. I'm not sure who authorized it but this is way over our heads so be careful."

"I will," was Jonathan's quiet reply. He had no idea what to do next and that made him extremely nervous, taking into account he had no control over the series of events that had taken place, wedging him in the middle of it. And, just when he thought things couldn't have gotten any more bazaar, they did.

Later that afternoon, the Muslims returned to the bank as promised. This time, Minister Muhammad arrived with his security advisor, Captain Darius X. They met in the hallway, which lead to the employees restrooms. The Captain warned the others. "Brothas, we need to be discreet if this place is wired. Watch everything you say."

As the men began their search in the lobby. Jonathan was curious about the black leather case hanging over Captain Darius' shoulder. He stopped the security advisor before exiting the long hallway. "Brotha Darius, you need a laptop to help you find what you're looking for?"

The man donned a glowing expression as he opened the case. "Oh this baby is a high frequency monitoring device. It's not only for spying. It's for spy bustin' too."

The device resembled an early model wireless radio. It appeared to be nothing more than a black box with an antennae and small silver knobs. However the transistorized box picked up soundwaves that were consistent with wire tap apparatuses and other hi-tech bugging mechanisms. Black Muslims had been in the espionage game for decades out of necessity. They picked up a few toys of their own to even the playing field.

Within moments, several breaches in security were discovered once the black box locked in to the radio frequency used. Jonathan's phone line had been compromised and four listening devices were placed throughout his office with the intent of going undetected. Someone had gone through great lengths to keep an ear to the ground. Jonathan's shadowy suspicions proved legitimate and if he had to guess George Morrell was the culprit, although he was clueless as to why the bank's top security officer was keeping tabs on him.

Captain Darius suggested a further search at Jonathan's plush downtown apartment leased by the bank. Jonathan shuddered at the thought of someone invading his home, regardless of who was paying the note. Apprehensively, he consented to having his apartment explored from top to bottom.

Once Jonathan parked his sedan in an assigned parking space in the apartment's large underground garage, he hit the rear stairs leading to the back door. His new split-level apartment was outfitted in earth-toned leathers with hints of red and crème. From the foyer throughout the second floor, furnishings were covered in shades of brown, rust, and amber. Soft lighter hues outlined the master bedroom that stretched from one end of the upper level to the other.

Two hours after they arrived, the Muslim's thorough search found nothing remotely suspicious. Jonathan was relieved. He assumed that Morrell had only taken measures at the bank to assure that he abided by the rules he had protested earlier. Jonathan hadn't decided how he would respond to the shady customers traipsing through his office. The best course of action was pretending to conform until the time came to bend the rules and change the way the game was played. In the meanwhile, Jonathan resigned himself to be vigilant. He had no choice but to watch and wait.

That night, George Morrell met Brian Tillman in the basement of the White Sands building. The operation was moving right on schedule. Morrell had received a call informing him the chemist finally perfected a synthetic drug that was relatively safe for consumption on the street.

"This is what I've been waiting Brian." Morrell held a small vile of sky blue liquid up toward the lighted ceiling. "A quiet storm that'll roll right through this country and revolutionize the drug distribution industry. After a few more weeks, we'll be ready for a world that won't be ready for us." He poured a stiff shot of bourbon for himself then one for his partner in crime. "I hope you're ready for lifestyles of the rich and infamous. More money than you've imagined in your wildest freakin' dreams."

Tillman fingered the fine crystal. He spent a few moments imagining his unimaginable future wealth. "Yeah, that's it. That's what I'll buy, a little island off the coast of Martinique and stock it with a private harem of a hundred suntanned beauties to treat me like a king. That's the lifestyle I'm after. Yes sir." He sipped from the cocktail glass then stopped as a thought came to mind. "Mr. Morrell, what about Jonathan Holloway? He could get in our way and gum up the works."

Morrell's eyes narrowed. "He doesn't know it but we go way back. He owes me in more ways than one and you're my security blanket. That's why I put you in his branch. You keep your friends close and your enemies closer. If it comes down to it, I'll take care of Jonathan and anyone else who makes the mistake of dicking with me. Keep an eye on him and I'll handle the rest. I've got this covered from the inside out." Morrell was confident to a fault. He was positive Jonathan would meet the same fate his father had, if he got in the way.

TWENTY-THREE

This Ain't What You Want

One month had passed since Jonathan's proverbial pedestal had been kicked out from underneath him. He had always prided himself on being in control of his own destiny and the master of his own fate but ASFB decided he was worth more to them estranged from the community he cherished since birth. His only means of detachment from the capsized world he once enjoyed was the daily phone conversations with Denise. He realized the old cliché, *absence makes the heart grow fonder*, was vastly underrated.

For the first time in Jonathan's adulthood, he actually felt a void down to the bone. He dialed her up one evening to convey how much he longed to hold her close again, so much so that he wasn't above begging for her to come rushing back if even for a brief moment. Denise reminded Jonathan of their formal agreement that she would not return to Dallas until ready to stay for a lifetime. Meanwhile, she worked diligently at tying up loose ends in California. It would take another month to finalize her divorce and settle vested interests in the health studio she owned with her husband. Although she spent her nights dreaming of Jonathan, who also captivated her thoughts during the waking hours, that wasn't nearly enough. The kind of love she needed was more than a phone call away. A divorce decree stood between them. A divorce decree and a long plane ride.

With construction at the bank completed, Tillman's new office was decorated with expensive leather and exotic wood furnishings. His business meetings were orchestrated by appointment only and conducted behind a stained glass and ebony wood door equipped with an automatic lock, which was operated by a small switch under his desk. No one entered his office without receiving his expressed consent or invitation. In the beginning, a few middle-aged businessmen came to call on him during office hours then he began seeing high-octane trust fund babies after normal banking hours. Each of them anticipated his escort to the steel encased room aligned with rows of safe deposit boxes.

To access the room, a special code was required. Tillman inserted an override key card as a secondary security measure. The set up was state-of-the-art and engineered to keep out those who didn't belong, especially Jonathan. Morrell took considerable precautions to assure all the transactions in that small room remained secret. Before long, business was booming for Tillman. Jonathan couldn't find any records of official bank business among the mill of paper reports he received for branch production. When curiosity got the best of him, he rapped on Tillman's office door only to be shooed away like a common housefly.

"Obviously you don't understand how important my work is or how much I value my privacy," Tillman growled. "Let me make this crystal clear. What goes on in my office and anything I do here is my concern and does not affect your business or your customers, not one iota. Maybe I need to put it in terms you do understand. Step Off!" Drunken with his newfound power, Tillman slammed the door in Jonathan's face.

"I know he didn't just," Jonathan heard himself say. "Oh it's on now. Somebody's gonna get hurt over this."

Jonathan paced the floor, fighting the urge to disregard all he had built and worked hard to accomplish. He envisioned himself kicking in that expensive door with the automatic lock then smashing Tillman's head in the process. That violent inclination was interrupted when his office phone began to ring with the urgency of a five-alarm fire engine.

"Yeah!" Jonathan spat into the receiver.

"George Morrell here. I understand you and Brian are having some issues with your new working arrangements. Remember what we discussed and don't fool yourself. You still like being there as much as we do having you there. So many people are counting on you. Don't forget that."

"I'm sure if I did, you'd be right there to remind me." A long bout of silence passed between them. "So, that it?"

"Yes, I think we're on the same page now. Brian may be a little hard to take in large doses but he'll settle down. I'll see to it."

Feeling alienated within the banking facility he managed from the ground up, Jonathan was caught between a rock and a very hard place. It seemed as though his world had been torn apart, bit by bit. A lesser man would have thrown his hands up and given in. Jonathan never learned to pull off either of those. Instead, he constantly asked himself if all the drama and upheaval was worth being there for the people, as Morrell put it. Adding insult to injury, Jonathan's role had been diminished to taking loan applications, later reviewed for decision by Tillman, if he took the time to review them before arbitrarily stamping decline on nearly every one.

Jonathan's loan approval rating took a sharp dive from eighty-seven to twenty four percent. The community was outraged with feelings of betrayal. Local business owners began stopping by to complain about the new, stricter, lending policies before taking their accounts elsewhere.

Later that week, Jonathan worked on the embarrassing production numbers he'd come to despise. He sat at his desk wondering how he allowed himself to get caught up in a corporate maneuver that stripped him of his power and a large amount of integrity. His moment of self–reflection halted when he noticed another of Tillman's customers outside the private office door. Another sharply dressed white man, who was quite representative of the new clientele. Jonathan recognized the man's Bostonian lace-up shoes as he peered over his desk to get a better look at the visitor's wardrobe. The customer exhibited apparent good taste in footwear, Jonathan admitted. He'd just purchased a similar pair himself. They weren't cheap. Nordstrom's sold them exclusively, priced at three-hundred bucks a box.

Tillman opened the door, welcomed the man with a handshake then escorted him into that pretentiously decorated office he was so damned proud of. Illusions of smashing that door to pieces came to mind again only to be chased away when Comphy wandered into the bank, causing quite a stir. He was draped in a maroon velveteen jumpsuit. Pink frills hung around the circumference of his matching wide brimmed hat.

Comphy looked ridiculous as he took slow calculated steps due to his near toxic consumption of alcohol. He paused just long enough to wave at his admirers, who yelled his name, encouraging him between bouts of gut busting laughter. Making a spectacle of himself didn't curtail his actions in the least. The resident drunk was glad to be around people having a good time, even if at his expense.

Once Comphy staggered over to the sign-in area, he plopped down in a chair and scribbled on a loan application. Jonathan looked over his shoulder, trying to decide what to do with the unrepentant soul who'd obviously lost his way and a piece of his mind along with it. After reading the answers Comphy filled in, Jonathan smiled for the first time in several days. *Place of Birth:* At Home. *Address:* No. I always wear pants. *Nearest Relative:* Jonathan Holloway - Friend. Comphy's answers and childlike demeanor humored Jonathan as much as they warmed his heart. At least there was one customer who still needed him.

"Ok, Comphy. Let's see here." Jonathan accepted the wrinkled sheet of paper. "Seems that you've left some of these spaces blank. How much do you want to borrow?"

"Mr. Jonathan, fifty dollars ought to cover it," he replied, like a sober dignitary.

"Fifty dollars huh? Comphy, we can't loan you fifty dollars."

Comphy ran a question around in that spacey head of his before letting it fly. "Say you can't do fifty? How about twenty dollars then?"

Jonathan folded his arms. "I don't think it's necessary but I'll explain it to you anyway. Your monthly Social Security allotment has already been depleted. You have no job, so you have no means of repaying a loan."

After pondering his options, Comphy stroked his narrow chin then delved into intense negotiations. "Ok, gimme ten dollars. No? Well lemme hold five." After Jonathan refused to loan Comphy any amount, he became insistent. "All right! All right! Be that a way then. I'll settle for a dollar."

Jonathan had grown tired of dealing with his dizzied patron although a dollar would have put some food in Comphy's stomach so he took out a crisp bill from his wallet and offered it. Upon identifying it as a single dollar bill, Comphy lashed out. "A Dollar! Somebody call 911. Man, you rippin' me off." As Jonathan made a move to put his money away, Comphy snatched he bill out of his hand for immediate inspection. "Hi'ya, lil' fella.'" Comphy kissed the dollar bill, thanked Jonathan then tipped toward the exit as carefully as he did when he arrived.

"Hey Comphy, that'll get you a two piece and a pepper from William's Chicken."

The spectacle in velveteen turned around with a sorrowful expression. "Mr. Jonathan, you know I gots a drinkin' problem and I sho feel a powerful thirst comin' on."

Jonathan frowned at Comphy. "I thought you told me you weren't going to drink anymore."

The drunk's natural wit shone through without missing a beat. "I told you how I don't drink no mo', nor no less. I fancy an even all day flow."

Jonathan knew better than to give a homeless alcoholic money for food. A real drunk often fed his urge rather than his stomach. It was like handing candy to a child who didn't deserve it. The simple act of giving over shadowed Jonathan's better judgment and it felt good. He needed that in a big way. Right or wrong, Jonathan needed it.

St. Augustine, Jonathan's barber, passed Comphy on his way into of the bank. He stepped into the teller line to exchange rolls of quarters for legal tender. Normally, he would have made time to stop by the manager's office to say a kind word or two. Unfortunately for Jonathan, things hadn't been normal around there for weeks.

"Saint Augustine, how's business?" Jonathan asked.

His long time friend articulated his opinion without raising his head or losing count of his change. "Ten, twenty, thirty. It's better than yours from what I hear," he replied bluntly, "forty, fifty, sixty… and my business is the only one that black folks trust other

black folks with exclusively, so that ought to tell you something."
Jonathan lowered his head, knowing full well what Augustine was
alluding to. "Why haven't you come by lately?" the barber asked,
finally raising his head to make eye contact. "Relax, I'm not gonna
ask you for a loan. I'll pass on getting turned down today. Son
look, you know I'm jokin' with you but other people 'round here
ain't laughin'. You got to do somethin' about that white boy they
got runnin' this place and start back to helpin' your own kind."

"I have a few things working but it's not just him. Something's going down. Something big. I can't call it yet but it
doesn't smell right."

Augustine pulled down on Jonathan's collar. "It's like I use to
tell your daddy. If it looks like a duck but it clucks…then it must
be a chicken because a duck don't cluck."

Traces of a smile played around the corners of Jonathan's lips
when he remembered just how close Augustine and his father
once were. And the advice he'd just been given affirmed what
he already believed. Morrell had gone to great lengths to sell
Jonathan on the appearance of business as usual, despite all the
recent changes. The real trick was seeing things as they were, not
as they appeared.

Afterwards, Jonathan returned to his office to take a call. "Hey
Jonathan, this is Marcus. You want to hit Club Matrix with me
later tonight? They gotta drink special. Every nice buzz you can
think of is only two dollars. Check it out, it's ladies night too and
you ain't seen no parts of a real ho-down since that busted con-
dom incident."

Jonathan almost dropped the phone when reminded of that
mishap. Stammering nervously, he worked at recapturing his
composure. "See-see, now there you go. Why'd you have to go and
bring that up? All the tests were negative and you know I've sworn

off ladies nights at Matrix since then. Besides, I have enough problems than making matters worse by pouring liquor on them."

"Uh-oh, I could be mistaken but you almost sounded like a puuunk," Marcus challenged with a mocking tone. "*I can't go to ladies night. I might get into some trouble. I have enough problems already.* Punk-punk-punk!" he teased. "Negro please, you should hear yourself. Is you is or is you ain't gonna punk out on me?"

After the flagrant assault on Jonathan's ego, he conceded. "Ok, ok. I'll go. I'll roll through at about eight o'clock. Be sure to get there on time. I don't care if some hoochie hides your car keys, your drawers and your shoes. Be on time."

Marcus agreed to arrive in a timely manner as not to have Jonathan appear to be a horny hound on the prowl. Conversely, he actually found himself looking forward to a romp shaking diversion to ease his troubled mind.

Minutes before closing, Comphy returned to the bank stripped down to his rusty worn underwear and army boots. He twirled a broken ASFB umbrella which Deidra had thrown out in the garbage the day before. The remaining customers were disgusted at the sight of him. They demanded Jonathan have him arrested for public indecency.

A distinguished older woman, who seemed to be more put off than the others, clutched her purse tightly while looking down her nose at him. "It's useless men like him who give black people a bad name," she cursed. "I'm tired of seeing his sorry butt up and down M.L.K. Boulevard begging."

Comphy reached down to gather his stained underwear but the elastic continued to unravel between his errand fingers. "Whoa, Mr. Jonathan! My goodies almost fell out and I ain't givin' no peep shows today."

Jonathan tried to defuse the situation. He tried to usher the intoxicated exhibitionist into the men's room. Comphy turned around sharply to lock eyes with his ardent critic. "Beggin'? Beggin'!" he shouted. "You won't ever have to worry about me beggin' for anything you got, Wrinkles!" After Comphy poked his tongue at the older lady, he amused himself in song. "Oh the girls, the girls, they love me."

The dollar worth of rotgut hooch he bought in the projects had him superbly lit. Jonathan felt partly responsible so he steered the man inside the restroom then feverishly collected various clothing items from the bank's lost and found box. Once the lobby emptied, Comphy was sent away to sleep it off.

Deidra stormed into the manager's office, pleading with Jonathan to get Comphy professional help. He vehemently objected. "You have to understand Deidra, Comphy is a flower. He needs the sunlight shining on him to survive. That's why he lives on the streets. He has assigned housing but he would rather sleep under the stars. It's just that simple."

"No Jonathan, it's not that simple," she countered. "I wish it was but it isn't. Remember when Comphy got beat up real bad by those kids for throwing rocks at passing cars? You know he gets on my last good nerve but we nearly lost him then, and there have been other close calls."

"I hear you Deidra but the last time someone tried to help Comphy for his own good, he ended up strapped to a table in the county mental ward. He tried to slit his wrists because he couldn't take being confined indoors. He's a flower, a flower."

Deidra stood back on her legs in opposition. "A flower? Oomph! More like a ragweed if you ask me."

"Well, no one asked you. And anyway, I couldn't do that to him. There are already more brothas behind bars than in college."

"Oh, and you think that fool belongs in college?" Deidra quipped. She threw her hands up then left the office in a huff.

TWENTY-FOUR

Bad Dreams and Evil Things

A man, yet another white one, in a charcoal gray business suit tapped on the glass doors with the keys to his Hummer. Jonathan walked over to the door and signaled with his hands that the bank was closed.

The man shouted, "I have an appointment with the manager. Would you please run and tell the man in charge that I am waiting."

Run and tell? Step and fetch was more like it. "I'm the manager here and I don't have an appointment scheduled," Jonathan shouted back. "You must be mistaken."

Due to security measures, none of the bank employees were allowed to open the front doors for anyone after closing hours unless they were known customers or expected guests of the manager. Jonathan continued exchanging shouts with the man outside until Tillman appeared beside him and casually unlocked the door.

"Mr. Lamar. I'm glad you could make it," welcomed Tillman.

"Outstanding facility," the man commented, with a heavy French accent. "I explained to this fellow that the manager was expecting me but I couldn't seem to communicate it properly."

Jonathan's eyes darkened with resentment. Hearing the Frenchman's comments infuriated him. He felt a sudden need to proclaim who, 'The Man' was but it was moot when Tillman and his dapper client withdrew to the locked commercial-lending office. Dejected, Jonathan collected his briefcase and suit coat then exited the building. He nearly stumbled over Comphy asleep in the parking lot.

"Hey soldier, wake up. Comphy, wake up."

"I'm not sleep," he barked, while rolling over and wiping a stream of saliva from his mouth. "I'm just getting a little rest."

"Hey, it's almost dark. I'm going home and think you should find another place to lay your head."

"I'm a rolling stone," Comphy offered proudly. "Where I lay my head is my home. That's how I roll." Because he had in fact managed to take care of himself despite his unconventional life-style, Jonathan started towards his Lexus thinking it best to leave well enough along. "Hey, Mr. Jonathan. Why 'you let that white fella come around here at night to look after the bank for you?" Comphy heckled. "I could do the job and I don't need no fancy white Cadillac to do it neither."

Jonathan was somewhat perplexed. "What white man Comphy? No one watches this place at night. You must have been drunk and seeing things."

"I see better when I'm drunk," he insisted. "What you talkin' bout. I see the same white man in the same fine white chariot every Monday and Thursday night, just like clockwork. He checks the inside for robbers and leaves with a hand full of those black eight-track tapes. Last week he dropped some aspirin and said I could keep 'em." Comphy paused to study the backside of his wrist as if hunting for a watch but he didn't own one. "Is today Thursday? Then he'll be here tonight."

Everything about Comphy's story seemed farfetched. With nothing else in his life making sense, Jonathan was tempted to inquire further. "What about the tapes, Comphy? You said something about some tapes."

"Yeah, those eight-track tapes y'all hide in that little room with all them TV's in it," he explained.

Realizing Comphy was talking about the video surveillance room filled with monitoring cameras and VHS tapes, Jonathan made a mental footnote but neglected to take the homeless man's accusations seriously. "Ok, ok Comphy. 'Next time you see this mystical white man in my bank, you tell him I said he's fired on the spot and to hand the keys over to you."

Comphy agreed that sounded like a plan he could live with. "That's just what I'll do! It's about time a black man caught a break. White folks always get the good jobs. That's just what I'll do."

Jonathan mulled over Comphy's ridiculous story on the way home before chalking it up to nonsense. "Some white man coming around the bank at night, in south Dallas," he thought aloud. "That's crazy."

Later that night, Marcus made himself cozy at the upstairs bar of Club Matrix. Ogling women clad in assortments of clingy dresses and snuggling skirts was his idea of a hot night on the town. "So, Jonathan, you ready to get yo' boogie on?" Marcus shouted, above the thumping music, while searching the busy dance floor for a potential victim. "Ahh man, look at that one backing that thang up against ole dude. The freaks really do come out at night."

"At two bucks a drink, it's no wonder this place is packed," Jonathan shouted back. "Since this was your idea, why don't you dip into your pocket and splurge. I could use about four dollars worth myself and some of these sistahs look to have a six to eight dollar head start."

"I'ma break a twenty-twin-twin and take somebody home tonight. You can bet on that. Wait a minute. That's Monique from the gym." Marcus pointed his finger at the young lady he'd embarrassed at the health club.

"Marcus, are you crazy or just plain stupid? You must have amnesia. That's the same babe you played to the left and I'm sure she's not going to let you forget it."

"Yeah I remember but you forget one thing. Once I get 'em, I got 'em!" he answered confidently. "She can't deny this here and I miss the way she wraps her feet around my head." Marcus slid both hands down the front of his pants, suggesting that women wanted the whole package. "Order me something cold, man, while I go over and get thangs heated up. If I remember correctly, it won't take long."

"Don't do that to yourself. Hey! Hey!"

Marcus darted off to chase Monique in the crowded nightspot. Jonathan did his best to discourage him from making a criminal mistake. Unfortunately, Marcus had his mind made to act a fool and he wasn't going to let anybody stand in his way of getting it done so Jonathan hailed the bartender's attention instead. As soon as he'd put in an order, the commotion started. All he could hear above the music was a chorus of high pitched squabbling.

"You must be out yo' mind if you think I have anything to say to you after what you pulled on me," Monique screamed, in Marcus' face. The DJ noticed the argument. He disrupted the song so he could get an ear full of Monique's tirade. "If you were the last man on earth, and I do mean the last, I wouldn't let you have another whiff of this pussy. And, don't try begging me neither 'cause it ain't gonna work this, Tiny!"

She stormed away, leaving Marcus in a cloud of humiliation in the middle of the dance floor. Over a hundred people stood around pointing at him and laughing. The worst part of it was his pitiful walk of shame all the way back to the bar. When he finally crossed the dance floor, Jonathan patted him on the shoulder.

"I tried to warn you bruh'. I know that Hell hath no fury like woman scorned but that's nothing compared to a sistah who's pissed."

"Jonathan, you hear that? She tried to loud talk me," Marcus mumbled. "All that wasn't even necessary, I was only tryin' to give her another shot." He turned up a twelve-ounce long neck bottle of beer and contemplated. The humiliation he'd served up to Monique came full circle and returned home just as ugly as when it left.

Marcus usually shelled out twenty dollars on liquor treats and by the night's end felt like his money was well spent. This time, he coaxed Jonathan into tying on a good one to help blow off some of his nine-to-five steam. While kicking up his heels on the dance floor, with one more than willing participant after the next, Jonathan caught a glimpse of someone who seemed familiar standing at the downstairs bar. The man Jonathan saw favored Brian Tillman but the dim club lighting and smoke filled haze obstructed his view. Another look confirmed his suspicions. It *was* Brian Tillman. Jonathan's strained attitude, saturated with several adult beverages presented an opportunity for tragedy. When he abandoned a woman on the dance floor to head downstairs on a wild tare, Marcus caught up to him as he reached the bottom of the winding staircase.

Marcus grabbed him by the arm. "Hey man! Hold on! What's got you so worked up? Hey! Where'r you goin'?" He'd never seen Jonathan appear so determined. "Here man, drink this and chill out." Marcus handed him a bottle of beer, blocked him from moving forward, then turned toward the bar area in search of the source of Jonathan's tension but he didn't spot anyone who looked out of place.

"I need to get somethin' off my chest," he snarled. Suddenly, Jonathan slammed the beer bottle down on a nearby table and shoved Marcus' thick frame aside as if he were made of paper. He started out for the bar again, where Tillman lounged with a man twice his size and a whole foot taller. Marcus threw both arms around Jonathan and spun him in the other direction.

"Another time brotha, another time. He's got his peeps with him tonight. That's his bodyguard."

Jonathan was confused. "Bodyguard? Who's got a bodyguard?"

Marcus recognized Tillman from another arena. "That's the X-Man, a drug dealer to high-end clientele. That's who you want to thump with?"

"Man, let me go." Jonathan shook free from his friend's hold. He'd heard Marcus clearly but the words didn't add up. "X-Man? You must be drunk or think I am. Naw, he's a banker not an ecstasy dealer. I work with his trifling ass down at the branch."

"Jonathan look, he's a known pusher but the narcotics squad hasn't been able to pen anything on him. He's got help on the inside but nobody knows who, yet. Maybe by day he's who you think he is or maybe you've got him mixed up with someone else. That dude over there is bad news and might not be the man you're after but I'd better get you home before you get somebody hurt, including me."

Once inside Jonathan's car, Marcus glided through the streets while an attractive woman, who he'd sweet talked on the way out of Club Matrix, followed closely behind them in his car. Jonathan had passed out along the way and had to be helped upstairs. After catching his breath, Marcus eased Jonathan's listless body down onto the sofa and threw a blanket on him. "You're on your own now, rookie. If you can't run with the big dogs, stay that ass on the porch." Marcus rushed back downstairs to take care of his own business, which waited patiently outside in the car.

Jonathan had sufficiently proved that he belonged on the porch. Two-dollar drink night was for serious elbow-benders, whether rumors regarding the club's watered down cocktails held merit or not. Either way, he drank more than he should have, motivated by a long day that hadn't cut him any breaks.

When Jonathan arrived at the bank, the tellers were busy counting their money drawers and preparing for the day. He sat his briefcase down and began to water the ivy plants in the office. As he parted the long vertical blinds, hanging against the window in his office, an old rusty van idled directly outside the bank's front door. The motor ran continuously, spewing thick exhaust from a shaky tailpipe. It occurred to Jonathan that there was something peculiar about the van sitting there before business hours but it was too late to investigate when things got out of hand.

Jonathan heard a blood curling scream as a hooded man worked feverishly to muffle Deidra's cries by holding his gloved hand over her mouth. Three other men, who also wore ski masks and para-military battle gear, sprinted toward the teller cage brandishing semi-automatic rifles. With precision timing, they fastened large metal hooks to the sides of the Plexiglas plate partition, which encased the tellers work area.

Jonathan ran from his office, helpless and concerned for the safety of his associates. "Everybody calm down. Hey you, let her go," he demanded. "Deidra, try to relax. All they want is the money. Nobody has to get hurt."

A fifth robber sauntered into the lobby as if there wasn't an ounce of urgency. He paused casually for a moment then motioned for his men to rip the two-inch thick glass partition down. Three of them tugged on the ropes and then ran toward the front door. When the slack from the long ropes stiffened, the large plate of glass fell onto the floor. Bank employees were amazed and disappointed at how easily it came down.

As the gunmen yelled for the tellers to empty the cash drawers and safes into the green trash bags they'd brought with them, Deidra issued orders to comply. "If y'all do like Jonathan says, we're all gonna be fine."

The bank-jackers acted like common crooks up to that point but after Deidra referred to the manager by name, the lead gunman trained his weapon on Jonathan. "Ahh yes, Jonathan Holloway," he said routinely, while in the distressed manager's direction. "Glad you could make it to our little soiree'." He removed his mask to reveal himself. When he did, Jonathan remembered seeing that face before but it was of no consequence when the gunman released the safety on his weapon and prepared to fire.

Jonathan dove for cover as the robber squeezed back on the trigger. Fiery bullets blasted from the gun. Fragments of exploding furniture flew in the air. Employees begged and screamed as the shooting continued. Several bullets blew chunks out of the walls. One of them caught Jonathan in the chest. Shrieks of terror echoed into the deadening silence as their manager laid flat and still, blood soaked clothes holding his chest together. His eyes opened slightly then fluttered faintly like a drowning man who'd lost the will to survive. Jonathan felt his lungs congesting with his own blood while it became increasingly more difficult to shuttle oxygen through them. Others looked on as he struggled through his final labored gasps for breath. When Jonathan sighed for the very last time, the room was void of sound. Jonathan's world had diminished into nothing more than still silence. Deidra trembled uncontrollably until her emotions forced her to turn away.

Suddenly, Jonathan sprang up clutching feverishly at his throat and chest. As the sun peeked over the horizon, he gasped for breath while climbing off his leather sofa. Jonathan had merely been dreaming. Regardless of how real it felt, he was relieved that it was only a terrible dream.

With widened eyes, Jonathan studied his surroundings as if he didn't know where he was. After having fallen asleep the night before, his sweat drenched party clothes took him back to something Ms. Harris told him when he was a child plagued with nightmares. She advised him that dreams were often times premonitions that spoke to troubled souls in order to protect them, sometimes from themselves. Jonathan's dream spoke loudly and said all the wrong things. It was too real, much too real to be ignored.

TWENTY-FIVE

Killers and Drug Dealers

The sun offered its customary hellos to another Friday morning, only on that particular day, Jonathan wasn't looking forward to the weekend. The previous night provided enough weekend flavored festivities to last him a while. One hell of a hangover constantly reminded him of that.

He showered, changed and took his time driving to the bank. Forgetting all the events from his vicious nightmare was a good start. But the odd story Comphy told him about some mystical white man in a Cadillac kept running through his mind unabated.

When Jonathan reached M.L.K. Blvd., a multitude of red and blue lights stopped him in his tracks. He couldn't help thinking that perhaps his dream was a premonition or things to come when his eyes found a white sheet covering what had to be a dead body resting on the bank's doorstep. Jonathan hoped it was a failed robbery gone awry without any of his employees getting injured in the progress.

While approaching the scene with reserved apprehensions, he asked the policeman standing over the corpse what happened.

"No big deal," the officer replied. "Just another homeless stiff got done in last night." He went back to reviewing the crime scene and scribbling notes on a hand size note pad.

Despite the pool of blood staining the entranceway, Jonathan's initial feelings mirrored the officer's indifference concerning the dead body until a homicide detective walked up and pulled the sheet back to get a look at the victim. Jonathan's heart skipped a beat after he saw the homeless stiff was Comphy. His remains rested in a puddle of deep crimson after enduring a tough life of daily struggles. Although Comphy lasted far longer than most of the city's throw-a-ways, that was no consolation to a dead man.

Jonathan figured Comphy's death was caused by a random act of violence until the uniform cop said different. "The victim's throat had been slashed deep enough so that his tongue could be pulled through the slit. It was an execution."

The lead detective agreed. "Back in Miami, I saw this sort of thing all the time. Drug dealers are notorious for this type of homicide. They call it a Columbian necktie. This poor fella' must've seen too much or had too much to tell. In either case, he sure did piss off the wrong people. Whatever secrets this guy knew, died with him. Case closed."

"Case closed?" Jonathan protested. "'You're telling me there'll be no investigation to find if anybody saw anything?"

The first officer smacked his lips and rolled his eyes. "Are you kidding me? In this neighborhood, nobody ever sees nothing, hears nothing... tells nothing. But you can see by the way the heavy blood trail leads from around the side of the building to here, the attack took place back there." The officer pointed toward the ATM while drawing a diagram of the bank to further exercise his theory.

The detective moved closer to Jonathan. "Hey, looky here," he exclaimed, like he'd just won a prize. "Check out this guy's hands. Yep, looks like this one went down swinging. And, he may have gotten some of his attacker's skin underneath his fingernails."

Hope returned to Jonathan's face. "Good, then you do have a lead?"

"I'm sorry but unless the killer checked himself into a hospital last night with deep lacerations and said, *hey I just got these cuts by doing somebody in over at the bank in south Dallas*, then this case is closed."

Jonathan told the officers Comphy's real name, Elsie Hart, and where to find his remaining articles. Unfortunately, they blew him off and were not shy about doing so. "Yeah, uh… we'll get right on that," was their sarcastic reply in return for his information. Perhaps they had seen too many dead vagrants to give Comphy special consideration.

Jonathan picked himself up and made his way inside the branch. He encountered several of the female employees sobbing. He contacted the Employee Assistance group, to come out and visit with his grief-stricken staff. Even though Comphy was a nuisance at times, he was somewhat of a fixture around the banking center and even more so in the community.

After the body had been taken away, Jonathan placed a call to Walter Delaney to inform him of what had taken place and to get clearance to close the bank temporarily. Delaney had already received word but neglected to tell Jonathan how or when. Instead, he asked his subordinate to hurry downtown and bring the surveillance tapes from the bank's security system.

In compliance with his boss's instructions, Jonathan entered the ATM room. He stopped the VCRs and collected all the taps from the previous night and some others that were dated two weeks prior to the murder. Jonathan's thoughts were clouded when transporting the tapes to corporate headquarters but at least bank officials appeared more interested in solving the murder than the Dallas Homicide detectives.

Filled with sorrow and remorse for not having taken Comphy seriously, Jonathan rode the elevator up to the forty-second floor. Lauren Stanton was waiting on him when the doors opened.

"Jonathan, don't get off. I need to talk to you," she said hurriedly. Her stern expression suggested that he not argue. Lauren shoved him back then stepped inside the elevator with him. After they descended, another young lady attempted to get on with them on the next floor but Lauren wouldn't allow it. "Sorry honey, this one's full. There will be others, trust me." The lady pouted in objection as the doors slammed shut.

"What's up Lauren?" Jonathan asked, once they were alone again.

She didn't answer until they stepped off on the basement level in the underground parking garage. "I need to fill you in before Delaney gets to you." Lauren crossed directly in front of Jonathan and locked eyes with his. "Remember when I told you Delaney and Morrell had it out in Delaney's office?"

"Yeah, so?"

"Well, this morning, when I got in around seven forty-five, the feathers were flying again. They shouted back and forth for over ten minutes behind closed doors so all I could make out was something about a murder at your branch. During the last part of it, Morrell was doing most of the talking, then they fought for another few minutes until Morrell stormed out and slammed the door. I overheard that weasel Delaney say he was washing his hands of the whole thing. He was terrified when he came out to get a drink from the water fountain. Shortly after that, you called in. I don't know what's going on but if I were you, I would put some serious consideration into finding another job or blowing town before whatever they're up to gets on you."

"I'll go right up and make Delaney come clean," Jonathan threatened.

"No, you have to play it smart. If you get rough with Delaney, they'll have you thrown out before you've gotten to the bottom of it. Promise me you'll keep your head."

Begrudgingly, Jonathan agreed and gave his word although his mind traveled so fast it was impossible to process all the information Lauren had just dropped in his lap. He needed time to sort it out. There was a lot to consider and too many pieces of the puzzle were missing to get a clear picture of what was happening, a puzzle involving him. Jonathan assumed the fight between Delaney and Morrell had to be over negative publicity the murder was sure to bring, once the news hit the streets but that was merely speculation.

During the elevator ride up, Lauren got off on the lobby level and headed for the snack shop. Jonathan waved goodbye but his mind traveled to several places at once. He'd forgotten to push the button for the forty-second floor and ended up on fifty-seven instead. When the doors opened, he was confused until it occurred to him that he was on the executive dinning floor. He spotted George Morrell and Brian Tillman having breakfast after ten o'clock. They acknowledged him with dual head nods and matching devilish grins, as if they expected him to appear. The doors closed quickly but it seemed like an eternity for Jonathan. Those two were apparently up to something and very cavalier about it.

Once on the correct floor, Jonathan headed for the row of executive offices. Delaney paced back and forth inside of his. Not like a ferocious jungle cat but more like a scared antelope moments before a ravenous lion snapped his scrawny neck.

Still shaken by his previous encounter when Jonathan entered without knocking, Delaney sat down behind his desk. He offered his visitor to do likewise. "Thanks for coming Jonathan. Have a seat."

"Walter, you wanted me to bring these tapes?" He held up a bag with six tapes wrapped inside it. "On the way over I had time to think. Do you want to know what I believe is on them?"

Delaney sat quietly for a moment with a blank expression. "I'm not certain but maybe a murder Jonathan," he mumbled somberly. "Maybe a murder."

Shocked by Comphy's death, Jonathan didn't initially think of the ATM surveillance cameras capturing the incident on film. When it dawned on him that Delaney was demanding potentially rock-solid evidence, he popped to his feet. "I've got to get these to the police right away."

Delaney summoned him back. "Jonathan, wait! Please come over here and sit back down. Thank you. Now listen to me carefully." Beads of sweat mounted on his balding head. "You don't know what's on those tapes and neither do I but before you take them anywhere you need to think about the serious repercussions."

Now even more suspicious of Delaney's true motives to control the investigation, Jonathan lost it. Without warning he catapulted himself out of the chair and dismissed the promise he'd made to Lauren about remaining calm. "So that's it? You've got something to do with the killing? Is it you on these tapes? I wouldn't have pegged you for a cold-blooded killer."

Delaney stood from his chair. He hurried over and placed both hands on Jonathan's shoulders. "Don't do this Jonathan!" his shaky voice bellowed. "Don't got mixed up in this and take it to the next level. These people are treacherous!"

A peculiar smile hung on Jonathan's face. "These people? What people?" Jonathan challenged. "Huh, what people Walter?' he grunted at Delaney and snatched him up by the collar. "Yeah, I know how to shake it out of you. My friend was murdered on the front door of my banking center. I figure that mixes me up in it pretty good." He grabbed Delaney's arms and begun feeling them up to his shoulders while his accusations came out as loud powerful rants. "Where did he scratch you Walter, huh? On the arms, huh? On the chest?"

Walter Delaney feared retribution. Jonathan's large stature dwarfed his much smaller boss when he pinned him to the desk. Delaney panicked and wailed. His stubby arms flailed wildly. "It wasn't me! It wasn't me! I didn't do it. It was…" The brief skirmish ended abruptly when Delaney's door flew open with Morrell and Lauren gawking in from outside the office. They saved the contemptible regional manager from the beating of his life. Jonathan hadn't killed a man before but the rage coursing through his veins could have easily changed that with a few blows from his bare hands.

Eventually, Jonathan backed off. Delaney climbed off the desk and straightened out his wrinkled clothing. He was bewildered by what almost happened to him yet he offered advice while Jonathan collected the tapes. "Jonathan, this is big. Too big for you to get involved in. Don't fight a battle you can't win!" he pleaded. "I'm begging you. Let it go. They'll win. They always do."

Jonathan heard Delaney cackling then rendered his own advice to everyone in general. "If you think I'm going to let this go, you've got another thing coming. You bet against me and you're gonna lose." He turned to stare down Morrell before pushing his way past the man whom he suspected of playing a part behind the scenes. When he refused to move aside for Jonathan's passage, the velocity nearly toppled Morrell, who grimaced and clutched his arm after having been slammed against the door frame. Lauren wisely retreated to her desk to escape the enduing aftershock as Morrell floundered into Delaney's office and closed the door behind him.

Morrell calmly antagonized the unglued executive banker. "I thought you said you could handle him Walter."

Delaney sniffled and mist up around the eyes before he could respond. "That was before I knew there'd be killing. I didn't sign up for this. If the damned company wants to do creative financing that's one thing but murder and drugs. Why did you have to go and kill the homeless man, George? He was mentally ill for God sake. He couldn't have interrupted your operation."

"I had to shut him up," Morrell snapped angrily. His wrath was so naked, it startled Delaney. "That idiot remembered seeing me taking the video tapes from the branch without notifying Holloway then the fool demanded my keys. Can you believe that? When I didn't hand them over, he tried to bite me and I…" Morrell laughed with dizzying amusement despite his throbbing arm. "I did the old bum a favor. I put him out of his misery."

Delaney shook his head, fearing what might come next in the way of a reprisal, either from Jonathan or the police, who were sure to come sniffing around sooner or later. Delaney knew that Jonathan was relentless in helping people from his community and Morrell would stop at nothing to ensure the success of his synthetic drug program. An irresistible force was heading toward a collision with an immovable object. A big bang was inevitable.

"I was afraid if Jonathan caught on, no amount of money or company perks would keep him quiet," Delaney contended, with his head drooping down.

The ASFB top security officer leaned back to settle against the leather chair. He gazed beyond Walter Delaney to observe the Dallas skyline through the large window. "Well, we tried to do it nice and quietly but the old fashion way works just as good. There's nothing like a nigger out of his place to agitate things, no offense. But then you're not really black are you Walter? As I recall, you sold out a long time ago. Hell, I guess awards and money doesn't buy nearly as much as it used to, huh?"

Delaney was more ashamed than angered by Morrell's comments because there was some truth in what he'd said. Delaney's lack of support to the black community and other African Americans working within the company was well-documented and common knowledge on the streets. After he sank to his chair, recalling the conversation he'd overheard between Morrell and Tillman on the night of the banquet, Delaney was sorry not to have warned Jonathan when the chance first presented itself. "So that's why you fixed the award?" his soft voice muttered to Morrell. "I could have told you before all this got started that money wouldn't manipulate Jonathan. He's not like us."

Morrell's tired expression soured. "What the hell's gotten into you?"

"I want out. That's all there is to it. I'm not cut out for this and I know things will get a lot worse before you're finished."

"You're a part of this whether you like it or not. For once in your life have a backbone and see something through. There's no way to straddle the fence on this one. Either you're with us or against us, an asset or a liability. Which will it be, Walter?"

Walter Delaney had heard of people getting in Morrell's way, some of them later showed up on the front page, framed inside a white chalk line on the ground. Comphy got in Morrell's and caught the same fate. Delaney didn't want to follow suite and become the next victim.

"Just stay calm," Morrell told him. "Holloway doesn't know about the bank's agreement to sponsor my drug campaign but it won't matter in a couple of days."

"Whuuut about the tapes? Jonathan took them," Delaney Whined.

"Don't concern yourself with that,' Morrell suggested. "I'll clean up this little mess, my way. If money and prestige aren't motivators for our unscrupulous Mr. Holloway, then I'll just have to find out what are. There's something he cares about. There's always something men don't want to lose." Morrell had the presence of mind to doctor the tapes. That's why he left them at the scene. If the murderer had taken them after the attack on Comphy, it would have smelled of an inside job. When Morrell exited the office, he warned Lauren to forget all that she had seen and heard. The ferocious manner in which his directives came across, convinced her to do just that.

Jonathan drove aimlessly around the city for hours until Deidra reached him on his cellular phone. "Jonathan, some police detectives were looking for you. They were asking for the tapes from the surveillance cameras."

"The tapes? Oh, oh yeah, the tapes. I'm on my way to the police station now. There's someone I need to speak with before I hand these tapes over to anybody. I'll get with you later. And Deidra, be careful." He drove to the southwest police precinct, where he'd spent numerous days, detained as a juvenile offender. Sergeant Rideau, the white office, who derailed Jonathan's one-way ticket to Harmsway as a mad-at-the-world youth, stood at the information desk. "Hey there, it's Jon-Jon Holloway. Put 'er there, podner." They shook firmly like old friends. "You haven't been around here in a month of Sunday's but it's good to see ya. 'Looks like you're stayin' in shape too. 'Been hitting the heavy bag?"

"Nah, I haven't been in a boxing gym in years but thanks though," Jonathan answered, quietly. His disturbed demeanor went unnoticed.

"Fifteen years later, but I can still see those iron fists of yours blazing away like it was yesterday. Old times eh? You were really somethin' special, kid. 'Could've gone all the way if you had half a mind ta." The sergeant pulled a cotton handkerchief from his back pocket when reminiscing over old times overwhelmed him. He stared at the trophy case behind Jonathan. "That National Championship Cup is the pride of the department but you can take it home any time you want, you know that. We had some good fighters since you but none of 'em had the raw talent or your passion for knocking their opponent silly every time they set foot in the ring."

"Nah Sergeant, you keep it. Besides, this is where it belongs." Jonathan refused just as he did each time the old police officer got too emotional and offered it to him. They went through the same ritual whenever Jonathan stopped by to visit. He came to understand that the championship cup meant so much to Rideau because it reaffirmed that all the work he'd put into helping countless boys, with too much anger to contain, stay out of prison. The well-deserving cop had earned the right to come to work and have a constant reminder staring him in the face that his life meant something to a lot of grateful people.

Rideau was a master at sensing when someone was in trouble. And after he'd wiped his eyes, he saw a restless man standing before him. "Hey hotshot banker, whut did cha' get another speeding ticket you want me to take care of?"

"It's not that simple this time. A friend of mine got himself killed at the bank last night."

The Sergeant appeared puzzled. "I didn't hear about no robbery."

Jonathan explained what occurred then asked where he might find detectives Orangello and Caffey, the names that two men had given Deidra when they came for the VHS tapes. The chunky officer shook his head and regretfully informed Jonathan that someone was up to no good. "Jon-Jon, I wish I could help ya but detectives Orange Jell-O and Coffee are made-up names cops used in the old days when they were moonlighting for extra money off the clock. Someone's pulling your chain."

"Orangello and Coffee," Jonathan repeated slowly. "Yeah, I guess someone's trying to put one over on me." Now that he knew someone sent two men to pose as cops looking to get the tapes, he assumed it had to be someone other than Morrell and Delaney because they were with him when the fake detectives called on Deidra. Brian Tillman was as good a place to start as any after Jonathan reasoned his banking center nemesis had to be mixed up with Delaney. "Sarge, I'm getting a bad feeling about this. I need you to run a name for me. Try Tillman. First name Brian. That's Tillman. Two L's. Yeah, just like it sounds."

The officer typed the name into the computer to initiate a quick search. He came up empty. "Sorry, Champ. Nothing's coming up. No priors. Nothing at all. Not even a summons. Looks like you've got the wrong guy. This Tillman's clean as a whistle." Sergeant Rideau duplicated his efforts on Walter Delaney. Again nothing. Two pitches, two strikes. Jonathan figured a man like Morrell must have gotten caught doing something outside the lines in his past. Men with power often do took risks that came back to bite them when they least expected it. "I might be wasting your time but try this last one for me. George Morrell. That's two R's, two L's."

When Rideau heard the name, his eyes narrowed. He recalled what he knew about the man he remembered from long ago. "M O R R E L L. George Morrell! Jon-Jon, I don't have to wait until that name comes up. I can tell ya anythin' you want to know about that snake. They don't make many like him. Morrell's long history of illegal interrogations and racketeering got him booted out of the FBI. He even killed a man in his custody once, beat him to death with a telephone book while he was cuffed. Morrell said it was self-defense. I say he's bad news. Even heard he was a freelance arms dealer for a while, for our side and theirs. He's got no conscience. A real bad seed."

Jonathan couldn't disguise his surprise when he heard Morrell's track record and couldn't understand how a man like that could become a top level security advisor for a national bank. It took a thief to catch a thief, he surmised although ASFB had to know they were taking a chance crawling into bed with him. Jonathan hadn't planned on going up against a suspected murderer with ties to overseas terrorists. A man willing to betray his own country was dangerous and capable of most anything. In order to survive, Jonathan had to become equally dangerous.

TWENTY-SIX

Jail Time and Chalk Lines

Before Jonathan left the police station, his old friend cautioned him. "Don't you go gettin' tangled up with the likes of him. He's a heartless animal who has killed before and wouldn't think twice about takin' a man's life. We'd all be better served if someone put him in the ground. But until that happens, you steer clear of him like your life depended on it 'cause it just might."

Jonathan acknowledged Rideau's warning then headed back to the bank. When he arrived there, the property management's cleaning crew had removed all signs of a vicious slaying. It was as if Comphy's murder never happened but Jonathan would never forget him lying there with his still, lifeless, body traced by crime scene chalk.

"It's been crazy around here all day with people calling and stopping by," Deidra said wearily. "And those detectives said they planned on coming back. Those cops seemed serious about getting their hands on those tapes too."

Jonathan filled Deidra in on what Sergeant Rideau told him about Morrell and the others. Her startled expression was haunting. The idea of men impersonating cops was terrifying by itself, speculation that they were off duty officers doing the bidding for someone else was frightening. But Jonathan was too mad to be scared as his frustration swelled. If someone wanted the tapes back badly enough to come after him, Jonathan decided to invite his Muslim associates to the party. He paid Minister Muhammad a visit on his way home so they could view the tapes from the bank together.

He traveled to the Dallas Mosque, where the Minister was very interested in hearing about the day's activities. Jonathan told him all that transpired, leaving nothing out. Captain Darius X and Reggie Brown were called in along with other members of the nation's security force, The Fruit of Islam. Jonathan recapped the events for the men. They immediately carved out plans for his own safety.

The entire consortium traveled to Jonathan's new apartment. At the Minister's behest, Captain Darius brought along their high-tech equipment again for another clean sweep of the place. Jonathan popped in the VHS tape recorded on Thursday night, the evening of Comphy's death. It was rolling but didn't substantiate any evidence of a murder. However, the Minister noticed something odd. Jonathan's big scene showed the Minister as he approached the machine, accompanied by a guard. He inserted his card, placed the receipt in his checkbook then turned and walked way. That same transaction appeared three times within a thirty-minute sequence, down to the second. In addition, the Minister insisted that he'd stopped by the bank on the previous night and still had the receipt to prove it. Not only was it proof the videotape had been doctored but someone went out of their way to set him up as a prime suspect. He was fuming because that tape could have implicated him for being at the crime scene around the victim's time of Comphy's death.

After viewing the other five tapes, Reggie noticed how the same three men carried identical briefcases. They continually entered the bank after it was closed for business. "They act more like drug dealers than businessmen if you ask me," Reggie suggested. "And I should know. I'm willing to bet my life they've got gravity to sell, something that'll bring brothas down even further." That reminded Jonathan of Marcus' accusations of Tillman's drug distribution.

"So, that's why he had a bodyguard in the club that night," Jonathan thoughts aloud. "I guess I didn't want to believe it. More drugs coming in here, to my neighborhood? And, through my own damned bank. I can't go out like that. They brought whatever junk they're peddling to the wrong backyard. Somebody's gonna pay. I guarantee it. Somebody's gonna pay." Jonathan was amazed after processing the notion of pumping drugs into the community through his branch. However circumstantial the evidence, it was stacking up fast.

As ordered, the Minister's men searched every inch of the apartment. One of the Muslims found a listening device and a miniature video camera in the large common area they were meeting in. The entire conversation about the tapes had been recorded.

"Brotha Jonathan. You have to leave this place," Captain Darius alarmed. "They're sure to come after you if they think you're on to them or getting to close to the truth. Those hoodlums who took out that homeless man wouldn't have no problems getting next to you in order to keep their drug thing going good in the hood."

Jonathan knew right away who had the capability and motive to bait his home with covert devices. If he'd lacked just cause before, an inexcusable invasion of privacy gave him more than he needed. Morrell had violated his home and retribution was owed.

Jonathan stood up and marched over to the small camera, hidden behind a West Indian voodoo mask hanging on the wall. "Show's over!" he announced adamantly, before snatching the wires out of it.

In the upstairs business office of White Sands Upholstery, George Morrell cursed as the surveillance camera he planted in Jonathan's apartment blacked out. He'd hoped to peek in on Jonathan and stay one step ahead of him. In utter disbelief that everything he had worked three years to set in motion was coming undone because of an unrelenting branch manager. Morrell let out a thunderous growl before hurling a stapler through the large office window. "Webley!" he summoned, "there has been a change of plans. You'll have to break down the entire system for mobilization at a moment's notice. I have to exterminate a very annoying pest. It seems that our little fly in the ointment has decided to invite a few party crashers. Niggers and flies I do despise but I goddam hate Muslim cockroaches." Morrell grimaced while rubbing his sore arm. Slowly, he unbuttoned his white oxford shirt which had accumulated bloodstains on the right sleeve. He replaced it with one that was clean and pressed. "And get Tillman on the phone. Tell him to prepare to liquidate all the assets, if necessary. He'll know what to do. Our L.A. connection is standing by to move money if need be."

Back at the apartment, the Muslim Security Captain quickly rewired the small camera to the Mosque security room. From that point on, anyone who crossed through Jonathan's living room would be picked up by the miniature wide-lens camera.

"Let that be a lesson to you," the Minister suggested, "beware of Greeks baring gifts, or any other white folks for that matter." He also shared his thoughts for shaking up things to bring about a desired outcome. "When a wise man desires to bag a serpent in the bush, he must first seek to flush it out into the open. Never go to war with something that deadly on its terms. We could entice that snake to come out for something it values or we could cast an imposing shadow and convince it there's another venomous animal wishing to impede on its turf. Either will do. Greed and domination, my brothas, both will entice the heart of a serpent. You can count on that."

The men sat around the spacious room mapping out a game plan to snare the man who had the gall to wire Jonathan's home. Reggie and Jonathan utilized the equipment left by the Minister's crew to place sensors at the apartment entrances. Jonathan paged Marcus and waited for the call to be returned. He was so twisted by visions of murder, drugs, Tillman, Morrell, Delaney and unrivaled deception that he didn't hear the telephone when it rang. "Jonathan… Jonathan!" Reggie yelled, from the adjoining room. "You gon' get that? It's the phone!"

"Oh, I got it. Hello. Yeah Marcus, thanks for getting back to me. No, nothing pressing yet but we need to know how many snakes we're dealing with. I'm all right but the good brothas found a listening bug and spy cam in my living room. Yeah man, in my own house. They've been walking the dog all along."

Marcus had seen his share of dastardly deeds in the streets to believe that criminals were often capable of anything they put a mind to. "The kind of people you're about to get with ain't concerned about who they have to setup or take down to keep the money rolling nor are they concerned about how far they've got to go to get it done. That's the same way we got to come at this."

"I never thought I'd be putting myself in a position to kill a man but it looks like things are beginning to boil," Jonathan said evenly.

"They killed your friend Comphy for whatever reason. They took him out. Maybe he knew something, maybe not but they really did a number on him too. The autopsy indicated a foreign toxic substance in his digestive system, which would have killed him sooner or later anyway. That's right, poison. The same stuff they've been finding in dead inmates that nobody's supposed to know about," Marcus revealed.

"Harmsway?" said Jonathan, as calmly as his own name.

"Yeah, how'd you know that?" Marcus asked suspiciously.

"A little bird told me, one who just flew the coop."

"I'll tell you something I bet you didn't know. The medical examiner found extreme trauma to Comphy's genitals. Skin on his penis was scarred and severely damaged. And I'm sorry to be the one to tell you this but he's not the only one to turn up like that at the morgue. Theo Manus is down here too."

"Tee-Man?" was the only thing Jonathan could say. It was his childhood friend that never seemed to grow up or kick his appetite for illegal substances. Closing his eyes to lend way for a silent prayer, Jonathan felt that those who wanted to control him had taken personal steps to break his spirit while getting at people in his inner circle.

"There were several others over the past two to three weeks," Marcus continued. "I'm not liking this at all. It has all the markings of an epidemic. Before you know it, there'll be hundreds of bodies stacking up and city officials don't have a clue what's causing it. From what I hear, compared to the toxic chemical content, it makes crack cocaine look like aspirin."

"Aspirin?" Jonathan repeated with great resolve. "That's it! That's what Comphy said that night before he died, that some white man in a Cadillac was taking videos from the branch. He also told me the man dropped some aspirin and Comphy kept them. Damn Marcus, he tried to warn me but I didn't listen to him. I couldn't make sense of it. Just figured he'd been hallucinating again. Hell, the last time he had an episode it was ten-foot spiders." Jonathan felt terrible that he hadn't earnestly considered what the dead man said but Marcus helped to keep things in perspective.

"Listen man. Don't go getting all bent about not taking him seriously. I know he was a regular down at the bank but he was also a career drunk. He wasn't that reliable. Think about it. You can't change what's happened but we can step to it and stop this madness before it does become an epidemic. And, you know where is it'll hit the hardest. When America catches a cold, people in the hood come down with the flu."

"Yeah, in the heart of our community too," Jonathan answered. "Hey Marcus, thanks. It might take a couple of days before the snakes start to get a little jumpy so I'll need you to be on standby, in case it kicks off sooner."

"I'll be there for you Jonathan, believe that," Marcus asserted. "I'm pulling a double shift tonight so hit me on the hip if there's trouble. Page me, code 007 and I'll know it's you. All right then. Keep your head up and eyes opened." Parenthetically, his beat was patrolling the underground streets beneath the downtown district, which was a few blocks away from Jonathan's apartment.

The newscast came over the television while Jonathan and Reggie prepared sandwiches and other snacks for what could have possibly been a long night. The slim female news announcer, who looked as if she was dipped in foundation makeup, came on the screen with the shocking lead-in story.

"In this evening's news, American South Financial Bank's bids good bye to regional manager Walter Delaney, who was discovered by a cleaning lady today in his Highland Park home, hanged to death. Details are sketchy at this time but evidence suggests it was a suicide although no known note has been found."

The well-dressed anchorman took over the next story. "In world news tonight, the French government has its hands full as it attempts to regulate the sale of a new age sex drug, Sextine Unitral or commonly referred to as Sex Units. The bio-synthetic designer drug is said to be safe if used as directed but many knock off imposter drugs are being chemically fabricated and distributed without proper research, testing, of clearance from France's Pharmaceutical Board, the equivalent of America's FDA. Some ingredients in the imposter street drugs have been prone to cause irreversible nerve damage and neurosis."

Reggie matched Jonathan's bewildered expression with one of his own, acknowledging they both realized what the motivation was behind the bodies piling up at the morgue with contusions on the users' genitals. There was an untapped market in the U.S. for powerfully addictive drugs that constituted a period of euphoria while simultaneously increasing the user's sex drive, imagination and stamina. ASFB had allowed Morrell to test a new designer party pill in the south Dallas community when it hadn't been FDA approved.

Jonathan loaded two handguns which had been locked away in his downstairs storage area. When he offered Reggie a loaded weapon, the ex-con regrettably declined. "Nah brotha', I can't be caught with a loaded gat. I'm a felon on parole. If I get busted with that peacemaker, they'll put me in a death grip and I ain't doing twenty-five to life for nobody." Jonathan understood Reggie's decision to roll with a less lethal weapon. "But, I will get me some of this here Louisville Sluggah'," he declared, while taking a full swing with the wooden baseball bat.

TWENTY-SEVEN

Demons and The Dope Man

As Reggie stepped up for batting practice, the telephone rang. Denise was on the line calling from Oakland. She had been going through withdrawals since returning home after having been joined at the hip with Jonathan while in Dallas.

"Jonathan, I'm sorry but I'm finding it harder to stay away any longer. Now, don't say anything. Just listen. I can't think about anything else but you. I'm not productive here and I feel so empty. I need to see your face, Jonathan, and feel you next to me. I know what we said but I need some reassurance. What I really need is you."

Jonathan was pleased to hear her voice and the excitement wrapped up in it but he was fittingly apprehensive about having her in town when something bad was about to go down. "Sweetheart, I'm missing you too but now is not the time. Trust me, please. There's too much going on and I can't have you caught up in it, Denise. Its better this way and it'll soon be over and done with."

"Then tell me what's going on," Denise insisted. "At least I'd feel better about whatever it is that's got you all tied up all of a sudden. Jonathan, you can't keep me in the dark like this. It's not fair. I care for you too much not to know what's gotten you acting out of pocket."

Jonathan wanted to share what peril awaited just around the corner but his better judgment prevailed. There was no way Denise could have been prepared for the murder and mayhem that had taken place since the last time she shared his warm embrace. So many variables had changed. "Denise, baby... you must know how I feel about you, about us. But, I can't explain it to you right now and I need to be going. Promise me that you'll wait until I call and tell you that's everything has been settled. It might take a few days."

"A few days?" she objected adamantly. "Jonathan, what could be so important that it'll take that long to handle? Honey, you're scaring me. I don't like this, not at all. You've been open since we met and now you pull this few-days-stuff on me."

"I'm sorry but it's got to be this way. Baby, I need to go. Just try to understand that I have to handle something very important that can't wait."

Denise couldn't let it go nor could she promise him she would stay away. She became more insistent on knowing what had him so distant and evasive. "Jonathan, if you're not going to tell me what it is, at least you could ease my troubled mind. Tell me if you've found another woman to take my place. I can handle that, I'm a big girl." She was sensing the heaviness weighing on the man she'd quickly learned to love. The aching between her legs had worked its way up to her heart. The sister had it bad. Even worse, it had her too.

After a failed attempt to end the phone call, Jonathan tried to satisfy Denise's last request. "Another woman? No, it's nothing like that. You're the only woman I'll ever need, the only one I'll ever want. Remember that. I'll contact you in a few days, ok?" Denise held the phone in silence, still pouting on the other end. "Denise, are you there?"

"Uh-huh… I'm here," she answered quietly.

"Question. Do you believe in me?"

After another long bout of silence, a soft voice replied, "Yesss, I do." Jonathan placed the phone in its cradle then laid his pager down next to it. Just his luck, it would have gone off at the worst possible time and gotten a lot of good people killed.

When Denise finally managed to lower the receiver from her ear, she walked the floors of her upscale penthouse until she decided to get a second opinion regarding her impending dilemma. Her girlfriend Angie answered the call on the first ring.

"What's going on, are we still shopping tomorrow?" she belted out in one breath. "Gucci-West is having a mark down sale on all shoes from a model showing last week in Paris or somewheres."

Denise passed on the invitation to power shop. Instead, she assessed the situation that hijacked her joy and kept her away from Jonathan. She had found her knight in shining armor who had openly shared his fears as well as his hopes and dreams until suddenly slamming the door shut to all of his personal affairs. "Why is this happening to me?" Denise cried.

Angie took a more intricate approach and sorted out the details. "Lemme get this straight. That fine man says he misses you and wants to see you? And, you feel the same about him too? But, he's been distant and vague about what's keeping him so busy? And, he wants you to come to him but he wants you to wait until he can straighten something out? Uh-huh. I'm sorry to be the bearer of bad news so don't shoot the messenger, but it sounds like he's got someone else giving up the booty he's not getting from you."

Denise immediately objected to her friend's twisted rationale. "Angie, he loves me and cares for me. I can't see him getting with anyone else. He's not like most brothas. There must be some other reason he doesn't want me there. Maybe he's just been real busy with work. I don't know anymore but the last couple of weeks... just weird."

Angie saw fit to express her philosophy about men and their priorities. "Dee, I would give my right arm to see you happy, you know that. You deserve it more than anyone I know, except me maybe, but the truth is a man can be extremely preoccupied with whut-ever but don't nothing beat out sex. If he isn't gettin' it from you... Well, you know he's still gettin' it. Let's be real about this. Sex only comes second to sleep and sometimes not even then."

There was a pause in the conversation while Denise deliberated. True enough, Angie wanted Denise to be happy but she was limited to drawing from her own past experiences. It just so happened that her personal experiences involved too many men who couldn't be trusted.

The stars must have shifted because Angie had an epiphany. Her hope for that often time mystical, 'Call me when you get home, in the morning, when you get settled at the job, then we'll do lunch, and I need to see you tonight,' kind of love was restored. Her fantasy of finding *Mr. Be Good to Me, Be Good for Me,* still existed after all and somehow superseded her usual pessimistic belief that all boy-girl relationships were train wrecks just waiting to happen. Subsequently, she encouraged Denise to hold firmly to her shot at real love.

"Dee, I may be wrong about this Jonathan of yours and maybe my faith has been shaken a bit by what I've gone through." She fought back tears before she could go on. "But... if he is the one brotha who can keep his pants up when his woman ain't around then you need to know that too. Do yourself a favor and go to him. Hell, do *me* a favor and go to him. You tell him that you came to help, to be with him, and be there for him. You are every woman. Remember that."

As Denise wiped her eyes, she thanked her confidant. "I knew I could count on you. He doesn't know it yet but he does need me. Just like I need him. To hell with a few days, I'm on my way to Texas. You're the best, Angie."

Denise gathered her things and left on the whimsical advice of her dearest friend. She tossed lingerie and personal necessities into a small tote bag, thinking she'd improvise on anything else she needed once she arrived. Before she talked herself out of it, Denise was on the next Dallas-bound plane to be with the man she loved.

Back in Dallas, the Muslims worked out the Minister's plan to perfection. They hit the nightclubs to spread some juicy rumors on Jonathan's behalf. Some of them hung around glitter filled dance halls in Oak Cliff while others lurked near the hot spots on the north side of town. Each of them posed as representatives for a high roller looking to move some major weight for a rising star in the drug trade, who was rumored to have a vault full of illegal party favors. Their mission was to shake enough bushes until the right snake heard rumblings of stiff competition. Within a couple of hours, their scheme came off without a hitch.

Later that night, one of the Minister's men was relieving himself in the restroom of Club Matrix. Brian Tillman stepped up to the urinal next to the young man and casually struck up a conversation. "What's up playa'?" Tillman saluted. He sniffled continually while wiping at his nose with the free hand. His cool street attitude was a direct contradiction to his expensive Brooks Bothers suit. "I heard you know who can get some primo blow at a good price, if a man was interested that is."

The Muslim recognized that snake right off, from the photo Jonathan provided. "Yeah, you heard right. Who's askin'?"

"If the price is right, I'm askin'. The name's Smith, John Smith." Tillman didn't want to alarm Jonathan's people if the rumors of him entering the game were true. "Who you representing?"

The Muslim replied that he'd rather finish up his business then talk over business at the washbasins. "Holloway's the man now. He's got the kite. A bank vault full of it, so you know the price is right. If you're serious, I'll set it up and you can look over the goods."

Tillman's was seething. "A bank vault full, huh? Well, I've got the money so let's do this. Where's the meet?"

"Not far, not far at all. What time you want to do this?"

"One thing before we move forward. This Holloway, he's a short bald guy, right?" Tillman asked sheepishly. "I think I know him."

"You've got it twisted, Money. He's a tall GQ smoove type. He talks the talk while walking the walk."

Now Tillman could barely contain his temper. "My bad. I must have been thinking of some other Jonathan Holloway but that's cool." When Tillman slipped up and said Jonathan's first name, the young Muslim knew the snake had taken the bait. Tillman gave his husky bodyguard a quick wink and a nod. "Yeah, I'm in but I need to deal with the head guy, this Holloway. And to answer your question, I'm serious as a whole in the head."

After the young man finished washing his hands, Tillman handed over his compact cellular phone to the black man who was headed toward a pay phone with a pocket full of loose change. "Thanks man," he said, taking out Jonathan's business card with his home number written on the back of it.

Jonathan answered on the first ring and agreed to make the deal at four o'clock that morning. The Muslim middleman complied with the instructions given to him then ended the call. As he handed the tiny cell phone back to Tillman, he handed over the business card with Jonathan's bank information printed on the other side. "This is the address. Four o'clock sharp and don't be late. Mr. Holloway don't play when it come to money. You'll be sorry if you don't show."

"Oh, you don't have to worry about that," Tillman assured him, with a tightly knitted smirk. "I'll be there. Yeah, I'll be there all right."

After the trap was set, the young Muslim marched back to the bar area where his contemporaries stalked about. He held up his left hand, like a crossing guard, to signal the others in his crew. Without hesitation, the other three men filed out of the club expediently, in military fashion. They had successfully accomplished what they were sent there to do.

Tillman walked laps around the men's room floor voicing frustrations to his paid muscle standing guard near the entrance. "I can't believe that black bastard. Jonathan Holloway's stealing from me. Me! And, from right under my own nose." He shuddered at the thought of someone going through his pockets, especially Jonathan. "So, that do-gooder act he's been running all these years was a front. He ain't nothing but a back-stabbing thief." Tillman rolled a small glass cylinder between his fingers, twisted off the top and dabbed a healthy portion of a white powder onto the back of his left hand. In one quick whiff, he snorted the entire mound and threw his head back before devising a plan of his own. "If he's gonna make a major move, he'll have to enter the vault, my vault, break into the deposit boxes and package up *my* dope. I can't believe I'm saying this. He's gonna try and sell me my own blow. Well, that homeboy has another thing coming. I can wait to slap his uppity-black-ass back into his place."

Although it appeared that he'd stumbled on Jonathan's ploy to rob him, Tillman still found it hard to believe the information he'd been fed about Jonathan being a big-time dealer, so he pushed redial to settle any doubts. Just as it had moments before, Jonathan's phone rang. And just as he'd done before, he answered it on the first ring.

"Yeah, this is Jonathan," he said, not expecting a response from the caller. He smiled to himself thinking how stupid Tillman was for using his personal cell phone. "Hell-o?" When the line dropped off, Jonathan was sure Tillman would show up at the bank and get what he had coming to him.

After Tillman recognized Jonathan's voice, he hung up quickly and smashed his fist against the wall mirror. He shook with pain while pulling a handkerchief from his jacket pocket to wrap his bleeding hand. While looking at the splatters of blood on his new suit, he acknowledged Jonathan's tenacity. "That spook's got balls, Fred. You gotta give him that. Sellin' my product, out of my office!"

Tillman's hired help flashed a long switchblade knife. "Too bad we gotta cut 'em off though," Fred decided. "Hey, boss. When are you gonna tell Mr. Morrell about this?"

"No, this one's all mine. Morrell has enough to worry about. Plus, he doesn't know about my side hustle. It's better that he's kept in the dark about this." Tillman flashed Fred a sinister smile as they exited the washroom. "I want to catch Jonathan Holloway with his pants down so I can pump a few hot slugs up his ass."

TWENTY-EIGHT

My Pocket Got the Mumps

Inside of the bank was as dark as an autumn night. Tillman and his rugged thug entered with flashlights glaring. After punching the security code on the mag-tech pad, located on the vault's door, they opened it and entered. Tillman slinked wearing a pensive expression. He was in sheer agony from the pain shooting through his hand but he refused to get it stitched up in a nearby hospital emergency room. His clothes were disheveled and perspiration streamed from his forehead. "Hey Fred, help me get the money over there in this briefcase. My hand feels like it's on fire."

Beefy Fred followed directions while Tillman took another hit from his little glass bottle to help him cope with the searing pain. When Fred finished stuffing the briefcase with neatly wrapped stacks of one-hundred-dollar bills, there were still several bundles of cash left over. "Fred, you can keep those extra stacks for yourself. You're about to earn every penny."

Again, Fred was happy to do as he was told. He loaded his pocket with as many bills as they could hold. "Look boss. My pocket got the mumps," he joked.

Jonathan, Reggie and two of the Minister's men ducked out of sight in the bank lobby. They positioned themselves with guns drawn, waiting for the right time to strike. Tillman left the vault door opened and unknowingly walked right passed the men in hiding when he couriered the briefcase outside the building. He staggered with uneven strides as he checked his surroundings. Then, he headed toward the rear of the bank and placed the case inside the rear compartment of his prized utility vehicle. Tillman set the alarm to protect it even though his bushwhacking scheme wasn't supposed to take more than a few minutes to execute.

Slowly, he sauntered back through the lobby and once again passed mere inches from Jonathan's crew. Fred eyed him peculiarly when he reached the vault. "Why'd you take the money out there? Wouldn't it be safer in here with us?"

"Nah, I didn't want it weighing us down if we need to make a fast get away. It could get rough but I plan on ending this thing before that happens. We'll light him up when he opens the vault door and leave him in here to rot. No one will find him until Monday morning, dead and with locked up with enough drugs to make his admirers wish they never trusted him. Thieving watermelon-seed-spitting niggers, I hate 'em."

"Hey boss, I's just wondering… how much oxygen you think this room holds?"

"Probably about five or six hours but Holloway won't need any after I'm done with him."

As they settled in to wait for a drug deal guaranteed to go bad, Tillman paused to take another hit of nose candy while pulling the large steel door closed. He desperately spooned out the last bit of cocaine when he felt the heavy door being pulled from the other side. He reached hurriedly in his waistband for the .45 caliber canon he'd brought along but he couldn't get his blood-soaked fingers to cooperate. Tillman was scared when he turned around, not knowing what to expect. The corners of the heavily stained handkerchief began to shake. Two of the meanest looking black men he'd ever seen stood inches away when his eyes met theirs. Tillman's nerves were shot. His left foot tapped the floor erratically and there was no way he could get it to stop. He imagined going for his gun but thought better of it because he'd also imagined being shot by the military assault rifles they pointed at him.

Jonathan strolled up behind the men he'd in sent ahead to secure the vault. He eased toward Tillman slowly. "Nice forty-five," Jonathan said, before he snatched it from Tillman's possession with his left hand and punched him on the mouth with his right. The drug dealer's leg's buckled. He fell hard against the cold cement floor. Jonathan inspected the impressive widow-maker. "I always wanted one of these. Since you won't be needing this one, I'll just keep it as a memento. That all right with you, Brian?"

Tillman rubbed at his face and grunted sorely. "Ouch man, that really hurt!"

"Yeah, I imagine it does," Jonathan replied with a grim chuckle. He surveyed the vault for the first time. "So, this is it. A little drugstore? Not a bad set up but you know where all this lead, don't you? Either hell or jail."

"For sho'," added Reggie, who was a living testimony.

"But you'll never make it to jail Brian. See, I've got other plans for you and fat boy over there."

Fred's hands were held high in the air the entire time. He was afraid to move. Reggie threw the shivering hired muscle a satisfied grin, flashing his coveted gold-capped tooth. "Looks like your last job was a bad career move, big man. You should have gotten on at the post office. They' always hiring."

Fred assumed what his fate would be. He went for his gun but the two warrior-sized Muslims were prepared to squeeze off enough rounds to rip his body to shreds. Fred instantly got the message and quickly tossed aside his large chrome plated pistol. "Ok-ok. I put it down. Just don't shoot me," he begged. Then, he cowered back against the far wall, anticipating the worst.

Reggie wielded his baseball bat, as if it had anything to do with Fred's decision to give up his firearm. "I'm glad we have an understanding. I'd hate to have to use this," he chided.

Tillman peered up at Jonathan standing over him. He grimaced from his sprawled position on the floor. "Why'd you hit me?" he whined, noticing that his front tooth jiggled when he spoke. "If you wanted the dope, I'd have cut you in."

Reggie laughed while pointing at Tillman's mouth. "See, now you gotta get you one of these." He ran his thick tongue over his own flashy tooth to show Tillman what he had to look forward to, if they decided to let him live.

"Yeah, what do you say Jonathan? Let's do business together," Tillman pleaded. "I'll talk to Morrell for you. I'm sure he'll break you off a piece of the action." His feeble words confirmed what Jonathan knew but couldn't prove. The man behind all of his troubles was George Morrell.

Jonathan shook his head. He was disgusted with all he endured at the hands of a man he once looked up to. "Hmmm... I think I'll let you keep the drugs. I would hate to be thought of as, uh what was that he called us a minute ago?"

Reggie used Tillman's fabricated Ivy League diction. "I believe he said we was *Thieving... watermelon-seed-spitting Niggers*, as it were."

Jonathan let out a light chuckle. "Let me hip you wanna be *good fellas* to the law of the land. For two white men, that's ya'll, the penalty for bringing drugs up in this here neighborhood is death by firing squad." Honestly, Jonathan didn't know what do with the two cowering dope slingers but it sounded good to him at the time he said it. Reggie whistled an eerie tone while carrying in a box filled with small candles. He and the other men lit each one then placed them throughout the vault. Tillman watched with a peculiar look on his face until he felt compelled to ask what was going on. "Don't take this the wrong way but what's with the candle. Is it a black thing?"

"Shut up!" Jonathan barked. "Slide farther away from that gat."

Reggie started whistling again as he reached inside the box and came out with a can of black spray paint. Now everyone watched as he tagged the floor with a large satanic pentagram in the middle of it.

Tillman's eye bugged out like they were about to roll onto the floor. He was antsy and at the mercy of Jonathan, who had him out numbered and out witted. "Uhh-uh Man, this is getting way too weird."

"Don't sweat it Brian," Jonathan reassured him. "We're just sending you home in style. I know yo' daddy can't wait to get you back. Devils belong in Hell!"

In a fit of panic, Tillman made an ill-fated move for Fred's gun that lay several feet away. As soon as Tillman's hand clutched its pistol grip, Jonathan mashed it with the heel of his shoe. The loaded gun popped off twice. Bang! Bang! Stray bullets ricocheted off the stainless-steel walls. Jonathan's crew ducked out of the vault for cover. Once they were all safely accounted for, Jonathan slammed the door shut then locked it. His eyes narrowed with immense concern.

Reggie couldn't figure out what Jonathan was thinking. "Jon-Jon, what's got your face all twisted up? You're not changing your mind about Tillman and his boy, are you?"

"No. They'll get what they deserve but something just occurred to me," Jonathan answered. He appeared more perplexed than before as he shook his finger in the direction of Tillman and Fred, still locked inside. "Correct me if I'm wrong but was that punk was going to shoot me."

Reggie backed up his suspicions. "Yeah. He was gonna do you in, brotha. Probably 'cause you pimp slapped the taste out of his mouth. And, I ain't seen no body get chumped like that since Shaft did it and you know he was a bad mother…"

"Shut yo' mouth," Jonathan chimed in.

"I can dig it." Reggie slapped him five on the brown side and topped it off with the soul shake they knew well as kids.

The lock had been changed on the ATM room where the video recorders were stored. Jonathan was forced to break in to collect the tapes, which had just recorded what happened to Tillman and his henchmen. The tapes were quickly obtained and shoved into a black leather bag before Jonathan made his escape from the place he helped to erect from an empty lot to something the neighborhood was proud of.

Engulfed in a pit of horror inside the vault, Tillman cocked the hammer back on Fred's gun and braced himself for Jonathan's return. "Shhh… did you hear something?" he whispered. The only sound heard was Fred sucking up the oxygen.

Jonathan scampered to the back of the bank. When he looked in the window of Tillman's expensive SUV. Suddenly, the car alarm sounded. "Please step away from the car! You are too close to the car!" it blared loudly.

"Hey Regg', hand me that bat?" With one powerful swing, Jonathan shattered the back window into hundreds of tiny pieces. The thrill of destroying something that belonged to Tillman felt so good, he wanted to do it again. There went the window on the driver's side. Wham! "Now I'm inside the car!" Jonathan replied, as if he'd somehow gotten even with the annoying alarm. Then, he reached in and yanked the alarm's speaker wires from beneath the dashboard. Reggie searched the rear compartment until he came across the briefcase Tillman stashed earlier. When he opened it, his knees weakened. "Oh my God! Thank you, God. Thank you!" A half-million dollars was more money than Reggie had ever seen.

"Oh yeah. The money," Jonathan said, matter-of-factly, while looking over Reggie's shoulder. So, you're praising God, now? What happened to Allah?"

"This kind of money ain't got nothing to do with Allah. These crisp Benjamin's say, 'In *God* We Trust'."

"Hey man, I know it's a lot of cheese but that's blood money. We got to do the right thing and burn it."

Reggie's breathing shortened when he imagined handing the money over to Jonathan. "Oh, hell naw, we ain't got to burn all of it!" he protested. "How 'bout we light up a couple of hundred-dollar bills and call it a night?"

"Just kidding Reggie, we're keeping all the money. I just needed to get your mind back on breathing before you passed out. I'm not carrying your big ass to car."

"Whew. Jon-Jon, you play too much. Man, don't scare me like that."

"Look man, why don't you and those two brothas take half of this money and help the Minister do some good with it. I'll get back to the apartment and wait for Morrell to make a move. Some things a man's got to do alone."

Reggie was offended that Jonathan would charge into a dangerous situation without offering him a chance to come along for the ride. "Jon-Jon, don't make me hurt you. I've been your best friend since before I could pee off myself and now you don't need me no more? Don't forget, it's still another very bad man out there who wants you dead. And when he finds out you killed his boy and took his grip, he's gonna be pissed. I need to have your back when Morrell comes knockin'."

Jonathan was moved by Reggie's unyielding loyalty. "No matter what I say, you're not leaving are you?"

"Uh-uh," Reggie answered insistently. "Not even thinking about it."

"Then I won't bother trying. Send those brothas to the Mosque and we'll put in work, like we used to."

TWENTY-NINE

Page me 9-1-1

A few hours earlier, Denise sat on a plane diligently trying to reach Jonathan on the jet's air phone. On her third attempt, she decided to leave a message although it would ruin her surprise to fly in unannounced. "Hello Jonathan... by the time you get this message, I'll be closer to you than you think. Actually, my plane lands at one-fifty this morning. I know it's late but the red eye is all they had left. Don't be upset with me, ok? I just had to see you. Please be there to get me, baby. DFW, Terminal B, Gate 21. I've got something with your name on it. See you soon."

Denise's anxious expression faded when the plane landed and she hadn't been contacted by the man she was rushing through her divorce to begin a new life with. While her recorded message played on Jonathan's answering machine, a dense cloud of cigarette smoke filled the living area at his apartment. When the message concluded, George Morrell dropped the smoldering butt on the floor then smashed it against the hardwood with the heel of his expensive Italian loafers. He immediately erased the message and lit up another Marlborough before casually excited through the front door. Morrell's original plan included easing in to the apartment undetected, just as he had twenty-five years earlier, to leave another dead Holloway in his wake. His interception of Denise's voice message provided an alternative strategy that fell into his lap.

After Denise stepped through the secured area of the terminal, she called Jonathan's home again but the answering machine picked up after the third ring. Now she was concerned with Jonathan's whereabouts so late into the night, as well as with whom. Maybe Angie was correct about men when she suggested that Jonathan might have enticed other women to help pass his time. Several minutes of waiting outside near the passenger pickup area had gotten the best of Denise. After a number of men, who couldn't help but notice her tightly fitting crème colored pantsuit, offered to take her where ever she needed to go, Denise felt down right foolish for taking a long flight without clearing it with Jonathan first.

Morrell sped all the way to the airport to intercept Denise. A pile up on I-35 caused him to be later than he anticipated but he spotted her just as a Yellow Cab pulled over to answer her summons. Morrell gave the long sidewalk a thorough check for airport security in the event that she wouldn't go peacefully. He was prepared to get physical if Denise required convincing.

"Hey, Denise," he yelled, as the cab driver hopped out to open a car door for her. "Denise, it's me. George Morrell. Jonathan's friend from the bank." He was all smiles and charm to spare. "You're much too beautiful to be out here all alone at this time of night. Jonathan sends his apologies. 'Official bank business. It was something about an emergency down at the branch. Alarms going off and such." Morrell gathered that his pitch sounded desperate so he took a deep breath to compose himself. "I know I'm not as handsome as Jonathan but he asked me to swing by and take you to his apartment. He'll join you there as soon as he can break free."

Denise studied Morrell a while, longer than the cab driver thought necessary as he awaited her decision. "Go on without me," she told the cabbie eventually.

Morrell's artificial smile was polished enough to divert further suspicions. Denise was ultimately satisfied that Jonathan sent him, she figured or he wouldn't have known she'd be waiting there.

"Good," said Morrell. "Then I didn't leave a hot poker game for nothing. Jonathan is all torn up about this. I'm sure he'll make it up to you."

"Humph, he'd better," Denise asserted playfully. With diminished reservations, she climbed in the white Cadillac and looked forward to seeing her fantasy man again.

Morrell delivered Denise to the apartment building as promised. This time he entered through the parking garage to see if Jonathan's Lexus was in its assigned space. When there were no signs of it, Morrell parked in the back of the lot in the section allotted for visitors. He popped the trunk from the inside, retrieved a small doctor's bag that was hidden near the spare tire and then helped Denise out of the car. Instead of taking the elevator he led her up the back stairway.

When no one answered the doorbell, Morrell used a duplicate key to enter through the service entrance. "Guess Jonathan's not quite finished yet but the branch is not far from here. He should only be a minute." Since Morrell had the place under surveillance before Jonathan moved in, he knew Denise had never been there before.

Once inside, she marveled at the extravagant furnishings. Morrell quickly pointed out that he had helped to handpick the entire décor. That meant he knew every inch of the place, as well as Jonathan did. Although everything appeared to be on the up and up, Denise couldn't get comfortable with the idea of being alone with Morrell. Something about him rubbed her the wrong way so she excused him from his duties and showed him the door. "Thank you so much for seeing that I made it here safely but you can run along now. I'll be sure to tell Jonathan you were the perfect gentleman."

Denise turned her back when she picked up the phone to page Jonathan. Morrell quietly sneaked behind her. He grabbed the phone cord then ripped it out of the wall. Denise spun around as Morrell snatched her by the wrist and tried to kiss her on the lips.

"Let me go!" she screamed, while fighting off his advances. "What in the hell do you think you're doing?"

After growing impatient, Morrell slapped Denise with a brutal backhand across her face. Denise stumbled backwards then crashed against the floor. The security executive stood over her, peering down, as she writhed in pain. "Oh, playing hard to get. Is that it, bitch? I wish I had the time to enjoy this."

Denise continued to roll around, holding her throbbing face. She had no idea why Morrell thought he could get away with sexually assaulting her. When he drew back his hand to strike her again, Denise pretended to give in. "All right, all right but a girl likes to be handled softly," she grumbled. "You don't have to get rough to get what you want. I'll cooperate."

Morrell's ego allowed him to underestimate her shrewdness. He extended his hand to help Denise to her feet. She forcefully thrusted her size nine sling back pump into the middle of his crotch. Morrell sank to his knees, grunting miserably before toppling over.

"Guess you didn't know I'm from Hotlanta. We don't play that shit." Denise mule-kicked him in the face for good measure then grabbed her bag from the sofa table. She ran toward the front door to get away. She jiggled on the knob but nothing happened.

It was locked with a deadbolt that required a key to open it. She was trapped.

Morrell stumbled towards the front door then clutched a handful of Denise's hair. Disappointed with himself for misplacing his trust, Morrell struck her again with a closed fist. Denise flew across the room when his powerful blow snapped her head back. She laid unconscious, sprawled out on the floor.

Morrell limped over to the stocked wet bar then poured himself a stiff drink. "Not bad Denise, for a girl."

The entire incident had been observed in the Mosque's security room by Minister Muhammad's men. The attendant on duty was hesitant to wake his boss but couldn't find a way around reporting it immediately. "Excuse me, Minister Muhammad. Sorry to wake you. This is brotha Lawrence down at the Mosque control room. I know it's late but there's something you should see right away."

Morrell had no idea others had witnessed his evil deeds. As far as he knew, the camera he'd installed had been rendered inoperable. That was his second mistake. Getting on Jonathan's bad side was his first.

About the same time the double-cross concluded at the bank, Minister Muhammad pulled himself out the bed to view the recorded version of Morrell putting his hand on an attractive black woman in Jonathan's living room. In the time it took the tape to rewind, the minister made two calls to Jonathan's cell phone but to no avail. Darius X remembered giving Reggie a two-way pager, so he'd be equipped if something went awry. Meanwhile, the Minister issued orders to rescue the distressed woman in Jonathan's apartment from impending doom. Within minutes, four armed members from the Nation of Islam jumped into a long black suburban then sped away.

Reggie was counting tall stacks of money when his pager went off. "I need a nap Jon-Jon. This undercover bid'ness is harder than I thought. A nine-to-five plus all this overtime, I'ont know how you do it. Almost make a brotha wanna start hustling again. Hold on...." He read the small screen. *911 at Jonathans.* "The Minister's tryin' to reach us, Reggie announced. "We need to get over to your place quick. I don't know what jumped off but it can't be good. Give me your phone. I'll call the Mosque."

Jonathan floored the gas pedal, thinking Tillman had somehow freed himself from the vault. He checked the car console for his cell phone remembering he'd turned it off while waiting on Tillman to arrive at the bank. "What could be going wrong at my place?" Jonathan thought aloud.

THIRTY

All Money Ain't Good Money

T ires squealed against the concrete as Jonathan rolled closer to the parking garage at his building. Reggie listened intensely to Minister Muhammad on the phone. "Yes Sir, Brotha Minister. Yes Sir. I will, Sir. Here's Jonathan." Reggie's expression hardened as he handed Jonathan the telephone. The Minister quickly explained the need for urgency.

"Brotha Jonathan, I'm glad I caught you. That corporate devil, George Morrell, broke into your home earlier tonight. And Jonathan, that's not all. He had a woman with him, a beautiful sistah. She fought him but..." he said, with his words trailing off remorsefully.

"Denise!" Jonathan bellowed. He hoped she headed his serious warnings about coming to Dallas. This was the worst way to discover she didn't. "There's no telling what Morrell will do to get at me." Fearing he might get there in time to stop Morrell from doing something he couldn't get over, Jonathan tried to contact Marcus. He paged the officer twice but there was no response. Marcus's pager was clipped his waistband as sat in a restroom stall reading the sports section, with his pants resting around his ankles. It was vibrating softly so he couldn't feel the subtle trimmers beckoning him.

Jonathan whipped the car around the north side of his apartment building, facing McKinney Avenue. He slammed on the breaks, nearly ramming into the back of a street maintenance crew working the night shift. Huge cement mixing trucks and various heavy machinery blocked the entrance. The road was under repair, due to be completely resurfaced by morning.

Jonathan maneuvered through the construction barriers and around an enormous vat of scalding-hot tar being prepared to pour onto the road. Fearing he was trapped, Jonathan orchestrated a tight U-turn in the middle of the avenue then parked on the curb before sprinting from the car. He and Reggie raced through the parking garage on foot until they reached the elevator. They stepped on with caution, gasping for breath as the doors closed.

The door to Jonathan's apartment was wide open. As soon as they walked into the large living area, Jonathan drew his pistol then flicked the lights off. He sneered when smelling stale remnants from Morrell's cigarettes. "Shhh… Reggie," he whispered. "If that punk is still here, he might not be alone so be careful. And watch your step."

They agreed on splitting up to probe the apartment faster. Jonathan sneaked around his own home like a common burglar. There were no signs of an intruder in any of the downstairs rooms so Reggie crept upstairs to the second level, keeping his back to the wall as often as possible. That was one thing he had grown accustomed to while in prison.

Once Reggie reached the second-floor landing and felt confident that no one lurked in the darkness, he lowered his trusty baseball bat to open Jonathan's bedroom door.

Morrell eased closely behind him. "Hey homeboy," Morrell whispered, before cracking Reggie over the head with a metal flashlight. Reggie's body made a solid thud against the floor, followed by the clattering of his bat falling against it. Jonathan heard the noise but there was no way to know who had gotten the short end of the stick or how many men Morrell might have requisitioned to help him.

Despite his apprehensions, Jonathan was drawn in. Moments after reaching the second floor landing, he endured the unnerving backdrop of silence as he stepped over his friend's body. Jonathan wasn't sure if Reggie was still alive but it wasn't prudent to expose himself while examining it. Jonathan had to remain composed as he continued on with his expedition. He faced an imminent threat to his own mortality.

His eyes narrowed as he approached the bedroom door like Reggie had done moments before. Out of nowhere, a blinding white light flashed inches away from Jonathan's face. Jonathan threw up one hand up to shield his eyes. He aimlessly waved his handgun around but feared Denise was inside the room. He was reluctant to fire his weapon.

Through his blurred vision, Jonathan caught a glimpse of Denise. She was bound and gagged to a chair. Before he took a single step in her direction, he was greeted with a stinging blow across his back from the bat that Morrell took off Reggie.

Jonathan cringed as the pain zigzagged between his shoulders. He staggered toward a wall to maintain his balance. He heard someone laughing but it sounded as if it came from a far off place, which suggested he was swatted harder than he thought. Suddenly, someone kicked him in the small of his back. It sent him barreling into the wall. The gun he struggled to hold onto to had flown from his hand. Dazed and hurting, Jonathan tried to lift his head to regain his bearings. Seconds later, his eyes stung when bright lights suddenly filled the room.

Once items in the bedroom came into focused, Jonathan's eyes landed on Denise. Her jaw was swollen and bruised. There was a thin trail of blood dribbling from her mouth as her chin bobbed slowly against her chest.

"Denise, wake up. Wake up baby…" Jonathan pleaded.

She recognized his voice but lacked the where with all to utter a single word. When Jonathan studied her face, his eyes locked on her eerily-blank stare. He recognized that dazed expression all too well. She had been drugged.

Jonathan whirled around when he heard an insane chuckle reverberating throughout the room. Jonathan wheeled his body around to get a line on where the laughter emanated from. Morrell was leaning against the wall nonchalantly. He coddled a gun in one hand and a hypodermic needle in the other. When Jonathan made a rash decision to charge him, Morrell popped two slugs in the drywall to discourage it. Both bullets whizzed Jonathan's head. He was wise to him down.

At the police substation, Marcus received a call over the radio as he washed his hands in the sink. "Metro three, metro three, multiple gunshots fired at the 1200 block of McKinney. Repeat, 1200 block of McKinney. The Novella Towers Apartment Building." Marcus dashed out of the restroom stall. His partner met him in the hallway just outside. "Isn't that the call we've been waiting for?"

"Yeah, just hope we're not too late." Marcus had forewarned his partner that trouble was brewing and a close friend was deep in the middle of it.

A few minutes away, the Muslim Mobile weaved in and out of the passing lane while it zoomed down I-30. Captain Darius instructed the driver to exit the freeway on a grassy off ramp when they discovered an overturned car was backing up traffic. After three near collisions with other motorists who had the same idea, they caught a break.

Hardwood Street was clear but all the traffic lights were against them. "Turn right here, turn right here," Captain Darius demanded. Time was running out.

The Suburban fled into the darkness without obstruction until a strange rumbling became increasingly louder. One of the men braced himself in the backseat and yelled at the top of his lungs, "Brotha' Captain! A traaaaaaaaaaaaain!"

The driver overreacted. He jammed his military styled boot against the brake pedal. The long SUV skidded down the deserted street, throwing up a mountainous cloud of dust and trepidation as the screeching tires slid against the dirt road. The train rumbled toward the intersection without slowing. The SUV glided out of control and didn't seem capable of stopping before it reached the railroad crossing. When the train conductor feared the worst, he sounded his horn to warn them. Each of the men clung for dear life to anything bolted down.

"Allah, be merciful," the Minister prayed while the Suburban continued to drift helplessly toward the steel tracks.

The train's horn blasted urgently as the speeding locomotive hugged the cold rails. Finally, the SUV came to an abrupt stop near the tracks. It shook back and forth amidst the weight of heavy freight cars passing two inches in front of it. For the next seven minutes, the men watched in amazement and waited. Never had a group of men come so close to meeting death and lived to tell about it. They were forced to contemplate the frailty of human life and Jonathan's fate.

"Jonathan Holloway… tisk-tisk-tisk! How many times will I have to hear that detestable name in my lifetime?" The infamous

George Morrell shook his head disapprovingly while lecturing Jonathan on meddling in his affairs. "Don't you go getting any more ideas. I'd hate to shoot you when I have other plans for your bringing about your elimination. But first, I'm interested to know why you couldn't find it in yourself to be a good little boy like I said. I wasn't asking for much, not really. Just wanted you to play by the rules, mine. Everything would have worked out for you in the long run but no, you had to go and get self-righteous on me. If I had known you'd be so much damned trouble when I killed yo' daddy, I would have snapped your neck like a twig while I was at it."

Jonathan was still dizzy when he lifted his head. He was baffled about Morrell's confession, although he'd heard every word. His father was found dead from an apparent heroin overdose. Jonathan remembered the horrible scene that played in his head dozens of times. There was a needle stuck in his father's arm, much like the syringe Morrell was holding in his hand. Jonathan's chest swelled with emotion when it all made sense to him. He didn't want to believe he had spent his whole life resenting his father for not being there during the toughest parts of it. Morrell had taken both parents away and robbed him of his childhood.

Although hazy, Jonathan began to muddle his way through all the lies that accompanied him through years of isolation and shame. "You killed my father? Why would you ruin an honest man and destroy his family?" He felt just as grief stricken as if the incident had recently occurred instead of twenty-five years ago.

Before Morrell had an opportunity to answer, Jonathan charged him in a wild fit of rage. He was yelling like a mad man with nothing to lose. "I'll kill you if it's the last thing I do!" Morrell squeezed the trigger once. Bang! Then he pulled it again. Bang! The loud shots rang out in the apartment. Two rounds exploded against Jonathan's chest. Puffs of smoke rose from his jacket where the hot lead found their target. Time stood still as Jonathan laid on the floor with his lips quivering. Subtle movements in his fingers dissipated within seconds as he stared blindly toward the ceiling.

Morrell inched closer to inspect his fallen prey. "Like father, like son, I guess. Looks like the stress of carrying the world on your shoulders was too much to bear, even for a stubborn asshole like you," Morrell mocked. "That homeless bum that kept pestering me too and he had to be dealt with. I did him a favor and put him out of his misery. But did he thank me? Noooo! The ingrate just laid there, bleeding and choking on his own blood. What the hell. His life wasn't worth living anyway." After his brief tirade, Morrell sat his gun down on the floor next to Jonathan. He needed both hands to prepare his latest victim for the same untimely death that he successfully executed several times before.

After Morrell tied a thin rubber hose around Jonathan's arm, he rehearsed the act he would perform for the police when they eventually arrived. "Yes officer, it was a pity that Jonathan became involved with drugs. Yep, just like his dear old dad. Drug are such a terrible scourge on society. This was likely a drug deal gone wrong and we had such high hopes for this guy. You can give and give but these people refuse to get off the junk. Whadda ya gonna do?" His babbling continued as he knelled over Jonathan's body preparing to inject him.

Without notice, abrupt pain shot down Morrell's back. He howled after hearing his bones creak. For the first time since his near fatal run in with Jonathan's father, Morrell actually feared death calling his name.

Reggie took his sweet time to antagonized Morrell while warming up for an old school beat down. "Whadda ya think about that? Huh? That was a base hit. Here's a home run." The bat came down again. It smacked Morrell with another powerful blow to the head. Blood seeped from the gash after he crashed face-first against the floor.

Reggie congratulated himself on his solid follow though then tossed the bat aside to attend to Jonathan once Morrell was no longer a threat. "Jon-Jon? Jon-Jon? You know you hear me, man. Get up! You gotta get up from there." When Reggie worked feverishly to resuscitate Jonathan, he was saddened to discover his favorite childhood friend was no longer breathing.

Quietly, Morrell rolled onto his side. He wiped away streams of blood from his face as he struggled to his knees. He searched the floor for Jonathan's gun until he managed to locate it. With a shaky aim, Morrell pointed at Reggie and pulled the trigger. Reggie hollered as the bullet tore through his left shoulder.

Reggie grabbed at his shoulder then turned towards Morrell, who was barely standing and bewildered. He flinched when hearing a thunderous outburst from downstairs. As the front door came crashing in, Morrell made his way to edge of the upstairs loft. He released the cylinder on Jonathan's revolver to count the remaining bullets. There were two rounds left.

When he saw four black men storming up the staircase, he shot once to deter them from advancing further. The men took cover and returned fire. Reggie crawled to the other side of the room and hid under the bed. Morrell lurched toward the window to escape. He rested the gun on the dresser as he struggled to pry the window open.

Jonathan's eyelids fluttered. He was disoriented but alive. He felt even more fortunate that Morrell was still in the same room with him. He took a labored breath and gathered himself to finish a deed that was at least a quarter century past due. Naked revenge motivated Jonathan to get up. Resolve drove him past the pain. The chance to set things right guided his steps.

"Hey Asshole," he murmured, while stepping toward the window that Morrell couldn't open. "Oh yeah, the window sticks. I've been meaning to talk to somebody about that."

When Morrell snatched the gun and turned around, Jonathan rammed his fist into the older man's gut. Morrell doubled over and dropped the gun. He was winded and clutching at his stomach. "Please Jonathan. Don't hit me again. Okay, I'm begging," he said in a pleading tone. "Isn't that what you really want, me groveling at your feet?" Morrell coughed violently before continuing. "I'm trapped. Wow, you punch like a sonofabitch. I know when I'm licked and you've won. I give up."

Jonathan stared down at Morrell. He wondered if that black-hearted killer preferred prison over an immediate death sentence. He was face to face with the man who admittedly murdered his father in cold blood. George Morrell was wonder if Jonathan had the stones to kill an unarmed man, regardless of what he had done. There they were, two men committed to ending it on their terms. Jonathan was confronted by a once in a lifetime chance at reckoning with his father's murderer and subsequently his mother turning to the streets for survival. Years of unconscionable deceit, a mountain of treachery, and suffering had culminated in that defining moment. And, Jonathan didn't think it was worth it to become what he despised. He decided to trust the court system to deliver justice for his parents. However, Morrell wasn't so willing to let it end that way, not with both men left standing.

"Get up!" Jonathan shouted. "You're going to jail for the rest of your pitiful life."

As he turned to signal an all clear to his backup to enter the room, he noticed Denise was starting to regain consciousness.

He was relieved to see her eyes opening. Morrell viewed it as a small window of opportunity to fight his way out, so he took it. He reached at his pant leg to remove a small revolver from an ankle holster. As he raised the weapon to fire from his crouched position, Denise saw Morrell taking aim at the back of Jonathan's head.

"Jonnnnnathan!" she screamed, with her eyes gazing past him.

Jonathan spun on a dime. He backhanded Morrell across the face then belted him again in the nose with a stinging jab. That powerful blow wobbled Morrell. He refused to loosen his grip on the gun although he lacked enough strength to lift it. Rather than give up, he lit in with a barrage of insults despite a trail of bloody drool suspended from his chin.

"'That all you got, boy? You hit like your daddy and I outright whipped his ass," Morrell bragged. He threw a feeble left hook that Jonathan easily dodged. Blood seeped from both nostrils as Morrell mustered enough determination to fire his gun.

Jonathan recoiled. His eyes widened with surprise after being shot a third time. Visions of his childhood played in his mind like a slow-motion reel to reel. All the birthdays he endured without a father to share them with and his mother's rapid descent to the grave flashed before his eyes. The thought of Starla's alcohol and drug abuse, which lead to her scandalous demise, ushered him to a place he didn't know existed. It was the point of no return. Unwittingly, Morrell had taught Jonathan one very valuable lesson. Some deeds were so despicable, so repulsive, they were actually worth getting yourself killing over.

Without regard for his own life, he attacked Morrell, who shot him in the chest again. Minister Muhammad and Captain Darius tried to step in to save Jonathan when he coughed and sputtered. Reggie help the men back.

"No-no-no. Jon-Jon's got to end this his way," he explained nervously.

Jonathan hissed and scowled like a prize fighter in the last round of a title bout. His fists flew in swarms of thunder. With each devastating blow he delivered to Morrell's face, his head snapped back-and-forth helplessly. Jonathan threw a bone crushing combination when Morrell attempted buckle. Whack! "That's for my mother." Whack! "That's for Comphy, the last brotha you'll ever hurt." Whack! Whack! "Begging won't help you either. I ain't accepting no apologies today," he taunted.

Morrell couldn't hear a word past the kettledrums banging in his head. His scrawny legs gave way but Jonathan propped him back up against the window. Reggie nodded his approval. "Yeah, that's what I'm talking about Jon-Jon. Don't let that devil tap out yet."

"And this is for my father…" Whack! "Who never got the chance to see his son grow up to kick… yo'… ass!" Whack-whack-whack! Jonathan gave that beating everything he had then collapsed on the floor.

Morrell's broken body went crashing through the large plate-glass window, plummeting toward the street below. He screamed all the way down with both his arms flailing and grasping at air. His head burst wide open like a ripe melon when it splattered against the hard concrete.

On the edge of night, the morning sun witnessed it all then conveniently looked the other way when a man who had committed one sin too many was forced to settle up with his past. His debt was finally paid in full. Morrell had to realize at some point that he couldn't cheat the devil. He had merely been avoiding the inevitable, a date with destiny that required soul.

Captain Darius X stood by the landing while the other men untied Denise and attended to Reggie's shoulder wound. Minister

Muhammad peered out of the shattered window, reflecting on the long night and everything that transpired while the darkness eagerly kept watch. Jonathan laid still on the floor, littered with fragments of broken glass.

"Minister... did he make it?" Jonathan uttered sorely.

Surprised that Jonathan was alive, the tall man eyed him peculiarly then shook his head. "No," he replied evenly. "No, he didn't. Looks like a position just opened at the bank though."

A faint smile found its way onto Jonathan's lips. "Outstanding," he groaned quietly.

Reggie scurried over to unfasten Jonathan's jacket. "Jon-Jon! Jon-Jon! You can make it, man. Just hold on..." After Reggie searched and failed to find a single drop of blood, a tired expression accompanied a strained sigh of relief. "What the heck...? See, I told you. You play too much Jon-Jon." Reggie poked at the bulletproof vest that protected Jonathan's chest. "What if that fool was to shoot you in the face."

Jonathan took a long look at Denise seating in the chair. "I didn't think of that. Had something else on my mind." Reggie fell back on his behind and laughed a long time.

Marcus arrived with his partner eventually, ready to do battle but they found quiet after the storm. Marcus stepped closer to the epicenter of all the action. He feared the worst when he saw Jonathan flat on his back. Thankfully and despite Jonathan's adamant resistance, Marcus insisted his friend wear a bullet proof vest if he was determined to go up against drug dealers. It took some convincing but as it turned out, Marcus was a lifesaver in the end.

"It's a good thing my head is harder than yours," Marcus reminded Jonathan while looking him over. "Good thing Morrell didn't shoot you in the face."

"Yeah, I keep hearing that," Jonathan joked.

"Not a scratch on you. Wish I could say the same for your sweet crib though. You can forget about that security deposit. Your landlord is gonna freak."

Two emergency medical teams sorted through the shot up apartment. Reggie was transported to the nearest hospital. He finally got that long nap he'd been waiting for. Denise was under observation then eventually released when the drugs she had been given cleared her system.

Oh yeah, Brian Tillman and bonehead Fred had long since concluded that Jonathan wasn't coming back for them and neither was anyone else until Monday morning. Unfortunately, the following Monday fell on a holiday. The branch employees didn't get a whiff of their corpses until after a three-day weekend.

It's been two years since the branch was aired out and turned over to Jonathan's trusty assistant, Deidra. A few other things have changed in the 'hood as well. Drugs are still there but that issue is being dealt with accordingly by Marcus' the newest narcotics detective on the force. The Muslim Mosque just completed construction on their building annex, mainly due to the gift of a quarter-million dollars from an anonymous philanthropist. The General Motors manufacturing plant is up and running. As a result, several major corporations pledged to do likewise and built production facilities in south Dallas.

Jonathan lost his fervor for banking but he agreed to do some consulting work for a financial startup that loaned money to black businesses. There was a huge market for small companies who agreed to pool their resources for lower rates. Minister Muhammad managed the lending consortium while Jonathan cultivated his love for Denise. Within a year, everything fell into place. Denise was granted an amicable divorce and immediately began planning a marriage ceremony performed by Minister Muhammad, who was certified by the state.

When it was all said and done, Denise and Jonathan's lives were brought together by fate, saved by grace. They named their firstborn child after his father.

The End

A note from the author

Victor McGlothin - The Writing Coach

Would you like to write your first novel and finish in half the time? Visit my personal website **www.VictorMcGlothin.com** to get free novel writing tips: *Six Keys to Starting Your Novel Fast and Finishing*

Made in the USA
Middletown, DE
16 August 2020